THE OFFER: BOOKS 1, 2 & 3

THE OFFER: BOOKS 1, 2 & 3

THE BILLIONAIRE'S LOVE STORY

LILY ZANTE

ISBN: 978-1-914467-53-0

AUTHOR'S NOTE

'The Billionaire's Love Story' is a contemporary billionaire romance serial set in New York. There are nine installments and each book must be read in order.

This boxed set contains **Books 1, 2 & 3 of The Offer.** The other books in the series are:

Reading Order

THE OFFER, BOOK 1

The Billionaire's Love Story (#4)

CHAPTER ONE

I'm sorry I rushed off but something urgent came up. I'll be back tomorrow.

She'd sent that text to Briony as soon as she had arrived back home, not long after lunchtime.

Tobias's words cut into her, sharp like shrapnel, leaving her so devastated that the only thing she could think of was to get the hell away. She couldn't run the risk of seeing him again. She'd tried to soldier on at work, had managed to stumble along for a few hours but his unpleasant words and that venomous look on his face refused to leave her and made it unbearable for her to remain there.

The hours had crawled miserably towards lunchtime. She'd gone out to grab a sandwich but had ended up coming home and cleaning her oven instead.

It was spotless now. Because when all else failed, when she couldn't stop replaying that scene over and over in her mind, or stem the endless recording of his words, her urge to clean, the desire to put order into things she could control, helped focus her mind. So she had cleaned her oven until she could see her face reflected in the shiny windows of the oven door.

I'll fuck you for hours and pay you well.

His words stabbed into her psyche, throwing her into further misery. Each time her mind drifted to *that* scene again, she scrubbed harder, forcing herself to concentrate on the task at hand.

It was bad enough that money worries kept her from sleeping ever since she'd found out how much the hospital bill had come to. This morning she had worked herself into a frenzy as she'd left for work and was already hesitant about asking Tobias for an advance. Yet he had so graciously helped her through a tough Christmas period and it was this that had convinced her to go forward with her request.

But she hadn't been prepared for his response, which had knocked the life and breath right out of her, as if he'd landed a solid punch to her midriff. She had rushed away, unsure which was worse: Colt's punches, or Tobias's words.

She never wanted to see him again. Never. Sucker that she was for attracting only jerks and douchebags.

Her cell phone rang, snapping her back to present and when she saw Briony's number, she was half-tempted to ignore it, but she knew she couldn't do that to one of the few people she liked and trusted.

"Hey, Briony."

"Is everything okay? I just got back from a meeting and I saw your text."

"I'm fine," said Savannah, eager to put her boss's mind at ease. "I'm sorry I left but something came up."

"Are you okay?"

"Yes." *No.*

"I wanted to make sure. Tobias was looking for you earlier; I didn't know where you were."

"Does he know I came home early?"

"He's been in meetings all day. He wouldn't even know if your room caught fire."

Savannah feigned a laugh. "I'm sorry. I can explain tomorrow when I come in."

"Don't worry about it. I know you've had enough to deal with recently. Is Jacob all right? I thought for a moment—"

"Jacob's fine. Thanks for asking. What did Tobias want?" Her anxiety began to climb. What more could he have to say after the disgusting accusations he had leveled at her?

"I'm not sure and I didn't care to ask. He didn't look too happy."

"Maybe he had a problem with his Word templates," Savannah suggested, knowing that it wasn't the reason he'd come looking for her.

"I don't know why Candace can't deal with those problems," Briony muttered. "But that's not important. I wanted to make sure that you and Jacob were okay."

"We're fine." Savannah reassured her, quickly glancing at her cell phone screen when she heard the beep of another call waiting. Her eyes flickered with excitement. Bella from Southwood Select, the new recruitment agency she'd been dealing with, was on the line. "I've got another call coming through," she said. "Do you mind—?"

"No, go. I'll speak to you tomorrow." Briony told her. Savannah quickly switched to the other call.

"Savannah?" Bella's crisply efficient voice greeted her, raising her hopes. "I've got good news."

"Yes?" Her mood suddenly brightened.

"You've got the job!" Words that lifted her from her misery.

"I did?"

"You sure did. They loved you. It wasn't only your experience to date and the fact that you've held this position before, but they liked your personality. They think you'll fit right in." Savannah placed her hand on her chest as if she was unable to contain her happiness. This news was more than a small ray of sunshine in an otherwise shit-filled day. "That's the best news I've heard all week! I'm so excited. I really am." She felt a lightness in her chest and couldn't help but smile. "How soon can I start?" *Tomorrow?* She hoped. She was desperate to leave Stone Enterprises at the first opportunity.

Bella laughed. "You *are* eager to start. I like that! Unfortunately not tomorrow, but maybe in around two weeks' time. I've been told that they're looking at the start of February."

"Are you sure?" asked Savannah, suddenly anxious again. "Because when I spoke to the manager during my interview, he told me that they needed someone as soon as possible."

Bella paused. "I'll look into that for you. I can ask, certainly. But first, let me get the paperwork over to you—"

"I can come by during my lunch hour and sign all the necessary paperwork." Forget waiting until lunchtime, she might even rush out an hour after she arrived at the office to get that paperwork signed.

"That works for me. I'll see you tomorrow. Congratulations, once again."

"Thanks." Savannah put the phone down and hung her head in sheer relief. It was strange how today life had shown her two extremes on the emotional spectrum. *Not only two*, thought Savannah despondently, hugging her arms around her body. She'd suffered a whole heap of emotions in between. So much so that she was now ravenous, as well as drained, after the tumultuous ride that the day had turned into. She still hadn't eaten lunch.

Feeling happier, she opened the refrigerator and pulled out some cheese and a jar of relish with which to make a sandwich.

As she opened the lid to the jar, she was again reminded of Tobias Stone; this had been in the Christmas gift basket he'd sent her.

Back when he had cared.

CHAPTER TWO

H̲e had to claw his way out of this hole which was as wide as a crater.

Tobias pushed out of his chair and stared vacantly out of the floor-to-ceiling windows of his Park Avenue duplex. He scrubbed his face as he considered the options for getting himself out of the category five shitstorm he found himself in.

How the fuck was he going to get himself out of this one?

He had a battle ahead of him. Making it up to Savannah Page was going to be more than difficult, if not goddamn impossible, especially when the woman wasn't giving him a chance. But he had wheedled his way out of tighter corners before and he would do so again.

When he'd first seen her this morning, when she'd told him she needed to speak to him, he had assumed it was because she wanted to discuss more personal matters. She'd been coy, almost hesitant when she had approached him, and wishful thinking made him believe she'd come to talk about *them*.

No way had he been prepared for the request she'd hit him with and in his instant anger, he hadn't been able to hold back either. Then at the day's end, when he'd finally sought out the solitude of his office, Matthias had shown up and delivered the bomb: that Jacob had been sick and in the hospital. And that was when Tobias had discovered the real reason Savannah had come to him.

Discovering his mistake, he couldn't concentrate, couldn't think, and couldn't function. Letting his emotions spiral out of control with Savannah the way he had was dangerous and he wasn't used to it. But her request for an advance had been so unexpected that it had completely derailed him. Always on guard for people wanting and expecting things from him, Tobias had reacted to her as he would have for any unsolicited request for money.

But he saw now that his paranoia, along with his feelings for her, had blinded his judgment and had made him jump to the wrong conclusion. He should have known better. Savannah Page wasn't that kind of woman.

Of course he'd gone to find her, needing to apologize to her, feeling guilty and haunted by the look on her face and the way her body seemed to crumple under the weight of his harsh words. Seeing the damage he'd inflicted on her had left him with a bitter taste he couldn't get rid of. But when he went to her office, she was nowhere to be found. Briony told him she had probably left for lunch.

His day had progressively worsened. One goddamn meeting after another; sucking his soul and draining him dry. How the hell were they supposed to attract new clients and find new companies to invest in if they spent so much time analyzing the minutiae of every decision?

He walked away from the windows and sauntered into his state-of-the-art kitchen. A copy of the WSJ lay spread-eagled on one of the white Corian countertops along with some paperwork he had been looking through.

He had been trying to read, to focus his mind elsewhere but

he couldn't. He'd been unable to think of anything else and now, with the time approaching almost ten o'clock at night, he was going crazy still thinking of her and of what he had done. A proudly independent and steely woman such as Savannah must have been in a desperate place to come to him for money.

He reread the report that Ludwig, his trusted head of security, had prepared and dropped off earlier. He turned to Ludwig whenever he needed intel and the man always delivered. Savannah Page had money worries—nothing overly major—$10,000 on a credit card and a hospital bill for just over $3,500. With that jerk of an ex-husband up to his eyeballs in gambling debt, she wasn't going to get any help from him. Twenty-eight years old, soon to turn twenty-nine in three weeks' time, she was the sole provider for Jacob Samuel Page.

He had to fix this soon, before it was too late. It didn't matter how he went about it, what mattered was that he fixed it.

Showing up at her apartment now was the only way to do that. He'd been thinking about it ever since he'd returned home but the idea had seemed so preposterous that he'd pushed it to the back of his mind. Yet here he was three hours later, still thinking about it.

He *had* to see her. He had to make sure she was going to be all right, because she had looked anything but all right by the time he'd finished with her. There was no point summoning Morris—not at this time of night. Picking up his car keys, Tobias rushed out of his apartment and headed towards Sunnyside.

He and Savannah were going to figure this out tonight.

CHAPTER THREE

"I'm sorry to ask you, but I was wondering if...if...there was any chance you could... loan me some money."

Because there's no one else I can ask. She cringed inside, wanting to disappear into a black hole, hating that she had to beg to make ends meet. "It's just that..." her voice trickled to a whisper, "I need to pay a hospital bill." Savannah squeezed her eyes before opening them. Sitting alone at the kitchen table, she gripped the phone, her head lowered.

She had hit rock bottom and it was impossible to go any lower.

"A hospital bill for what?"

"For Jacob. He had an asthma attack last week and had to be hospitalized for a few days."

"You never told me," said Kay, her tone one of accusation.

"I'm sorry. There's been a lot going on. He was at home for a few days and I was going crazy with worry trying to—" she gulped. *Trying to see if Colt or her parents could help financially.* "Trying to figure out what I was going to do."

"I'm sorry, Sav. That's sounds hard on you. How's he now?"

She breathed easier. "He's fine now. Back to his usual, energetic self." That was all that really mattered, in the end. Begging and scraping to pay the bill was something she could do, but seeing her son sick in the hospital was difficult to bear. "I hate to ask you, Kay, and I've been avoiding calling you for that reason." Asking Kay for money had been as difficult as asking Tobias—almost. Maybe it was because she and Kay were roughly the same age; her cousin was a few years younger. Asking her for money made Savannah feel like even more of a failure than she already did.

"How much is the bill?" Kay's voice was solemn.

"It's $3,583.95."

Her cousin spluttered at the other end. "You're freaking' kidding me?" Silence fell, making Savannah even more uncomfortable. "Don't you qualify for government assistance or something?" Kay's reminder of what she *should* have done now made her burn with regret.

"I held off on signing up for it," she whimpered "I thought I'd be able to land on my feet and find a permanent job soon enough."

"But, Sav, you can't make those kinds of assumptions, not with a young child to take care of. It was never going to be that easy." Kay's words twisted into her gut like a scythe.

"I know." Savannah *did* know it but she had been so determined to land herself on her feet, that she'd gone about it all wrong, thinking it would be far easier than it really had been. But perhaps it wasn't too late and even with the promise of the new job, she could still qualify for aid. It was time to throw away her pride and start filling out the paperwork for government assistance.

"We'll figure something out," Kay told her as she struggled to compose herself; her shoulders slumped as she stared down at the floor.

"I know it's a lot of money, and I'm sorry to burden you with my problems."

"Shhhhh," Kay soothed, but it did nothing to help her feel any better. What a loser she was. She couldn't even call Kay on her cell phone, but had texted her cousin to call her back from work.

How low was that?

She was digging for cents, scrambling to survive. This was no way to get by in life, not if she wanted to provide Jacob with a life that was worth living. A dull and heavy ache settled in her chest, dragging her spirits even lower.

"Give me a week or so to see what I can do, Sav. Don't worry."

"Thanks. I owe you."

"Take care of Jacob and don't be sad. We'll figure something out. I think I might be able to lend you half at least."

She put the phone down as tears slid down her cheeks. Where was she supposed to conjure up the rest of the money from? Walking into Jacob's room where he lay fast asleep, Savannah pulled the bedspread, which he had kicked away, back over his body.

A deeper sadness settled over her as she watched her sleeping son. She was a complete failure and yet he thought she was the best mother in the world. He had no idea that she could barely keep it together. He could never know. She rubbed her tears away and walked out, gently closing the door behind her.

Worry still settled over her. It would be a huge help if Kay could lend her half but how was she going to make up the rest of the payment? The new job, as great as it seemed, wasn't double the salary and if this agency paid anything like her current agency did, then she would have to work a month without getting paid.

She could go back to waitressing in the evenings and maybe

work at the supermarket on the weekends. It would be difficult but it would only be until she'd earned enough to get out of this rut. Lost in deep troubled thoughts of how to claw her way out of the darkness, Savannah jolted when the phone rang again. She answered it quickly.

"Arnold?"

"Sorry to bother you, Ms. Page. But there's someone here who wants to see you. A gentleman by the name of Mr. Stone." She backed away in fear at the mention of his name.

Tobias Stone.

What was he doing here and at this time of night? She shrank back, panic seizing her insides and squeezing her chest until she felt like she couldn't breathe anymore.

Why, oh, why, oh, why was he here—in her apartment building, downstairs in her lobby? She had nothing to say to him.

"Ms. Page?" Arnold's gruff voice didn't hide his concern. "If it's too late I can—" Time slowed down as a myriad of conflicting emotions coursed through her body, paralyzing her senses. She wasn't in the right state of mind to deal with him and yet she had plenty to say to him, especially now that she would be leaving. Maybe this would be her final chance to tell him exactly what she thought of him.

When she didn't reply, because her body seemed to have gone into lockdown mode, she heard Arnold's faraway voice. "I'm afraid this isn't a good time."

"Wait." She spoke up. She had things she needed Tobias Stone to hear and it would be better to say them now, outside of Stone Enterprises, before she walked away forever. "I'm coming down."

She slipped a sweatshirt over her black lounge pants and stringy vest and then slipped on her sneakers. Her hand automatically lifted to the plastic clip which held her thick hair in place but she thought better of it. There was no point in shaking her hair loose.

She wasn't hoping to impress Tobias Stone—she was hoping to give him a piece of her mind.

CHAPTER FOUR

The wizened old man gave Tobias the kind of stare which would have made a lesser man jump.

Instead, Tobias turned his back to him and stared out of the lobby door, fixing his eyes on the sleek, black Porsche Panamera that was parked outside. It seemed like a safe enough neighborhood, but this wasn't Upper Manhattan and he could never be too relaxed. Not that there was any need to worry. His bodyguards would be parked somewhere close by; he peered up and down the street, looking out for their car. He often forgot they tailed him twenty-four-seven.

The elevator's metallic 'ding' sounded and his heart skipped a beat when any moment now he would see her again, for the first time since *that* meeting. He turned around slowly, his nerves jangling like nervous pups. She stepped out, wearing an oversized top with dark, casual pants and somehow she looked smaller. Her face was set hard and she looked as though she had been crying. The muscles around his heart clenched and he bunched his shoulders, hating himself even more.

She didn't even glance at him once as she walked over to the concierge. He heard her say something about Jacob and as he slowly approached the desk, walking up behind her, he heard the man reply. "I'll go right on up, Ms. Page. Don't you worry about Jacob. I'll wait outside the door." The old man gave him another skewering look before he headed towards the elevator.

Savannah turned around stiffly, her arms still folded. A weighted ball landed in the pit of his stomach and her all too obvious distress made the weight of his guilt double as it settled heavily inside him. "Why are you here?"

He slowly removed his hands from his pockets and was at a loss with how to proceed. Placing them on his hips seemed too casual, and with his insides churning away with full-on discomfort, Tobias felt anything but casual. He clutched his car keys even tighter.

"I came to apologize, Savannah." He wanted to reach out and touch her, but her body language told him to get lost. Standing his ground, he stared at her face. She looked different with her hair scrunched up and held in place with a brown plastic clip. "I am sorry for the things I said, for the way I behaved, for the way I hurt you."

She snorted at him. "It's becoming quite a regular thing, isn't it? You apologizing all the time. Maybe if you didn't jump to twenty-foot-long conclusions in the first place, you wouldn't hurt people's feelings."

He bowed his head. "That's why I came. I can't live with what I said and I'm ashamed of how I treated you." She gave him a cutting look.

"It's done and you can't take your words back. You can't repair the damage."

"I can, if you'll give me a chance."

"Give you a chance? *Give you a chance?*" She said slowly, her eyes bulging. "You can't buy respect and forgiveness. I know you think you can, because you live in this glass bubble where you think you can buy anything, but you're wrong."

"Savannah, I'm sorry. I can't tell you how—" She put her hand up at him, halting him mid-flow. "You were so off the mark, Mr. Stone. Paying for sex is what you do in *your* world. It's not what happens in mine. You really thought I was going to blackmail you? Kiss and tell? You think I came to you for sex?" Her furious words lashed at him. "Do you seriously take me to be that kind of woman?" She pinned a brutal stare on him, leaving him speechless. "Times are hard," she continued, rage spiking her words, "but I'm sure there are other ways of earning good money. I'm not quite in the gutter yet that I need to consider doing *that*. Not even for you, Mr. I-Can-Buy-Whatever-The-Hell-I-Want. I hate the sight of you." She twisted the knife further. "I wish I'd never met you and I resent the fact that Jacob thinks so highly of you when you're nothing more than a jerk."

Her words landed like a whip on both cheeks: hard, raw and as good as leaving blood marks. He stared at her, ashamed to hear the accusations she now flung back at him. But she was right. "I was a jerk."

"*Was?*"

"I *am* a jerk—but not all the time. I have my redeeming moments." He lifted his lips slightly, trying to smile at her but she held her chin high and her nostrils flared. He had to back off in order to calm her down, before he lost her forever. "It was, it *is* unforgiveable."

"You're damn right it is," she snapped, her eyes, bloodshot and angry, blazing at him. "I don't even know why you're here. What difference do you think it can possibly make now? You can't take back what you said. You can't *unsay* those words." He stepped towards her and saw that she flinched. He stopped, clearly aware of the depth of her hatred for him.

For him to fix this, he would have to tread lightly.

God damn it, anyone else, anything else, he wouldn't have

bothered but for the life of him, he could not walk away from Savannah Page. Not with this—his wrongdoing—hanging over him. He had to at least try but in the face of her obvious reluctance to forgive him, Tobias was more determined than ever to do whatever it took to win her back.

"I can't take back what I said, but I can fix it. I said things in the heat of the moment—"

"Sometimes people speak the truth in the heat of the moment. This isn't the first time you've jumped to the wrong conclusion, Mr. Stone. You accused me of taking something from you once, do you remember?"

The Dalton file, how could he forget?

"What is it that makes you want to punish me each time?" Her composure was calm, but her voice was spitting rage. He could see she'd been bottling it up inside her; he would even hazard a guess that she had probably resisted coming down to see him at all. Maybe she saw this as her only opportunity to have her say without Matthias, Candace or Briony interrupting, or the office logistics and dynamics getting in the way. It was what he'd been hoping for and the fact that she had at least come to see him told him that his battle to win her back, although likely to be long and strewn with obstacles, was not entirely lost. Not yet.

"It's not you," he said, looking down, guilt thrashing over him like the spray off a waterfall. She was always so good at highlighting his flaws and his inadequacies. He'd come to apologize but he should have known better, should have been better prepared for her attack. She smacked him back in the face with his shortcomings and there wasn't a thing he could do but listen and agree. The psychological and business tactics that he used so effectively on his employees and other businessmen, bending them to his will easily, didn't seem to work so well on Savannah.

"It's not you, Savannah. It's me."

Not only had he never been able to get her to do what he wanted, she never seemed afraid of letting him know exactly what she thought of him—traits he found attractive, especially when everyone else around him was always eager to do his bidding.

He had tried to temper down his feelings for her, unsure himself of the attraction between them—but it was there, invisible and strong, and undeniable. After what seemed like a long spell of keeping his head down and focusing on his business, he was finally coming out of a long, slow hibernation and had connected with this woman who didn't fall at his feet, or try to fall into his bed, as easily as many before her had tried.

It made him want her even more.

"I don't trust many people."

"No shit."

"Please listen," he said, anxious that she heard him out. "I don't open myself up to them, or expose myself in any way which might hurt me."

"We're not so different, then." Her voice still carried that hardness, but she had a point. He could see she was tough outside, that she needed to keep that hard shell around her, but unlike him, she was made of softer, warmer stuff, despite how she saw herself.

"I'm going to make it up to you," he told her.

"You can't."

"Give me a chance."

"I don't want to."

"Please," he begged, something else that didn't come easily to him.

"Why?"

"Because I messed up. Even more than last time. Let me, Savannah."

Her face reddened. "I don't want anything from you."

"Let me try." He would plead, beg and cajole—things he never did—but he would do them for her, if that was what it took. She shook her head. "No."

He started to speak but something about the way she stared at him told him he'd already lost her. He clenched his hands together, tightening his stomach instinctively, as if to prepare for the blow that he felt was coming.

"I can make it up to you. I hurt you, I know I did. The accusations I made were unacceptable. I—" But she'd started to walk away, as if she didn't have the inclination or the desire to stay another minute. He shook his head. "Where are you going? I'm not done."

"I am." She pressed the button for the elevator but he walked over and stood in front of her, blocking her entry to the door. "You do things to me, Savannah." His words floated from his lips in a soft whisper but she narrowed her eyes at him as they stared at one another. He wasn't given to revealing his innermost secrets, but he had to lay his feelings on the line because he might not get another chance. Now his gut, which had been as unsettled as his nerves from the moment he'd arrived, turned to a jelly-like mess.

"*I do things to you?*" Her tone was almost mocking. The 'ding' of the elevator heralded its arrival and as the doors slid apart, she moved forward but he beat her to it, barricading entry to it with his body. "I heard about Jacob. About the asthma attack and I'm sorry I had no idea he'd been that sick. How is he?" If she was surprised by the way he'd prevented her from leaving, she seemed to take it in her stride.

"Fine now."

"I understand he was in the hospital for a few days." She nodded, looking away. He stepped away from the elevator and the doors closed. Facing each other, standing next to the closed doors, he needed to know before she tried to flee again. "That's why you came to me for help, wasn't it?" This time she turned to face him, her expression unreadable, and her face hard, as if it was made of lead. "Wasn't it?" he asked again, needing a reaction, anything.

"What if it was? I don't need your help anymore."

"But I *want* to help. I hate that not only did I shoot you down, I got it so badly, badly and unforgivably wrong." He stepped towards her again, and noticed that this time she didn't flinch. He decided to take it slow, so as not to push her away. "Take the advance you asked me for earlier. I can arrange it, just say the word." His eyes, so full of remorse, now fixed onto her face and he was tempted to reach out and take her hand. But they weren't at that juncture yet; they could have been, had he not messed up.

"I don't need your help, Mr. Stone."

"It's back to formalities is it, Ms. Page?" he asked, his voice hardening again. It was excruciating, dealing with someone who refused to budge, even a little. How was he ever going to make amends with her? "You have to give me chance, Savannah."

"I don't have to give you a damn thing."

"And yet you did, willingly." She stared up at him, her hazel eyes glistening under the harsh lobby lights. "That day, you and me," he reminded her. How could she forget so easily when that moment had taunted him for days?

"The kiss?" She snarled, baring her teeth.

"Tell me it didn't mean anything."

"It didn't mean anything," she shot back.

"I don't believe you. You felt something, I know you did. I could see it in your eyes. I've been pretending it didn't exist, but I think about you and that moment more than is healthy for me." He felt tempted to thumb her lips, to run his fingers through her hair as she stood with her arms folded in that ridiculously large sweatshirt. He didn't doubt that she was soft and warm underneath that tough metal exterior and he yearned to hold her and set everything straight again but one thing was clear: winning Savannah Page back wasn't going to be easy.

She placed her hands on her hips in defiance. "You have to understand something about me," she said, the corners of her lips curling up into a cruel smile. "I'm lousy when it comes to picking men. I'm a magnet for attracting the ones who hurt me the most." Her hazel eyes burned into him fiercely as she licked her lips, staring at him provocatively. Was she taunting him? "I haven't been in a relationship for years. I was desperate for a man's touch." The last words were a whisper that spoke directly to his core. "The way I reacted to you, I'd have done the same if it had been Matthias." Tension inched along his spine, pinching the back of his neck with its spiky fingers.

"Is that what you tell yourself?" The breath sucked out of his body, as if she'd punched his solar plexus and he almost struggled to breathe. It wasn't true. It couldn't be. He knew the way she had kissed him that night.

"Believe it," she hissed. "I haven't tasted a man's lips in years. That wasn't me reacting to *you*. I'd have done the same with anyone else. *We* don't have anything, Mr. Stone. Don't mistake that kiss for deep attraction or lust. I'm like a dried-up, abandoned well that's suddenly found water again."

His mouth tightened and he refused to believe her. But he couldn't resist asking, "Who's going to help you? Your husband?"

"That loser?" Her expression hinted at surprise even though her response was sharp. "I told you, it seems I only ever attract men who hurt me. Men whose self-esteem is so low the only way they can feel good about themselves is by making others feel worse than bad." Her words knifed him and he clutched his car keys desperately, like a man who was on his last legs. Once more she had managed to hit him where it hurt. He grabbed her arms, his fingers lingering on the fabric of her sweatshirt as she shuffled her arms free and out of his grip.

"It's not my self-esteem I have a problem with, I assure you," he told her, trying to keep his voice even. She'd embittered him further by her reference to Matthias. "Don't mix me up with the type of man you married." He couldn't say too much without alerting her suspicions.

And he didn't believe her when she said she wasn't reacting to him. Enough women had hit on him that he could tell deceit from full-on emotional entanglement, and even though Savannah Page could deny it all she wanted, she'd felt something for him that evening. He had to find a way to show it to her again. "I can give you the advance and not only for a few months—for a year, whatever you need. I can—the company can pay for Jacob's medical bills and you'll have all the healthcare benefits too." He'd been thinking of how he could help her and had the loose bare bones of something unraveling in his mind. He would have to act on it immediately.

She shook her head. "It's too late. I never want to see you again, Tobias Stone. I don't want to work for your company and once I've worked out my notice, you'll never see or hear from me again. I can't wait for the day when we won't ever have to cross paths again."

"What do you mean?" *She was leaving?*

"I have another contract with a new agency and it starts in a few weeks' time, hopefully sooner, if I can convince them to take me on." With those words, she punched the air out of his lungs.

"With who?"

"Southwood Select. They came through for me in the end. So you see, Mr. Stone, you don't need to concern yourself with putting things right for me. I'll be out of your hair in no time."

He almost stepped back, fighting the shock of her words as they bulldozed through him. He struggled to accept the reality of her words, a reality which left him winded. He couldn't let her walk away now, not when he finally believed he had a chance at something.

"Goodnight." She turned and pressed the button to the elevator, and this time, when the elevator doors flew apart, she stepped in and was gone, leaving him with his knees liquefied and his steps unsteady.

By the time he staggered outside, Tobias's jaw had set harder. She thought she'd be out of his hair, did she? He climbed into his Porsche and called Ludwig. "Southwood Select, it's a recruitment agency that has offered Savannah Page a job. I want the details on my desk by eight in the morning."

"I'm on it, Tobias."

He hung up. *I can't wait for the day when we won't ever have to cross paths again.*

As if he was going to let that day arrive.

CHAPTER FIVE

A s she took the elevator back to her floor, Savannah
pondered over Tobias's visit and held her stomach tightly
—as if the contents of it would suddenly fall through her body if
she didn't. It was crazy enough that the man had come to her
apartment at all, let alone this late at night.

As tough as she had tried to be, blocking Tobias's attempts
to make it up to her had still been difficult. With the paperwork
on her new job not yet signed, she was hardly in a position to
turn anything down but she was still hurting, and her pride got
in the way.

They had been cruel, the things he'd said and all she could
remember in that moment was that they had hurt more than
Colt's punches. But seeing him again just now had shaken her
resolve to show nothing but contempt for him. Like a Swiss
army knife to his neck, she'd wanted to hold a bitter grudge
against him. But the more he spoke and the more his words
seeped through to her heart, the harder she found it to retaliate.
She had sensed genuine remorse from him, even though she'd
pushed back.

It was easier to deal with the man she knew—the one who

was as hard as steel and as cold as ice—than the one who had come to see her tonight. She couldn't stare into his metallic blue eyes a moment longer, not when he continued to tell her that he was sorry and that he wanted to make it up to her. What was that all about? Offering her an advance and paying for Jacob's medical bills as well as providing her with healthcare benefits? She was a temp and therefore had no access to those benefits or perks.

So what if he'd found out about Jacob being in the hospital and remorse had poured out of every wrinkle and furrow on his face? She would not allow herself to believe any of his words. Having been within firing range of his roller-coaster moods, she knew how temperamental the man could be.

In the end, there wasn't that much difference between him and Colt; the way they changed suddenly and without warning. She had vowed never to put herself through that kind of mental torment again and she owed it to herself not to give into a man like Tobias—even if he left her heart racing and her body reacting in ways that were so alien to her. She *wanted* to believe him but she also had a duty to protect herself. Being with such a temperamental man would be bad for her health and she wasn't about to expose Jacob to that kind of life again.

She stepped out of the elevator and walked towards her apartment. "Not even a peep, Ms. Page," Arnold announced as she approached the door to her apartment. He had been guarding it loyally and it was as if he had read her mind and known that she would be worried about leaving Jacob alone.

"Thank you, Arnold."

"Is everything all right?" he asked, looking at her with concern.

"Yes." She forced a smile.

"You didn't look so pleased to see him." He frowned and his

face puckered into even smaller lines. "Was that young Jacob's father?"

"No," she replied quickly. "He doesn't even know where I live." Arnold gave her a knowing look.

"You're safe here, Ms. Page. I'm always on the door, most nights."

"I know, Arnold, and I feel better for knowing that. Thank you, and goodnight." He nodded and walked away as she stepped back into her apartment with relief. Though there was no chance she would get any sleep tonight.

Today had to rate up there along with her list of worst days. It wasn't anywhere as bad as the day her drunken husband had tried to force himself on her as she lay sleeping with Jacob. When she'd fought back, the smack he tried to launch at her face had missed and his hard hand had fallen and hit Jacob instead. It had been the day she'd lost it completely.

She didn't have days like that anymore. Thankfully, she was in a better place now but still, as far as days went, today had been a new low in her new life. First the penthouse and now this. She'd seen two completely different faces of the same man, and she wasn't even sure if they were the same person.

"You're back!" Briony exclaimed, when she returned to work the next day. She had barely been at work five minutes when Briony rushed through the door. Savannah looked up in surprise as her computer flickered to life. The notepad and folder she had taken out, in preparation for the day's work, lay suspended in her hands. Briony stood in front of her desk with her hands on her hips, as if she were awaiting an explanation. "What happened?"

She had been so consumed by yesterday's events, and

especially by Tobias's appearance last night, that she'd forgotten to figure out what she was going to tell Briony this morning to explain her sudden disappearance yesterday. The idea of lying to her friend didn't sit well with her but there was no way she could tell her the truth. "I had some issues to deal with regarding my ex-husband." She glanced at Briony quickly before setting the folder on the desk and opening her organizer.

"Oh, hon," said Briony, pulling up a chair and sitting herself down. Savannah blanched. She didn't want an in-depth discussion about it. "Did you get it taken care of, whatever it was?"

Savannah's attempts to appear nonchalant seemed pointless in the face of Briony's apparent concern. She tapped the desk with her fingers and put on a somber expression. "I think so."

"Any time you want to talk about things, hon, you let me know," Briony said. Savannah heard more than an invitation to open up and share but there was nothing she *could* share. Everything that had happened between her and Tobias, not only yesterday, but before, had to remain a secret. But she could offer a morsel to her friend whose genuine concern made Savannah feel better. It was comforting to know that Briony cared. "I made the mistake of calling Jacob's father and asking him to help pay towards the hospital bill but he refused."

Briony shifted forward in her seat, her face the perfect picture of feminine solidarity and disgust. She shook her head slowly. "Men are pigs, aren't they?"

"The ones I meet seem to be," replied Savannah, agreeing. "But I'm fine. I'm used to it. I don't know why I did it. I mean, I guess I do. But I had to try." She gave Briony a small nod and a smile, hoping this would be the end of it.

"Are you having a hard time making the payment?"

Savannah faked a smile. "Kind of. But I think I might be okay." She wanted to tell Briony about the new job and that she would be leaving soon. She felt obliged to tell her even before she told her current agency but first she needed to go to Southwood Select and sign the paperwork. Only then would she know it was real. "My cousin might be able to help me out." She stared at her computer screen knowing that Kay hadn't promised anything definite and only half at best. "We'll see what happens."

"I could have a word with HR," Briony suggested. "I'm sure the company could help you—"

"No," Savannah interrupted. "No, please don't."

"But, hon, are you in a position to dismiss it so easily? I can see you're stressed out. I've seen you this last week, what with the worry over Jacob, and now having to deal with this. Let me —"

"No, Briony, please don't do anything on my behalf." She pleaded. The last thing she needed was for Briony to go rushing off to HR, or, god forbid, to Tobias, on her quest for assistance. She wanted no more involvement from Tobias but then it hit her like a falling boulder. *He already knew about her leaving.* What if he told Briony before Savannah herself had had a chance to? Dare she email him or call him or go see him to tell him to keep this news to himself? A new worry settled heavily in her chest.

Briony seemed annoyed. "I don't understand your logic," she said, glancing at her watch. "Don't worry, we can talk later. I have a heap of things to do and then a meeting with Tobias and Matthias before lunch."

"With both of them?"

"I'll update you soon enough," Briony said, giving her a strange grin and with those ominous words hanging in the air, she stood up.

"I need to see you about something later on," Savannah said as breezily as she could manage, given the nature of the news she needed to impart.

"Why didn't you tell me now?" Briony asked.

"It can wait. It's not that important."

Briony moved towards the door, shrugging. "I think it's about time you had some me-time, Savannah. You should come out with us for a drink one evening, you, me and Max. You work way too hard and I can see that you need to relax."

"I have a young son—"

"I know, I know. But that doesn't mean that you can't put any time aside for yourself. You have a babysitter, too, don't you? Once in a while it would do you some good to get out and meet with people socially. You've been looking too worked up lately and I'm starting to worry about you."

"Please don't," Savannah rushed to reassure her. Everyone worried about her, it seemed.

"I want to keep you on, and I'm doing my best to make it happen. The last thing I want is for you to get sick on account of the stress and that dumbass ex of yours." Savannah raised her chin, feeling somewhat uplifted. But she felt even more uncomfortable than ever at the thought of telling Briony that she had another job lined up. There would never be a right time to tell her.

She'd have to do it as soon as she had the requisite paperwork in her hands.

CHAPTER SIX

"No Matthias?" Briony looked surprised when she walked into his office.

"No," Tobias replied, closing the door behind her. This wasn't the meeting he had planned with the three of them. This one was a very last-minute meeting and involved a slight change of plans.

"Sit down, Briony," he ordered as he stood behind his chair with his hands in his pockets. He'd been figuring it out all night and his plan was almost perfect. It depended on how Savannah Page reacted. "I've been thinking about the position for this new candidate you want to hire," he glanced at her.

"I'm seeing HR about it later today," Briony replied. "I'm anxious that we move on it quickly." She sat back in her chair with her notepad balanced on her lap.

"I know you're interested in taking on Savannah Page."

"Yes. For reasons I've mentioned before. She's hard-working, honest, rel—" Tobias nodded.

"You've mentioned her work ethic before and how satisfied you were with her performance." He inhaled deeply. "About a year ago we spoke about my requirement for having someone on hand to conduct preliminary research on companies that caught my attention?"

Briony looked puzzled at first, her brow creasing and then smoothing out. "Last year, wasn't it?"

"That's right." He placed his hand in front of him on the headrest. "I have an urgent requirement for that position right now. For a part-time researcher." Briony's eyes widened as she gave him a what's-this-got-to-do-with-me look.

"But I want someone I can trust. Someone who is capable, honest and hard-working and who can work alone, without being spoon-fed every hour." He could see that she still hadn't grasped it, even though he had tried to set it out in a way that would make sense and not raise too much suspicion. It was a simple enough requirement, but granted, it was still out of the ordinary, especially for a man like him to be dealing with such trifling matters. Still, he had to get this right from the onset so that later on if anyone questioned his motives—people like Matthias or Candace—he was more than prepared for them.

"I don't understand," Briony responded, shuffling in her chair. "What does this have to do with the position I want to fill? Is there a cap on recruitment numbers?"

"No cap," replied Tobias. "But I was hoping you could take this on imminently. As in starting this week."

"This week?" She jerked her head back, disbelieving. Tobias leaned forward.

"Or next week, I'll leave it up to you. It's a small project, and we can pass it to the research teams once I need a detailed analysis but you could have Savannah Page carry out the initial research for two days a week."

"Savannah Page?"

"That's who you're thinking of taking on, isn't it?"

Briony nodded.

"It's not something I can give to Candace, nor is it specific enough to give to our research teams. I'm fully aware we have people with college degrees who perform market and risk analysis on companies but that's not what I need, not when I come across a company I'm merely curious about."

"I see," said Briony slowly. "We talked about it briefly a year ago." It was coming back to her. Back then it had been more of a nice-to-have resource. But now, with him needing to make serious amends with Savannah, he'd found a way to do that and have it be something that would help them both.

"It makes sense for you to run this since it falls under your area and I also think that Savannah Page would be ideal, especially with her knowledge of how things work, especially here on the twenty-first floor, and with your and others' recommendations about her character and reliability. I'd rather not waste any time going out to source another person when you already have someone. Do you agree?"

Briony appeared to consider his offer. "This is not a reflection on Savannah, in fact I'm actually pleased that you have an opening that might be beneficial for her. She's had a hard time of things lately and I'm not sure I have enough work for her as quickly as she needs it. But it seems as though we're hiring when we already have a department in-house."

Tobias forced a smile. "I don't want to take a resource from another department, when I don't have a full-time position for them. You have a temp for whom you don't yet have enough work. Why not fulfill both our needs and give her a full-time job?" He didn't want to touch on the real reason, nor did Briony need to know. Thankfully, she seemed to know that Savannah was in need of financial assistance. He leaned forward. "I've also heard that she's having a hard time lately."

"Her son had to go to the hospital last week," Briony told him. "She's a single mom, too. I don't think the boy's father is around and I get the feeling that she's struggling."

"I know it's not our duty to act as welfare agents, but we have the need for more work and she seems to be suitably qualified. It makes sense to have her do the job."

Briony nodded. "It does."

"I would rather this didn't leave these four walls," he cautioned. "I met her son when she brought him to work once during the holidays because she had nowhere else to leave him. I understand her position and if I can give her work that she needs, and for which I now have a pressing requirement, then it appears to be a perfect fit. And by the same token, I'm certain that Savannah would not want to accept charity." In case Briony needed any more convincing. "She seems to be the right candidate only because you trust her implicitly and you know how paranoid I can be."

"I think we all know that, Tobias."

She nodded. "I guess it makes sense. In fact, I don't have enough work to keep her busy right now."

"It's your project, Briony. We'll meet sometime next week to discuss a project plan and what I expect from you. As I've already mentioned, it's not a huge project and it shouldn't ruffle any feathers but I expect it might." He looked at her, knowing that he could trust her. "But maybe you can let Ms. Page know about the position today?"

"I'll have to resubmit an amended job specification to HR first, based on the new requirement."

"I've already taken care of that. The paperwork is here." He handed her a purple plastic document wallet which she took before slipping him a surprised look.

"I know this seems fast but I had to bypass the usual routes to hiring. I want this started as early as possible."

"It works out perfectly. You haven't mentioned any of this to Savannah?" Briony asked. That was the tricky part.

"No," he replied, staring out of the window at the dull gray skyline among a lifeless sky devoid of the sun. "I needed to run it by you first." He turned and faced Briony again. "Of course, if she's not interested, we'll advertise internally, and failing that, put it out to an agency." Briony tapped her pen against her lips, frowning as she scribbled some notes. "I know I've thrown this at you without any prior warning and if you need to take more people on, you still can."

This seemed to cheer Briony up. "We have the budget to take on a second admin person?"

"Yes."

Briony's face brightened. "Thanks."

"That's all, Briony," he said, dismissing her. She got up and moved towards the door. "When do you plan to tell her?" he asked, turning to face his computer screen.

"I was going to tell her now."

Tobias nodded. "Don't forget, you decide how this is run. Savannah Page reports to you as usual. I won't be having any dealings with her."

CHAPTER SEVEN

"Hi," said Savannah, grinning widely as she stood in front of Bella's desk. Unable to wait a moment longer, she had braved the lunch-hour madness to make her way to Southwood Select. "I've come to sign the paperwork," said Savannah brightly but the way Bella dipped her chin to her chest and avoided looking at her suddenly made her wary.

"Come with me," Bella said, getting up and motioning her into a windowed cubicle away from the open-plan office.

"What's wrong?" Even as she asked the question, Savannah knew she wasn't going to like the answer. A sinking feeling dragged her spirits down like a lead balloon.

Bella looked at her with large, pitiful eyes. "I am *so* sorry to tell you this but the company retracted their offer."

"They did what?" Fear stole into Savannah's skin like a New York chill. "What do you mean *retracted?*"

"I mean they took it off the table." The slim-built, delicately framed young woman wiped her hand over her cheek and looked at Savannah full of remorse. "I'm sorry. I got a call this morning and I forgot that you were going to come by. I've been trying to find out what happened but I can't get any more information out of them other than them saying that they're reconsidering their options."

"But why?" Shock froze Savannah to the spot, and she stared at Bella in confusion. As if she didn't have enough shit to be dealing with right now. "What did they say exactly?"

Bella looked away, as if she was killing time or trying to find the right words, Savannah couldn't tell which it was.

"They didn't call me," Bella whispered. "They told my boss, and my boss told me. That's all I know. I don't know if they filled the position from somewhere else or what. I'm sorry, Savannah. There is no job to offer you."

She felt her body lurch backwards, as if someone had yanked the carpet out from under her feet.

No job? She had made plans based on this new position. She had even—oh, good god—she had even told Tobias Stone that she would be leaving. She had been so high and mighty in her responses to him yesterday. "Do you think there's a chance they might reconsider?" She prayed there would be, even as she asked the question, but Bella shook her head.

"I'm *really, really* sorry. It's happened before. Sometimes companies fill a vacancy internally and then they don't have the balls to tell us the truth. I feel truly awful for you because you sounded so happy yesterday when I told you that you'd gotten it."

"Do you have any other positions at that level that I could go for?" she whispered, retreating back into herself. Somewhere in the dark islands of her soul, where her hopes often languished, she still held onto the belief that there was light at the end of all this, that even amid her setbacks, she was still moving forward to a better place. But with the years flying by fast, especially now that she had Jacob—a child whom she desired to raise into a decent young man—there were many bleak and lucid moments which revealed the starkness of her reality. That she was a single mom, very much on her own, without a stable job or income and no savings. In these moments, it became harder to believe in the light.

"I desperately need a longer contract or a full-time job, Bella. I'm in a shit broke place right now and I'm going to have to think hard about going back to waitressing and working in the supermarket on weekends so that I can make ends meet. I *need* a job, a better paying job, now more than ever."

Bella pulled at the collar of her blouse, her fidgety fingers betraying her poise. "Right now I don't have any positions that are suitable for you. You're too overqualified for most of them."

"I don't mind. I'll take anything." But she needed something that paid more and had a longer contract and with the chance of becoming permanent.

"Look, Savannah. I've heard that Stone Enterprises is a good place to work. They're known for paying well. I wish they'd use our agency instead of the same one they've used for years."

Savannah glanced down at her shoes. "I need to leave. I can't stay there much longer. Please, can you continue looking for me?"

"Are you serious?" Bella gave her a stare that was so penetrating, she flexed her knuckles tightly. "You're already working at a great company. Do you have any idea how hard it is to get a job there? If I were you, I would try to stay there as long as I could."

"I *am* serious and I am desperate to leave," Savannah insisted. *And I don't intend to explain why.*

Bella rolled her shoulders, indicating her incomprehension. "I'll keep an eye out for you, but don't expect a miracle. You won't find the kind of job you already have."

But Savannah wasn't prepared to listen to Bella for a moment longer and after excusing herself, she walked out looking defeated. Her shoulders were hunched together and her movements were slow, nothing like the eager young woman who had swept in less than fifteen minutes ago. It had seemed to become a regular thing for her now, one setback after another. Whenever things seemed to be turning around in her life, something bad lurked around the corner.

She'd been back half an hour but work was the last thing on her mind. Staring at her screen, Savannah hadn't even noticed Briony slip into the room until her friend spoke. "I'm beginning to get worried about you," said Briony, instantly bringing her back to the present.

"Sorry, I was miles away."

"On another planet, by the looks of it."

Savannah looked perplexed.

"Turns out that things happened a lot quicker than I expected."

"What things?" Savannah asked, curious now that Briony had shaken her out of her recent melancholy. Closing the door behind her, Briony made herself comfortable once more in the empty chair.

"It won't take long," Briony assured her. "It's good news actually. *Very* good news for *you*." Her last words caught her attention.

"Good news?" Savannah asked, dubiously. "For *me*?" She doubted that such a thing existed and was certain that whatever it was, Briony's mention of good news would do nothing to lift her spirits. Yet Briony looked like she was about to explode with the news she seemed unable to contain. For a moment Savannah was reminded of Jacob when he had something he couldn't keep to himself.

"Tobias has—" Briony started, then paused, "*we* have secured your position and would like to make you an offer."

"We?"

"Stone Enterprises," replied Briony, looking more than pleased with herself.

"What offer?"

"The offer of a permanent position."

Savannah sat up, her eyes widening dangerously, as if she was about to scream. "I thought you were still working on the paperwork for that."

"Tobias wants things rushed through quickly. He said he didn't want lack of resources or money to get in the way of our results this year."

"But why didn't you say anything to me this morning?"

"He didn't confirm it until our meeting later, that's why."

"What's the position for?" Savannah asked, curious.

"A researcher, two days a week but the position is with me. Same as what you did before, pretty much." Briony handed her a thick envelope. "Here's your offer letter. It's a generous offer and to be honest, I'm surprised at it myself, but I think it's on par with what we're paying new trainees in the research department. You're not in the research department, but you come under my remit, and I report to Tobias so... I guess it has its advantages."

"What do you mean?" Savannah ripped open the envelope and skimmed over the contract quickly, flicking through the pages until her eyes found and settled on the salary.

And she nearly stopped breathing. This was more money than the job that she'd *almost* had. "Is this for real?" She stared at Briony, not wanting to be sucked into more false hopes. Her biorhythms wouldn't be able to take it.

"Like I said, it's on par with what the trainees get." Briony repeated. "What's wrong, Savannah?"

"Healthcare and perks, gym membership..." murmured Savannah. Hadn't Tobias mentioned these very things to her last night? This new position made the job she'd lost at Southwood Select pale in comparison and this position was *way* out of her league. Something about it seemed highly suspect and she was already wary about the man who could do whatever he wanted and control whatever he needed. She read through the contract quickly and imagined that it would be the type of job that college graduates pinned their hopes on, or summer interns.

And she was getting a chance at this?

"Didn't you want someone to do admin stuff? I thought it wouldn't be much different from what I did before?" She looked up from the offer letter and challenged Briony.

"I'm sensing hesitation on your part, Savannah. I thought you would be thrilled?" Briony gave her a pointed stare. She *was* thrilled, but an offer such as this, too good to be true, seemed shady to her.

"Is this something Tobias put together?"

"It's a project he mentioned to me a long time ago. We'd spoken about it briefly but out of necessity, he's had to bring it forward. You know things aren't working out with deals abroad. He wants to concentrate more on companies closer to home. He and Matthias have been looking at this new direction for the past year. Matthias is of the opinion that global markets and the Far East will be fine whereas Tobias takes a more cautious approach."

"It seems too quick."

"Excuse me?" Briony's mouth fell open. "What do you mean?"

"I thought you were stuck in red tape? That it was taking you a while to get everything together?"

"Tobias wants someone to devote two days per week on this. You're the ideal resource and I don't have a full week's work for you, not yet. That will change a month or two down the line. With you working two days a week on the new research tasks and doing stuff for me on the remaining days, it means we can take you on now. We can offer you a permanent job and for more money than I could have given you if you only worked for me. I think you get paid more because the research element requires extra skills."

"Which I don't have."

"But which you can be taught. What Tobias prizes, for those working with him, is trust and I've told him you're reliable and trustworthy."

"Will I be working with him?"

"No. You report to me. You'll have no dealings with him. What's wrong?" Briony asked. "This isn't the reaction I was expecting from you."

"It's kind of sudden, that's all," replied Savannah slowly, not wanting to come across as ungrateful just because she was being wary. But it was sudden. She'd gone from being a temp, to almost getting a job elsewhere, and to now being offered this too-good-to-be-true position. Something didn't feel right. "How come you managed to move it along so fast, within a couple of hours?"

"That's typical of Tobias, he's sharp. He won't sit around waiting for red tape to slow things down. If he wants something done, he makes sure it happens."

That was what she was afraid of. Savannah lowered her head, thinking about it. That man could make anything happen and for a moment she'd been afraid that this was his way of making it up to her. But if he'd discussed this with Briony a long time ago, and she'd heard rumblings about the Far East deals from the others then maybe it had nothing to do with him trying to make it up to her? She was worrying for no reason.

And even if it was—she was now no longer in a position to

turn her nose up at an opportunity like this. "It's great. I—I'm grateful to you for making this happen." She had to stop sabotaging herself and stop thinking that everything that happened to her, every good thing, was Tobias Stone's doing. Accepting this offer could mean a lot of things for her. She still had to figure out how to get the other half of the money for the hospital bill, assuming that Kay could help. Things no longer looked as bleak as they had a day ago.

"So are you going to take the offer or not? Because, looking at you, I can't tell if you're pleased or not," Briony said.

"I'm sorry, it's a lot to get used to, especially after all the stuff that happened yesterday and I'm scared to get excited in case it disappears."

"That's an odd way of looking at it," commented Briony. "You need to loosen up, hon. Hopefully, accepting this offer might be the start of good things for you."

"That would be a welcome change," said Savannah, feeling sheepish about her muted reaction. "I guess I'm surprised that it's happened so fast when I'd resigned myself to thinking it might take weeks or months."

Briony grinned at her. "Like I said, Tobias can push things through super-fast."

"Would you mind if I took the paperwork home tonight and read through it properly? Of course I'm going to accept but I'm just cautious and I need to read all the fine print carefully."

"I understand. I don't have everything mapped out just yet for the new project. I'm meeting with Tobias in a few days' time to discuss project milestones. This is all new to me too but I have enough so that we can at least start, maybe towards the end of this week or early next week. It depends on when I can meet with Tobias."

"He's running this?"

"No, I am," Briony told her firmly. "Do you have enough work to keep you busy for the next few days?"

Savannah nodded.

"I'd better get back and rejig my project schedule to accommodate for this," said Briony getting up. "By the way, what was it that you wanted to see me about?"

When Savannah looked at her puzzled, Briony added, "This morning you said you wanted to see me about something."

There was no point in telling her about the job that hadn't materialized. Instead she changed tack. "I was thinking of taking you up on that offer, you know, going out one evening with you and Max for drinks or something."

"Great!" The corners of Briony's red matte lips lifted upwards. "We should put a date on it."

"Let me figure out my childcare plans."

Briony flashed a dazzling smile and left, leaving Savannah in a blanket of happiness.

She would put the news from Southwood Select behind her and focus on the future, a future that was suddenly bright again. She couldn't wait to tell Jacob. So caught up was she in her thoughts that it suddenly came to her like an electric shock out of nowhere. She wasn't going to leave Stone Enterprises, nor see the last of Tobias Stone. In fact, with her working on a project for Tobias, even if it was through Briony and just for two days a week, it was still two days too many of running the risk of seeing him again.

CHAPTER EIGHT

"You're away for the whole week?" Candace asked, scribbling in her notepad.

"The whole week," Tobias confirmed as he rolled down his sleeves. "Come in," he shouted, when he heard the knock at the door.

But when the door opened, Savannah Page wasn't the person he expected to see even though he'd been wondering how she might have taken the news about the job offer. He had pushed his attraction to her out of the way and tried to find a way of making it up to her without it looking as if he had masterminded the whole thing. Even for someone as sharp-minded as her. Looking at the way her lips were now pursed together tightly, he wasn't sure he had succeeded.

"That will be all, Candace," he said, dismissing his PA with a nod. She got up haughtily, muttered something about his pre-dinner drinks with a client but he ignored her and pinned his gaze on Savannah as she hovered around the doorway.

"I can come back another time." She looked as though she was ready to bolt.

"Don't forget six o'clock at The Oasis with—"

"I heard you the first time," he replied brusquely, throwing Candace a withering look. "Close the door on your way out."

But Candace paused as she headed towards the door. "Is this about more Word templates?" she asked him, turning around.

"Leave now." He growled, his anger rising. Savannah stepped to the side, leaving barely enough room for Candace to glide past her. He felt sure there was no love lost between the women. Unfortunately, his PA seemed to have the kind of territorially hostile reaction to most women he came into contact with. Her reaction to Savannah didn't surprise him.

Savannah walked in and let the door slam shut behind her. "I need to know." She said, not moving from the doorway.

"Need to know what?" he asked, slowly standing up and unrolling his shirt sleeves all the way down, just to have something to take his mind off the way she stared at him. It must have been difficult, he imagined, to have heard the news today. Losing that other job.

She walked towards the center of his office. "This new position—working for you two days a week—"

"You're not working for me." He thought he'd made that clear to Briony. "You'll have nothing to do with me. It's for work I need done but everything will go through Briony."

She fixed her stare on him, her face solemn, and all hard edges and brittleness.

This is your doing, asshole, he told himself.

"Did you create that role for me?" Her voice wavered as she asked, and he couldn't help but cast his eyes over her. Damn it, she was a fine-looking woman, all the way from the loose-fitting, pale gray top she wore, with the same black skirt she seemed to have on most of the time, right down to her sling-back heels. And here she was trying to unravel him. Why had he assumed she would have bought it, no questions asked? She was nothing like the vacuous women he usually met, the outwardly pretty empty heads over whose eyes the wool could so easily be pulled.

"Create a position just for you?" he asked easily, his voice smooth like molasses as he secured his bullet-back cufflinks in place. "You're being slightly presumptuous again, aren't you?"

"I wouldn't put it past you." Her voice was cold and flat, as if she didn't believe anything he said.

"If you must know, it was a project that Briony and I had talked about a while back. I brought it forward. You probably want to know why?" He slipped on his suit jacket, conscious that he had gone through the motions of getting partly dressed in front of her.

"I'm listening." She folded her arms, resting them under her breasts, the loose top now snugly in place, drawing his attention to her in ways which didn't help him. All too aware of the effect she had on him, he slid his hands into his pockets. It always seemed a safer option—it meant he couldn't be tempted to reach out and touch her. Everything about the last week, the highs and lows and things best forgotten, now stared back at him, reminding him of what he had lost.

"It's due to market changes and needing to look ahead. The work you've been given is something I need done. But you're leaving anyway, aren't you?" he asked casually. "We can fill that position internally, if you aren't interested. Don't worry," he whispered, leaning towards her slightly, "I didn't divulge to Briony what you shared with me last night."

She gulped but said nothing.

"When do you leave?" he asked, sounding more casual than he felt.

"I don't. I didn't get the other job."

"You didn't? I'm sorry to hear that." He grabbed his cell phone. "Briony wants to offer this position to you first, and you are more than welcome to turn it down. I'm sure you've got plenty of other opportunities coming your way."

"I'm not sure."

"About this job?" He narrowed his eyes. "If you're worried about working with me, don't be. The work will come through Briony. There's no need for any interaction between us."

Her lips moved but she didn't say a word. "One more thing," he said, as she turned to leave. "If you still need that advance, assuming you take the offer, it's still available but you'll need to speak to someone in HR."

She seemed to consider his advice. "Thank you." Then, without looking at him, she slipped out of his office and left him standing there, all dressed up for drinks at The Oasis.

"What was that letter about, Mommy?" Jacob asked, stretching his mouth into a yawn that showed her all of his teeth and the back of his throat. She'd been reading it again while they ate dinner.

"I've got a new job," she announced, smoothing the bedspread over him. She'd read through the contract twice, not so much to check the fine print, but because she had never had a job which paid this much, or which had offered the kind of perks that would make a difference in her life, and she wanted to double-check it all. "I was going to tell you, once I accepted the offer." It was a marvelous opportunity and of course she was going to accept. Not only that, but when she went into work tomorrow, she was going to take Tobias up on his offer and see someone in HR. Any help with that hospital bill was a godsend —if only because it meant she could sleep peacefully at night not fretting about where to get the money. With a permanent job, she knew she would be able to pay it all back and she couldn't help but feel happier. Depending on what HR offered, she might not even need to borrow any money from Kay.

"A new job?" Jacob asked, sounding disappointed.

"It's a good thing! For us, it's a great thing. Why do you look so sad?"

"You're leaving Mr. Stone?" His reply threw her for a moment.

"No. It's a permanent job."

"What does that mean?"

"It means that before this, I was a temp. I was there for a short time, like they were trying me out, and I was trying them out."

"And now?"

"Now they like me and I like them and they want to keep me there all the time." She thought for a moment how it would have turned out had that other job not simply vanished. Jacob was looking at her curiously. "I said yes. Or rather, I will say yes, when I hand that letter back tomorrow."

"You're staying with Mr. Stone's company?" His expression brightened up again.

"Yes, I am and it means..." How was she to explain to a six-year-old that it meant peace of mind for her? "It means we can go ice skating more, and we can go to the movie theater, and..." And pay her debts off and buy him things when he needed them instead of waiting for them to be discounted, and go on a mini vacation somewhere for a few days.

"Cool!"

"Though maybe not ice skating just yet." She didn't want to run the risk of him having another asthma attack.

"Why not?"

"It's bitterly cold outside at the moment, honey. I don't want to risk triggering your asthma." Which reminded her of something she'd been meaning to find out. "The doctor at the hospital told me you weren't using your inhaler when you should have been. I found that hard to believe. Is it true?"

Jacob slipped under the covers. "Jacob Samuel Stone," she said, her voice taking on a teacher's solemnity. But he giggled in response.

"Mommy, you said Jacob Samuel *Stone!*"

"Page, I meant Page." Of course she meant Page.

"Jacob Samuel Stone," repeated Jacob, giggling even more until she pulled the bedspread down. His floppy hair was all mussed up.

"Your inhaler," she said, forcing a stern look and addressing him in the strictest voice she could muster. How had she made that enormous error? Choosing not to think about it a moment longer, she tried to focus on what she needed to uncover. "I want to know why you're not using your inhaler."

His lower lip trembled.

"Jacob."

"He said I was a wuss and that I couldn't breathe properly by myself 'cos I was weak."

"Who?" Even as the question left her lips, she already had a good idea who.

"Henry Carson."

Goddamn it, that devil child seemed hell-bent on making her son's life hell and she was powerless to do much about it. Savannah's mind spun with images of the brat whose cruel words had hurt her boy before. She wanted to shake Henry Carson by his shoulders and tell him to leave her son alone.

"Oh, honey," she said, trying to think of the best way of dealing with this. Being a single mother was hard. What she wouldn't give to discuss such things with a partner, to have someone else to share her worries with. But that was a fantasy she could never have and there was no use dreaming about it, just the way that there was no point in looking through holiday brochures or beautiful homes she saw on TV and in magazines. She gritted her teeth together "Henry Carson sounds to me as though he's out to make trouble. Why are you paying any attention to what he says?"

"Because everyone else does. Everyone likes him and..." Jacob's eyes crinkled up. "Nobody likes me, Mommy." Her insides sliced into slivers to hear him say it. Instantly, her hand slid over his baby-soft skin, trying to soothe his hurt by the power of touch. "That's not true, Jacob. You told me you play with Lenny mostly. He's your friend, isn't he?"

He nodded.

"See! I bet he doesn't like Henry Carson much." She'd met Lenny once at a party and had been secretly pleased that Jacob counted him as a friend. He wasn't riotous and seemed to have a similar temperament as her son.

"He can't stand him. He thinks he's a show-off."

"There you go, then. How about I set up a play date for you both?" Already her mind was thinking ahead as to how she could solidify their bond, how she could fix it so that her son would feel more secure and happy, even if Devil Child Carson felt the need to pick on Jacob in order to make himself feel better. If this didn't stop soon, she'd have to go see his teacher but she was trying to help Jacob to stand up on his own two little feet, to not always rely on her to fix everything. "We could get him to come over one weekend."

"Can we, Mommy?"

"Of course we can." He seemed appeased, calmer and she tucked the bedspread under his chin, running her fingers gently around the shape of his eyebrows. "You mustn't let any child stop you from using your inhaler, Jacob. You could have been really sick." It could have been fatal. She'd heard and read of too many cases where someone didn't have their inhaler to hand when their airways had constricted. The consequences had been fatal. "Not using your inhaler was wrong. I know it matters to you, at this age, what people think." Heck, it mattered to an extent at any age. "But you can't let Henry Carson bully you into doing the wrong thing. I want you to try to stand up for yourself, especially when it comes to important things. I thought you were Iron Man?"

He gave her a searching stare. "I'm trying, Mommy."

"And I love that you are. Goodnight, honey."

"'Nite."

Once the financial pressure was off to some extent, she could stop worrying about their future and concentrate more on Jacob and his friends and what was going on at school.

Compared to worries about debt, Henry Carson was a pushover.

CHAPTER NINE

"Are you sure you don't want a drink?" Matthias asked him, as he poured himself another bourbon. Tobias shook his head.

"It's a little early, isn't it?" he asked, looking up from his paperwork.

"Relax," his colleague told him, walking over to the bar area of the cream and gold accented interior of Tobias's private jet. "There are no meetings lined up today. Only dinner."

"An important dinner," Tobias reminded him. He'd lined up to meet with the founders of a few tech startups as well as those of companies which were now in their third to fifth year of operation. Having survived this far, they were of interest to him and as always, Tobias wanted to meet with the founders, to get a feel for the personalities and brains behind these operations and to assess whether he thought they had what it took to remain strong and flourish. "Drinks and dinner, and what, a getting-to-know you exercise?"

"Tonight, yes," Tobias commented. "For the rest of the week, we've got meetings lined up and I'm hoping we can determine which of the companies we want to invest in by the end of it. It didn't take as long as I thought it might to get them all together tonight."

"A man of your stature and wealth—I'm sure they wouldn't have missed this opportunity. Is it wise to invest heavily in tech right now, Tobias? You know how fast technology changes. We could be sinking money into a never-ending black hole." Tobias lifted his face and stared at the large TV screen to his right, between two large windows. In front on him, a large chestnut table bore fruit and flowers and papers he had been going through. His mind was deep in the figures he'd been analyzing, or trying to, without Matthias's constant interruptions. His colleague seemed eager to make conversation. "Technology is a part of our life now, it's embedded into our DNA. It's not going anywhere. If it changes, we need to make sure we're up to date with it."

"I know we've been slowly looking at changing our investment portfolio for over a year now, but do you think it's wise to drop our current investments, especially those which have been so lucrative, and from which we have made so many good relationships—do you think it's smart to suddenly cut them?"

"I didn't set out to make friends. This is business." Tobias replied icily. "And if I sense fluctuations in the foundations of a company, I don't give a fuck about the business dinners and friends I made while courting that business. I will always do what's best for my clients, and the company."

"For you, you mean."

Tobias frowned. "Not me. But Stone Enterprises. What are you implying?" He wasn't sure what Matthias was getting at. "What is it? Are you questioning something?"

"I'm not questioning your motives, Tobias."

"Aren't you?"

"What the hell is that supposed to mean?" Matthias asked.

"You seem distracted, that's all I'm saying. Yanling is still waiting for a decision."

Tobias snapped the folder of papers he'd been going through. "I'm not distracted. I'm thinking things through. At the moment, I'm still undecided about him and the Far East and I'm in no hurry to give him a decision one way or another. What we're doing this week is more important."

"We've been keeping him hanging on for weeks," Matthias retorted.

"The market conditions remain tough and global equities have been rocked by China's slowdown," replied Tobias evenly. He didn't understand Matthias's insistence on partnering with this man. "I'm not ready to make a final decision, so please don't press me for one. You know my stance on it." Tobias placed his paperwork on the table between them and stood up and stretched out his shoulders. He walked over to the bar area where he poured himself a glass of water. He turned around to find Matthias watching him carefully.

"I heard about the new position," Matthias said, broaching the very subject Tobias had been waiting for.

"Which one?"

"The one for Savannah Page." Matthias replied, smoothing down his tie. Tobias had been wondering when his colleague might comment on this. It hadn't been a grand announcement. It was, after all, a low position and had barely warranted a minor mention in the twenty-first-floor email group as well as a small entry in the corporate newsletter.

But it was two days' worth of work that would make a difference to Savannah Page's life. It wasn't going to affect his business in the slightest but it was his company and he could do what he wanted, as long as he didn't put his clients' best interests at risk. Giving Savannah a job that was permanent, instead of temporary, and one that gave her more money and perks, was something he could do; something he needed to do to make up for his mistake. His conscience was clear now. As far as he was concerned, he had done as much as he could.

"Because I was under the impression," Matthias continued slowly, "that Briony and I were supposed to put together a case for hiring someone. I have a lot of client data that I want Briony to segment for targeting purposes."

"I haven't taken that away from her. In fact, this new requirement I have isn't going to impact Briony that much." He'd made sure that he hadn't compromised Briony's work. "Nothing has changed much for Briony and she's assured me that it doesn't affect the work she's doing for you."

"It doesn't, especially since you've given her the go-ahead to hire a second person."

"Briony needs a second person. She has too much on her plate as it is. She was starting to struggle towards the end of last year and things were beginning to slip. She's taken on too much on and I wanted to alleviate that."

"Savannah Page," said Matthias, letting the name hover in the air. Tobias returned to his seat and sank into the cream luxury leather, easing his head back against the headrest and closing his eyes. "What about her?"

Matthias continued. "She's done very well, getting the sort of position that our college graduates would kill for."

Tobias opened his eyes, unsure where this conversation was leading. "We reward hard work and effort—at least that's what I like to think. But I didn't realize you'd taken such an active interest in our recruitment campaigns...or in Savannah Page."

"I've always had a thing for pretty little things. You should know that about me, Tobias."

A lump, as solid and as cold as ice, formed in Tobias's chest. "Do you never think of settling down, Matthias? You're what—

in your mid-thirties now? Don't family life and commitment call out to you?"

Matthias almost choked on his bourbon. "Me?" He stared at him then threw his head back and barked with laughter. "In all the time you've known me, when have I ever given you the idea that I was a settling down kind of guy?" It was true; Matthias was not that type of man. In the decade that he'd known him, from the days when they had both worked with Becker Schwartz, the man who had taken a liking to Tobias and employed him in his small company, Matthias had been a ladies' man through and through. Six years older than himself, it wasn't long before the two became firm friends. It had been a friendship that had survived Tobias becoming Schwartz's new prodigy in the trading world, and had seen Tobias through both his happiest and bleakest times.

"I thought that with the passing of time you might see things differently," said Tobias softly. Matthias partied hard but he couldn't do that forever.

"I love you as a brother," said Matthias, slugging down the rest of his bourbon, "but women are like cars to me, I get bored with the same one after a while. I need the newest model on a constant basis. I don't do commitment. I'm not *you*. You have the Midas touch and you had it all..." Matthias looked away, stopping sharply in his rambling.

"Had it all?"

Matthias turned to him again. "I meant with Ivy. I don't know where that came from."

"It's all right," Tobias shrugged. There was a time when he didn't want to talk to anyone about Ivy, wanted to keep her memory and all his thoughts about her deep inside him. But now, thinking about her didn't envelop him in complete darkness, not the way it used to.

"I know you cared about Ivy."

"I still think about that time, and I still wonder how you cope." Matthias clunked the empty glass onto the table and sat back, staring out of the window. "I don't ask you anymore, because I don't want to take you back to that dark place. I hate to see you in pain, but I don't want you to think that I don't care."

"I know you care," said Tobias. He would never forget that Matthias had been there for him the entire first year. He had been the one who had shown up at his apartment daily, picking up the bottles of whiskey and empty glasses littered all over the floor. Matthias had been the one to drag him out of bed and throw him under a shower on those never-ending days when he wanted to bury himself under his covers. He couldn't face the world, not a world without Ivy, and he would never forget that his friend had helped him through it.

"I know you don't like to talk about it, and I haven't asked as often but this past year, I think you've started to move on. Maybe Naomi has helped with that."

Tobias stared at the powder blue sky and the cotton candy clouds, and listened to the quiet, controlled humming of the engines. "I had to move on. I couldn't stay in that place forever." Those days had been dark, the mornings and the nights, and everything in between; a huge, rolling wall of blackness where he hadn't known one week from the next. Each moment had felt as though someone had pierced his lungs and heart with a fish hook and tried to tug them both out through his throat.

"I haven't seen her around much lately," Matthias ventured. "I notice you didn't go away this Christmas like you'd hinted. What's going on?"

Tobias shook his head.

"What?"

"Nothing."

"She's good for you, isn't she?"

Tobias shrugged. "She was." She had been.

"*Was?*"

"We're not together anymore." He stood up and returned to the bar, this time pouring himself a glass of whiskey. "Another bourbon?" he asked Matthias. His friend nodded.

"What do you mean you're not together anymore?" Matthias joined him at the bar.

"We split, before Christmas."

"That's why you've been so up and down lately?"

"Have I?"

"Miserable as fuck one moment, and easygoing the next. We didn't know what was up with you."

"We?"

"Your friends, your colleagues."

"You and Candace," Tobias guessed.

"She noticed too. How could she not? She's your goddamn PA, and I'm one of your closest friends, at least I like to think I am."

"As my closest friend," Tobias offered, "this goes nowhere."

"Go on," Matthias leaned closer, in anticipation of receiving a shiny new secret.

"She was never a girlfriend."

Matthias's mouth hung open. Tobias elaborated. "Naomi is a high-class escort."

His friend's eyes opened wide. "What?"

Tobias nodded. "It's true."

"You can have any woman you want and you paid for an escort?" Matthias gasped. Shock creased the furrows on his forehead. "Why?"

"Because I didn't want to deal with all that other stuff." Tobias replied, in a voice that reeked of boredom, of having to explain his reasons. He thought a man like Matthias would understand since he wasn't so hot with emotional involvement either. Matthias's face turned softer. A glimmer of understanding and admiration graced his features.

"Ingenious," he said. "You paid someone just to screw her? Freaking ingenious. That's exactly the type of service I need." He slapped a congratulatory pat on Tobias's back. "You're full of surprises, Tobias. I would never have guessed. Do you have her card?"

Tobias rested his hand on the bar cabinet. "Don't."

Matthias's eyes narrowed, "The penthouse—was that where...?" Already Tobias had regretted telling him.

"Enough," he said. "This goes nowhere, do you understand?"

Matthias sobered up immediately. "Of course not but does this mean you're single again and missing pussy?"

Tobias gave him a cutting look. "You can be unbelievably vulgar, you know that?"

Matthias held his hands up. "I'm sorry," he grinned. "It can't be easy going from a pro to nothing. She must have been something in the sack."

"I wish I hadn't told you," Tobias replied, regretting his confession.

"I'm sorry. It's come as a surprise, that's all. Your secret is safe with me but we should check out the night life here."

"I'm not interested."

"And yet you paid a whore for sex!" Matthias exclaimed.

"We were together for a few months. It hardly qualifies as being as sordid as you make it out to be."

"So why not just get a regular girlfriend? Hell, Tobias, you had enough women throwing themselves at you."

"I didn't want complications or emotional crap to deal with. I didn't want commitment. I don't want to talk about it anymore."

Matthias picked up a newspaper and screwed his face up at

the headlines. "Silverstein is giving away more millions to fund Third World vaccines." He shook his head in disgust.

"It's a noble cause," Tobias countered.

Matthias snorted. "I don't understand it myself." Then, after a few moments, he folded up the newspaper again. "And all this time I thought she was your girlfriend."

"Enough," Tobias thundered.

CHAPTER TEN

"We should have done this a long time ago," said Briony, wiping the last crumbs of her hot turkey sandwich from her mouth.

"Ummmmm," mumbled Savannah, biting into her buffalo chicken sandwich and chewing. It was moist and tangy and the chicken melted in her mouth. Divine.

"Maybe next time we can have a proper hot meal. Come to think of it, why didn't we do that today, while the bosses are away?"

"As if it mattered to you where they were," retorted Savannah, wishing that she'd bought the large sandwich instead of the smaller size.

"It doesn't," Briony replied, sitting back and letting her hands rest over her stomach. She let out a contented sigh. "But it always feels nicer to know you can go out without a heavy meeting to deal with on your return. How's it been, your first two weeks as a full-time employee?"

"The same, and not the same." Things didn't seem so different for Savannah. She still worked in room 218 and all of her interaction was with Briony. Even the new job, the two days when she researched a list of companies that Tobias had taken an interest in, wasn't all that different or taxing. Briony had shown her the types of information she had to collate and the graphs and charts that were needed for the final report which Tobias would get. It wasn't too difficult once she had done it a few times. But she barely saw Tobias. "But I'm enjoying it," she told Briony. "Are you growing it out?" She noticed that Briony's hair wasn't as spiky as before.

"Max likes it short, but I feel like I need a change. What do you think? Long or short?" Savannah shrugged. "I'm used to spiky, but a change can do wonders."

"I love your highlights," Briony commented appreciatively.

"I needed a change," said Savannah, touching her hair. And what a result that change had produced. It was not long afterwards that she and Tobias had shared that kiss.

Settling into her new role easily, she sometimes found herself wondering what might have happened if she had never asked Tobias for an advance. If they had never exchanged harsh words, would anything have developed between them?

As the days passed, her anger had slowly melted and with her immediate stress and worries over the paying of the hospital bill now gone, she felt better about herself, and happier. It meant that she found herself thinking of Tobias Stone more instead of fretting over how to find some money.

She had thought that she might see him in meetings at least, or that he might send her an email requesting something, or that he might call her for something. He had plenty of opportunity now—where he hadn't before. But there had been only silence and this week he and Matthias had been away from the office.

She regretted telling him that she never wanted to see him again and that his kiss had meant nothing.

"Isn't this all nice and cozy?" asked Candace, suddenly appearing in front of them from nowhere. Savannah and Briony turned and stared at her in unison, an invisible bond binding them against her. Candace stood before them holding a take-out bag in her fur-lined leather gloved hands. "Congratulations," she said, fixing her gaze on Savannah.

"For what?"

"Your promotion."

"That's old news, Candace. It's *so* last week." Briony muttered in a put-on bored voice.

"It wasn't really announced, more like swept under the table," Candace returned. "One minute we have a temp, and the next, the temp's managed to land a dream job summer interns would fight over."

"Are you bored, Candace? Or is it your time of the month? Or is this another one of your drive-by snipings you're subjecting us to?" Briony asked as Savannah shifted uncomfortably in her seat. Candace's words, though laced with a hint of jealousy, weren't any different than what she sometimes thought.

"None of those things. But people are wondering how come you got the job?"

"Briony was always looking to expand her team," replied Savannah, unable to sit in silence any longer. "You've had more work than can be expected of one person, haven't you?" Savannah asked her friend but Briony gave her an I-can-handle-this look.

"Not that it's any business of yours but Tobias discussed this work with me last year. However, if it's getting your panties tied up in knots thinking about it, why don't you bring it up with him?"

"I'm sure Matthias will have by now," Candace replied smugly.

"I'm sure they have far weightier things to discuss," said Briony, "than what Savannah's working on."

"You'd think so. Enjoy your lunch," Candace said. "Are you planning to return to the office in the afternoon or...?"

"We're undecided yet," Briony told her and they watched Candace leave in a puff of overdramatic disgust.

"What's with her?" Savannah asked, as they watched her slink out of the door.

"She's jealous," Briony muttered. "You helped Tobias with some stuff, didn't you? I think she's feeling threatened. It doesn't help that she's got the hots for him."

"For Tobias?" Savannah asked, trying to keep her voice level.

"Blatantly. Haven't you noticed the way she preens herself whenever she's around him? She's been able to hide it because she's his PA and needs to be around him most of the time but I'm sure he thinks of her more like a cheap deodorant smell that he can't seem to get rid of."

"I don't think Tobias would wear cheap deodorant," replied Savannah. "And I don't think Candace is cheap."

"Dripping in designer," said Briony. "Shall we pay up at the counter?" They got up and slipped on their coats before paying their server. "She's high maintenance," confirmed Briony. "Paid $200 for an oxygen facial during her lunch hour last week."

"I didn't know," said Savannah, feeling a little put back. *Wow, $200 on a facial?* Briony slid on her thin red gloves as they sauntered out of the warm, oven-baked atmosphere of the sandwich shop. The chilled air, sharp like a knife's blade, cut into their faces, turning the warmth that they had been basking in to instant ice.

"That woman probably doesn't need to work, not like the rest of us, and it wouldn't surprise me if she's hoping to get her claws into Tobias while she's here."

"How long since his wife passed away?"

"Four or five years."

"Did you ever meet her?" Savannah asked, lowering her voice. Asking these questions made her feel like a spy, as if she was uncovering intelligence or some deeply hidden secret.

"She passed away before I joined. Candace didn't meet her either, only Matthias. He said she was beautiful, and not only in the way she looked, but in her heart. She grounded Tobias." Briony's words crushed Savannah's heart. It hurt to hear about Tobias and someone else—even if it was about someone he'd been with before her time.

Before her time. As if the brief moments she'd shared with Tobias were of any significance.

"Why?"

"No reason. I just wondered what she was like," said Savannah.

"Candace started a year after me but I'm telling you, she's got her eye on one of them."

"Who?"

"One of the Stone brothers."

"And you?"

"Me?" Briony chuckled to herself. "I've got Max." She hooked her arm through Savannah's as the two of them shivered together. "I don't need a Stone."

I didn't want a Stone, thought Savannah. But now...now she wasn't so sure. She had no idea how things were between them or if there would ever be a chance for anything to evolve. Conflicted and unsure, she'd been looking to Tobias for a sign, for a glimmer of remembrance but she'd barely seen him.

She was no longer sure if she dreaded running into Tobias again or looked forward to it. Such was his changeability that it was difficult to ascertain how things would be. It was impossible to see how a conversation with Tobias Stone would turn out, let alone anything else.

She was in trouble—not the financial kind of trouble any

more—but something as unsettling. Not only was she still working for his company, and indirectly working for him, she couldn't erase the memories of intimacy with him. The more she thought about it, the more she wondered what it would take to get it back.

"Savannah?" They'd stopped at the light and Briony looked at her searchingly. "What're you thinking of now? I was saying, how about that drink?"

"Drink?"

"One evening after work—you can finally meet Max and you can bring along your significant other."

"I don't have a significant other," she mumbled, staring ahead and waiting for the light to change.

"I thought as much," Briony said. "But I wasn't sure. You never know. The perfect partner might be waiting for you out there, though you're not going to meet him sitting inside." Savannah rolled her eyes. Briony and Kay seemed too uncannily similar in their romantic outlook.

"With a child?" She shook her head, dismissing the idea instantly. "Who do you think is going to be interested in me?" Yet Tobias Stone had been. Not only that, he'd showed genuine affection for Jacob to the point that her son now adored the man. "But a night out might not be such a bad idea," she agreed. "How about sometime next week?"

"Tobias is back next week and it might be slightly hectic. We could do it a week or two after that? Valentine's Day is coming."

They crossed the road, chattering away among the sound of people and traffic stacked up with engines roaring. Savannah didn't mind when; Valentine's Day had lost its allure for her years ago.

"It's my birthday a few days before," she let slip by accident.

"What date?"

"On the ninth," replied Savannah, as they approached the Stone building.

"Is this the big 3-0?" Briony asked her as they both stepped through the same revolving door segment.

"That's next year."

"Twenty-nine is still worth celebrating," Briony replied, sounding a little too excited for Savannah's liking. "We'll celebrate your birthday then."

"I don't want to make a big deal about it." Visions of a grand affair masterminded by Briony suddenly scared her. If anything, she wanted a few drinks and that was about it.

"We'll keep it small," Briony promised.

Savannah wondered if it would seem out of place if she invited Tobias along. Whether he came or not would be a different matter. At the very least she wanted to thank him for suggesting the advance from HR.

Maybe she ought to send him an email first, to test the waters.

CHAPTER ELEVEN

Walking towards the Stone building, Tobias reread the email once more. It had shown up on his cell phone a few hours ago when he and Matthias had boarded his private jet to return to New York. Matthias had slept most of the time, recovering from partying hard while in San Diego, and Tobias had spent the entire time going through the financial figures of more new startups he'd heard about from the new business contacts he had formed.

Tobias,

HR gave me a generous advance that will more than help cover the cost of the hospital bill. I am extremely grateful to you and to Stone Enterprises for helping me out. I'm sorry for anything I might have said rashly before, when I was under stress.

Savannah

But every now and then he had looked away from his

financial data and read Savannah's email, as if trying to second-guess the motivations behind her sending it.

She had been the first one to reach out. *It seemed to be working.* He had planned to remain distant, to stay out of her way and give her the space she so wanted. Maybe she was starting to reminisce, as he so often had, about what they had shared for one brief moment. If she was still interested, if she wanted more, it would be up to her to make the first move.

And he would be waiting.

It was Friday evening, soon after 5:30 p.m., when Tobias walked into the Stone building after Morris had dropped him off. He didn't consider it strange to be coming to work when so many were leaving for the weekend. For so long now, this had become his second home. He avoided going home to an empty apartment with a schedule that was mostly free over the weekend. There was only so much boxing and running, and reading of the newspapers and various magazine articles that he could do. Although next weekend would be different.

Still thinking of his impending weekend, when he'd be taking his private jet to Martha's Vineyard, he stepped out of the elevator on the twenty-first floor and found himself face to face with Briony and Savannah.

"I didn't expect to see you until next week," said Briony, surprised.

"We landed twenty minutes ago," he replied.

"And you're coming to work *now*?" Briony asked. The elevator doors closed as other people climbed in and left the two women and Tobias standing in a small circle outside.

"I have some things to catch up on." He glanced briefly at Savannah and noted that she had said nothing. He tried to read her expression, knowing that he hadn't yet replied to her email. Something told him—maybe it was the way she looked away quickly when he turned to her—that she was uncomfortable.

"Was it a good trip?" Briony asked as Savannah pressed the elevator button again.

"Time will tell," he replied, conscious of the fact that Savannah hadn't looked at him or said anything. "I must get going," he said.

"Don't work too hard," Briony cried out as the women stepped into the elevator.

"I won't. See you on Monday." See you *both* on Monday, he wanted to say, but didn't. Keeping his distance seemed to be working. As hard as it was to ignore her, that's what Tobias had to do.

———

"That man never lets up." Briony commented, belting up her thick cashmere coat. "He doesn't know how to relax." Savannah said nothing as she reconsidered her plan. Would it be too obvious if she pretended to forget something in her office just so that she could go back upstairs and seek out Tobias? If she could somehow make it appear that she had run into him again by accident. He hadn't replied to her email, and even now he'd barely looked at her, had barely noticed her. As if that wasn't bad enough, the sight of him with that darkened stubble, rough and rugged, albeit in a sharp suit, wasn't going to help her forget him.

Had he always looked so hot? He was a concoction of danger and mystery mixed together with a splash of intrigue. She inhaled deeply, thinking how the lack of men and romance in her life now seemed to drive her towards taking desperate measures. It didn't help that Tobias Stone looked more attractive to her every day. It didn't help at all that the longer she worked here, the harder it would be to forget the feel of his hands around her waist and the hard press of his lips on hers.

Her insides turned molten again, as they always did when she thought of him. "I wonder if he's broken up with Naomi?" Briony wondered. "Come to think of it, I haven't seen her around in a while."

Savannah shrugged. "You think so?"

"We used to see her around his office a few times, not much, but she'd come in towards the end of the day, every so often."

"She did?"

Briony nodded. "And she came to a few Christmas parties."

"How long have they been together?"

Briony shrugged. "Maybe a couple of years. I'm not sure. They went away last Christmas, I can't remember if they were together the year before."

A couple of years? He'd paid for sex for a couple of years? In Savannah's books that sounded more like a relationship, rather than an exchange of services.

"Are you sure you don't want to have a quick drink tonight?" Briony asked. "I feel as though your first full week in your new job needs to be properly celebrated."

"How about we save that for the next time, when we're going out for my birthday?" Savannah replied, becoming more anxious with each passing minute that took her away from Tobias. "I don't believe it! I think I've forgotten something upstairs. I need to go back."

"It can't be that important," Briony exclaimed. Lying was not her forte, and Savannah was already hesitant about her crazy idea. What if Tobias saw straight through her? He had before, he would again, and she would look like a real fool. Blowing hot and cold with him—like a high-school virgin who wasn't sure whether she was ready or not—was further compounded by the realization that a lot depended on his mood. He'd told her he couldn't stop thinking about her that night, but did he still feel the same way now?

"It's...my organizer," she said weakly, coming up with an excuse which was as pathetic as her motivation for needing to go back up.

"You still write things down?" Briony kissed her on the cheek. "Try to enjoy your weekend." She winked.

"Drinks next week. My birthday is on Tuesday but I can't go out that night. How about next Friday?"

"In time for Valentine's Day weekend." Briony smiled.

"Valentine's Day hasn't meant anything to me in years," Savannah sighed as they hovered around in front of the revolving doors. She wasn't even sure what she was going back up for, but she felt a pull and she needed to speak to him, alone. "Next Friday, I promise, and I'll arrange childcare."

"Okay, hon. Have a good weekend." Briony slipped through the revolving doors leaving Savannah hovering. She walked slowly towards the elevator bank, trying to think of reasons why she shouldn't go and seek out Tobias, but her pull towards him—made all the more stronger because he'd completely backed off from her—drove her to hit the elevator button. But when the elevator arrived, it was Tobias who stepped out. Seeing her, he appeared to do a double-take before plucking at the cuff of his jacket.

"Oh, hey—" she stammered as someone pushed past her and got into the elevator she'd been waiting for.

"I thought you were leaving?" he asked, and she could feel it already, his all-too-inquisitive gaze running over her face. Heat warmed her cheeks and she wondered if he could see through her little ruse.

"I am. I was. I forgot something," she managed to blubber. "I thought you had things to do?" she asked him, unable to look away from him. His face wasn't as smooth as usual, but rough and coarse and she resisted the urge to trace her fingers over his dusting of dark hairs of stubble.

"I did but I have an impromptu dinner date and it's been a while since we've met."

An impromptu dinner date? She instinctively knew it was with a woman. Men didn't do *dinner dates.* For one thing, they wouldn't call it that. "Oh...that's...that's...nice." It felt like someone had skewered her heart. Was he seeing Naomi again? Or had he moved on to someone else? She stabbed the button to the elevator, determined to go upstairs on her fool's errand.

"You and Jacob have a good weekend," he said breezily, and walked away, leaving her to wait for an elevator she didn't want, and an office that she had no reason to return to. She made her way to the twenty-first floor anyway, only to stay in the elevator and travel the entire distance back down again. As she walked out of the Stone building, she checked her cell phone and saw that Tobias had replied to her email only a few moments ago. Her heart jumped for joy.

At Stone Enterprises, we strive to do our best for our employees. Briony has updated me and is pleased with your progress.

That was it? She shoved her phone back into her handbag in contempt. That was all he had to say? Nothing that she could reply to—or cling to? Nothing that had hidden meaning, or an ulterior motive. Nothing that she could take away and analyze.

Nothing.

Instead he'd given her a few lines of cold and impersonal; something hollow and meaningless, as if it had been taken from the company's marketing brochure.

She knew the real reason she was so mad. It was because he hadn't said the things she'd been wanting to hear. She was left feeling hollow and knew what it was that she missed: the other Tobias, the one who had shown an interest in her and seemed to care.

CHAPTER TWELVE

"Aren't I the lucky woman tonight—having dinner with Tobias Stone?"

"It's a shame Dad couldn't make it."

"He's meeting me at the Manhattan Theater Club at 8:00. Why don't you come along? I'm sure we can get you a ticket." Tobias shook his head. Meeting his mother for dinner on such short notice was one thing, spending the rest of the evening with his parents was another. He was tired from his trip and not in the mood for dodging his mother's prying questions.

"Thanks, but no. I've had a tough week and need to go home. How is he?"

"Your father is very well, despite having two sons who seem to have forgotten their parents." Millicent Stone sucked on the olive from her martini while Tobias felt his neck tense up.

"That's not true. We haven't forgotten you. I admit I've been slightly lax, but Xavier makes an effort." *He's got nothing much else to do,* thought Tobias. His mother pursed her stringy lips together, disagreeing.

"If you can call that an effort. As for your father, he's

meeting an old friend and I thought it would be a good time to catch up with my elusive son."

"I've been busy, Mom." Tobias explained.

"Too busy to make Christmas or New Year's visits?"

"I saw you at Thanksgiving!"

"Tobias," his mother dipped her chin and gave him a death stare. "I only have two boys, and both of you seem to have forgotten all about me." Even if he saw her every week, it wouldn't be enough.

She seemed to want more of them as they got older and he had a feeling that she was rather lonely, despite her seemingly busy social life. His father kept himself busy with his friends but his mother seemed to go through moments when she wanted to know what they were up to and wanted to see them more often. She seemed needy in a way his father wasn't.

Even Ivy had found her a little interfering and intimidating at times, and he understood why. She wanted to know everything, be involved in everything, and found it difficult to let go. He had shielded Ivy from accepting one too many dinner invitations from her, or from committing to spend every Christmas with his parents. It didn't matter who he was or that he ran a company that made billions of dollars, or that he counted well-known business leaders as friends close enough to send Christmas cards to, Millicent Stone was a formidable woman. Even he found her imposing at times, and he'd had plenty of years to get used to her.

"I thought you might bring Naomi with you?" He picked that moment to fill his mouth with a big chunk of steak and spent several moments chewing it slowly. Millicent waited, her wine glass cradled in her leathery, silver-braceleted hand. Her thin lips didn't give any indication of what she was thinking about or of what she knew.

He knew, even if she hadn't said it in as many words, that

his mother didn't like Naomi very much. To this day, he had failed to understand the reason why. Naomi had been 'properly dressed,' she'd dripped from head to toe in designer labels that his mother would have approved of, and she looked 'right' in all the right parts though her hair was dyed a shade of blonde that didn't quite match her eyebrows. Still, there was no way that his mother would have known that she was a high-class escort.

"I just got back from San Diego, Mom." He didn't want to get into a conversation about Naomi.

"She must have been busy tonight if you've been away for a week, was it? And you've chosen to have dinner with me instead of with her." She didn't miss a trick, his mother.

He nodded. "It was a week." If he told her he had split with Naomi, she'd be lining up daughters of friends from 'the right type of people' she knew. His father didn't interfere, and in his own quiet way managed to touch base with him, even if all that passed between them was a 'how's it going?' followed by a nod. That's what he loved about his father. Ellery Stone didn't pry; his mother, on the other hand, wanted not only details, but times and measurements along with it. He wondered if it would be rude to get the bill immediately after he'd finished his dinner. "What time is your show?"

"Not for another hour. We have time for coffee."

His shoulders slumped. "I saw Xavier on New Year's Eve," he said, trying to catch the waiter's eye and get the order hurried along. His mother sniffed discontentedly.

"We saw him last weekend when he introduced us to a Russian waif, Petra Something-or-other-wich." Tobias couldn't help but smile. Xavier had some balls bringing his girlfriend over to meet his parents.

"He brought her over to meet you?"

His mother dabbed the corners of her mouth with a napkin. "Yes. For Sunday lunch. You recall that family tradition we used to have, way before you both discovered sex and girls and then disappeared into your own lives?"

"What was she like?" he asked, ignoring her comment.

"Very skinny and extremely tall," his mother murmured, her face a blanket of displeasure. When they were younger, she had seemed softer. When he quickly reached the echelons of the super wealthy, Tobias had set his parents up in a beautiful home in Connecticut as well as a townhouse in New York. They seemed happy with their lives, traveling and socializing between their two homes but he'd noticed a gradual change in his mother. "We used to live in Queens before, or have you erased all those memories from your past? I hope you're not ashamed about where you came from."

"I don't have any airs or graces." He raised an eyebrow, unconvinced. "You should leave Xavier alone and not interfere."

"I just think he can do better."

"I rest my case."

She threw her napkin to the side in protest. "You make me out to be a monster, Tobias." Thankfully, a waiter appeared, ready to take their order.

"Filter coffee for me, and—?" he looked at his mother.

"A mint tea." The waiter nodded and scurried off. But he was still curious to know.

"What was she like?" he asked, trying to imagine Xavier and his new girlfriend at what could only have been a painful meal. There was only so much diplomacy his father could dish out.

"She reminded me of Ivy, only taller and with longer hair, and she talked funny." Tobias's lips clamped together tightly at the mention of Ivy's name. "But, he does seem happy and I hope this one lasts longer than his previous attempts at finding a girlfriend. It's about time he thought about settling down."

"I don't think he's looking for a lifetime commitment," Tobias contended.

"Why not? You were married and settled at his age." He looked away. He'd been happy, so deliriously happy that he'd taken it all for granted.

"We're not the same, Mom. He's not ready to settle down. I'm happy for him." He wasn't sure if the girl his brother had been with on New Year's Eve was this new one. That evening seemed a long time ago, even though it hadn't been. For him, so much had happened during that time. "Thank you." He said, as the waiter placed their hot drinks on the table. "Naomi and I split up." Something forced the words out and he watched his mother's face freeze over.

"Thank heavens for that," she murmured finally.

"You never really liked her, did you?" he asked, watching her knobbled fingers as she stirred the mint in her tea.

"She wasn't the right type of girl for you, Tobias."

"And what would the right type of girl be?"

"Someone like Ivy, of course. Good family, nice parents."

Tobias snorted loudly. "You used to say I could do better before I married Ivy, and you never liked her parents much either."

"But she was perfect for you."

"You never acted as if she was, when she was alive."

"She was." His mother insisted. "She was the best of them all."

"I never had many girlfriends, Mom. We met at sixteen, or have you wiped that from your memory as well?" He'd had many girlfriends before Ivy, but that didn't count, and after Ivy, there had only been Naomi. He wasn't sure yet whether he had won Savannah Page back. But the signs looked promising.

She placed her leathery hand over his. "I might not have been as understanding as I could have, Tobias. But even I could see that Ivy was a gem. I feel for you, my darling. You don't talk about it anymore."

"I don't want to," he said, moving his hand away and drinking his coffee quickly. "She's gone and I have to move on."

Much to his surprise, his mother didn't come out with a list of possible matches for him. "It makes me very happy to hear that. You don't need to rush into anything, Tobias. You take your time."

"I'm not rushing into anything, Mom," he replied, dropping a brown sugar cube into his coffee. He thought back to his encounter with Savannah just now. As with most of his interactions with her, he couldn't tell for sure but she'd looked as if she wanted to talk to him. Maybe the tide was turning and Savannah Page was trying to reach out to him. If he could play it cool a little longer, things might turn around completely.

"Nor should you, not with what you've been through, my darling."

He smiled as he remembered the day at Bryant Park with Savannah and Jacob. "What's so funny?" His mother's hawk eyes examined his face.

"Nothing," he replied quickly. He didn't need his mother's opinion on Savannah and Jacob. Sometimes, he wondered himself if he was trying to recreate his past.

"It can't be nothing if you're smiling like that." His mother persisted, fishing for information. Tobias shrugged and lifted up his cup of coffee.

"Just a young boy I met recently."

"A young boy?"

"A friend's son. He reminds me of myself, a little."

His mother's face hardened. "He reminds you of yourself or—"

"Don't go there."

"Tobias."

"Don't." He replied, staring at his coffee and taking the last sip quickly. "Look at that," he said loudly, glancing at his watch.

"You're going to be late for your show. Let me call you a cab because I've sent Morris home." He didn't care whether she had finished her mint tea or not.

Reluctantly, Millicent got up as Tobias settled the bill. A waiter rushed over with her white fur coat. "Next time, don't leave it so long."

"I won't," he replied, thanking his lucky stars that he'd gotten through the evening relatively unscathed.

What, he wondered, would his mother make of Savannah?

CHAPTER THIRTEEN

"You don't need *any* of it?" Kay's voice rose to fever pitch.

"No. I...it's all taken care of," Savannah replied, as she narrowly avoided treading on Jacob's Marvel fighter plane. She picked it up and remembered that this was the toy Tobias had bought for her son for Christmas.

"How come? Did your parents help out?"

"Uh, no." *Not exactly.* "I meant to tell you. I've got a permanent job now."

"You do? That's fantastic news, Sav. Well done!"

"It is," she agreed, walking around the living room and picking up Jacob's coloring books and pencils from the floor while he lay on his stomach on the sofa watching TV. "They made me a permanent member of staff there, at the same place where I've been contracting at since before Christmas. Sorry, I should have called and told you sooner but everything happened really quickly." The weeks had rushed by like wildfire and all of this week, just as Briony had predicted, had been madly busy. Tobias had returned from his week-long trip with a million things for Briony to work on, and in turn, she had barely seen Briony much either.

"That's okay," replied Kay wearily. "I know all about being busy. My social life is practically nonexistent now that I'm enslaved by the bank."

"It's not like you to allow anything to get in the way of your social life," Savannah remarked, "Even if you're working fourteen to sixteen hours a day."

"Yeah, well. I don't know why I thought it was a good idea to go into investment banking."

"You shouldn't have made such an impression when you landed your summer internship." Kay was smart and gorgeous and a lot of fun to be with. She also *had* a lot of fun. Sometimes Savannah envied her, though she would never trade that life for one without Jacob.

"Where are you working?"

"At Stone Enterprises. Have you—" She was about to ask her cousin if she knew of the company but judging from the way Kay squealed, she clearly had.

"Stone Enterprises? Get out of here!" Kay shrieked so loudly that Jacob looked up at her.

"It's only Aunty Kay," Savannah whispered to him. "You know how she gets excited." She traipsed out of the living room and wandered into her bedroom, closing the door behind her.

"You did well to get a permanent position," Kay replied. "I've heard it's difficult to get a job there."

"This is nothing high up or important," Savannah assured her. "It's only an admin role."

"Even so, I've heard that college grads find it hard to get temp work there. Oh, my freaking god...tell me, tell me, tell me!"

"Tell you what?"

"Tell me about Tobias Stone. Have you seen him yet? Oh my god, you lucky woman! What I wouldn't give to be in the same building as that man."

Savannah contained her smile.

"What's he like?"

"Who? Tobias...Stone?" She tacked on the surname in case Kay became too suspicious about her familiarity with the man. She wasn't ready to tell Kay about Tobias yet. Come to think of it, she wasn't sure there *would* be anything to tell, with the way things were going—or not going—between them.

"Yes, Tobias Freakin' Stone. Can I come and meet you for lunch or something when I get back? Oh, god, just to sneak a look at him. Do you know he's always on the hottest new bachelors list every single freakin' year?" Savannah let her cousin drone on. She sat back on her bed with her legs spread out in front of her and continued to listen to Kay's fangirl outpourings. *How would Kay react if she found out that Savannah had kissed Tobias Stone?*

"Have you?"

"Have I what?" Savannah asked. She'd let her mind drift off again.

"Have you seen him yet?"

"Uh—I've caught a few glimpses of him, yes."

"You probably don't work anywhere near him though. Do you know he has holiday homes in Miami, Barbados and the Hamptons? Those are just a few of them, and he's got a private jet. And he has a team of security guards following him around everywhere."

He had no such thing, not the security guards, anyway. "How do you know all that?" asked Savannah, curious. She felt sure Tobias would be shocked to discover that a person whom he knew nothing about had the full details on him.

"It's not hard to find out. Come on, Sav! We have the number one hottest guy living in the city. It would be a sin not to stalk him. Online, I mean."

"Hmmmm," Savannah murmured in reply.

"So how come you don't need me to loan you any money?"

"The company advanced me a few months' salary. I pay a little back every month."

"Freakin' generous," gasped Kay, the envy dripping from her voice. "Maybe I need to get a job there. Now there's a thought."

"Don't you need to work in an investment bank?"

"It's finances. If it meant working near Tobias Stone...I'm sure I could find something to do."

Savannah laughed. "You'd change your career just to be in the same building as him?"

"To work for a gorgeous, single and currently unattached billionaire." Kay corrected her. "Damn right I would."

"How do you know he's single?"

"You never see him with anyone and he's never reported in celebrity columns or magazines with anyone."

"Clearly you've researched him thoroughly."

"What I wouldn't give to search *him* thoroughly." Kay gave a dirty laugh. "Do you know he trains downtown at a local gym? Hangs out with normal people?"

"I'm sure he's a normal person himself," replied Savannah.

"I bet he's got a glorious body. Hard, and firm and ... ummm," Kay let out a moan that would have made Savannah blush, were she not already preoccupied in her own heated thoughts about Tobias's body. "I'm getting excited just thinking about him," Kay whispered. Savannah clamped her lips tightly together to stop herself from laughing. If only Kay knew...

"I hear he was at The Oasis on New Year's Eve."

"I have no idea," Savannah replied. How the hell did Kay know that, all the way in Hong Kong?

"Social media. Someone posted a photo of him leaving the club. I can't believe you don't know this."

"It's...hardly news worth knowing." Savannah replied, dumbfounded by her cousin's obsessive level of interest. And to think, she'd put her arms around his neck and felt that gloriously hard chest against her body.

He was a great kisser, too.

But she kept these thoughts to herself. "Thanks, Kay. For offering to help me, but I think I'll be okay for now."

"You stay put until I get back. I'm going to be meeting you for lunch and after work at the Stone building. It makes me very happy to know you're working *there*."

Savannah smiled to herself as she hung up and lay back on her bed. How was she going to find a way back to Tobias Stone?

CHAPTER FOURTEEN

The day of her twenty-ninth birthday was upon her and if Savannah had been hopeful of resolving things with Tobias by now, she had been severely mistaken.

She had barely seen him in the week following his return from San Diego and there had been no further interaction between them. Of course, with Briony as her boss, and a buffer between them, there was never any real reason for her and Tobias to meet.

Not even on the pretense of fixing a Word template.

Either Candace was now well versed in these things, or Tobias wanted nothing more to do with her. With a sinking heart, Savannah suspected the latter. If he had so desired it, he could have found an excuse for summoning her. Her flimsy attempt to find him alone had been thwarted and in the process she'd discovered that he'd most likely met with a woman for a dinner date. She had no choice but to let it rest.

"Tobias is supposed to be joining us," Briony announced. "We'll give him a few more minutes, otherwise we'll continue without him." How could she really let things rest when there was always the possibility that she might see him around?

Like today.

Savannah had been looking forward to this first proper meeting with the three of them but as she sat in the conference room, just her and Briony, she felt nervous knowing that he would turn up at any moment. She tried to contain herself.

She had made more of an effort with her appearance today, not only because it was her birthday. She had upped her game since she'd started here a few months ago and these days she chose her outfits with more care; she also had a few more clothes to choose from, having splurged at the sales. She wore light make-up and made an effort with her hair, today more so because of this meeting and the chance that Tobias would be there.

Her only plans for today were a movie with Jacob tonight. She'd wanted to do that over the weekend instead of a school night but Jacob had insisted. He said her birthday was as special as his and she couldn't say anything to that.

Briony had bought her a box of chocolates with an extravagant hand-made card that probably cost as much as the chocolates. "Are you sure you can't do drinks today?" Briony asked.

"I promised to take Jacob to watch a movie tonight. We're watching *Alvin and the Chipmunks*."

Briony made a face. "That was your choice, was it?"

"No. It was my choice to stay in but Jacob insisted we do something."

"Enjoy."

"They're really funny," Savannah insisted. "Have you heard them sing?"

"The last time I saw a chipmunk it was on the National Geographic channel. I don't do chipmunks. Or kids' movies."

"Then you're missing out on a magical time."

"There are plenty of other magical times to be had," Briony

murmured under her breath, but loud enough for Savannah to hear. "Don't you think about dating again?" Briony asked, making Savannah feel conscious all of a sudden. "Don't you get lonely?"

This wasn't a conversation she particularly wanted to have right now when the risk of Tobias walking in was sky high. "I don't have time to get lonely," she replied. She hadn't been lonely until Tobias had left his indelible imprint on her lips that day and then continued to steal into her dreams at night. Though her financial troubles were now held at bay and she was settling into her new job just fine, she still felt uneasy. Only this time it wasn't so much the lying-awake-at-night-worrying-about-debt type of uneasy. This was more a tightening-of-the-stomach-in-anticipation of seeing Tobias kind of uneasy. It was worse than being in high school and experiencing for the first time the highs and lows of having boyfriends.

She hadn't worried too much about being single or dating until Tobias Stone had stolen into her thoughts. The more he kept away, the more she was drawn to him.

"But when you're watching TV, when Jacob's asleep?" Briony asked, frowning. "Don't you miss having someone around?"

"Not really," she lied. Lying was turning out to be a normal thing for her these days. How could she ever tell people what had happened between her and Tobias? "My life is pretty full." Briony would never understand. "Friday night is going ahead, is it?" she asked, changing the subject.

"At least that's something to look forward to," said Briony, puffing out her cheeks. "Candace mentioned The Oasis—some new rooftop bar she went to."

"Who invited her?" Savannah asked, bristling. Briony turned beet red.

"You didn't!" Savannah shot back, heat rising to her face.

The last person she wanted to spend an evening with, especially celebrating her birthday drinks, was that plastic mannequin. She wasn't sure how they did things here and had no idea whether she was expected to foot the bill for everyone, but she didn't like the idea of visiting a place that Candace had suggested. "I thought it was only you and me and that I was finally getting to meet Max."

"Chloe and the others overheard, so I kind of invited them along. I had to!" Briony exclaimed when Savannah gave her a scathing look. "And, er...Matthias is coming, too."

"Matthias!" Savannah hissed. She doubted whether any of Briony's coworkers had overheard and whether Briony, whom she knew liked a good night out, had simply gotten carried away and asked everyone on the twenty-first floor. "I'm sorry. Look, if it helps, we all contribute towards the pot. And because I now feel so bad for inviting so many people, the first round of drinks is on me."

Savannah felt her gut clench. This was fast turning into something she wanted to avoid. "I wanted it to be a small celebration," she said, louder than she had intended, hoping to make her point heard. But the door opened and Tobias walked in. The icy look he gave her told her that he'd heard. Heat pinched her cheeks and she glanced quickly at Briony before staring at her notepad.

She had been toying with the idea of asking him a few days ago, but with interactions between them almost nonexistent, she'd slowly talked herself out of the idea. Maybe Briony would ask him now. She'd asked everyone else.

As he hovered around the door, not taking a step further, Savannah crossed her legs, wondering where he would sit around the circular six-seater table.

"I'm in a conference call and I can't get out of it. I'm sorry but you'll have to continue without me."

Briony seemed to take the news in her stride. "You're impossible to get hold of these days, Tobias."

"I'm sure you can manage without me," he replied smoothly, not even looking Savannah's way once. "Was there anything in particular you wanted to discuss?"

Briony shook her head. "We're fine. Savannah has compiled a report on that new startup in Seattle," Briony looked at her. "You did, right? And she's gone through their company reports and—"

"I haven't finished it yet," Savannah whispered, hating the sound of her suddenly meek and mouse-like voice. "I have to put the charts together and then you can have it." She stared at Tobias but those metallic blue eyes that had once burned into hers so passionately now seemed to barely register any recognition.

"That's fine," he said, almost dismissively. "Whenever you're ready."

He turned to Briony again. "I have a list of the next few companies I'd like you to look into."

"Let me have it and we'll get started," she told him.

"Will do. I have to go." And he vanished as fast as he had appeared.

"When you've done—" Briony turned to her and started at the same time that Savannah spoke.

"You didn't ask him—"

"Ask him what?"

"To go for drinks on Friday night. You've asked almost everyone else on the twenty-first floor."

"You already said I was asking too many people."

"Why not him?" She blushed, hoping that Briony wouldn't catch the nervous note in her voice. If she did, she cleverly hid it. "I would hate for him to think that I had purposely left him out," she explained, "when it looks as though I've asked everyone else. It wouldn't be right. Getting this job has been life-saving, and I would hate for Tobias to think I'm ungrateful."

"Fair enough," replied Briony. "I'll ask him. Just make sure you get the report to him as soon as it's finished."

"Do you want me to run it by you first?"

"No, you seem to have grasped the idea well. All the others looked fine. Please make sure he gets it today."

A chance to see Tobias in his office? Adrenaline started to pump through her veins at the opportunity.

S he went over the report more times than was necessary and it was just as well he didn't need it in a hurry.

Later that afternoon, the time came that she was ready to hand it over to him. With butterflies dancing inside her chest, she made her way to Tobias's office only to have her excitement sink to the floor when she saw his door wide open. She stared at the back of Matthias's head as he sat in the chair facing Tobias. The two men appeared to be laughing about something and the moment she appeared by the door, the laughter stopped.

"Ah, it's the birthday girl," exclaimed Matthias, looking over his shoulder at her. "Happy Birthday."

"Thank you," she said and saw Tobias lift his head and turn his full attention on her as she stood nervously in the doorway, looking like an unsure twit. She wasn't sure whether she should come in or not.

"How many years is it?" Matthias continued, pushing her into further misery. "Twenty-four, twenty-five?"

"It's rude to ask a woman her age," Tobias chimed in smoothly, rescuing her.

"Savannah won't mind, will you?" Matthias turned his chair to the side slightly, so that he could see her better. She still hung around the door, not daring to enter.

"I'm sorry to interrupt," she said, wishing she'd come much later or much earlier, instead of sitting around worrying about the right time to see him. She'd built the visit up to be something big and as it had now turned out, she wasn't going to get to ask him anything. "Here's that report you wanted." She walked towards his desk and handed it to him.

"I hear we're helping you to celebrate your birthday on Friday night. Is that right?" Matthias boomed, giving her a shit-eating grin.

"I guess," she replied, hating Briony with a passion at that very instant. She stole another glance at Tobias who seemed immersed in the report. "You're both more than welcome. You too, Tobias," she said, making a pointed reference to him even as he seemed to be doing his utmost to avoid eye contact with her.

He looked up briefly and muttered a "Thanks."

So much for her chance to catch him alone. She'd hoped to get an idea of how things were between them—but it was plainly obvious to her now—there was nothing between them. "Let me know if anything needs changing," she mumbled as she walked out.

"I'd better be off," she heard Matthias say as she walked out of the door. "What time on Friday?" Matthias asked, walking quickly to catch up with her.

"I'm not sure," she replied in a dull voice. "Briony has all the details."

"I'm more than looking forward to it," Matthias said, casting his eyes over her blouse and making her cringe. "We finally get to have that elusive drink and celebrate your new promotion."

"It's hardly a promotion," she managed to utter. "Friday, then," she replied, walking away quickly.

CHAPTER FIFTEEN

I t was as infuriating as hiccups and as maddening as hell that he seemed not at all interested in her anymore.

And even more irritating was the fact that she was doing it again, that thing where her mind was more on Tobias than anything else. She'd been secretly looking out for a 'happy birthday' email from him yesterday but there'd been nothing. He hadn't even appeared remotely interested when she'd invited him to her birthday drinks.

Her problem was that she couldn't easily forget about him and the situation irritated her. It was difficult not to think about the man who sat a few minutes' away from her.

At least watching the movie with Jacob last night, followed by pizza, had taken her mind off what *hadn't* happened on her birthday.

Today was a new day and she was determined to wash that man's memories out of her system. She watched her PC come to life and got out her files and journal, determined to have a normal working day, and not one where she hit the refresh key on her email inbox checking to see if anything had come from him.

But this morning, an email from Tobias teased her as it sat in her inbox. Her insides jolted to life as she rushed to open it.

I would like to see five years' worth of data reflected in the chart on page 6.

Tobias

This infuriated her even more because these were not the words she wanted to hear from him. When the phone rang in the next moment, she answered it quickly, her eyes still on the screen as his words taunted her.

"I've got a day of meetings," Briony announced with a sigh. "This is one of Tobias's days, isn't it? Do you have enough to keep you busy?"

"Yes, I've got plenty." The two days she was supposed to be working on researching companies became known as 'Tobias's days.' "He wants me to make an amendment to the report I handed him yesterday."

"I'll leave you to it."

Savannah hung up. Five years' worth of data, coming up. Determined not to give him a further reason to complain, she worked hard for the next few hours and when the report had been amended as he had requested, she printed it off and arranged it into a professional-looking report, with its plastic front and back and a plastic spine to hold it all together, as Briony had shown her.

She marched towards Tobias's office and rapped her knuckles hard against the wooden door.

"Come in." He was sitting down, with his chin resting on his closed fist and his other hand hovering around his mouse.

"I made the changes you requested." She approached his desk with more confidence than she felt, and handed the amended report to him. He lowered his chin and flicked through it quickly.

"You didn't make any changes to the charts on pages 13 and 17."

"You didn't ask me to."

"I did."

She swallowed, feeling her throat dry up as she stared into his cold blue eyes and forgot to breathe.

"I sent you an email right after the first one."

Shit. She gritted her teeth together but forced the corners of her lips up into a smile. She had been so determined to get to work on the change he had requested that it hadn't occurred to her to check her email for subsequent updates.

Like a horny teenager, she'd been preoccupied with the thought of seeing him again. "I didn't check. I'm sorry." And now he probably thought she was totally incompetent. He handed the report back to her and sat back in his chair as if he was assessing her.

"Before you change your mind again, do you have any other changes to make?" She couldn't help herself.

"Only the ones I emailed you about this morning," he said tightly. "It's always a good idea to make sure there aren't any further amendments required." He made her feel even sillier now, as if he was telling her the Basic 101s of doing her job. "My requests are always likely to change, so I suggest you get used to it."

She forced herself to inhale slowly and smile, and to keep her mouth shut.

"How was yesterday?" he asked, causing her heart to jumpstart to life again. He *did* know about her birthday and he'd been waiting for the right moment to ask her about it. She felt suddenly lighter, as if a summer breeze had just kissed her cheeks.

"We went to see *Alvin and the Chipmunks* and then had a pizza and..." She noticed his hardened face and stopped talking.

"I meant the meeting with Briony." She took a deep breath as his words landed like a fist to her sternum.

"I'm working my way through the new list you gave her," she said, in a voice that was a little too loud, a little too bright, and a little too false. Yet she'd managed to string together a perfectly coherent sentence even though her pride lay in tatters around her ankles, making her feel as bad as if as if her panties had dropped.

Tobias Stone didn't give a hoot about her birthday or what she'd done last night to celebrate it. "Good," he replied and picked up his pen, as if he was ready to get on with his work.

A fireball of emotions started to burn way down deep in the pit of her stomach, threatening to come hurtling out of her throat. Shame made her want to hasten back to her office and hide. "I'll make those changes," she replied, trying to keep her voice strong as she left his office, her jaw clenched tightly. She rushed back to her office and checked her inbox.

There it was. Another email sent three minutes after the first one, requesting the changes.

Please also fix the graphs on pages 13 and 17. Five years' worth of data for both.

Tobias

With humiliation burning her cheeks at her terrible faux pas, for thinking he was even remotely interested in her or her birthday, she couldn't help but fire back a reply.

Before I begin to make the proposed changes, do you have any more? I'm conscious that your requests are prone to changing.

Savannah

He replied in less than a minute:

Any more what?

Tobias

Frowning, her fingers flew across her keyboard.

Surprises.

Savannah

He replied, equally quickly.

I'm full of surprises, when I want to be.

Tobias

Her fingers hovered over her keyboard, her heart rate galloping as she found herself being reeled into a luscious web of flirtation. He *was* flirting with her, wasn't he? His responses no longer sounded like marketing spiel.

You've surprised me enough times, Mr. Stone.

Savannah

Should she send it? Her breathing turned fast, her mouth open as her finger hovered over the 'Send' icon. Damn it, why not? She hit 'Send' before the logical side of her brain stopped her.

And she waited, and waited, and waited, her nerves a mangled wreck of anticipation. But he didn't reply. After a good few moments, the fluttering in her belly petered away. Disappointed, she made herself concentrate on the report solidly, rechecking that she had done as he asked, and refreshing her computer screen constantly. But there were no further emails from him.

Perhaps he was busy.

Of course he was.

She rechecked his last email, rechecked her report again, reprinted it and rebound it once more. Curious and nervous, she got up and made her way to his office one more time. She stood at his door, not having knocked yet, and tightened her quads in a bid to stand tall and strong.

"What's that?" Briony asked, walking up behind her.

"The report Tobias wanted me to fix."

"I'll take it," said Briony, holding out her hand. "I'm about to meet with him and Matthias now."

"Uh—" Her body tensed, not wanting to relinquish the chance of seeing him, not after their recent flurry of emails. She wanted to know if he felt what she did. She needed to look into his eyes, to discover if there was any difference in his demeanor from how he had been when she had first seen him this morning to now. Briony grabbed the report, taking with it her hopes.

"Thanks," said Savannah, and headed back to her office, mission unaccomplished.

CHAPTER SIXTEEN

"You're not coming?" Matthias asked, hovering around his door. Tobias looked up from his computer screen and saw the top of Candace's hat behind him, rising like a furry ferret from her head. "Since when do I come to these events?" Tobias asked. It was Friday night and there seemed to be a relaxed mood around the office which he had noticed in his late afternoon Friday meeting.

Of course, he knew the reason for it.

"I've got things to finish up," he said, giving his excuse, "then I'm flying to Martha's Vineyard this weekend."

"Nice for some."

"There's nothing stopping you from doing the same things," Tobias reminded him. He'd made the man a millionaire many times over.

"We'll have a drink on you," Matthias replied, and raised his hand in a wave before he and Candace disappeared out of view.

Tobias drummed his fingers on the table and reconsidered his decision not to attend. He felt sure that Savannah would wonder why he hadn't shown up. She would want him there, he was sure of it. He rested his clasped hands behind his head and examined the events of the past few days. She was so honest and transparent, and he could see right through her. He knew she was confused about his aloofness.

It seemed to be working.

The truth was, he wanted to go but it would look odd, especially when he didn't usually show up at such events.

If they could somehow turn back time and return to that night when they had kissed, if he hadn't ruined things with his accusations, perhaps he might have been in a position to fly her away for the weekend with him. Maybe he could have helped her to celebrate her twenty-ninth birthday in style. Instead, he had to sit back and pretend he wasn't interested.

W as this her second or third glass of champagne? Savannah took a sip. For sure it was the best she had ever tasted and if Matthias wanted to order another bottle, who was she to say no? She looked around at the familiar faces from work, at the people she was slowly coming to know. Most of them were here. Except for him.

"Having a good time?" Briony asked her.

"I am. People are much more relaxed outside of work."

"See what you miss out on when you're busy watching kiddie's movies."

"I celebrated my birthday with my son and I don't regret a moment of it."

"And why should you? Now, tell me, what else are you doing to celebrate?" Briony asked.

Savannah shifted her neck back. "What do you mean?"

"I mean, what else do you have planned?" Savannah shook her head. There was nothing else. There never was. Though she had thought about taking Jacob ice skating tomorrow.

"Friends, family? Cousins?" Briony persisted.

"They're far away," she muttered, trying to figure out if Briony felt sorry for her or was genuinely interested. "But my parents should be coming down hopefully over the Easter break. I'll do something with them then." She took a big sip from her champagne glass, almost emptying it and found Matthias was by her side in an instant, refilling her glass.

"Excuse me," Briony said, looking up from her cell phone. "I think Max is outside trying to find us." She rushed off and left Savannah and Matthias standing alone. It wasn't that she didn't like him but his interest in her was too intense at times. It was as if he was trying to find out more about her, and she wasn't prone to revealing too much about herself. There was only one man she seemed to have permanently on her mind these days but she'd pushed him too far away from her now, and she regretted it.

"Happy birthday once again, Savannah," said Matthias. "I must say, you look absolutely gorgeous this evening." He raised his glass to her, and she smiled, feeling embarrassed. She'd worn a new long-sleeved polka-dot dress she'd found at a sale. The shift dress, made of silky material, was a good few inches above her knees and shorter than the length she usually wore, especially with nude tights instead of her usual thick black ones. And while the silk fabric of her dress wasn't the best for this type of weather, her thick new coat helped keep the chill out. Wearing high-heeled ankle boots, she was confident in her new clothes. It was amazing what a difference it made—she felt good because she looked good, or did she look good because she felt good?

"Thanks," she muttered, feeling uncomfortable with the way he seemed to undress her with his eyes.

"And how are you finding your new role?" he asked as Candace breezed over to join them.

"It's fairly interesting."

"*Fairly* interesting?"

"You did well to land such a position." Candace reminded her.

"We're similar, in that respect only," Savannah shot back. "You did well to land *your* position." Candace stiffened visibly, unable to come back fast enough with a reply.

"And what sort of training have you had?" Matthias asked,

"Training?"

"For your new role."

She wasn't sure what he was asking. "What do you mean?"

"I mean, have you studied risk theory, financial theory, the markets, quantitative analysis?" He waited expectantly for an answer while she floundered. He seemed to be questioning her right to the job and it surprised her, this, coming from him. Candace, yes, but Matthias? She hadn't expected it.

"I don't need any of that. I'm still doing admin tasks, with some analysis thrown in."

"What did you do before?" he asked.

"I was an office manager in my last job and I handled payroll and helped out with that from time to time." This close examination of her suitability for the job made her uneasy.

"Payroll?" asked Candace.

"It's slightly different than word processing," Savannah replied drily.

"Well, by all accounts you're doing a fantastic job. Briony was telling me how she showed you what to do once and you'd taken it all on board. Excel has a million different uses, so I applaud your efforts. I still can't get my head around pivot tables, but you seem to be getting along fine. Besides," he said, giving her the type of smile that would have charmed the panties off a less resilient woman, "who am I to question you?"

"Pivot tables?" Candace's perfectly shaped and arched brows shifted north.

"They don't come with chairs," Savannah replied smugly. Her remark sent Matthias roaring into laughter.

"What have I missed?" asked Briony, entering the fray. "Max is here!" she announced as a tall and slender woman appeared in view. Savannah almost spit out her drink. She was smartly dressed with patent black high heels and a killer business suit to match.

"*This* is Max?" She'd never expected to see a woman.

Max exchanged greetings with Matthias and Candace whom she had obviously met before. Then, turning to Savannah, "You must be Savannah. I've heard a lot about you."

"I bet you have," murmured Candace.

"Nice to finally meet you," Savannah replied, still not used to Max being a woman. She tried to think back to all the conversations she'd had with Briony where she might have noticed, but no. There was nothing.

"Thank you, darling." Max took a glass of champagne from Matthias.

"It's been a while since you came out to play, Max," he replied, giving her his usual charismatic smile, even though it wouldn't win him any favors.

"This woman works me too hard," Max complained, turning her face to Briony before raising her glass to them all. "Happy birthday, Savannah." They all raised their glasses to her, while she shrank into herself, managing to murmur her thanks. As the chatter started up again, Max and Matthias struck up a conversation while Candace hung around like an extra accessory. Briony whispered.

"I did want to tell you before, but I wanted to see your reaction."

Savannah blushed accordingly. "Thanks," she replied. "But what were you afraid of? That I wouldn't talk to you if I knew?"

"No, I couldn't care less what you thought. You either like me or don't, and if you don't because of *this*, that's your problem. The reason I didn't tell you was that I didn't think it mattered."

"It doesn't," Savannah replied, and stared towards the door when a suited man walked in. Her eagle eyes and ratcheted-up senses had been on alert for any signs of his arrival. But the man wasn't Tobias.

"It doesn't look as if Tobias is coming," she said, clutching her champagne glass for comfort.

"He doesn't show up to these things. I wouldn't take it personally." Briony comforted her.

"Tobias?" asked Matthias, looking ruddy-cheeked as he caught the tail end of the conversation. "He's off to Martha's Vineyard for the weekend. I'm not sure who with. You can never tell with him." Savannah didn't like the tone of his voice, or the implication he made. Or the idea that Tobias was going away with someone for the weekend. Matthias eyed her carefully but she kept her mouth closed, sensing that it wouldn't do to stand up for Tobias, not now, not in front of everyone, not with the way she felt about him.

"I don't think he's with Naomi anymore," Candace offered, sliding her fingers around the base of her glass.

"You'd know about that," Matthias agreed. "You keep close watch on him, don't you, sweetheart?"

She cut her eyes at him. "And you don't?" she snarled back.

"He was working late tonight. Looking over some financials again. That man loves numbers the way most men love lingerie."

"You love lingerie?" quizzed Briony.

"I love admiring it when it is worn well," he replied. "Max looks hotter and hotter each time I see her," he said, as soon as Briony's girlfriend left their group and walked over to join the other women from Briony's office. It surprised Savannah that he seemed to have forgotten his seniority, the way his tongue had loosened.

"I'll be sure to pass on your compliment," said Briony, playfully nudging him with her elbow. "Though she certainly wouldn't give you a second glance."

"Pity," he murmured, looking longingly at her. Savannah wrinkled her nose in disgust.

"Maybe you could ask Tobias for Naomi's number?" Candace suggested. "You wouldn't mind having his cast-offs, would you?"

"Now, now, Candace. Remember we have new people on the team." Matthias reminded her gently. Savannah didn't like the way the two of them were talking, as if there were a hidden meaning to his words. Did Tobias know they talked about him like this? "Come with me," he said, slipping his hand into Candace's and pulling her away. "Let's go mingle."

"Do they always talk about him behind his back?" Savannah asked Briony.

"Who? About Tobias, you mean?"

Savannah nodded. "I thought they were friends."

"They rib each other. I wouldn't take it to mean anything else. He and Tobias go back a long way. And you haven't heard Tobias. He can be sharp when he wants to be." Savannah already knew that, but she couldn't help thinking that Tobias would tell people to their face, instead of talking about them behind their backs the way Matthias and Candace had done.

Maybe she was being overly protective of him because she cared.

She suddenly felt no real desire to be here. The champagne made her feel happy but she'd have been even happier if he'd walked in. She looked around her and the truth hit; the one person she would have liked the most to be here was nowhere to be seen. If only he'd shown up, it would have given her an opportunity to tend to unresolved business.

The emails which they had sent one another a few days ago had stopped suddenly, without explanation. She wanted to know why. Not only was he not here, he was going away. Tonight? Tomorrow? For Valentine's Day weekend? Who with?

Pain mixed with fury and knotted deep in her belly. It hadn't taken long at all for him to find someone else. She checked her cell phone to see if Rosalee might have called and instead found an email from Tobias.

Her insides trembled.

I have checked the report and I have one final request. Apologies. Please change the colors for the chart on page 6, they are hard to tell apart.

Tobias

Was he kidding? She was already pissed that he wasn't here, already worked up that he'd left her hanging by not replying to her email from days ago, and he expected her to believe that he was looking at her report now? On Friday night? Without thinking, she emailed back:

I will do that tomorrow. How sad that you're nitpicking over my report so late on a Friday night, of all nights.

Outraged, she didn't even bother to sign her name. Putting down her champagne glass, she moved to a corner waiting for his reply to light up her mail icon.

"What are you doing hiding over here?" Chloe asked, stopping for a moment, presumably on her way towards the ladies' room.

"I'm checking in with my babysitter." Savannah lied easily and waited for the other woman to disappear. When she looked at her cell phone again, Tobias had replied.

Tomorrow is Saturday but you are more than welcome to come into work if you so wish.

She noted that he also had omitted to sign his name.

Shouldn't you be on your way to Martha's Vineyard for the weekend? I'd hate to think my report was holding you back.

Quick as a flash, his reply came through.

News travels fast.

She jabbed at her keypad:

People talk. You'd be amazed.

He replied:

I don't think so.

She wondered what he would make of it if he'd heard Candace and Matthias talking. She doubted that he had any idea of what others said behind his back and worried that it would come as a shock to him, especially because he was so paranoid and trusted no one anyway.

I would love to continue this conversation, but we are all here at my birthday drinks, to which you were invited, but I notice you didn't show up. You must be getting ready to leave for your weekend away and I am sure you have better things to do than to text me all night long.

She hesitated, noting the innuendo, unsure whether to leave it or not. She bit her lip as she reconsidered. Then let bravado take over and sent it.

I have better things to do than to text you all night long. But if you want to continue this conversation, you are more than welcome to pass by my office when you leave. I'll be here until way past your bedtime.

Savannah smiled to herself, his words making the heat rise to her cheeks. She licked her lips slowly.

Now *that* was an invitation and a half.

CHAPTER SEVENTEEN

She'd only lasted another thirty-six minutes after Tobias's last email, to which she hadn't dared to reply.

Instead, she'd mingled with everyone, while trying to think of reasons why she should or should not go see Tobias at his office this late on a Friday night.

And none of the reasons mattered.

Too late, she was there now.

"Savannah?" He got up slowly, his forehead a crisscross of creases and his eyes pinning her in place from a distance of twenty feet. She slipped through his door which had been ajar, and closed it behind her. Something hot and slippery coiled around inside her, making her legs weak as she stood watching him.

"So you decided to take me up on my offer?"

"Here I am," she replied, breathless from the sheer shock of being here in his office once more, alone with him. And she was probably about to make a complete fool of herself. She had to get her heartbeat under control, her breathing too, before he did that thing he did so well—which was to display a cool air while she whimpered internally in his presence.

"And here you are," he said softly. He looked tired, she decided, as she stepped slowly towards the center of the room. His pale blue shirt didn't look as sharp as it normally did, and though his eyes sparkled, the skin around them looked tight. Moving his hand to his cheek, he scrubbed his face, as if he was still surprised to see her.

"You didn't come?"

"Where?" He was playing ignorant now, was he?

"To my birthday drinks. I invited you." She waited breathlessly, even though she must have sounded like a four-year-old waiting for her party guests to arrive. She took a few slow and tentative steps towards him, hearing only the whooshing of air in her ears.

"So you did," he replied slowly, moving around his desk and taking a few steps towards her while heat raced along her body. It wasn't so much that he was advancing closer, or the way his gaze burned right through her, or the way his lips parted. It wasn't even the way her body was reacting to him—it was the anticipation of what might follow—what she wanted, and she had a pretty good idea that he wanted the same thing. A reconnection, a sign, a flicker of that same interest flashed before her eyes.

"Then why weren't you there?" she asked, in a low whisper.

"Are you disappointed?" he asked, slipping his hands into his pockets while his gaze locked onto her. He stood not more than a foot away from her now, and already the slow burn of liquid heat started to spiral inside her, spreading out towards her chest and stomach.

"Everyone else was there, Briony, Matthias, Candace, Chloe...and some of the other managers I didn't invite."

"I didn't know you were planning such a big celebration."

"I wasn't. I didn't want it but Briony seemed to think it

might be a good idea. It was supposed to be a small affair but it seems to have quickly grown."

"You met Max?"

She grinned at the recollection. "I met Max. I had no idea." His lips curled up in a knowing smile.

"I'm sorry I didn't come," he said and she wondered if his words marked a possible return to how he had been before. He had a softer edge to him now, or was she getting it wrong again, with her body leaping ahead? She bit the bullet.

"I didn't think it mattered—you not being there but if I'm to be honest, it did." Now that she'd put her feelings out for him to see, she waited while her insides tumbled like a crazy sea, awaiting his response for the glimmer of something more.

"I don't usually—"

"Attend these types of events. I know. Briony told me."

"You asked Briony why I wasn't there?"

"Not exactly."

"Not exactly," he echoed, his voice soft as silk. "I've been respecting your wishes, Savannah. You said you wished you'd never met me and you wanted nothing to do with me." She swallowed. *So that's what he'd been doing?*

"Well...I...," she tried to weigh her words carefully. "See, the thing is—" She looked at the egg-shaped glass paperweight on his desk, and tried to calm her insides down before she dared to look at him again.

One, two, three...

She lifted her eyes to him then, withering under the weight of his stare. Dare she lay her heart on the line? Tobias Stone had reawakened feelings in her which she thought had been buried for good after Colt and what he'd done to her. Men, romance and relationships hadn't figured too high up on her list when she'd been preoccupied with trying to pay bills and survive. In despair, she'd sometimes wished for someone to be there, to help with raising her son, but a partner, a confidante, a lover for her? No, that part of it hadn't shown up on her radar.

After Colt, she had no longer wanted to put herself in such a vulnerable place again. But now...now this man had awakened her dormant desires. He'd helped her birth newly created sexual fantasies and surely she owed it to herself to sample whatever he offered, in whatever flavor, for however long?

She could no more close her mind to the emotional tie that bound her to him than she could ignore the physical reaction of her body to him.

"The thing is?" he asked softly, as her gaze slipped to the top of his open shirt. He'd taken off his tie and her eyes fell to the hollow dip below his Adam's apple. She stared back at him, not trusting where her mind was taking her or the way her body was loosening up around him.

"Now that things are better for me, now that time has... taken the edge off what you said to me..." Damn it, why wasn't he interrupting her so that she wouldn't have to twitter on? He watched her intently, making her conscious of herself until heat made her face blush, with lust, or desire, or from embarrassment, she wasn't sure which. "Now that I...I'm...I..." In a fit of exasperation she threw her hands up in the air, brushing her fingers against his chest by accident. "I don't understand this myself. I don't know what this is."

He stepped closer to her, so that there was no more than a passage of air between them and she dared not move back. It was now or never.

"You don't know what this is?" he asked, his voice so low it could have been a vibration. His breath, hot and minty, kissed her skin, and the smell of woody cologne teased her senses, making her breasts heavy, her insides light and stealing the breath from her lungs. He was responsible for this nuclear reaction of emotions in her body and mind, and yet he stood here so calm and unshakeable. How the hell did he manage to do that when she was melting to liquid inside?

"Don't you have anything to say?" she asked, desperate to know about his feelings.

"I said what I needed to say that day. And it's still the same," he said softly. She shook her head once, her eyes zoning in on his lips.

"And what was that?"

"That I need you. I still want you." He slipped his fingers around a lock of her hair and pushed it behind her ear. The feel of his skin against her face jump-started her memories, making her pant faster.

"You do?" she murmured, seeing only his lips, and yearning to taste them again. He nodded.

"You feel like that still? The way you did before?" she asked, wanting to know for sure.

"How was I before?" He dropped his head and his hooded eyes stared back at hers, burrowing deeper into her soul.

"Interested."

"You think I'm not interested?" His lips were a finger's width away, her body craving his touch.

"I can't tell with you," she murmured, letting his fingers entwine with hers. "You're always so unpredictable."

"Does that make you uneasy?" His lips almost grazed hers.

"*You* make me uneasy." She could feel his breath, hot against her skin.

"And does that excite you?"

"*You* excite me."

"That's quite a change in opinion, Ms. Page," he murmured, this time his lips brushed against hers fleetingly, only for a second so that she wasn't even sure she had imagined it.

"Don't you go starting on that *Ms. Page* business," she said irritated, and then because she couldn't wait a second longer, "Kiss me." His lips fell onto her mouth and she moved into him, relaxing and falling into the hard feel of him, and taking in his taste and smell, and his familiarity. His was the touch she had missed and dreamed about for weeks. He parted her lips with his tongue and swirled it over hers.

"You taste like champagne," he said, when they finally broke apart, his lips wet, his husky voice setting off alarm bells in her lower region.

"You taste like mint," she breathed, fixing her arms around the back of his neck and forcing him to dip his head towards her again. As their kissing became more intense, she felt his excitement against her heated body.

Now that there was no interruption, now that the office was empty and it was only the two of them, now that she knew exactly what she wanted—she felt shameless. "Take me here, like you promised," she breathed nibbling his ears and the soft skin underneath. His cologne promised excitement and desire and took her back to that first time when she had accidentally ended up on the thirtieth floor.

"Savannah." He moved his face away, surprise lighting his features. "You don't mean that."

"I *do* mean it. It sounds forward, I know, but it's what I want. I don't say things like this, I don't do things like this, Tobias, but you make me..." He slammed his lips into hers again, their bodies tight, hard and desperate against each another. She felt his hands slide under her coat and move slowly over the curves of her waist and hips and she hitched a breath as sparks crawled along her skin. Her nerves fizzed with excitement.

"God, you drive me insane," he rasped, resting his forehead against hers to take a breath.

She let her hands slip down and rest on his biceps, her

fingers feeling along the contours of his hard and thick muscles. "I need to feel you inside me," she gasped, drunk on desire, her body on fire. It was intoxicating, being around him, feeling and tasting him and she was desperate for all of him, needing him with an urgency that almost scared her. She wanted him to fill her up, to plunder her body, to do those very things she had been thinking and dreaming that he would do to her.

"But...but..." it was the first time she'd heard him stutter. The first time that Tobias Stone had lost his smooth lines and ice-like composure. "We don't have to do this now, Savannah."

His hesitation infuriated her, especially with his obvious hardness betraying his noble excuses. "It's all I've thought of for weeks." She'd said it out loud now and she couldn't unsay it. She could no longer keep her feelings in check, even knowing who he was, and how he could be. She wanted him; she wanted to put the past behind them and to start again. "Don't *you* want this, Tobias? Is it just me?"

"I want you," he croaked, his fingers deliciously piercing into her bottom. She instinctively ground her hips into him, her need for him almost uncontrollable when he stared at her like that, his hands sliding over her body. He seemed to be weighing up his options.

What was he waiting for? "If you think I've come here to blackmail you or —"

"Shush," he said, pulling her tightly against him so that her breasts squashed up against his chest. "Let's not restart any of that. I told you I was sorry."

"Then show me that you're sorry." She was being upfront, but the dirty thoughts she'd been secretly harboring about him now rose up and staked their claim. All the pent-up frustrations and feelings that had accompanied her sleep, or run amok in her brain while she sat at work trying to take her mind off him, now flared out of control. She had been a passionate woman once, before Colt had beaten it out of her. "Show me, Tobias, before I get embarrassed and change my mind."

"I would love to show you," he murmured, nestling his lips along her lower lip and biting it. "I've wanted you the whole time." She mewled against his mouth and snuggled closer to him, feeling the hard line of his chest and stomach, and his hands, big and strong, now resting against her lower back. He leaned in and gave her a slow, lingering, teasing kiss. The kind of kiss that set her insides on fire. The kind of kiss which made her ache for his mouth on her breasts and his fingers lower down. She slipped onto his desk, forcing him to lower his head and lean forward so as not to break their kiss.

"What do you say?" she asked, pulling away and starting to lean backwards.

"Not here," he rasped and grabbed her wrist, pulling her off the desk. He moved towards the door but when he opened it she heard a voice outside. She froze, hidden out of sight behind his body.

"Tobias. Are you still working here, this late?"

"You can talk. I had last-minute things to work out." The shadow of a moving body flitted by. Savannah stayed behind him while he stood at the door with it open a little, so that it exposed only his face. She couldn't help but run her hands down the fabric of his shirt, her excitement at the idea of what was to come making her body suddenly alive, as if sparks of electricity danced across her skin.

"I'm heading home. Enjoy your weekend," the voice sounded far away.

"I will," Tobias replied. As if the sudden lull had cranked up his desire, he turned and grabbed her hard, kissing her with such force that it took her breath away. Like two people who had never kissed before, they went at it and she was sure he was going to take her here now, on his desk, or his couch, or even on the floor. It didn't matter where because she was so wet for him, she could no longer wait for him to glide inside her. Lips and mouths sucked and nipped as his hands slid over her body.

"Follow me," she heard him mumble before he pulled her along and walked towards the elevator. She knew exactly where he was heading.

And about time too.

Her heart thundered like the shot of gunfire and she was vaguely aware of him fiddling around with the elevator buttons. As soon as they were inside, once the doors closed, he was on her. Another kiss, wet and languorous, engulfed her in heat from her breasts all the way to her toes. Her nerves tingled with sultry pleasure, and every inch of her skin ached for the touch of his lips.

And then she remembered what she had on and pulled away in shock.

Off-white underwear.

She couldn't let him see *that*. If ever there was a show-stopper, this was it. She would have made an effort if she'd had any inkling that her night was going to end like this. But oh, dear god, off-white old panties and an unflattering bra? A man like Tobias, she was sure, had bedded models in the real classy stuff she saw in magazines. Naomi would have been all satin and lace.

She couldn't compete.

"What is it?" he asked, sensing her hesitation as the elevator doors slid open. He was still holding her hand as they crossed the thickly carpeted hallway and she stared at the black wallpaper. She had a feeling that once she passed through that door, that there would be no going back. "We don't have to do this if you're not ready," Tobias told her, his voice solemn.

To hell with it. She was ready; she was so slick with heat

and lust and it wouldn't matter—not for too long—what color or state her undergarments were in.

"I'm sure," she breathed, as he opened the door to the penthouse. "Are you?"

CHAPTER EIGHTEEN

W as he sure?

Hell, yeah. His pulse raced and his fingers trembled as he worked the key to the penthouse door. It didn't help that Savannah's fingers teased along the waistband of his slacks and shivers scampered along his back.

He pushed open the door and with his hand on the small of her back, pushed her in. She glanced around, her eyes widening as she looked around, taking in the windowed wall at the far end and the spiral staircase. She looked around in awe, breathless and speechless, the way most people were when they first came up here. He caught the motion of her chest heaving fast and furious and saw that her eyes were bright, her skin translucent.

She looked at him with pure desire. Closing the door behind him, he walked towards her and took her by the fingers, gently pulling her to him. She was heat and softness, and he didn't know how long he could hold back.

"Welcome to my penthouse," he said, cupping her cheek with one hand and sliding her coat off with the other.

"It's...it's..." He knew. The light and space up here, the wood and windows, the metal staircase, all of it left people speechless. But she hadn't come here to admire the setting. He raked his fingers through her hair and she pushed herself up against his chest, her soft body driving his hard one insane. Soon enough, if they didn't slow down, he would reach the point of no return.

"It's beautiful up here," she murmured.

"Hmmmm," he moved his hands to her face and fingered the outline of her lips with his thumbs. "Do you want to talk about what happened? Now that you've calmed down and hopefully forgiven me."

"I've been wanting to talk to you for a while."

"I know. I kept my distance deliberately. I wanted you to have your space."

"Why did you stop emailing me that day?" she asked. Their emails had quickly taken on a more personal tone; writing words behind a screen was easy but he needed to see her face to face, to make sure things were fine once more between them. "I wanted to be sure you weren't still angry with me."

"I'm not angry with you."

"I'm forgiven?" he asked.

"Completely. It's all in the past." Relieved, he bent down and slipped a kiss on her lips again. She tasted heavenly, of champagne, and lust and his thoughts soared into overdrive, an image of her naked body flashing into his mind. Her mewling, as she ground her hips into him, sent the blood rushing around his body. Engorged, he needed release.

"Is this the champagne talking, Savannah?"

She shook her head. "No. It's me. I think about you more times than is good for me. We've said things to one another in the past but I don't think it's what we meant to say. I know I lashed back at you. But it's not the way I feel now." This was music to his ears, that she didn't play games, didn't hold back but laid her heart on the line. He'd have to be careful he didn't crush it carelessly again. He didn't intend to.

"It's not?" he asked, knowing that she was right but not able to tell her, just yet, of how he felt. He slipped his arms around her waist.

"Make love to me." Her hooded eyes stared up at him from behind thick mascaraed lashes.

Anticipating the next hour, his mind still managed to function. "What about Jacob?"

"I have a babysitter." He struggled to maintain control, especially when all he wanted to do was to rip her dress off and get dirty with her. "What do you want to do?" he asked, as an image of her lying spread-eagled on his bed upstairs tempted him.

"How about we discuss the charts I created earlier," she whispered, sucking his lower lip. He pulled his head back, his fingers frozen on the curve of her hip.

"Charts?" he asked, he could never tell with Savannah Page.

"Don't be silly," she replied, her lips slinking into a smile as her fingers raked through his hair. He could smell the zingy scent of her perfume and his body tensed in preparation. They lingered once more, entrenched in a kiss so deep, so molten, that he found himself falling deeper into her, his mind and senses being swallowed whole.

"I want you to screw me senseless," she whispered.

The blood rushed south, emptying his mind of normal thought. "We don't have to rush things, Savann—"

"Stop. Talking." She breathed. "Before I change my mind." He heard the urgency in her voice, could feel it in the way she kissed him, with a thirst and a hunger he hadn't come across. He wanted it slower, upstairs in bed; wanted to take his time with her, to examine every inch of her, to undress her slowly, revealing each part of her in turn, he wanted to work his mouth and tongue over every crevice of her body because for weeks she had lingered in his thoughts and now his moment with her had come.

But she didn't look like a woman who could wait. Her boldness and brashness, her heat and want, excited him beyond reason. He wasn't used to this, to having someone else control the timing and pacing of his lovemaking, but then he'd always known she was different.

"Do you have—?"

"Yes," he replied, walking away to a chest of drawers on which a bright green and navy blue vase rested. He fumbled inside the drawer and felt her hands around his waist as she hugged his back.

"You have protection placed strategically throughout your penthouse?" She giggled, and he felt her breasts against his back. She peeked around his arm, her lips grazing his bicep with a small kiss.

"I have to be careful," he replied, slipping the foil packet into the pocket of his slacks as he turned around to face her. "Are we really going to do this now? Don't you want to wait for a more opportune time?" In answer she lifted on her tiptoes and kissed him on his lips, letting her tongue swirl around his lips and running her hands down the side of his ribs.

He was going to explode if this continued. She pulled back and stared at him with bedroom eyes. "I'm a single mom, Tobias. I don't have a lot of time, or many *opportune* moments. Not that I make a habit out of doing *this*."

And that was when he grabbed her wrist.

"Where are you going?" she asked, as he moved towards the spiral staircase.

"Upstairs."

"Upstairs?"

"To bed. I want to enjoy you slowly, Savannah."

"I don't want slow," she told him as she tugged at his hand.

"But I want our first time to be special, I want to take my time with you and be gentle." He pulled her towards him, his hungry hands squeezing her bottom once more and pushing her body further into his hardness.

"I haven't had sex in almost three years, Tobias. Slow and gentle aren't the things I need right now."

Holy shit. His jaw tightened when her hands started to undo his belt. He took a deep breath, fighting the urge to rip her dress off, and needing to restrain himself now that her confession made *him* feel like a man who hadn't had sex for years. "Then I will do my best to screw you senseless," he murmured, nipping her lower lip and dragging her towards the corner, near the curved TV screen and the sectional sofa pit.

He threw her onto the dark gray velvet sofa which was larger than a bed. Orange and green brocade cushions bounced as she moved back up on it, inviting him with those sultry eyes. Her dress rode up, only barely covering her thighs, and Tobias licked his lips. His breathing was ragged as he peeled off her tights, taking her panties off at the same time. He wanted to savor the sight of her but as he reached for the hem of her dress, unsure how to take it off, she pushed his hands away. He wanted to strip her down to nothing, but for now, for today, for this first time, he was going to respect her wishes and do it her way. He'd have his chance later. He sat back on his knees and pulled out his foil packet when she shimmied forward and undid his belt. He got up and almost groaned in agony when she pulled his boxer briefs and slacks down. He shrugged them off as she lay back, propped up on her elbows, watching him sheath himself. His heartbeat rocketed as he caught her staring in this most intimate moment. He had no qualms, or worries or outrageous accusations to make. He'd been missing something in his life and this woman had somehow managed to make herself fit right into it. He didn't know how, he didn't know what would happen next, all he knew was that he needed her, and he liked to think she needed him too. His soul warmed at the thought of their need for one another.

She moved her legs apart and threw her head back, giving him a look that made him want to crawl all over her like a spotty teenager, except that he was now schooled in holding back, in maintaining his control. He climbed onto the sofa and gently lowered his body over hers, at the same time lifting her dress up and feeling her wet nakedness for the first time. She arched her back, letting out a long and drawn-out sigh as his mouth melted into hers. He was more turned on than ever by the sound of her moans, long and low. Her soft breasts rested against his chest and he longed to suckle them, but there was no opening on her dress and he couldn't find the access he so craved. He was desperate to see her naked, to feel all of her against him but she threw her arms around his neck, clinging to him like her life depended on it.

Three years?

He moved his thumb around her swollen wetness, getting even harder when he found her soaking wet. Slipping into position, he met her softness with his hardness and dipped his head down, kissing her deeply. His tongue meshed with hers and as each mewl escaped from her mouth, it became harder for him to hold back. He lifted his head and stared at her, and then she groaned; a guttural sound, hungry and deep. That was it. He rammed into her with one smooth thrust, all the way to the hilt, making her scream, before he pulled out slowly. And again and again, slipping out slowly, sliding in hard and fast; the wet and sloshy noises of their union mingled with her cries of rapture and took him to a place where they were one. Raw and animalistic, this felt like more than making love. Her cries rose with every thrust, making him want to do it over and over again.

Three years?

His deep frustrations, built up in the weeks he'd stayed away from her, now melted away with every stroke, every push and every pull. He never once took his gaze off her; she was hot and wet, her thighs moist with sweat. As her dress bunched up around her waist, his gaze fell to her face, to her open mouth and closed eyes as she whimpered and sighed loudly, bucking wildly, easily and fast, and all he could do was watch as she came, shuddering and throbbing, her face flushed pink as her knees hugged his waist. She was too far gone, too deeply immersed in her own world as he stared down at her, allowing himself to be completely swallowed up by her. It took all of his control not to explode as he watched her release. When he came, moments later, it was violently and with a release that drained him to his core.

After a short while, they turned on their sides, facing each other. He stared into her bright eyes, losing himself in them and giving himself up to a connection so deep, he could almost feel it in his heart.

She smiled. "I've never felt that before," she murmured, stroking his hair. In answer, he bent down and seared her lips with another deep kiss. He would want her again, and again, and again.

He didn't know how long they lay there, except that she suddenly sat upright and glanced at her watch. "Jacob!" she gasped. "I have to get back. I told Rosalee I'd be back by ten. It's almost ten thirty." The anxiety in her voice forced him back to reality. He reluctantly moved off the sofa as she hunted around for her things. He found her panties behind a cushion and gave them to her.

"Thank you," she whispered, turning her back to him as she hopped into them.

"Hey," he said, once he had pulled on his slacks and made

himself decent. He grabbed her hands and forced her to look at him. "Was that...was that worthy of your three-year hiatus?"

"Couldn't you tell?" she asked, smiling back at him. "It was definitely worthy."

"No regrets?"

"None." She said, picking up her coat, in an obvious hurry to get away. "You?"

"None." He waited for her to slip her shoes back on before he pulled her to him and kissed her again. He couldn't help but slide his eager hands around her thick coat. "I don't want you to go."

"I don't want to go," she said, placing her hands on either side of his face. "But I have to. I'm sorry."

"I want to see you again. This isn't just a one-night stand...is it?"

She paused a fraction too long before answering. "I hope not."

"It's not. I want to see you again, Savannah. Not just for *this*," he explained, not wanting to get things off to a wrong start. "I mean you and me, being together, not just *this*..."

"*This* was pretty great," she said, a smile dancing on her lips. "As far as *this* goes, we all know that whatever Tobias Stone wants, Tobias Stone gets." She lifted her lips and kissed him again.

"Not always," he murmured. "But most of the time."

"It could get complicated," she said.

It would be complicated. He had yet to own up to his part in orchestrating her decision to remain with his company. She would hate him for it, for controlling her in this way but he'd done it because he believed he'd given her a better alternative. Of course, she would have another opinion on the matter.

It still wasn't going to deter him. Nothing would. He liked that she didn't play mind games or speak in riddles. "Are you glad I came?" she asked, her gaze dropping once more to his lips.

"Literally or figuratively?" he asked, wishing she wasn't wearing that coat and wanting to feel her skin beneath it.

"Both," she replied, the glazed expression in her darkened eyes telling him that she was hungry for him again. He wanted to spend the night with her, and not only the night, but the whole weekend too. "Come away with me this weekend," he urged but she had moved away from him, as if he'd said something hurtful.

"I'd forgotten that you were going away."

"I'm going to a friend's wedding in Martha's Vineyard. Come with me."

"I can't do that, Tobias, as much as I would love to," she seemed suddenly flustered. "I have Jacob. I can't up and go whenever I want."

Of course she couldn't. "I understand."

"Is that going to be a problem?" she asked, looking worried. He slipped his hands around her waist, needing her to know that it wasn't going to be a problem.

"Not at all, I promise you."

"It sounds like a nice weekend," she said quietly, as she fished her cell phone out from her bag.

"It would have been even better with you there." But she was staring at her cell phone, her face tightening in an instant. "Savannah," he said, tracing his finger along her cheek. "What's the matter?"

She shoved the cell phone away. "Nothing. I thought Rosalee might have called. But she didn't."

"So?" *What had scared her?* "Savannah?"

"My, uh...my ex called." She laughed nervously.

"What did he want?" He inclined his head, his breath catching in his chest.

"I don't know. I missed his call and anyway," she dismissed it with a blink of her eyes, "he probably called me by mistake." But Tobias was wary. He knew enough about her unsavory ex than to dismiss it so easily. "This wedding on the weekend," she said, tugging at her earlobe, "is it just you going?"

"If you won't come with me, then yes, I'll go alone." He grazed his lips against hers, the urge strong to turn the light kiss heavy. He pulled away reluctantly before she made him hard again and cupped her face in his hands. "I don't have anyone else in my life, Savannah. You know that but maybe things will be different now." She turned her lips towards his fingers and kissed them. "Maybe."

Maybe this could work.

"I have to get back," she told him. "I've never been this late before." The thought of not waking up with her tomorrow, of only having her for such a short amount of time, just about killed him.

"I'll drive you back."

"Thank you." She seemed anxious to get back to Jacob. He didn't know what that felt like anymore—being responsible and caring for someone. But now he was determined to take away her worries and the harshness of her life, and make things better for her again.

When the time was right—and if she was okay with it—he'd take her away somewhere, only the two of them; somewhere where they could be alone. Later, when she was ready, and if things went well, they could all spend time together, Jacob too. He would take the lead from her.

For the first time in years, Tobias Stone dared to believe that all was not lost, and that maybe this was the start of a new beginning.

THE OFFER, BOOK 2

The Billionaire's Love Story (#5)

CHAPTER ONE

"I guess I'd better go," she murmured, not moving her hand from Tobias's.

"I guess you'd better." His lips grazed over her cheeks before his mouth found hers and he gave her another one of his deep, lingering kisses. Sparks ignited over her skin as the sizzle went straight to her belly. His mouth slid over hers, capturing her bottom lip and sucking gently. Tobias tasted of warmth, and sweetness and mint, and when his lips trailed softly from her mouth to her neck, she had a hard time remembering that she needed to leave.

"You're...making it ...incredibly difficult for me to get out of this car."

"Ummm-hmmm," he murmured, his lips sucking her neck gently, making her toes curl. Held captive by his kisses, his words and his touch, she had been unable to leave even though she knew Rosalee would be waiting. She was already late. Dragging herself away from this man was as impossible as not breathing. Her heart surged with a happiness she hadn't known since Jacob had been born.

He lifted her hand to his mouth and kissed her fingers. "You sure I can't come in?"

"Jacob would be asleep," she replied, wishing she could let him come upstairs but not ready for Rosalee's questions.

"Even better," he muttered, his voice soft, his eyes glistening in the darkness that was partially lit from the fading light of the lampposts. With Rosalee leaving, and Jacob asleep, they would be able to...

"You're tempting me," she whispered. Sex with him had been like nothing she had ever known; a level of connecting she had never experienced and it had touched her on more than just a physical level. It was something deeper, something magical.

"I'd settle for a cup of coffee," he said, stroking her wrists gently and lighting a fire in her body. "While I would happily worship your body, we could just sit and talk." She hated turning him down, especially as now, she sensed he was lonely, as if he didn't want to go home. But things were complicated and she wasn't ready yet.

"Tobias—"

"It's fine," he said, moving away. "Another time."

"I'd have to explain to Rosalee, and Jacob, I hope he's sleeping but if he isn't..."

"You don't have to explain, Savannah. I understand. I know it's going to be complicated; it's going to be tricky at work, too, but we'll get through that. Okay?"

"Okay." But she was secretly wary of what people would think; never mind what Briony's reaction might be, she knew she would need nerves of steel to deal with Candace and Matthias. Yet it was hard not to believe him when he stared at her like that, with desire burning in his eyes. He seemed to carry an air of quiet conviction that everything would work itself out.

"I wish you could come away with me this weekend. You and Jacob. It's not too late if you decide to change your mind."

It sounded tempting, if alien to her, the idea of flying off for the weekend in his private jet to attend a wedding. How would he explain her to his friends? And what about Jacob? As tempted as she was, Savannah knew she couldn't even entertain the idea. "Jacob would have a million questions."

Tobias kissed her hand again. "And?"

"He adores you, Tobias. I don't want to get his hopes up."

He sighed loudly enough for her to hear. She could tell from his expression that this wasn't the answer he wanted. "I understand. It's not easy for you. Not yet, then."

Not yet? She stared at him, trying to decipher his intent. She was sleeping with her boss's boss and she was in murky territory, even though there was nothing illicit about them being together. She hadn't done this because she was trying to get something from him, and he hadn't come after her because he was using her. He wasn't. This was just two people getting together, drawn towards one another, at least that was what it was for her.

Was it the same for him, she wondered?

"What do you mean, 'not yet'?"

"In time. We can't hide this forever."

"It's not going to be easy, what with me being an administrative person and with you being who you are." Forget Jacob, and Rosalee and Colt, sleeping with the CEO was going to brand her as a slut. She wasn't ready to deal with any of that. And Kay.

Damn it.

How was she ever going to explain herself to Kay? Tobias wasn't even aware that her cousin was his number-one groupie and here she was having sex with him. Her cousin would never forgive her.

"Is that how you see us?" he asked, suddenly serious as he stroked his thumb across her cheek. "You captivated me from the start, Savannah Page. Meeting you has been one of the best things to happen to me." Startled by his words, she pulled back a little, frowning. He wasn't prone to revealing much about his feelings, and his admission took her by surprise. "I don't care what others think."

"But I do, Tobias." He lived in a world where he made up his own rules. She had to live by them. "Social media would go crazy. You would break the internet. Can you imagine the women following the most eligible bachelor lists?" Her mouth curved into a smile at the idea of her cousin having a meltdown.

"Those blasted lists," he said, pressing her hand as it lay in his. They sat in silence for a few moments in the quiet darkness. Fluorescent rays of light danced across the sleeping street.

"Rosalee's waiting." Savannah said, giving his hand one final squeeze. In reply he pulled her closer, parting her lips with his tongue and leaving her with a sizzling kiss that left her breathless.

"And now I want you even more," she whispered. Disappointment spread over her like a second skin.

"Hold that thought."

"Enjoy the wedding," she said, then opened the door and stepped out. Rushing towards the apartment main door, she turned and gave him one final wave, feeling like a teenager who had come home way later than she should have. She smiled at the concierge and got into the elevator. Luckily, Arnold wasn't at the desk tonight.

She stepped into her apartment and bounded into the living room. "I'm sorry I'm late," she cried, feeling guilty as she saw Rosalee with her eyes closed.

"You're back," her babysitter replied, jerking wide awake and getting up slowly from the couch.

"Did you fall asleep?" Savannah glanced at her watch. It was nearly eleven o'clock. Guilt washed over her in buckets. "I'm sorry, Rosalee. I got...carried away." She felt bad that her own pleasure had put this woman out. Rosalee slipped her arms through her coat and smiled.

"You're glowing," she remarked. "You must have had a good evening."

"It was nice to get out." Savannah clapped a hand to her face, as if trying to hide the tell-tale signs of her evening. "Wait, Rosalee. You can't walk home now. I'm going to call you a cab." She'd never had Rosalee stay so late before and even though her babysitter lived a few blocks away, Savannah didn't feel right about her walking home alone at this time of night.

"Nonsense." Rosalee wrapped her scarf around her neck, slipped on her gloves and pulled on a thick woolly hat. "It's only a few blocks."

"But it's late. You can't walk home by yourself," Savannah insisted, not yet having taken her own coat off. "I'll walk you home." The elderly woman shuffled closer to her and looked at her as if she'd lost her mind.

"Then I'd have to walk you home to make sure *you* got back safely." The elderly woman shook her head. "I won't let you leave Jacob home alone." Rosalee had a point. With Arnold not being here either, Savannah was loath to leave the building.

"I'm calling you a cab," she fished her cell phone out of her handbag but Rosalee had already opened the door.

"Go to bed, my dear. I'll text you when I get home, if it makes you feel any better."

"I won't be so late again."

"A late night every now and then is not a problem." She kissed Savannah on her cheek and walked out, leaving her alone in the apartment, with happy memories of her evening. She'd forgotten all about her birthday drinks at the bar. Her cheeks burned at the memories of Tobias and the penthouse, and what they had done. She wondered what it would be like to spend all night by his side.

Unable to wipe the huge smile off her face, she walked into Jacob's room and gazed at her son who was soundly asleep. She sat on the edge of the bed, kissing him on his cheek and stroking his face, happy with the way things were unfolding in her life.

When she turned in for the night, sliding into an empty bed, she wished Tobias was here, lying beside her.

CHAPTER TWO

Arriving back in New York in his private jet sometime late on Sunday afternoon, Tobias was anxious to see Savannah again. It was Valentine's Day and he hoped that he might get to see her, maybe even to just have a hot dog at Bryant Park.

The whole time he'd been at the wedding, he'd not really been there; he'd been thinking of her and he couldn't wait to get back. He was hoping to meet with her this evening but even though he'd called her many times during the day, she hadn't answered or called him back. He knew it wouldn't be easy to get the time and the opportunity to see her, but he wasn't one to give up so easily.

Her silence made him uneasy.

Was she starting to have regrets?

Back in his apartment, he found it difficult to concentrate on anything when the object of his desire was only a thirty-minute drive away. Not wanting to call her or intrude too much, he'd gone for a session at the boxing ring with his trainer. When he returned a few hours later, sweating like a pig in an August heatwave, he was too worn out to lift a finger. But his energy soon perked up when he saw that he had a missed call from her.

"Hey," he said, his voice immediately soft. "I was beginning to get worried."

"Sorry. I saw all the missed calls but I was helping a friend with her son's birthday party. He's a good friend of Jacob's."

"On Valentine's Day?"

"Children don't care what day it is. A birthday is sacred no matter when it falls," she declared. He could already see her smiling from the way she spoke. "How was the wedding?"

"Cold, with six inches of snow. It looked like a winter wonderland."

"It sounds beautiful."

"It was stunning." The wedding had been beautiful but for all its beauty, and the snow-kissed trees and gardens and the white Christmassy twinkle lights, he would want somewhere hot and exotic if he ever got married again. "I missed you."

"I missed you too," she whispered.

"Happy Valentine's Day." He wasn't sure if it was too soon, or too mushy, or too much but he hadn't said those words in a long time and right now he felt the urge to say them to her. She giggled.

"Happy Valentine's Day," she replied. He heard a "why are you whispering?" in the background and contained a chuckle as he listened to her explain. "Because I didn't want to disturb you, honey."

"How's Jacob doing?" It had been a while since Tobias had seen the boy.

"He's suffering from the Sunday night blues. The weekend throws him and all of a sudden, returning to school on Monday doesn't seem so appealing. But he's tired from his friend's party so hopefully he'll settle down real quick."

"Settle down real quick," Tobias mused. "Is there a process involved?"

"Dinner, then bath time, then a bedtime story. It usually works well." It sounded as if her Sunday evening had been planned with military precision.

"Oh," he made a disappointed noise. "I guess there's no chance of meeting up today?" It was when she laughed that he knew there wasn't. "It's still not *that* late," he added, hoping to convince her.

"It's almost six," she countered in a tone that didn't sound as if she was about to reconsider.

It's still not that late, he thought, but decided against trying to persuade her further.

"What did you have in mind?" she asked.

"I was wondering if I could see you over dinner—both of you?" A long silence followed and made him wonder if she was reconsidering. "Not because it's Valentine's Day or anything," he added quickly. "I don't want you to think I'm turning all mushy on you."

"You turning mushy on me?" She giggled. "I didn't think that emotion was in your repertoire."

"You'd be surprised."

"True," she agreed. "You've surprised me before."

"The feeling is mutual." He heard her breathe out slowly, could almost see the contours of her lips and her mouth, and the dips and hollows of her neck.

"I'm sorry, Tobias. It's going to be difficult to make my way there now."

"Not even for a hot dog in Bryant Park?"

"The thing is, if I'd known earlier, I would have gone there instead of coming home. But now that we're here, it's going to be a hassle to get back out again."

"I'll drive over and pick you up."

"It's getting late and—" He was beginning to wonder if these were just excuses.

"Jacob's overtired as it is from the party and going to Bryant Park now would only make him even grumpier later on. And with it being a Monday tomorrow..."

"It's fine," he replied, unable to hide the mild irritation that had crawled along his skin.

"It's not." She paused. "I know it feels as if I'm making every excuse not to see you. I'm not. I've thought about you all weekend."

"All weekend?"

"Even today at the party when I was giving out cupcakes."

"What exactly were you thinking?"

"I was imagining how it would be if you were there too. Not that, you know, not that I'm expecting any type of commitment or anything."

Did she think this was a temporary fling? "Are you afraid of commitment?"

"Uh." She paused, and he could hear her struggle to find an answer.

"This wasn't a one-night stand for me, Savannah."

"I see." She replied, sounding more unsure than ever.

"You *see*?" What had made her doubtful all of a sudden?

"I just don't know how this will work out."

"In time." He assured her. "You seem to have lost faith," he asserted. "Why?"

"Why what?"

"Why aren't you expecting commitment?"

"Uh...well...because...my marriage wasn't the best exactly..." Her voice became softer, whisper-like, and he wished he was by her side to comfort her. "I guess I don't want to raise my hopes, that's all."

What little he knew of her ex made him fist his knuckles.

"Your ex-husband doesn't sound like the type of man you deserve."

"He wasn't so bad in the beginning," she replied, jumping to the man's defense. Silence filled the airwaves while Tobias waited for her to say something more.

"Can I see you tomorrow?" she asked. "To make up for today?"

She obviously didn't want to talk about her past. He understood that. "You've got no reason to make up for today."

"Can I see you anyway?" she asked.

"Are you really asking me that?"

"I'm really asking you that." She made a noise in her throat, like a half-hearted laugh. "I know what a busy man you are, Tobias. Could you pencil me into your schedule, do you think?" Her tone seemed more playful, and he was relieved to take her mind away from her past.

"I would make time for you."

"I wouldn't expect you to. I know you have a billion-dollar business to run."

"I'd make time for you." At the moment he said it, he knew it was true. He'd move mountains for this woman if he had to, because she never expected him to and that made him want to do it even more for her.

"If I can't see you today, then I must see you tomorrow."

"I could come by a little earlier...or I could stay late." Her voice turned silky, making him wonder if she was thinking of the same thing; the penthouse.

"Would staying late work for you?" he asked, mindful that Jacob was her priority. "Maybe we could grab dinner somewhere and—"

"Maybe we could go straight to your penthouse," she shot back. Her words sounded lighthearted, but there was nothing lighthearted about them.

"We could do that too," he replied, memories of her lying on his sofa, sticky and sweaty and calling his name, exciting him. Maybe he could take her and Jacob away somewhere for a vacation. At least if they went away, they might get to spend quality time together, instead of snatched moments. It would be the only time they stood a chance of having something that resembled a relationship. With his trip to Hong Kong less than a month away, he wondered how easy it would be to swap Savannah with Matthias and how it would go down with his colleague?

"Could do that?" she questioned.

"*Will* do that," he corrected. "You haven't seen the bedroom, and this time we get to do it my way."

She moaned lightly. "I look forward to it."

Not as much as he did, he was sure.

"I'll see you tomorrow, then," she whispered.

"Come by my office first thing, to say 'hello.'" Of course then would not be the time to tell her how he had orchestrated a way of keeping her at Stone Enterprises.

That confession would have to come later.

CHAPTER THREE

She'd never been this eager to get to work.

In the past, what with all their ups and downs, and Tobias's temperamental moods, Savannah had always felt anxious around him; way before she became aware of her attraction to him. But even then her anxiety levels had never been as high as they were today.

Now it was different. They had 'something' and it was real, not a figment of her imagination. The thought of seeing him again got her all hot and bothered and the elevator ride to the twenty-first was fraught with more tension than usual. Her insides tingled in delicious excitement as she eyed the button to the thirtieth floor.

She arrived at work early, feeling guilty about leaving Jacob earlier than usual at the Breakfast Club. She'd also asked Rosalee if she could keep Jacob for longer after school, telling her babysitter that she would pick Jacob up from her around 9:00 p.m.

She struggled to find time for Tobias, to give this relationship a chance to take hold, and she felt equally guilty for not spending time with her son. Not only that, it meant she needed Rosalee more. Savannah's dependence on her elderly friend made her uneasy and she hated that she had no one else to turn to.

Yet being with this man made her happy. Her moments of pure happiness were interspersed with moments of doubt. Was this the *right* time to have a relationship? She had purposely not gone looking for one but now that she found herself involved with Tobias, she was beginning to question if it would even work.

These thoughts plagued her as she arrived at work. Setting her things down in her own office first, she left her coat and bag there, then picked up her folder and pen and grabbed a report she'd been working on for Tobias, in case she needed an alibi for her visit. Smoothing down her corduroy skirt, she took a deep breath and made her way to Tobias's office.

She froze when she saw Candace's back as the PA opened the door to her office. As if she'd sniffed Savannah's arrival on the scene, Tobias's PA displayed an exaggerated look of surprise that would have been worthy of an Oscar nomination. "It's early for you, isn't it?"

"Even earlier for you," commented Savannah drily, and knocked on Tobias's door, turning her back to Candace. She entered on hearing his command.

Tobias gave her a smile that lit up his entire face and she noted how much softer he looked. "Good morning, Ms. Page," he said, getting up from his seat. She closed the door behind her and her heart skipped a beat as she walked towards his desk.

"Good morning, Mr. Stone," she replied, in the most provocative-sounding voice she could summon. They stood staring at one another across his pristine and polished desk. His eyes sparkled, his lips curved upwards and she tried not to let her gaze dwell too long on that naughty mouth of his.

"I'm glad you came by, Ms. Page," he murmured then slowly

walked around to her. Once again, he stood so that only inches of air separated them. Close enough for the woody aroma of his aftershave to kick her senses into overdrive.

"I missed you," she told him, and stared longingly at his lips, waiting for him to make the first move. She was suddenly shy and unsure again. The bravado of Friday night was a memory that now slipped away. Under the black turtleneck top, she felt her heart start to race and her legs turn to jelly. She only had to be within holding distance from this man and she turned to jelly. It wasn't going to bode well for their working relationship. It was difficult to focus on anything, especially when his glittering eyes flashed at her so provocatively. Trying to remain within their set boundaries, when her mind was filled with X-rated images of them together, was going to be impossible.

"I want to kiss you," he teased, his voice low.

"I wish you would."

"Later," he promised. "I'll kiss you all over." His words sent shivers along her spine as his hands slipped easily into his pockets. She'd been waiting for him to grab her, to show her how much he had missed her, so that she could return the favor. She'd been imagining, and had been hopeful for the feel of his lips on her mouth, for his arms around her, for the feel of his hard body against hers, but his cool and restrained manner painted a different picture. She understood. They could ill afford anything risky here and now. Friday night had been different. After hours, the darkness and the emptiness of the building had been intoxicating. Their desire had made them careless. It was so very different from this busy Monday morning as the Stone Building came to life amid a bright blue sky strewn with flashes of sunlight.

"Candace saw me come in," she told him. "I'm sure she's wondering what I'm doing here so early."

"You're paranoid," he said, his brow creasing slightly before the corners of his lips curved upwards. His eyes ran down the length of her body, resting slowly over her black turtleneck top, clingy and tight, and one she had purposely worn in order to garner this very effect from him. She could feel him undressing her slowly. Wished he would.

"That top fits you very well." He cleared his throat, bringing his gaze to her face. She smiled, impressed by his ability to make a simple compliment sound filthy. She hated that the day had only just begun.

"I'm glad you think so."

He swallowed, and she could have sworn he was fighting for control.

"Your PA wants my blood."

"Don't take it personally. She's not as important as she thinks. Here," he said, picking up a red and white paper bag from his desk and handing it to her. "A little something for you."

"What's this?" she asked, surprised, then opened it and looked inside.

"For Valentine's Day—I mean, I know it's not Valentine's Day today and I don't even know if it's the kind of thing you would celebrate but...I saw it in one of the gift shops." It had to be one of the longest sentences he had ever said. She pulled out a purple rubber jellyfish from the gift bag and threw her head back in surprise.

"It's...it's...lovely," she said, before breaking out into peals of laughter.

"I thought of you."

"A rubber jellyfish made you think of *me*?"

"Not exactly," he replied. He *had* been thinking of her. The thought made her feel warm all over. She leaned towards him.

"I want to kiss you," she confessed, her gaze dipping down to his lips.

"I know," he replied, a little too smugly.

She knew one kiss would not be enough, not for her and not for him. Knew that he would want to kiss her for the longest time, and feel her up and down, let his hands roam all over her body. And she relished that thought. He had awakened a hotbed of desire in her. One that had been asleep for years.

If they moved any closer together, she'd be in danger of having her arms wrapped around his neck. They couldn't go there, not here, not now. "Thank you, for being so thoughtful."

"You're welcome." His eyes turned dark once more, the way she remembered when he'd made love to her.

This was going to be difficult. Sweet torture, with him so close, yet untouchable.

"I told Rosalee I was staying late tonight."

"Good," he murmured. His smile said a million things. She had gone shopping this weekend and bought a few more sale items and some affordable but sexy lingerie—as fast as was possible to do so with a six-year-old in tow. Jacob made retching noises behind her and had walked around emitting loud and disgusted sighs, blatantly covering his eyes with his arms when she had picked up some lace lingerie sets.

"We could go for dinner first. Anywhere you want to go," Tobias suggested. Her smile faded. Dinner would be lovely but it meant that they might be seen together and she wasn't ready for that yet, and neither, she suspected, was he.

"Don't you think we should play it cool for a while, Tobias? What if someone saw us together? Are you ready for the million questions?"

"Are you worried about Jacob?"

"Not just Jacob. What about you? You're a well-known man. You're the CEO, you have a reputation and..." Those goddamned eligible bachelor lists Kay kept going on about. If anyone saw her with him, if news got out, and went viral, not only would it make things difficult for her working here, but one of her worse fears would be realized. Colt would find out where she was and so far she'd managed to keep her exact location a secret from him. He knew she was working and that she was in New York and that was more information than she was comfortable with him knowing. Damn. If only she'd changed her cell phone number when she'd left her hometown.

Stupidly, she'd taken her mother's advice at the time. "You never know when you might need him for something, Savannah."

As if she ever would need him.

New York was a big city and finding her in it would be difficult—as long as she stayed below the radar. There was no reason for Colt Brookes to intrude into her life now that they were finished as a couple and as a family. He hadn't shown any signs of trying to fix things when she'd left and moved in with her parents and there was no way he was going to come looking for her now. Liquor and loose women were his salvation, according to one of her friends from back home. He couldn't hurt her now but even so, she didn't want to put that theory to the test.

"It's not going to be easy," he agreed, reaching out and pulling her fingers into his "Not initially. Maybe we'll leave the dinner for now. How late can you stay?"

"I told Rosalee I'd be back by 9:00. Is that going to be a problem?"

"Nothing with you is ever going to be a problem with me." He stared at her lips and they were caught up in a frozen moment, caught up in their desire for one another until a sharp knock on the door made Tobias spring apart. Savannah picked up her notepad and pen.

"Good morning!" Matthias's voice boomed loud and intrusive, upsetting the intimacy they had shared.

"Hi," Savannah replied, giving him a smile.

"So sorry," he looked at them both in turn. "I didn't know you had something going on."

"We're done," Tobias replied tightly. "Did you want something?"

Matthias appeared to pause before replying. "I was going to ask you about the wedding."

"If you could take a look at this and let me know if anything needs changing." Savannah handed him the report she had luckily brought with her.

"Thank you," Tobias replied, taking it from her.

She walked out quickly, grateful for the few moments they had shared.

CHAPTER FOUR

"I thought you'd already gone home?" Briony asked at the same time as she turned on the hand dryer, thus saving Savannah an explanation. She'd been counting down the hours until 6:30 p.m., the time when, Tobias had assured her, most people would have left the office.

"I had a few things to wrap up," Savannah replied, raising her voice above the electric hum of the dryer. The heels of her shoes made tic-tac noises against the tiled floor of the ladies' room as she made her way towards a cubicle. The day had dragged on forever and the idea that Tobias was a short walk away, the penthouse a few floors away and knowing what awaited her—made the day stretch out far too long.

When the noise of the dryer stopped, she walked out of the cubicle expecting the all-clear only to find Briony waiting. Her hopes spiraled south as she forced a smile. Now it was her turn to ask. "What are you still doing here?"

"Waiting for you. We haven't had a chance to catch up yet." Briony had been holed up in meetings for most of the day.

"I noticed you were busy." Savannah wiped her hands with a paper towel and held back on freshening up before meeting Tobias. "How come things have turned so hectic suddenly?"

"It's one of the hectic times again. It turns crazy if Tobias has an important overseas trip coming up."

"Are *you* going?" Savannah asked.

Briony laughed. "I wish. Unfortunately, we don't get to attend such high-level meetings. It will only be Matthias and Tobias. Anyway, let's not talk about work. What happened to you on Friday night?"

"Um—Friday night?" Savannah ran her fingers through her hair and sneaked a quick look in the mirror.

"You disappeared halfway through the evening." Briony stared in the mirror and ran her fingers through her hair, pulling her reddish tufts up into spikes.

"I told Rosalee I'd be back by 10:00," Savannah explained.

"I'm sure you left earlier than that."

"Did I?" Savannah feigned surprise. "I don't remember. I didn't want to keep my babysitter waiting too long." She turned her back to the mirror and faced Briony. "It was a good night though, and it was great to finally meet Max."

"Yeah," Briony smiled. "She said it was good to finally meet you, too." Briony pouted and carefully applied her bright red lipstick. "I'm leaving. Are you coming?" Savannah opened her handbag and pulled out a tissue, busying herself in the act of unfolding it and getting ready to blow her nose.

"I have to log off, yet. You go. I'll see you tomorrow."

Alone once more, she checked her face, sprayed some mouth freshener and teased her fingers through her unruly hair. She swept her bangs to the side, then decided she liked them better behind her ears, then decided that her ears looked huge, then rearranged her hair so that her bangs fell over her ears again. She smoothed down her skirt and straightened up her body as she carefully examined herself in the mirror, taking one final glance before she stepped out of the room. She wondered how she was going to get to the penthouse. Did Tobias want her to go to his office first?

As it was, Tobias was hovering around outside the elevator bank with his nose deep in a newspaper. "Good night," she said breezily, hitting the elevator button to go up.

"You don't have your coat," Tobias replied, his gaze taking in her appearance with an appreciation that she had come to recognize.

"Will I need it?" she asked, as they slid into a thankfully empty elevator. The doors closed and his lips grazed her ears.

"You won't need *any* clothes, where you're going," he whispered. The intention floated around the walls of the elevator like an aphrodisiac on steroids. There were no words, no touches and no kisses exchanged, only thoughts as they stared hungrily at one another in silence. Subtle smiles danced on their lips as the anticipation and the promise of lust and love and sweltering sex made her giddy. She wondered why Tobias wasn't ravaging her the way he had done on Friday. Maybe he didn't want to take uncalculated risks. Maybe he, too, was being cautious.

But he grabbed her hand as soon as they walked out onto the gray and thickly carpeted hallway of the thirtieth floor. She ran the fingers of her free hand across the silky black wallpaper. "I'll have to get you a key," he murmured, his voice already dropping to a more sensual timbre.

"My *own key*?" she asked, exaggerating her excitement. "You mean I can come up here whenever I want?"

"Whenever you want. Hopefully, when I'm up here, too."

"There's no point otherwise," she replied, playfully swatting him across his back as he opened the penthouse door. As soon as the door closed, he turned primal. His mouth slid easily over hers, the gentleness disappearing within seconds as urgency took over, making her gasp. She dropped her handbag to the floor as he pushed her against the door, pulling her arms up above her head, pinning her against the door. She felt his body, hard and toned, against hers, and the restraint they had bottled up for days now unleashed with a force they could not control. Kisses, long, wet and deep bound them together. His hands slowly released her wrists so that her arms fell to her sides and he rested his head against her breasts as they took a moment to draw breath.

When her cell phone rang, Tobias moved back and she groaned, quickly bending down to answer it. The sight of Rosalee's name jolted her sharply. "What's wrong?" her breathlessness gave way to concern, which was always the case when she heard from the school or Rosalee, whenever Jacob wasn't by her side.

"Nothing's wrong," Rosalee laughed. "Don't sound so worried. I wanted to ask you if he can have mac and cheese."

Cheese seemed to exacerbate his asthma so she avoided giving it to him but every now and then, he was fine. "Sure, he can."

"That's all I wanted to know. I'm sorry to disturb you at work." Rosalee's words floated into her ears as she felt the heat of Tobias's gaze on her, as if he was waiting for an update.

"You didn't disturb me, Rosalee. Thanks for checking." She hung up and turned to Tobias. "Nothing to worry about," she explained, running her fingers along his lower lip. "She wanted to check that it was okay for Jacob to have mac and cheese. It sometimes sets off his asthma."

"He'll be okay?"

"He'll be fine. He's fully recovered now."

"That's a relief." Tobias replied, his voice soft as he reached for her hand.

"Rosalee told me to get on with my work." She gave him a mischievous look as he pulled her towards him.

"Work wasn't what I had in mind." He grabbed her wrist and pulled her towards the spiral staircase.

"Are we going upstairs?" she asked, remembering where he had wanted to take her last time.

"It's more comfortable," he assured her, and waited while she kicked off her shoes. The cold metal steps sent a chill through her heated body as she followed Tobias upstairs, her heart thudding wildly in her chest.

She gasped as soon as she set foot upstairs. The color scheme here was completely different. It was warm and inviting and she thought she'd stepped into a different place altogether as her feet sank into a bronze and mocha-colored thick carpet.

It was so typically Tobias—two different sides to the same space.

Warm bronze mingled with cream and gold as she stared at the enormous bed. The ornate bronze headboard was against an accent wall—its wallpaper metallic with some kind of print, tempting her to want to run her fingers over it. Large golden crystal-shaped pendant lights hung on either side, above the bedside cabinets. Her senses were seduced just by being here.

Tobias grabbed her by the waist and pulled her close to his chest, kissing her deeply and passionately until all she could do was melt into him. He pulled away, his breath hot and sexy against her lips. "I have waited all day to be alone with you."

"You're not the only one who's been waiting," she breathed, letting her cell phone slip to the floor. "I ran into Briony in the ladies' room," she murmured and started to unbutton his shirt, feeling the all too familiar arousal as her body fell under his spell once more. In between the slow and sensual removal of one another's clothes, he stopped every so often to kiss her deeply, and his fingers traced around her wrists, or stroked her waist, skimming her bare skin gently.

He unzipped her skirt, making it fall to the floor in a stiff pile. She shivered as his fingers dropped to the hem of her turtleneck and for a few moments he stood idly, staring into her eyes, as if he was purposely dragging the moment out painfully longer than was necessary.

She ran her tongue along her lower lips, heard her breaths escaping faster than usual, felt the slickness between her legs. He slid his other hand down and then lifted her top, rolling it over her stomach, then drawing it up over her arms before gently pulling it away from her head. Static crackled in her hair as the soft woolen garment fell to the floor.

Now he licked his lips as he stared at her in her lingerie. "You're beautiful." Her breasts spilled out over the top of her lace bra and his fingers slid up her bare back. He swallowed. "I don't intend to rush things tonight." His hand came up and pressed against her cheek as his parted lips nipped and sucked at the flesh along her lips, then her jawline, before sliding lower down to her neck. Heat curled along her body each time he touched her.

But the sharp ringtone of her cell phone intruded upon them like an unwanted public announcement and Tobias pulled away immediately. She sensed his irritation in the way the muscles around his jaw tightened even though his eyes showed softness. She was beginning to feel his moods, sense his thoughts, read him more easily than ever.

"Answer it," he told her. "It might be Rosalee." He was shirtless and tempting as he stood in front of her, with his naked chest, a wall of solid muscle. She could only stare back at him as she bent down to pick up her cell phone. But the name on the display was not who she expected.

"It's Colt." Her eyebrows twisted together.

"Answer it," he urged. "He's been bugging you since Friday."

"Hello," the irritation in her voice was hard to hide.

"Hey, sugar."

"Don't 'sugar' me."

"You're hard to get hold of." His rasping voice instantly transported her back to North Carolina, to the cramped one-bedroom apartment they had once shared.

"What do you want, Colt?"

"Why do you always sound so pissed?"

"What do you want?" she repeated, the muscles in her body tensing. She shivered, not from the cold, but from the touch of Tobias's fingers as he trailed them lightly along her collarbone, then down over her bra and onto her stomach. He positioned himself behind her and gently moved her hair to the side, his lips teasing the skin along her neck. She struggled to contain the soft moans that threatened to escape her lips—the sounds he always evoked in her.

"Only to wish you a happy birthday."

"You called for my birthday?" She snorted, her irritation now twofold from not only hearing the voice of a man she detested, but knowing that he was holding her back from making love with the man she most desired.

Tobias slipped his hand around her waist, the touch of his hand electrifying her bare skin. "Since when did you ever make an effort to remember my birthday?" Tobias led her towards the bed then gently sat her down. He kneeled between her legs, placed his hands gently on her thighs, and leaned forward to kiss the tops of her breasts.

"I'm making an effort now, ain't I? Happy birthday."

"Thanks," she muttered impatiently, feeling the delicious wetness of Tobias's lips on her skin. She felt emboldened that the new lacy lingerie, not black this time, but a deep red, was being admired and at such close range.

"That's all I wanted to say, sugar. I called you a few days ago and all." Colt's voice faded to the background as her body tingled with anticipation. Tobias smiled at her wickedly, and she existed only for him in that moment. Pushing her back so that she lay flat on the bed, he pressed his lips to her stomach, his hand exploring the dips of her hip bones before moving deliciously lower. Responding to her lover's touch, she parted her legs and arched her back instinctively and pinned him between her legs. She hugged his hips in a thigh hold.

"I have to go," she managed to say as Tobias's slow and gentle kisses sent electric signals through her body. The sensation was strange as he sucked her breast, first one, then the other, over the sheer lace fabric. It was like a fever each time he touched her, the heat in her body growing fiercer by the second, making her forget where she was.

"Did you find the money to pay the hospital bill?" Colt's question jerked her back to the present moment again.

"What?" Her eyelids flew open. *Why did he want to know?* Warm fingers pulled the straps of her bra down; Tobias didn't unclasp the back immediately but freed her breasts until she was topless and his mouth, warm and wet, claimed one breast sending heat shooting through her. "Aaah," she couldn't stifle the soft moan that escaped her lips as he teased her nipple.

"The hospital bill, for Jacob—did you get the money?"

"Uh-huh."

"So you're all paid up now?" His thick voice as unwelcome as thorns, disrupted the sensuality of the moment. "'Cos I was trying to get some money together to help you out." She stifled a moan as the sex god between her legs withdrew his beautiful lips and peeled down her panties, the thin strip of see-through lace rolled into a ribbon as he pulled it along her legs. Unclasping her bra, he now had her completely naked; the soft fur throw caressing her bare skin as she lay back.

She was in heaven and she never wanted to leave.

"Savannah? Are you there?" Colt's rough voice broke into her world as she stared at her discarded lingerie now lying like strips of flimsy lace on the bed.

"Why are you asking?"

Why now?

Somewhere in her mind, the fog cleared enough for rational thought to break free. Tobias got up off the floor and stripped off his pants. Her breath caught in her throat as he stood in front of her with the biggest promise of happiness bulging from his boxer briefs. She bit her lips as heat caressed her skin, eyeing him slowly as if she was ready to devour him.

"I want to help you out."

She wanted to get that voice out of her life. "We're fine," she shot back. "And we don't need your help. I have to go."

"Wait!" Colt shouted. Tobias stood watching her intently, irritation creeping into the fevered expression on his face. He seemed to be waiting for her to finish her conversation.

"What?" she snarled, lifting herself up to a sitting position. Conscious that she was now fully naked, she crossed one arm over her breasts, attempting to hide her nakedness now that an unfortunate interruption from her ex had turned the mood somber.

"Why are you so worked up? What in hell's name has gotten into you? I know I've been a bad husband to you and a bad father—"

"It's too late to make amends now."

"For you, yes, but I'm still Jacob's father. I'm straightening out now, Savannah. I want to get to know my son."

"It's too late for that, Colt. Leave us be."

"I won't leave you be. I have as much right to him as you do. At least let me help you. You shouldn't have to do this alone."

A cruel laugh died in her throat. "I've been doing this alone for years. Have you only noticed now?"

"I've been a total idiot. I know I was bad to you. I know I've done you wrong. Please, sug—Savannah," he pleaded, remembering in time. "Please let me help you."

"We don't need your help, Colt, we've managed fine without you."

"Where did you find the money?"

"Find the money? Under a flowerpot outside my door." She laughed at his words.

"I'm trying, Savannah. Stop busting my balls." She shook her head, gazing at Tobias as if to say that she was helpless. He moved her arm away, so that she could not hide her breasts, and pushed her gently back down on the bed. This time he pulled her down until her bottom was almost on the edge of the bed and he bent over so that his face nuzzled against her stomach. His hot breath kissed her skin, making her own breath hitch and when his fingers began their slow descent along her body the throbbing between her legs grew deeper still.

"Savannah? What in the Sam Hill are you doing? Are you still there?" But every delicious touch from Tobias took her further away from Colt's empty words. She was fully aroused and completely lost to the man before her. If Tobias didn't stop sucking her skin so hungrily, or leave his fingers from roaming over the delicate skin of her inner thighs, she would soon lose her mind, or her inhibitions, both of which she had been slowly discarding the moment she'd walked up the spiral staircase.

"Must be some job you've got there?" Colt asked. His questions and his refusal to disappear set off alarm bells in her mind. Her suspicions were roused, as her arousal started to wane.

"Don't worry about me, Colt."

"Where the hell did you get $3,500 from?"

"It's not your problem. Please leave us alone."

"A boy's got a right to know who his father is."

"You've never been a father to that boy. Don't ever call me again." She slammed down the phone.

"What is it?" Tobias looked up at her, his hands on her thighs.

"He wanted to know if I managed to pay the hospital bill."

"Was he offering to pay?"

"I have no idea." Tobias shifted closer to her until she felt his chest brush that most private part of her. Taking her hands in his, he entwined his fingers with hers. "And you said?"

"I don't want to see him ever again."

"Do you think he'll show up?"

"He doesn't know where I live. The only thing he has is my number."

"Then you don't need to worry about him." Tobias always made her worries disappear.

"You make everything better," she whispered, arching her lower back as his lips moved lower, to her stomach then below her waist and hips. She lifted her head sharply when he shifted further down the bed, his tongue skimming the insides of her thighs while his fingers stroked her softness.

"Tobias..." she murmured, but her protest was weak and her resolve even weaker.

"I've wanted to do this to you the whole day."

"You don't have..."

"I want to." When his hot tongue flicked against her, she arched her back higher, letting her thighs fall apart even more and moaning softly as she opened up to him completely.

CHAPTER FIVE

He loved holding her, loved the feel of her as she lay in his arms. This time, his lovemaking had been slow and deliberate. Gone was the raw, desperate lust they had given into on their first time.

He'd made her cry out even louder, even longer, as she fell apart over and over each time. This, now—lying with her back to his chest, his arms around her—this was heaven. He noticed that she kept glancing at the large clock which hung on the wall.

"I have to go soon," she murmured for the third time, disappointment thick as glue in her voice.

In answer he clasped his arm around her even tighter and groaned softly. "I don't want you to leave"

"Don't make this any harder," she pleaded, as he kissed her shoulder. He wasn't used to this, having someone he wanted to be with so much ration their time with him. He paid Naomi for her services and couldn't wait for her to leave. What he had with Savannah was something deeper, something meaningful, something that brought him back to life. He wanted to hold her the whole night and wake up with her the next morning.

After years of solitude, punctured only by the nights of

release when he'd called Naomi over, Tobias had forgotten what it felt like to truly be with someone. To not only be connected physically, but to have that invisible force that sizzled between two people, keeping them in one another's thoughts, making them desperate for one another. Now he had it with Savannah, and though it was the early days of their relationship, what they had felt different. Maybe her not being so accessible was what made him want her even more? Or was he substituting her for what he had lost? Had his mother been onto something? He pushed the thought away. She fiddled around with his wedding band, running her fingers over the smooth platinum and reminding him that perhaps it was time to take it off.

"We could have done this the entire time if you'd come with me to the wedding," he whispered, nipping her earlobe and making her squirm. She turned around in his arms and stared at him but he couldn't decipher the expression on her face. He stroked her cheek lightly.

"I couldn't though—" The idea of it, with just the two of them alone, was perfect. She could have brought Jacob along with her, if that had been her worry.

"Maybe another time?" he suggested. There would be another time, a better opportunity.

She propped herself up on her elbow, moving her face closer to his so that her hair fell forward onto his chest. He held a finger to her lips. "Before you say anything, hear me out. We can all go."

"Where?"

"Wherever you want."

"You mean just up and go?"

"I have a few business trips coming up."

"And? What explanation would I have for Briony? And Jacob?"

"You can bring Jacob with you. Seeing another part of the

world would be a worthy educational lesson for him. I bet it's better than anything he'd learn in the classroom. We'll take the private jet and wherever we go, my security goes with me. You and Jacob will always be safe, even if it's somewhere you've never been—"

"You have security?" Her jaw dropped as she looked around.

"Yes," he replied, as if it were the most natural thing in the world.

"They follow you around?"

"Twenty-four-seven."

"Can they see us?" she whispered, as if they might hear her.

He laughed. "I don't have cameras everywhere. No, the men are outside the building, sometimes they walk around. They're always outside my apartment, they go where I go."

"Are they on this floor?"

"No, they don't come up here. Only because I only give access to trusted people." She sat up in bed, clutching the bedspread like a life buoy.

"Do they know I'm here?"

"They might. I don't know. They don't follow me so closely in this building but—"

"The wedding on the weekend?"

"They were there."

"Bryant Park?"

He nodded.

"At the toy shop, when we first met?"

"Of course."

"At my apartment when you came late at night?"

"They were parked outside on the street."

She looked worried. "How can you live like that?"

"I'm used to it. I forget they're there. I forget about them. It's usually more for when I leave the city. You're derailing my point, Savannah. Come with me to Hong Kong. Don't say 'no' just yet. It will be in the first week in March, so you have plenty of time to make up your mind." He wasn't one to beg, but he loved having her around. "At least think about it?"

"Okay, I'll think about it."

Pretty soon, he would have to own up to that other thing he had to tell her. *Not yet,* he decided, not wanting to spoil this evening, as short and as sweet as it was. She dropped her lips to his and he couldn't help but kiss her deeply all over again. The taste of her was a mating call to his senses and he hardened as their tongues thrashed and her hand moved lower down his body. "Stay a little longer?" he asked in a broken voice, enjoying the feel of her fingers on his hardness.

She pulled her hand away. "I could spend all night with you but I have to go." She slowly raised herself from the bed. "I can't be late again for Rosalee." She dragged herself off the bed, turning her back to him.

"I won't be able to get you out of my head all night," he returned. She gave him a cheeky grin as she slipped her bra back on.

"I've got fifteen minutes to get back."

Fifteen minutes. He wanted her all over again. But he forced himself to look away, just the sight of her made him want to possess her. Her anxiety was starting to rub off on him and he dressed quickly. "I have to get my coat. It's in my office."

They left, coat and all, and he drove her to the apartment where her babysitter lived. Savannah disappeared into the apartment building to get Jacob while he waited in the car. A few moments later, they walked out and Tobias looked on, waiting to see at what point Savannah would tell him that they were getting a ride home.

And then Jacob looked up and stared at the car. Not that it was in any way a jaw-stopper. For that, Xavier's Ferrari would be the bomb. Unlike his brother, Tobias preferred to keep his wealth and status under the radar. Savannah opened the back passenger door and let Jacob climb in.

"Mr. Stone!" the boy yelled.

"Hey, Jacob." Tobias turned around and high-fived him.

"Cool car!"

"Thank you."

"Is it yours?"

"It is." Tobias couldn't help but smile.

"Cool."

"Want to drive it sometime?"

"Aaaaawww!"

Savannah got in beside him and gave him a steely stare. "Jacob is only six. He's too young to drive." From behind, he heard an exaggerated sound of disappointment.

"Even with him sitting on my lap?" Tobias asked, winking at the small boy.

"He's too big for your lap!" Savannah frowned at him dangerously and he heard Jacob titter as he drove off.

"Your mother's right, Jacob. You must never get behind the wheel of a car until you're old enough. How was your day, buddy?" He was anxious to change the topic, preferring to remain on Savannah's good side.

"I'm cool, Mr. Stone. How are you?"

"I'm very well and I'm even happier now that I've seen you again."

"Thank you for the ride," said Savannah, as he pulled up outside her apartment. His gaze fell to her lips again and it pained him not to be able to kiss her. He made do with a smile instead.

"Come inside, Mr. Stone," Jacob said. Then to Savannah, "Please, Mom. Can he?"

"Uh..." She seemed hesitant, and he had to take her cue.

He'd understand though, if she didn't want him to come up. It was late, and she probably had a ton of things she needed to do.

"How about we get together another time, buddy?" Jacob looked disappointed and he hated that.

"Another time, Jacob. Just like Mr. Stone said," Savannah said, putting her arm around the boy's shoulder.

"Promise?" he asked.

"I promise," Tobias replied.

CHAPTER SIX

"I'm still not sure that both of us are needed," Tobias declared once the managers had left the glass conference room after another meeting.

They'd been discussing strategy and the way forward concerning their Far Eastern investments. The last few weeks had been full of nothing but meetings with the research and analysis teams.

Tobias had studied the reports carefully and he was well aware of market sentiment. China's economy seemed to be declining, even though every now and then there appeared to be a slight upturn. His gut feeling told him to pull out but Matthias and a few of the other senior managers didn't share Tobias's view. They favored a gentler wait-and-see approach. Now the management team was split, and he and Matthias were on opposite sides.

Matthias turned his head sharply, his shoulders hunched as he stood up with his arms folded. "Of course we both need to go. Why? What are you proposing?"

"Maybe you should concentrate on the tech companies."

"That's your baby, isn't it?" Matthias's features twisted.

"Since when were we splitting the industries?" Tobias asked. "We have a lot to do, and I'm questioning whether both of us have to be there, especially if it looks as if we'll be withdrawing from those markets slowly."

"Except that we haven't fully decided that yet. We haven't concluded how we're going to move forward, and even if you think pulling out is the way to go, personally—I think you're wrong."

"Numbers never lie." Tobias defended his stance.

"Numbers paint a picture, but never tell the whole story. There are other factors you need to consider."

Tobias turned his head sharply at his colleague's words. "You think I don't take everything into consideration?"

"Things *will* bounce back, you wait and see. Of course, things will never return to pre-2008 levels, but we all know we'd been operating on a false economy back then, as well as a flawed banking system. This new low is the new normal."

Tobias examined his gray silk striped tie closely. "Except that China's economy only grew by 6.9 percent last year; it's been the slowest expansion in twenty-five years. Its quarterly growth has been the slowest since the global financial crisis. What more proof do you want?"

"They have an adjustment to make. Give them time. Look at the size of their population. Change isn't going to be immediate."

"That's one of my worries." Tobias countered.

"I'm saying theirs is a large economy and things don't move as fast for them."

"I like to play cautious when the figures tell me, otherwise I'm not averse to taking risks if I know the calculated odds are in my favor."

"We have an obligation to our business partners."

"The only obligation we have is to our customers, Matthias. Never forget that."

"I'm not as coldhearted as you. Yanling helped us when we were starting out and now that he's expanding, he's asking for the same."

"He helped us because it benefitted him, not because he thought he owed us anything."

Matthias's shoulders slumped. "Let's get out there and see for ourselves, huh?" asked Matthias, clasping his hands behind the back of his neck. "Keep an open mind, Tobias."

"I've always got an open mind."

"I know," replied Matthias, softening. "I'll rely on that while I smooth things out with Yanling for you. I know the two of you don't see eye-to-eye exactly but you don't want to piss him off for no reason."

"I can be polite when I want to be."

"A whole week in Hong Kong? You goddamned better be." Matthias returned. Tobias nodded his head, wondering how much more pleasant this trip would be if, by some lucky chance, Savannah came along but she hadn't exactly jumped at his suggestion. He realized how hard it was for her, and tried to understand, as hard as that was for him. His meetings and her commitments had kept them apart and they hadn't spent any time alone for almost two weeks.

This undercover romance wasn't easy. It was too soon perhaps, but it didn't feel like *too soon*. What he had with Savannah felt strong even for the short time they had known one another. For now, they had to make do with stolen glances and unsaid words during the day and phone conversations late at night.

He still had time before he left for the Far East—maybe they could snatch the opportunity to see one another before he left.

CHAPTER SEVEN

N ow that it had been eleven days since she'd last had sex, Savannah found herself thinking about it, and Tobias, all the time.

How had she managed to get by without it for three years?

Because pre-Tobias, it hadn't been important.

Pushing her hot and steamy thoughts to the back attic of her mind, she forced herself to examine the Excel spreadsheet of client names and data, a task that Briony was working on for Matthias. She hoped that total immersion in numbers would temporarily help her to forget the man who lived in her thoughts. Except that the very object of her preoccupation walked into her office, making her heart flip. She stared up at him in his white shirt, and slowly took in his wide-shoulders and torso which tapered to a V above his narrow hips. Absorbing the sight of him in one, slow, all-encompassing look brought back heated memories of this man naked and in bed with her. Not that they had spent many moments in bed. It had been that one time at the penthouse, or two, counting the sofa. And she was counting.

"To what do I owe this pleasure?" she asked, suddenly

brightening. Timing was such a bitch and this, not only keeping their romance hidden but trying to find the time to see one another, wreaked havoc on her well-being.

"Have lunch with me today."

Was he being serious? "Today?"

Tobias raised his arm and glanced at his watch. "Now."

She winced, and hated always saying 'No' to him but she had no choice. During the past week he'd asked to see her, not just for a penthouse visit, but to dinner a couple of times after work and each time she'd turned him down. She was beginning to feel that he cared less about keeping what they had a secret from others. But it was still new to her—not only being with him, but getting used to being with someone again, of being wanted. It was a shame that the man she was now with happened to be the most eligible bachelor in New York. Their romance would be difficult to keep a secret for long and so the only choice they had was to tiptoe around, as onerous as it was.

"I...don't think it's a good idea. What if people see us?"

"And what if they do?" Tobias shrugged and didn't seem too bothered about keeping things discreet, the way he constantly asked her to come for a meal with him but it mattered to her. Not only would it make things difficult for her, as his employee, she didn't relish the idea of rumors spreading like bed bugs through the office. Everyone on the twenty-first floor would have an opinion. It wasn't only Candace's bitchy words she'd have to listen to. The women in Briony's office—the ones who blushed when Tobias entered the room—would want to skewer her, she was sure. But she hated continuously turning him down because here at last was a man who appeared to not want just her body.

His face contorted. "Are you sure you're not purposely trying to avoid me?"

"I'm not. I'm trying to keep things quiet. If people see you and me together..."

"Then have lunch with me upstairs," he insisted. The only problem with that was when she got to the penthouse, she had a feeling that lunch would be the last thing she would want.

"Do you have a kitchen up there?"

"No, but I can get Candace to order in sandwiches or anything you might want."

"Candace?" No. Not Candace. He shrugged. She wanted to tell him to skip the sandwiches and what if they tried their luck and rushed upstairs now. *Skip the food part.* Yet the idea of sitting in his penthouse, looking out across the Manhattan skyline and having time alone with him to talk freely, suddenly appealed. They didn't get many of these moments to share a normal date.

"I'll go get the sandwiches," she said. "Now?" she asked again.

"Why not?" he asked, as if going to the penthouse during normal working hours, when people were everywhere and there was a greater risk of being caught, meant absolutely nothing to him. He pulled out a key from his pocket. "Your key to the thirtieth." She stared at it, then picked it out of the palm of his hand. "You know how to work this?" he asked. She nodded.

"I have a managers' meeting late in the afternoon." Tobias explained. "So we should go now."

"Which will give us plenty of time for lunch," she said, smiling as she got up and reached for her coat. He helped her into it, standing a little too close so that when she turned around, she pecked him on the lips. Faster than lightning, his hands slipped inside her coat, falling firmly around her waist and that was when he gave her a kiss that made her nerves tingle and stole her breath away.

"Later," she whispered, pulling out of his embrace, and

turning to open the door. As she stepped out with Tobias close behind her, Matthias's eyes settled on hers in surprise.

"Don't forget," Tobias told her, as he calmly walked past, "to include the previous three years' data. And don't you forget our three o'clock." He directed the latter at Matthias, leaving her unsure as to whether their plans had been derailed.

"As if I would," Matthias replied, another one of his charming smiles sliding from his lips. "Our Friday afternoon meetings are the highlight of my week." Savannah was left hovering by her door as Tobias disappeared down the hallway. She smiled back at Matthias and attempted to make her escape. "Data for which company?" he asked.

"For Dextronics. You visited them in San Diego."

He looked puzzled. "Ah, yes. Now I remember." She breathed easier. It was just as well that she'd worked on that report only yesterday but she sensed that Matthias was hunting around for information. Or perhaps she was being paranoid.

"I must rush," she explained. "I have to grab a quick sandwich before it gets busy." She whizzed past him and dove into the elevator, deciding to stick to the plan.

It was only as she rushed across the road to the sandwich shop that she realized she hadn't asked Tobias what type of sandwich he wanted. Taking a blind guess, she bought him a pastrami one and picked up a tuna salad sandwich for herself. She was back in the Stone Building in no time and as she stepped into the elevator, she prayed that her ascent to the thirtieth floor would be stress-free.

It almost was.

She had decided that she would wait until she was a few floors after the twenty-first floor before she inserted the key for the thirtieth floor, thinking that by then the elevator would have emptied.

"Are you going up?" The elevator stopped at the twenty-first and one of the other managers from her floor got in. She forced herself to laugh, unable to think of a good excuse on the fly.

"I nearly missed my floor," she said, trying to sound more cheerful than she felt as she stepped out. As she passed Briony's office, Briony appeared.

"Savannah, can I quickly check the dataset you used this morning? Matthias thinks he gave you the wrong one. Sorry," Briony pressed her hand to her cheek. "Could you change something before the managers' meeting this afternoon?"

That effectively killed her rendezvous with Tobias. Forget finding time to be together, she and Tobias weren't even able to share lunch in peace.

CHAPTER EIGHT

This gorgeous woman never ceased to surprise him. She'd come up with a proposal of her own and as he waited outside her apartment on a Sunday afternoon, Tobias became increasingly intrigued. His heart raced.

Their plans to meet for lunch two days ago had been derailed at the last moment and Savannah had taken it upon herself to 'remedy things.' At least that's what she'd told him when she'd called yesterday, barely able to contain the glee in her voice.

"Hey," he said, his breath catching in his throat at the sight of her. She wore a white summery dress with big red roses printed all over it.

"Nice of you to show up, and on time." She smiled widely, tapping her wristwatch.

"For you and Jacob," he said, handing her a bag as he stepped into her apartment. She accepted his gift gracefully.

"This is sweet, thank you." As soon as she had closed the door, he swooped in for a kiss, his blood on fire as soon as their lips met. She smelled like spring flowers and rainforest dew and she was his for four glorious hours. He felt as if the clock had already started ticking.

"Was Arnold on duty?" she asked, when they finally stopped kissing to draw breath.

"I don't know. I didn't think to stop and make conversation. I only had one thought on my mind."

"Hold that thought," she said, opening the bag he'd handed her and looking through it.

"What does he look like?"

"He's an elderly man, with a gap between his teeth. Champagne?" she asked in surprise, pulling out the bottle he had picked up along the way.

"Not to drink right now," he replied, reaching towards her again; she was irresistible in that dress. He ran his hands all over the globe of her bottom, while his tongue explored her mouth, his body stirring at the familiarity she now offered; the promise of more. "I love what you're wearing," he commented, standing back and taking in her appearance. "I can't wait to take it off you." She was barelegged, barefoot, in a dress which had buttons down the front and a loose belt. It was so very different from the strait-laced skirts and blouses she wore in the office.

"Lunch?" she asked, staring at him with amusement. "Did you want some? Since you're always asking." He wanted *her* for lunch, he decided, but her offer surprised him, since he was always the one to ask her. This time lunch could wait.

Or maybe not. Maybe he needed to get this thing over and done with, so that he could clear his conscience. But damn, she looked so hot.

"After," he replied, as she pulled him further into the room. It was small, with a coffee table and a couple of sofas and as he stepped into the center of the room, Savannah walked into the small kitchen behind him.

"You are always so generous. I don't need gifts, I only want you," she said, smiling at him as she took the champagne, flowers and a small Iron Man figurine out of the bag and placed them on the kitchen table.

"I like buying you things," he said, walking over to her and slipping his hands around her waist. His hands slid easily over her body in that silky fabric.

"Another Iron Man replica?"

"I don't know who else Jacob likes," Tobias shrugged in his defense.

She leaned in and kissed him. "Thank you. Jacob will be happy. There is no one else he likes, not as much as Iron Man." With the bag now emptied and his gifts put away, she clasped her hands together, wringing them nervously as if she wasn't sure what to do next.

With no time to waste, he grabbed her and slid his hands along her body and hoped she was wearing that lacy see-through lingerie again. The memory of it from their previous time together had haunted him ever since. She felt warm in his arms, soft and yielding, and his hands slid all over her dress, feeling the contours of her body as they kissed hungrily. His unfulfilled need for her, a dull ache, not only physical, but at a deeper, unseen level, now climbed to a peak. The frustrations of running on empty, of days passing with no physical touch, not even a proper moment to kiss—or eat a sandwich—was made all the more urgent now because even though they had the afternoon, he knew the time he had with her would never be enough.

Not enough to make up for the days they'd wasted. They kissed hard, feeling one another up and down like two hungry octopi. He might as well have had eight arms, judging by the speed with which his hands inched over her body, feeling, touching, and exploring the very curves and dips that he'd dreamed of each night. His hand slid over the silky fabric of her dress and he hardened as soon as he cupped her soft breast. This was no underwired or padded bra, he concluded, feeling delicate lace between his fingers. He groaned deep and low.

"We have all afternoon?" The blood drained away from his brain making him giddy.

"Four hours," she breathed, her fingers all over his face, caressing it softly, kissing him on his lips, his neck, his jaw as if she only had a few minutes left on this planet. She grabbed his hand and pulled him in the opposite direction from the kitchen, into a bedroom, and once inside, she slammed the door behind her.

Remembering what was important, Tobias shook his head, summoning up his reserves of restraint to make a suggestion. "How about we get something to eat, after all?" The idea hung in the air like the smell of dog poo and he pondered the lunacy of his suggestion given the size of his hardness.

"Is that the only thing you can think of?" she asked, her voice husky, her eyes dark. "I already asked you if you were hungry. I could rustle up something here. It will be quicker." She unbuttoned her dress to the waist. "I don't know about you, Tobias," she said, rubbing her body against his. "But I'm so horny right now, I could pass out." She let her dress fall open as it hung on her shoulders and revealed a strip of black lace. He stiffened, as if on cue, his breaths coming fast and shallow. When she moved closer and ran her fingers under his t-shirt, her touch made him tremble. Needing to get naked, he pulled his outer shirt off, then lifted his t-shirt off so that he was topless.

He instantly forgot his suggestion and the confession he needed to make; only one thing occupied his mind right now, and food wasn't it. While he didn't want her to think that he only ever wanted her body, his best efforts to show her that his intentions were noble disappeared when she undid the fabric belt of her dress and he undid the rest of the buttons. The flimsy material fell to the floor like rose petals at her feet.

She was such a goddamn beautiful tease, standing in front of him with her see-through lace which hid nothing. If anything, it served only to highlight the sweet flesh that it so enticingly tried to cover. Caught in painful deliberation, he froze for a second, until he buckled and went straight for her mouth, planting his lips firmly over hers and drawing a breath when her fingers flew to the buttons of his jeans. Between wet, sloppy, fevered kisses and impatient fingers, they undressed one another, pulling and tugging at each other's underwear. Time was ticking and he wanted to claim her, needed to make her his, and more than once. To make up for lost time. He pushed her back onto the bed, groaning from the feel of her skin on his; sweet respite after weeks of using only his imagination to recapture the smell, touch and essence of her. His heart rate rocketed sky-high, as did his manhood. But as she started to get comfortable, opening up to him, with her legs ready to cross over his back, he flipped her over on to her stomach. With his hands clasped around the soft flesh of her hips, he pulled her gently back until she was resting on her knees, the sight of her glistening excitement sending him over the edge as he slid on his condom. His senses were on fire as he thrust into her, felt the relief, the soft, warm and wet feel of her, and heard her animal cry as it resonated through the room. Unable to stop, he pushed into her, one hand on her hip, his fingers digging into her skin, the other hand around the mane of her tousled hair. She moaned in ecstasy each time he entered, each cry stirring him further towards that edge until he lost himself in her and with her.

When later they collapsed into bed, pulling the bedspread over them, they lay on their sides facing one another. She sighed dreamily, like a contented, overfed cat. "I feel complete when I'm with you," she murmured, tracing her fingers along his shoulder. There was no wrapping it up, no hiding her feelings, as she laid it out bare for him. He took her hand and kissed her fingers, his heart pitter-pattering away. "It's like I have this ache in my body the whole time I'm away from you and each time I see you, it aches even more."

He knew that feeling too. The longing, the yearning. "I know what that feels like," he said softly.

"But it won't be enough because even though we have the afternoon, I want you for the whole day." His sentiments exactly. The afternoon would be blissful while it stretched in front of them, but soon it would be over and the withdrawal symptoms would be even worse.

"And you?" she asked, running her hands lightly over his waist, making him stir again. "How do you feel?" He knew she was asking because he never opened up completely.

"You do things to me, Savannah," he whispered, inhaling the flowery scent of her perfume.

"I do things to you?" Her gaze settled on his lips as their legs entwined.

"You make me feel again."

She laughed. "You mean to say I've managed to melt you? The Ice Man." Her hazel eyes glistened. "I used to think of you as a glacier, cold, hard and impenetrable."

"I'm sure you had your reasons." Distancing himself from others had worked well for him, until she had come along. "And now?" he asked, curious to know.

"Now I see another side to you. I always had an inkling that there was more to you than met the eye." She ran her fingernails down his chest and drew patterns on it.

"That's what you thought?"

She nodded.

"Why?" he asked, he didn't recall being particularly gracious to her back then.

"The way you were with Jacob that first night at the toy store when you had that event for the children around Christmastime." She paused a moment. "Why did you decide on adoption centers? Are you adopted?"

"No," he ran his hands down her back, reveling in the intimacy that was now so natural between them. "It was an initiative suggested by the marketing department. A way of getting me publicity in a good way and doing something that meant something to me. Christmas time with children... I liked the idea that I could make it better for those less fortunate."

"It's a lovely idea."

"I wasn't keen on it at first, I thought maybe doing something else, like something at the homeless shelter would be a better alternative, but the marketing people thought that an event based around children at Christmastime might capture people's imaginations more. It sounds altruistic, and I have to admit at first I didn't want to do it but I'm glad now that we did." It had helped him heal. "I know now that it was the right thing to do." The quietness that settled inside him lingered for a few moments. "What would you do if you had more money than you knew what to do with?" he asked Savannah. The lines on her forehead creased as she considered his question but she shook her head and stared at him blankly.

"I don't know."

"There must be something," he insisted.

"I've never had that much money and so I've never been in a position to imagine what I'd do with extra because I never had extra." He slipped his arm around her waist and pulled her to him, feeling her warm body against his.

"What would have made your life easier?" he asked softly.

"Well...uh..." she exhaled loudly, her brows moving closer,

as if he'd given her a complex mathematical problem to solve. "Affordable childcare facilities."

"That would have helped you?"

"Having somewhere affordable where I could leave Jacob during the school holidays so that I could carry on working? Yes. Things like that, primarily for single mothers where we have no second income. Every little thing helps. Like the food banks so that people can..." She stopped, and he thought he saw a flicker of embarrassment in her eyes. He stroked her cheek, remembering that time when he'd seen her lining up at such a place. It was something he had never told her. It had been around the time she had piqued his interest, this normal woman who had stolen softly and quietly into his life. Except that she wasn't normal or average in any way; she was beautiful both inside and out and if he wasn't careful, she was going to claim his heart.

"I could lie like this forever," she whispered, changing the subject.

He dropped a soft kiss on her lips. Even though he knew it was a futile attempt, he still asked the question. "A last-minute change of mind about Hong Kong? Think about it, Savannah. We could spend the whole week together."

She shook her head. "I can't. You know my circumstances."

"I know," he said, resolving to let the matter go. He kissed the tip of her nose, not wanting her to feel bad. "A man can try. I just want you to myself all the time and that vision is hard to let go of." She looked up at him as if she was checking the intent behind his words.

"What would everyone think if I came along?"

"Who cares what they think? You're doing research for me."

She frowned in amusement. "Tobias, people aren't stupid. They'll know."

"So what? What's the worst they could say? I hate tiptoeing

around like this. I want to see you when I want to see you. Aren't you sick of this? Look at us now. You've had to ask your babysitter to take Jacob out for the afternoon so that we can spend some time together."

"I'm scared we might be moving too fast." Her fingers rested along his lower lip.

"Moving too fast?" He tried to keep the surprise out of his voice. "We've only managed to see each other a couple of times as it is. I see my PA more than I see you."

"Don't I know it." She pulled his lower lip. "That woman hates me."

"Want me to get rid of her?"

"No!" Savannah sat up in bed. "You're joking, aren't you? You wouldn't make that happen for no reason, would you?" His chest tightened and he wished he'd cleared up that minor issue which had been weighing on his mind.

"No," he said, then to change the subject. "What's this about moving too fast? This isn't moving fast. It's moving too goddamn slow."

"I know things are difficult because I have a child, otherwise I could see you every day. I'm not as free as—" She looked away.

"As?"

"As someone who was single."

"You *are* single."

"I mean as in someone who has no kids or responsibility. I can't forget about my son, Tobias."

"I would never ask you to." It hurt him that she would say such a thing. "I know what's more important to you and I am more than happy to be in second place, or even lower." He raised an eyebrow, waiting for her to say otherwise.

"Second place...?" She smiled.

"I'm happy in second," he said, cupping his fingers around her chin. "This can work."

"But it's not easy, is it?"

"Nothing worth having ever comes easy, and what comes easy isn't worth having."

"I'll have to remember that."

"Do you want to bail?"

"No." She rubbed the side of her head. "I feel bad that I have to keep turning you down all the time. Look what happened at work on Friday."

"That was down to bad timing. It was never going to be easy during office hours. I don't know what I was thinking."

"I tried to tell you."

"I can't think straight when you're around. I was desperate to see you and it wasn't even to have my way with you."

"I love it when you have your way with me."

"I noticed." She leaned in and kissed him deeply then, a kiss which said a million things, the same things he felt. *I want you, I need you, and I'm hungry for you.* She pulled away as flames of fire licked his skin and lust pooled between his legs. He could have her again and show her how much he needed her.

"My parents are coming down over Easter," she announced. "They've been promising me for a long time. I'd feel safe leaving Jacob with them, if you wanted to go somewhere for a few days, you and me." He liked the sound of that very much but the loud sound of a door closing, followed by a childish squeal somewhere in the apartment, made his skin tingle. It was nothing compared to the look on Savannah's face. Her eyes bulged as she threw back the bedspread.

"Shit!" she hissed, racing out of bed and trying to unravel her curled-up lingerie. "They're back!" She threw his clothes at him as he jumped out of the bed. He quickly climbed into his jeans and struggled to pull on his t-shirt while she quickly made up the bed.

"Mommy!" Jacob's shriek was right outside the door when

Savannah lunged toward the door at the same time as Jacob pushed it open.

"Mommy! We've got flowers and pop and another Iron Man!" Tobias barely managed to do up his zipper before Jacob stepped into the room and his gaze fell on him. "Mr. Stone! What are you doing here?"

CHAPTER NINE

"You're not wearing any socks, Mr. Stone!" Jacob giggled. It was at that precise moment that Rosalee emerged from the shadows and gave Savannah an all-knowing smile that made her shrink.

"You're right, buddy. I'm not," Tobias replied, completely unfazed. Savannah quickly did up her belt and wished teleportation was an option so that she could vanish to a far distant galaxy. With heat crawling along her skin, she was caught between embarrassment and guilt, and the uncomfortable idea of making introductions.

"We came back to get Jacob's scooter," Rosalee explained. "Is it all right for him to take it out, Savannah?"

Heat clawed at her cheeks. "It's fine, it's not a problem." Then, "This is Tobias Stone, Rosalee, and this," she said, forcing herself to meet Rosalee's eyes, "this is my wonderful babysitter."

"I'm so pleased to meet you, Mr. Stone."

"Is the Iron Man for me, Mr. Stone?" Jacob asked boldly.

"It sure is."

"Thanks! I can't wait to show Lenny." Jacob's smile could

not be any wider. "Mr. Stone is the best," he turned to tell Rosalee. "He got me that Marvel Quinjet for Christmas."

"Ah," replied Rosalee, putting her arms gently around the boy's shoulders. "That was a lovely gift basket, Mr. Stone." Savannah wondered how he managed to keep his cool as he nodded and smiled back. She stared down at her dress and double-checked to see if she had done up all of her buttons.

"Come on, Jacob." Rosalee pulled the boy away and closed the door behind her.

"Oh, shit," Savannah muttered under her breath, when they were alone once more.

"We were nearly caught in the act," whispered Tobias.

Savannah wiped the back of her hand across her brow. "What if they'd walked in when we were..." She was still in shock from the unexpected arrival.

"And to think I was getting ready for the next round," he told her in that dangerous and seductive voice he had.

Her eyes widened as she considered that scenario. "Something like that would scar Jacob for life," she replied, horrified by the thought of it. How would she ever explain *that* to him? Thankfully, he was too young to ask embarrassing questions but if he'd walked in on them in the middle of something, it would have been frightening for a young child to witness. "We have to be more careful."

"We *were* being careful," Tobias answered, placing his arms around her. "You see why whisking you away would be a good thing?" She fell into his chest and felt his protective arms wrap around her.

"I'm beginning to see your point. Getting time alone is almost impossible."

"Not almost. It *is*."

She buried her face in his chest and closed her eyes for a

moment. Lifting her head, she stared up into his cool blue eyes, now teal-colored. "I thought we'd at least have the afternoon."

"We'll go away for a few days when your parents come over. Don't worry, we'll figure something out." He cupped the back of her neck in one hand.

"We could go for that lunch now," Tobias suggested as they heard Rosalee's voice outside the door.

"Not now, Jacob! Just get your scooter!"

Savannah had a feeling that Jacob would want to spend time with them, especially now that he had seen Tobias. "I have a better idea. How about we spend the afternoon in Bryant Park? You, me and Jacob?"

"Great idea." Tobias seemed happy at the suggestion.

"Come with me," she said, not wanting to present the idea to Rosalee and Jacob by herself. When they walked into the living room, Rosalee's face was riddled with questions and Savannah knew that although she didn't have to face an inquisition right away, her babysitter would have questions at some point.

"There's been a change of plan for this afternoon," Savannah announced. "Who wants to go to Bryant Park?"

Jacob yelped for joy but Rosalee politely declined.

And so it was that Savannah's plans for enjoying an adult Sunday afternoon changed from sex and lunch, to sex and the park with her son and the new man in her life.

Walking beside Tobias as Jacob raced ahead on his scooter, there were moments when Jacob's back was turned that their hands would touch and their fingers would entwine and hold for a few seconds.

For now, stolen moments would have to do.

CHAPTER TEN

The sun had broken out from behind the gray clouds and brightness turned the day golden yellow, but a chill still hung in the air.

"Are you sure Jacob doesn't want to go ice skating?" Tobias asked when she quickly let go of his hand. Jacob turned around to wave at them.

"He's trying to impress you with his scooter skills," Savannah replied. He looked toward the boy and gave him a thumbs-up.

A ball hurtled towards them from the left, where a group of teenagers played football. Tobias ran over and threw it back to them. The park was teeming with families on this most normal of Sunday afternoons and he felt as if they fit right in; as if this was the most natural thing in the world—visiting a park over the weekend. Savannah looked around quickly, as if she'd seen something.

"What is it?" he asked.

"What if someone saw us?" She pushed her hands into the pockets of her coat. She'd worn long boots as well, needing to keep warm in the flimsy fabric that he had loved taking off her.

"Relax," he chuckled. "There are no press people here."

"You don't need reporters or the press. One normal person who recognized you and uploaded your photo to social media would be enough to cause damage."

"You sound paranoid," he exclaimed. "Why would anyone do that?"

"Because you're the number one most eligible bachelor in New York."

He snorted at that, dismissing it quickly with a nod of his head. "That's a stupid list that only stupid people follow."

"There are plenty of stupid people around." She looked around warily. "Where are your security men? I don't see them." She craned her neck, doing a full 360-degree circle as she scanned around the perimeters of the park.

"You're not supposed to see them." Tobias answered.

"Then how do you know they're here?"

"They are. Trust me on that. They're here. I don't want security men who look like big, bulky bodyguards. I'm a businessman and a hedge fund owner at that, not a rock or movie star. I consider myself boring in comparison. I don't have an entourage. Just one or two guys who follow me when I'm out."

"What's the threat?"

He shrugged. "People who want money. People who know what I'm worth and might want to try something silly."

"Doesn't that scare you?"

"I try not to think about it. Maybe if..." Maybe if Ivy had been alive he'd have been scared for her.

"Maybe if what?"

He paused for the longest time as they continued to walk. Savannah kept looking over to where Jacob was every few seconds, ever watchful, ever alert. After a few seconds had passed, he spoke. "I was worried when I was with Ivy that someone might try to hurt her. It wasn't a case of getting protection for myself. I was worried about her." He concentrated on a small patch of thick, green grass, feeling the urge to retreat into himself again.

"Who would hurt her?"

"Sick people have a way of using the ones you love to get back at you. That's what my advisors had told me. It was my duty to protect her and keep her safe."

"Did anything ever happen? Were you ever threatened?"

"No. Not in the way I imagined." He could see from her expression that his vague reply had piqued her curiosity. She opened her mouth as if she had another question but he stopped her. "I'm sorry," he told her. "I'd rather not talk about it."

"Sure. I understand." She reached for his hand once more as silence fell again. "This is nice, isn't it?"

"Yeah," he had to admit, it was nothing short of perfect. "What do you say to us going for dinner later on? Around 6:00 or 7:00?"

"That would be the perfect end to a perfect day." He nodded, almost leaning in to kiss her again, until she shook her head, warding him off.

"Sorry," he muttered, forgetting that they were still hiding being together. If not from colleagues at work, then from Jacob and his babysitter, and now from Joe Public.

"I'm sorry too," replied Savannah, looking more than a little disappointed. They stared at one another's lips longingly before turning away and keeping a watchful eye on Jacob.

"What does Jacob like?"

"He'll be happy with pizza. It's a universal favorite for kids."

"Pizza it is."

"Maybe you and I can watch a movie on TV or something, you know, make the most of the day, once Jacob is asleep. But no you-know-what," she added, scratching her nose.

"No you-know-what," he agreed. He was happy just to sit with her and watch a movie. He didn't need the lure of sex to be with her.

"It sounds like a dream date." She grazed her fingers gently against his hand.

It would be a dream date, if he owned up. He had to do it soon and there was no time like the present. Goodness knows he'd tried to get her to come out with him for a meal on many occasions. Jacob whizzed past them on his scooter, breaking his thoughts.

"Watch me!" he yelled, speeding away on the concrete pathway as they approached and sat down at an empty bench. Savannah took off the backpack she'd been carrying and placed it on her lap.

"There's something I want to tell you." He stared straight ahead as he said it. "I have a confession to make."

She looked worried, her eyes boring into his face. "A confession?"

He tried to swallow but his throat was bone dry. *Just say it.* "I lied to you."

"You lied to me about what?"

"About the job, about this role you now have."

"What about it?" She placed a hand just below her neck, as if to protect it, as if she knew this might change things between them.

"I *did* need a researcher and it was a role that I spoke to Briony about a while ago but—"

"But what?" Her face twisted, and he knew she wouldn't like any of it.

"I was responsible for making sure that you didn't get the Southwood Select job."

"What?" her voice rose up in shock and she edged away from him. "How did you know which job I—"

"I had intel. I have ways and means of finding out these things."

"No shit." Narrowed eyes cut into him. In the distance he thought he heard Jacob yell out.

"Look, Mommy! Look, Mr. Stone!" She turned and waved back at him, smiling as if nothing had happened. And just as easily she turned back to him, her face twisting with displeasure.

"You called and made my job offer with Southwood Select disappear so that I would have no option but to take the job Briony offered?"

He nodded.

Her steely gaze fixed upon his face. "Why?"

"I thought it was the right thing for you to stay at Stone Enterprises."

"Why would you think that?"

"Based on your circumstances." He tugged at the collar of his t-shirt, needing to let some air in.

"What's that supposed to mean?"

"It means I thought it made more sense for you to remain where you were."

She frowned, making her forehead crease into lines. "The man who can get whatever he wants, whenever he wants. You treated me like a commodity." He tried to grab her hand but she moved hers away before he could touch her, flinching away from him as if he was poison.

"No, I didn't. I wanted what was best for you."

"Best for me?" she shrieked. "How the hell would you know what's best for me? Don't you think you had an obligation to tell me?"

"I'm telling you now, Savannah. I've been trying to tell you every time we met." She shook her head, the disbelief clear on her face.

"I can't believe you did this to me."

"Did what?" he asked, surprised by her reaction. "I stopped you from taking a lousy job that was guaranteed for only a few months with the 'remote possibility' it might become permanent and gave you something much better. I gave you a position that made your life easier."

"It wasn't your decision to make!" She shot him a look of pure contempt, making his heart climb up his throat with thorns.

"As if you had so many other choices," he replied bitterly, the depth of her anger taking him by surprise.

"You don't get it, do you? Your drive to control, to make things be a certain way, to arrange pieces so that they fit in with what you need—it's selfish. It's *not normal,* Tobias."

"You're getting hysterical."

"Me getting hysterical? You don't think I have good reason to?"

"My intention was never to manipulate you. My decision was based purely on what would be the best outcome for you."

"Best outcome? You sound as though you performed a risk analysis on me. Without my knowledge, you decided to take the appropriate course of action."

"Yes." He bit down on his jaw. *What could she not understand?*

"You played with my life! You decided on what *you* thought was right for me."

"You're not thinking about this rationally."

"I'm not thinking rationally? I don't understand your way of thinking. How do you think it makes me feel to hear what you did? Don't you think you should have discussed this with me first?"

"I considered that option but I knew you would have been even angrier and you would have refused my job even though the perks and benefits and the advance helped you. I didn't want to risk that."

"You didn't want to risk it? Something so fundamental that affected my life and you *didn't want to risk telling me?"* She'd started to raise her voice and a few people around them turned and stared.

"Calm down, Savannah. We can discuss this without putting a show on." Her lips drew back in a snarl.

"I knew something didn't feel right, the way it all fell into place so quickly. I even came to your office and asked you, and still you lied when you had the perfect opportunity to tell me."

"I refrained from admitting the complete truth, yes. I own up. I should have told you sooner."

Anger burned behind her eyes. "What gave you the right to meddle? Do you really think my life is such a shambles?"

"Sometimes we make decisions that have far-reaching consequences. You were struggling, Savannah. I made things better for you. Is that such a bad thing?"

She stood up, slapping her hand to her forehead and shaking her head. "For the love of god, why can't you see that what you did was wrong?"

"How could it be wrong when it was the perfect solution for you?"

She clenched her jaw and he thought she was going to lose it. Glancing at Jacob over his shoulder seemed to calm her down. "You live your life playing by your own set of rules, making them up as you go along and doing what benefits you."

"I don't see it that way."

"Because you're arrogant, Tobias. You fail to see when you've done something wrong."

"I'm trying to apologize for not telling you sooner. I've been wanting to tell you for a while but I could never find the right time—I didn't think it would be that much of a big deal. If I knew you'd get on your high horse about it, I would have made sure you knew right away."

Children's cries and squeals of laughter in the background faded away as they hissed and spat their words at one another.

"Before you used me?"

He got up slowly. "Used you?" He cocked his head. "Used you for what?"

"For sex. Isn't that what happened? Once you got bored with Naomi, you moved onto me." He stared at her in shock. "I didn't fall at your feet right away so you had to keep me there until I did. Isn't that the real reason you wanted me at Stone Enterprises?"

"No, it fucking isn't." His voice was like ice, and his anger inflamed. He didn't care to curb his language, not if this was what she believed. "I can't believe you said that." He felt his chest constrict.

"And I can't believe what you did."

But before he had a chance to say anything, they heard Jacob's excited yelp as he flew towards them at breakneck speed. "Here I come!"

Immediately silenced, they watched as he came to a stop in front of them, looking more than a little pleased with himself. "I'm hungry, Mommy. Can I get a hot dog?"

"How about a pizza later, Jacob?" Tobias asked.

"I'm hungry now."

"We could go for pizza now?" He turned to ask Savannah, but her face had hardened and she looked away.

"I'll get you a hot dog," she said and stormed off before he'd even had a chance to stop her. Tobias flexed his fingers, knowing he could do nothing yet.

Beside him, Jacob flopped onto the bench, leaving his red scooter standing. "I could sure do with a rest," he exclaimed, sitting down and wiping his brow like an older person would. "That was hard work but it was fun!"

Tobias's lips shifted upwards as he contained a smile. In the distance he watched Savannah's figure getting smaller as she moved away. She obviously needed time to cool down, and he needed time to reconsider what she had said. He hadn't been prepared for this level of anger nor could he see why she failed to see that he'd tried to do the right thing. No wonder her life was such a mess. One wrong turn, that was all it took to fuck up a life. He should know.

"Who's your favorite superhero, Mr. Stone?" Tobias sat down beside the boy and pretended to think long and hard about it.

"I don't have a favorite," Tobias confessed.

"Not even one?"

Tobias shrugged. "Superman?"

Jacob looked disappointed.

Tobias tried again. "Batman?" These were the only two he'd grown up with and still he failed to impress Jacob. "Why do you like Iron Man so much?"

"Because he's strong and he can fly and I want to be like him when I grow up."

Intrigued, Tobias continued, "So that you can conquer evil?"

"So that I can protect my mom."

"Protect your mom? From what?"

"From my dad. He can get really angry real quick. He used to make her cry a lot." Tobias swallowed, his intestines twisting into knots.

"Mommy said he was like the Hulk and that he couldn't control it." The boy's words knocked the wind out of his lungs more forcefully than a blow to the stomach would have.

"Is that right, Jacob?" Tobias asked softly.

The boy nodded and then sprang up from the bench. "Will you watch me go around one more time?" he asked, hopping onto his scooter.

"Go ahead, buddy," Tobias answered, rubbing his thumb across the back of his hand and trying to imagine what kind of life the boy and his mother had endured. Jacob sped away, leaving a knot of anger sitting at the bottom of Tobias's stomach like days' old oatmeal that was hard to shift.

CHAPTER ELEVEN

S he walked back holding Jacob's warm hot dog in her hand and gazed across the field to see her son showing off again.

Trying to impress Tobias. She could see it clearly, how much her son wanted Tobias's attention; a father figure's attention. Her heart sank as she saw Tobias walking towards her. She wasn't ready to deal with this yet. The revelation was too new, too raw and she didn't want to discuss anything in front of Jacob. Least of all she didn't have the will in her to convince Tobias how wrong it was. How could she when the man himself couldn't see why she was so mad?

Yes, on the whole, the position he had offered her made sense. Even if she had taken the other job, it wouldn't have solved her immediate problem—of paying the hospital bill. She would have ended up drowning in more financial problems.

She wasn't so blind that she couldn't see what Tobias had done for her. The role, the position he had offered, with its salary and benefits and her ability to get the advance—it was perfect for her. She wasn't angry about that. But she was furious that he had gone to such lengths to orchestrate it. That he had been able to influence the people at Southwood Select. It was true then, that people with power, the ones with money, could treat life as a chess game, manipulating people like chess pieces, in order to score a victory, to get what they wanted. It was this—Tobias's below-the-belt manipulation of her circumstances without her knowing, that hurt her the most. Trust and honesty were important to her and he had abused both. Was it just sex that he wanted from her? She was no longer sure. Maybe his Christmas gifts and his interest in Jacob were part of his plan to get her to succumb to him.

"Hey," he said, walking towards her. "Are you all right?"

"I'm fine." She stared ahead, keeping her gaze fixed on Jacob. He continued walking with her, his voice gentler now.

"I was going to ask you to get one for me."

"Sorry," she murmured as Jacob came speeding up, wearing a smile as large as the hot dog. With one foot on the scooter and one foot on the ground, he attempted to take the hot dog from her. "You can't ride your scooter and eat a hot dog at the same time, Jacob." Her voice was unnaturally hard, and her anger wasn't intended for her son. "Let's go over by the bench." She was conscious that she hadn't answered Tobias's question, and that she was purposely avoiding looking at him as they walked over and sat by the bench again. She gave Jacob his hot dog and pulled out his water bottle from her backpack.

"We should head back after this," Savannah announced and out of the corner of her eye, she saw Tobias turn his head towards her.

"I thought we had plans for later?" Tobias asked, his voice was solemn, as if he already knew things had shifted.

She forced herself to look at him. "I've got some chores to finish up from this morning. Some ironing to do." It was a feeble excuse and she knew how pathetic it sounded, yet even though it was true, it wasn't the real reason she had changed their plans. With this recent revelation hanging over her, she needed time alone and she couldn't face the idea of the three of them going out for dinner.

"Can't Mr. Stone come back to our place and we can do something?" Jacob pleaded, his mouth dotted with mustard and ketchup splotches. Thankfully, she hadn't told him of their plans, so he was none the wiser.

Tobias answered. "Your mom is right, buddy. Maybe another time."

"But you always say that, Mr. Stone." Jacob retorted. "How come you came over when I wasn't there? It's not fair."

"Honey, Mr. Stone is busy and you've got school tomorrow." The boy's face dropped.

"I'll make it up to you, Jacob. Maybe we can hang another time?" Tobias suggested.

The afternoon, which had started off with such great promise, ended on a subdued note as Tobias drove them home in silence. Even Jacob was quiet but this, Savannah assumed, was partly because he was tired from all that riding around on his scooter. When Tobias parked outside her apartment, Savannah got out of the car with Jacob and then leaned over, putting her head in the passenger side window which Tobias had rolled down. Holding Jacob's hand, she leaned in, her voice low so that only Tobias could hear her. "Thanks for today but I need time to think things through."

"I can see that," he said, the anger he'd displayed earlier had all but melted. "Look, Savannah. I'm sorry. I never meant to hurt you."

She shoved her hair away from her face. "Still, I find it hard to come to terms with what you did."

"I don't understand why you're that upset, Savannah."

"And that's exactly why I'm so upset. You're not God and you can't play with people's lives." She knew it wouldn't be right to talk about things, not here, not now while Jacob was around.

Her son didn't know what was going on and she wanted to keep it that way. Things were already complicated enough.

"I wasn't playing with your life, Savannah. I was trying to make it better."

She was getting more irritated by the minute. "It's become second nature to you, bending people to your will—"

"Protecting those I care about?"

"You don't even see the fine line between protecting and controlling. I will always be grateful for what you did for me but you could at least have discussed the matter with me."

"As if it were so easy to explain things to you at that time. I tried. I came to see you that night but you weren't in a listening mood."

"So why not offer me the job first and let me decide?"

"You weren't thinking straight. You wanted to get the hell away from me at that time and you'd have taken any job just to get out of Stone Enterprises."

"Mommy!"

"One moment, honey." She quickly glanced over her shoulder, then turned back around to face Tobias. "I didn't want to talk to you then because I needed my space, just like I need it now."

"If that's how you feel, Savannah, then take all the time and space you need." She stepped away as he revved his engine then sped off like a boy racer.

Great example to set, she thought.

"Awesome!" Jacob shouted, a smile of pure admiration plastered across his face.

CHAPTER TWELVE

The following week passed by in a blur. Tobias was busy enough with meetings and preparations for his trip that Savannah didn't see him much. She also hadn't called him in the evenings either.

Perhaps it was a good thing that he was going away soon. She felt wary each time she walked down the hallway or got into the elevator, wondering if she would run into him again. And then what?

For the first part of the week, she continued working on the project Briony had given her—segmenting data for Matthias. 'Tobias's days' were pushed towards the end of the week and with him leaving for Hong Kong on the weekend, the chances were slim for them to resolve things before then.

After experiencing the short-lived high of their romance, her emotions were once more scattered in different directions as she experienced first-hand the bitter gut-churning ride of being in a relationship. She was starting to care for this man, had started to fall for him a little too quickly, had started to believe and trust in him more than she should have. She wasn't free-falling, but falling nonetheless, finding herself in a new low as she careened towards bleak and solemn days.

It was only Jacob who kept her mind off wallowing in too much self-pity. There were times when she wondered if she was making a big deal of what Tobias had done. Colt had tried to control her, had succeeded in the early days, when Jacob had been a baby and then a toddler. During that time, she didn't have the willpower or strength to stand up to him. That had come later. She owed it to herself not to let another man—even if he was wealthy and seemed to care for her—do the same thing. Tobias was nothing like her ex and she knew he would never willingly hurt her emotionally or lay a finger on her.

All he'd ever done was try to make things better. But it still didn't feel right and maybe all she needed was a little distance to put things right between them. Tonight, Rosalee was looking after Jacob at their apartment. Savannah knew what was coming; knew that she wouldn't be able to dodge the questions anymore by taking Jacob and rushing off as she'd been doing when she'd picked him up from the babysitter's home.

She walked into her apartment to find Rosalee getting up from the couch, as she always did as soon as she heard Savannah's key in the door. Tonight, however, her babysitter didn't seem to be in a rush to leave.

"Hey, Mommy!" Jacob came running and flung his arms around her waist.

"Hey, Champ. How was your day?"

"Busy," he replied, sounding all grown-up for a moment. "How was yours?"

"Busy, too." He ran off back to the sofa where his Marvel characters had set up home. Rosalee hovered by the door, her arms folded in her not-going-anywhere-soon pose. "Hey, Rosalee. How was he?"

The elderly woman nodded. "We've had a good evening.

He's eaten and I've saved you some. I made bean and sausage stew."

"I didn't know we had sausages."

"I had some at home."

Savannah bent down to get her handbag. "Let me give you some—"

"That's not necessary. I had to eat too." It was roughly once a week that Rosalee did this, even though Savannah had never asked her, but secretly she was always grateful. Coming home to the smell of freshly cooked food was wonderful.

"Thank you."

"You're welcome. Yours should be nice and hot." Rosalee told her. "How was work?" She examined Savannah's face closely.

"Good." Savannah smiled back, as she hung up her coat.

"And how is that wonderful Mr. Stone?" Rosalee lowered her voice.

"He's very well."

"Jacob's been telling me a lot about him." Rosalee nodded, smiling. "I knew there was something different about you," she said, nodding her head. "It wasn't only the new hairstyle, or the new clothes, but I couldn't put my finger on it. You've got a spring in your step." Savannah blushed. "I'm pleased to see that things are looking up for you."

"He's a good man," Savannah confessed. *Most of the time.*

"You must be careful, Savannah, especially if he's your boss." The way Rosalee said it made it sound like something illicit, as if Tobias was using her. Savannah's cheeks colored.

"It's not like that," she replied defensively, eager to stave off the stigma of sleaziness.

"He seems like a decent enough man but you have Jacob to think about. You have to be certain that the next man you meet is willing to take both of you on." Rosalee put her hand on Savannah's forearm and squeezed gently.

"He's fond of Jacob, and Jacob adores him."

"He seems to be," Rosalee agreed. "Jacob can't stop talking about him." She chortled. "I have a feeling he's good for you. I don't want you to get hurt again."

Savannah nodded and tugged at the collar of her blouse. She didn't want to get hurt either. "I know," she replied, feeling more unsure as the days passed and she and Tobias hadn't even spoken.

"I like seeing you happy," Rosalee continued, sliding her arms through her coat. "It's about time you started to enjoy life."

Savannah pondered Rosalee's words as the door closed. She had started to enjoy life again but with this rift between them suddenly turning things sour, her days descended into quiet misery.

If Savannah needed her space, she could have it, Tobias decided. He had other weightier matters to deal with. With Yanling and his business deals uppermost on his mind, Tobias was grateful to have something to occupy him, otherwise he'd have become steadily frustrated with the state of things between him and Savannah.

Jacob's words still haunted him and each time he thought of what he and his mother might have endured in the past, a fist of anger balled in his gut. He was desperate to talk to her, not only to resolve this current problem, but to find out more about her past. Up until now, he'd thought the pain of the past was only his to bear.

As the end of the week crawled by, and with his impending departure looming, Tobias caved in. He'd given her a week to simmer down and think about 'the wrong he had done' but when she hadn't even extended an olive branch, he decided that enough was enough and summoned her to his office.

He didn't want to leave with this bad atmosphere hanging between them. He wanted to see her, to see that she was all right even though he was more wary than ever that she might construe his actions in the wrong light. "Close the door, Savannah," he told her as she walked into his office leaving the door slightly ajar behind her. Her expression was tight, gone was the exuberance that had lit up her face that day he'd shown up at her apartment. Now she looked subdued and he could see that her armor was still heavy.

She closed the door and returned to his desk.

"Please, sit down," he urged. "I'm sorry if you felt I manipulated you. It was the last thing I intended."

She stared back at him, saying nothing.

"I wanted to give you your space these past few days, but I don't want to leave for this trip with us parting on bad terms." She seemed to soften, as if his apology had lifted a weight from her shoulders.

"I don't want to be like this, either."

"I guess there are some things we'll have to agree to disagree on," he concluded.

She threw him an icy stare. *Agree to disagree on?*

He wasn't going to admit to something he didn't believe in. "Look, Savannah. I still think I did the right thing, even if you seem adamant that I did it out of a need to control you."

"Don't you see, don't you *still* see, Tobias," she said the words slowly, clenching her teeth, "that what you did was manipulative?"

"I had to take things into my own hands."

"That's what my ex used to do and that didn't end well either."

"I'm nothing like your ex."

"I'm not so sure."

Her words jolted through him like a 100-volt charge. He was sure that he was nothing like her ex but if that was what she thought of him then he had nothing to say in return. He puffed out his chest. "Perhaps I was hasty in thinking we could work things out before I left."

"Why? Did you want another visit to your penthouse?"

His mouth fell open in shock and stayed there. "I'm not using you for sex."

She narrowed her eyes at him. "I'm not a stop-gap for Naomi?"

"Do you believe that?" He squared his shoulders, his hands fisting inside his pockets.

"I can see that it's all about the thrill of the chase with you. You want things you can't have and you take it as a challenge to plot and scheme your way to getting them. Maybe I'm one of those things."

"You're not a fucking commodity," he growled. *Christ, was that what she still thought?*

"You took the words right out of my mouth." She got up and walked towards the door. "Have a good trip, Tobias. Clearly we're not ready to discuss anything at the moment."

When she walked away from him, his heart threatened to shoot straight out of his chest. She couldn't leave; he wasn't ready to let her go. "We're not done yet. Savannah!" But she didn't turn around to listen and as she opened the door, Candace almost fell in.

"How long have you been standing there?" Tobias barked as Savannah walked out without even turning around to acknowledge him. He made no attempt to recover the situation. Candace fell silent.

"Well?" he snarled, eyeing his PA with contempt. "What is it?"

"They're waiting for you in the conference room," she whispered, and rushed out. Another goddamn useless meeting for another goddamn trip he didn't want to make in the first place.

CHAPTER THIRTEEN

With Tobias abroad, Savannah kept her head down and stayed in room 218 as much as possible. Part of this was fueled by her desire to avoid Candace.

She wasn't sure how much that vulture had heard of her conversation with Tobias. It was likely that the woman had heard nothing but it was the not knowing part that irritated her more than a flare-up of chickenpox. While Savannah didn't think Candace would stoop so low as to blabber to the press, she had a feeling his PA wouldn't be able to keep her news to herself.

More than ever, Savannah now looked forward to returning home in the evenings.

It was an uneventful and average Wednesday after dinner and she had only just pulled off her rubber cleaning gloves when her cell phone rang. Thrilled at the remote possibility that it might be Tobias, she grabbed it, only to find her hopes dive when she saw the caller ID.

"Hello, sugar." The sound of his gravelly voice sent shivers down her spine for all the wrong reasons.

"I told you, don't call me that." She glanced over at Jacob

who was lying on the couch watching TV and moved as far back in to the kitchen as she could. "What do you want now?" As soon as she spoke, she regretted her choice of words, but it was difficult to be polite when she felt nothing but hatred for the man.

"Why are you always getting so pissed each time you hear from me? Can't you even find a kind word for your old man?"

"We're divorced, Colt. We agreed to go our separate ways. I don't understand why you keep calling me."

"I'm passing by in a couple of weeks. It'll be a good time to see you both."

"I'm not sure that would be a good thing." She tried to keep calm, even though she felt an invisible fist smack straight into her chest and hold there.

"I want to see my boy."

"You're sure now that he's your boy, all of a sudden?" Her anger peaked as she remembered what he'd said to her the last time.

"'Course I'm sure. I know you ain't that kind of woman. Though...sheeeeet." His voice rose as if he'd made a discovery. "Are you all shacked up with some guy now? Is that why you can't wait to get rid of me each time I call?"

Her chest constricted. *Don't panic. Don't let on.* She laughed nervously. "I'm still single. You put me off men for life." She hoped her strong and steady voice carried conviction.

"I don't know. All of a sudden things are working out for you."

"What makes you think so?"

"You've got a job, you paid the hospital bill. Damn, you can afford to live in New York. It sounds to me like life is pretty sweet for you." She'd never told him she lived in Kay's apartment, had never let on that she'd lived with Aunty Sylvie either for fear that he might somehow track her down and find her, and she relied on her parents to keep silent if they ever ran into him.

"Things are still hard. It's expensive, being in the city, and I've struggled more than ever. I got government assistance to help with the hospital bill."

"That's not what you said before." Her brows snapped together as she tried to remember what she had told him. She was sure she hadn't given him any inkling of how she was doing, or what she did, or where she worked, or how she paid that bill off. He was fishing for information.

She lied. "I was out with my friends," she told him. "I didn't want to own up to it."

Her ex wasn't buying it. "What's his name? This friend of yours?"

"It was the girls from work." She'd been on the phone with him long enough. Luckily, she heard the landline ringing in the other room. "I have to go," she told him. "I don't want to see you again, Colt. Don't make me get a restraining order."

"Based on what? You never told the cops anything, why would they believe you now? I haven't done anything except call you a couple of times and it's only 'cos I'm worried about my son."

She laughed bitterly. That man never worried about anyone else but himself.

"I'm a changed man now, Savannah. You gotta believe me. Give me a chance."

"No." No chance. He didn't deserve one. She was better off without him. Nothing would ever change her mind regarding that.

"Savannah, please."

"Goodbye, Colt." She slammed her phone down on the counter and ran her hands over her eyes, blotting out the world and the light, going deep within herself to find comfort. To let

Colt back into her life would be a huge mistake, letting him in in the first place had been a mistake, but then she'd never have had Jacob. It was strange, and bittersweet, how her life had turned out.

Hearing Jacob's voice, she rushed into the living room, a small hopeful part of her wondering if Tobias would have called the landline seeing that her cell phone was busy. He put the phone down as she reached him. "It was Grandma, Mommy."

"She didn't want to talk to me?"

"I told her you were on the phone but we had a chat."

"Oh," she said, pleased that the relationship between Jacob and her parents was still strong.

His eyes shone as he broke the news. "She says to tell you that they are definitely coming to stay for a week at Easter."

"That would be wonderful." She liked the idea of having her parents over. So far they hadn't made it to New York since she had left and she looked forward to seeing them again. It was just as well that they were coming soon while Kay was still abroad. Easter was ideal.

She rubbed her forehead, feeling the tightness above her brows. With March upon them, summer would follow soon enough, and that meant it would be time for her and Jacob to leave the apartment, to leave Sunnyside, and perhaps even New York altogether.

CHAPTER FOURTEEN

P olite conversation and muted laughter mingled effortlessly with the faraway, fluttering and graceful notes of a piano being played somewhere in the background. On either side of them, at far ends of the opulent black marble bar, floor-to-ceiling bay windows watched over the Victoria Harbour as night fell over Hong Kong.

Tobias loosened his tie while Matthias refilled their whiskey glasses as they sat on surprisingly comfortable high bar stools. Lights twinkled like specks of glitter against a velvet blue-black sky and were reflected back along the black, glassy water.

Things hadn't gone as badly as he had anticipated. The share prices of Yanling's companies seemed to be holding, as were those of the other companies they had invested in. After much discussion, and with Matthias's reasoning, he hadn't yet pulled out of anything rashly. They'd walked away earlier this evening, with Stone Enterprises giving them another three months to see how they would fare, before he made his final decision.

"Cheers," said Matthias, lifting his glass.

"Cheers." They knocked their glasses together. He couldn't

fault Xian Yanling either. The man had been a gracious enough host, showing them the sights and sounds of the city and taking them out to the best restaurants and fine dining it offered. Still, Tobias was wary. The man seemed to be trying too hard to please him. But tonight Tobias wanted to wind down and not talk business on his final evening here. The sixteen-hour flight back to New York tomorrow would be tough and it would take him a few days to recover.

"That wasn't so bad, was it?" Matthias asked, knocking his whiskey back in two gulps.

"No," Tobias ruminated.

"It's never cut and dry."

"The data never lies." Tobias reminded him.

"Except that the data can't predict. It's a tool, and while we can only project forward, those projections don't always account for sudden fluctuations in global affairs or the economy." Matthias ordered another round of drinks.

"True. Very true, my friend." Tobias fell silent again. Now that the meetings were over, his mind once more settled to more personal matters.

"Why don't you stay on a few days longer with me?" Matthias asked, sitting back on the high stool and admiring the pretty, exotic-looking waitresses who walked around in their small black skirts and neat, figure-hugging black tops. More than once, he saw Matthias give a few of them long, appreciative glances.

"I might get in the way," Tobias replied, a grin causing his cheekbones to lift.

"But you're a single man now," Matthias countered. "When in Rome..." His attention drifted towards another beautiful young waitress who passed by. Tobias glanced at the petite woman with her finely shaped brows and bright, almost translucent skin and delicate features.

Though he could see the allure of her, no other woman triggered a response from him. He had eyes only for Savannah.

"Or is Naomi back on the scene?" Matthias seemed to want answers. Tobias remained silent and knocked back his whiskey quickly. He moved the empty glass away and slid the newly ordered full glass towards him.

"No," he replied, staring at the deep amber colored liquid.

"Is there someone else on the scene?" Matthias offered. "I'm all ears." But Tobias wasn't ready to share his news with anyone particularly when he himself wasn't sure what type of news he had. Were they together or not? Or had they reached an impasse? His attempts to resolve matters before he had left had failed, leaving him and Savannah at odds again.

"There's nothing new to report." He reached into his jacket blazer as soon as he heard his cell phone ringing. "Excuse me," he said, and moved to the other end of the bar to take the call. Not only because he wanted privacy, or because he hoped it would be Savannah, but because it helped get him out of answering Matthias's questions. Whatever Candace might have heard of his last conversation with Savannah that day, he knew it would have reached Matthias so he hadn't been surprised that his well-meaning friend was actively seeking answers. He had been subtly prying the entire trip.

"I'm in town," Xavier announced, crushing Tobias's hopes in an instant.

"I'm in Hong Kong," Tobias replied, staring out of the floor-to-ceiling windows. He glanced over his shoulder, half-expecting to see Xavier swaggering towards him. He never could be sure where his brother might show up next.

"In Hong Kong?"

"I'm flying back tomorrow."

Xavier let out a disappointed grunt. "I was hoping we could meet up for a drink tonight."

"Isn't Petra keeping you busy?" Tobias asked.

"Mom told you, huh?"

"How painful was the lunch?"

"Like having your balls tasered."

"Ouch." Tobias flinched. "What made you take her? You know what Mom's like."

"Yeah, well. My bad. It was the only weekend Petra was free, and I'd already arranged to meet Mom and Dad for lunch so I figured it would be worth the two hours of torture to be able to see her for the weekend. She's a model," he explained. "She doesn't stay around in one place long enough."

"Mom was wondering if she was a keeper."

"Who knows?" Tobias straightened up in surprise. He'd expected a dismissive response from his brother, not a 'who knows?'

"It sounds serious," said Tobias. *But how serious could things be with a model?* And one who wasn't around much.

"She's in New York today and I was wondering if you might want to meet up with us." *With us?* It really was serious. Tobias had met Xavier's girlfriends before when he'd met up with him and his group of friends, mostly at his brother's instigation. Meeting previous girlfriends had been an afterthought. This time his brother had actually mentioned a girlfriend upfront and it made Tobias all the more curious.

"I wish I could. Another time?" Tobias replied and was reminded of the phrase he often said to Jacob.

"It'll have to be, I guess. I'd like you to meet her though, bro," Xavier replied, confirming Tobias's suspicions that maybe Petra was more than a playmate.

"Mom says you and Naomi split up. How come?"

"No reason," replied Tobias guardedly. "It didn't work out."

"I had no idea. Things looked good between you two. It lasted longer than we thought it would."

"Longer than who thought?"

"Me, and Mom and Dad."

"I didn't know you were placing bets on me."

"We weren't," replied Xavier defensively. "I meant that after...you know..."

"After Ivy. You can still say her name. She was a part of my life and it's okay to talk about her." Except that he knew nobody did because he'd never been okay with it. He'd preferred to keep his thoughts about Ivy to himself. Talking out loud about her in the past tense cut him to the bone and he knew it was because of his past reaction that Xavier hadn't said her name now. "I'm sorry," said Tobias, realizing. "I know I've been a real bastard at times, and I haven't wanted to talk about her. I still find it hard to think about it."

"Don't worry. We all know what you've been through."

"It's getting easier," Tobias confessed. Being with Savannah had shown him that there was a way he could move on.

"You've had the worst thing happen to you, bro. It hasn't been an easy time for you, we know that, but you need to open up and let others in. Maybe that's why you and Naomi didn't work out."

"What do you mean?" Tobias was intrigued to hear his brother's take on the matter since Xavier was completely ignorant of the arrangement he had with Naomi.

"You might not know it but there's a part of you that you keep hidden. A part of you that's off limits, like a black box that nobody's allowed access to. You drive people away." Tobias thought about that for a while. Maybe that was why Savannah didn't understand his desire to control, his drive to have things be a certain way. He did what he did in order to ensure that nobody close to him ever got hurt again, or left.

"I can introduce you to some of Petra's friends," Xavier suggested, trying to be helpful.

"No," replied Tobias, shaking his head. "You've been helpful enough."

"She has great-looking friends."

I'm sure she does, thought Tobias. *But I already have someone like that.* "Catch you later, buddy. Gotta go before Matthias gets thrown out of the bar for making improper suggestions to the bar staff." As he walked back to his friend, a waitress hurried away and Matthias pushed a slip of paper, just big enough to hold a telephone number, into his pocket.

"That's your night planned out, is it?" Tobias asked.

Matthias gestured with his thumb. "I'm making sure I'm well looked after. There's nothing like the natives to show you a good time. Everything okay back at the office?"

Tobias swirled the whiskey around in his glass before taking a gulp. "The office? What made you think that was someone from the office?"

"No reason." They sat in silence before Matthias asked, "Do you want to stay here or go someplace else for something to eat?"

"I'm going to order room service and have an early night. You know how long that goddamn flight back is, and I never do sleep well on a plane."

"See you sometime next week," Matthias replied, as the two men patted one another on the back.

Tobias emptied his whiskey glass. "Don't get anyone pregnant."

CHAPTER FIFTEEN

S avannah thought he'd be in the office on Friday and all day she had been secretly looking out for him. She had even taken special care with what she'd worn to work, hoping to pass by his office at some moment and to resolve this air of unease that stood between them.

It was only later in the afternoon that Briony dashed her hopes by confirming that Tobias wasn't due to arrive in New York until late on Friday night. She returned home that evening feeling empty.

The week without him had passed slowly. Colt's phone call had shaken her, but she put it behind her and tried to keep busy. As busy as a woman moping around like a long lost dog could.

Tobias Stone had not only opened up a world of glorious sex for her, but he'd given her something she had never had; a desire to be with someone—a desire that went deeper and transcended more than just the physical. She thought of him more times than she cared to admit and now hated herself for how their last meeting had gone. That at his last attempt to make up, they had ended up in the same position, stubbornly stuck in their own misconceptions instead of giving an inch. It was only when he was away, in a different land, with not even the possibility of her running into him that she realized she cared for him too much to hurt him. She sensed that this man was already in pain. After his past, and what had happened to him, it wasn't difficult to see that he still suffered, no matter how well he tried to hide it.

With Jacob tucked in bed over an hour ago, Savannah settled down on the couch for a quiet and uneventful Sunday evening. She'd been sitting, not watching whatever was on TV, because her thoughts had been preoccupied by Tobias and the idea, the anticipation of seeing him tomorrow, when she was sure he would return to work. Distracted by the possible scenarios that might unfold at work tomorrow, she jolted when her cell phone rang. Lately, she'd jumped each time it rang, dreading the sound of hearing Colt's voice at the other end. But it was Tobias who called her now. And still she jerked back in surprise, her stomach spiraling towards the floor.

"Don't hang up," he told her. "Hear me out." She clutched the phone tighter on hearing his ominous words.

"What makes you think I'm going to hang up on you?" Something in his voice sounded lighter. Maybe he'd missed her, too. The distance and time apart from one another had changed things for both of them, which was crazy given that they had to fight and steal around trying to find the time to see each other.

"The way you were the last time we met."

"I didn't hang up on you," she pointed out.

"You didn't give me a chance."

He was right. "We were both being stubborn," she confessed. "I'm not solely to blame for that day." She hoped they weren't going to get off on the wrong foot again.

"You're right," he conceded. "You weren't to blame."

She jerked her head up, intrigued to know what more he had to say. "You're back in New York?" She already knew he was but she wondered when he had arrived back.

"I got back on Friday night but—"

Today was Sunday. *Why hadn't he called her sooner?*

"I had things I needed to figure out and..." He spoke slowly, with less of the confidence and conviction he usually displayed.

"How was it? Your trip?"

"It worked out well. Matthias is still over there."

"He didn't come back with you?"

"When I left him at the bar, he was busy exchanging numbers with a couple of waitresses." *So those were the kinds of things they got up to on business trips?* She didn't want to dwell too long on those thoughts and silence fell between them. It was quite the paradox. When he wasn't around, she missed him and yet when he was back in her life, they seemed to be at odds with one another again. Maybe she'd forgotten, and maybe it was such a long time but was this what being in a relationship was like?

"I wanted to ask you to do something." His voice shook her from her somber thoughts.

"Like what?"

"Can you come over?"

She looked at her watch. "Now?" She let out a snort, as if the man didn't already understand her predicament.

"Not now," his voice was gentle, his tone understanding. "Tomorrow. Take the day off."

"I haven't put in my request." She had to fill in a form and get Briony to sign it off in order to take time off work.

"Then call in sick."

"Why?"

"Because it's the only way we'll be able to talk without any interruption. There's never the time for us to talk properly."

"And come where?"

"To my apartment."

"Did I hear you right?" Savannah sat up on the couch,

uncurling her left leg from under her, placing it on the floor. She sat forward, resting her forehead in her hand. "You want me to take the day off work and come to your place tomorrow so that you can get me in bed again?" *The cheek of it.*

"I never mentioned bed in that sentence and from our past dealings, it's always you who wants to hit the sack..."

He was right. Changing tack, she challenged him. "I can't take the day off sick. That would be lying."

"Take it as one of 'Tobias's days,' that's what you call them isn't it—the days you work on my stuff?"

"And tell Briony I'm taking a 'Tobias day' *at your apartment*? Why don't you take an ad out in the *Wall Street Journal* and announce that you're seeing me?"

"It's not such a bad idea," he countered playfully.

"Now you're being facetious."

"I don't care. I want the world to know."

"To know that we're together?"

"Would that be such a problem?" He let out a sigh. "Please. It's important."

"You're taking the day off sick, too?"

"I own the company, I can do what I want."

"You do what you want anyway," she muttered.

"I'll send Morris to get you."

"I haven't made my mind up yet."

"If you could think about it and let me—"

"Okay. I'll come."

"Thank you. I'll send Morris to come and get you."

"I'm capable of making my own way there."

"So you are."

"Tomorrow, then," she confirmed.

"Around 10:00?"

"Around 10:00." She wondered what had prompted this. "Don't forget to text me your address."

CHAPTER SIXTEEN

The day broke and when the light poured through the window of his bedroom, Tobias felt remarkably alert, which was surprising given that he hadn't slept much.

The jet lag and adjusting to a thirteen-hour time difference, had been tough enough. But he'd also started responding to nonurgent emails that had cluttered up his email inbox the past week. His body was tired, but his mind couldn't switch off when there was so much to be done.

The idea of Savannah coming over compounded his restlessness and prompted him to get out of bed at an ungodly hour. He was working away at his desk by 6:00 a.m. So engrossed was he that when the buzzer sounded and Savannah announced her arrival, he scrambled up from his desk because he wasn't sure he was ready to meet her.

He had showered and freshened up, but that had been a few hours ago. Quickly checking his reflection in the huge handcrafted mirror in the entrance hall, he rubbed the spiky growth that had sprung up all over his jaw and chin, making him itch. He hadn't shaved in days. The sound of the doorbell stopped him from checking himself out any further and he quickly answered the door, his heart nervously beating behind his ribcage when he set eyes on Savannah. She looked bright and fresh, reminding him of flowers and sunshine, as she stood, gazing at him anxiously in her casual jeans and a white cotton shirt with a jacket.

"I called in sick," she told him as she stepped inside.

"Thanks for coming." He closed the door behind her, staring at her and taking his fill.

"Briony told me I'd been looking stressed out the entire week."

"Were you?" he asked.

"I thought I was remarkably stress-free."

"Maybe you missed me more than you thought you did," he replied, holding out his hand. "Let me have your jacket?" She slipped it off, eyeing him the whole while, as if she were trying to figure out why he might have called her over. He hung her jacket in the guest closet and watched as she wandered around.

"You have a beautiful home."

"Thank you."

She walked over to the hallway which was a whole wall of windows looking out onto Park Avenue. "And you have some of the best views in all of New York, between this place, your penthouse and your office."

"I can't complain."

She looked around wide-eyed, every now and then stealing a glance at him. "You look tired."

"You look amazing."

"You look rough," she replied, staring at his face, making him self-conscious. He lifted his fingers to his bristly stubble.

"Thanks for coming."

"You already said that." She trailed her fingers over the shiny windows. "What is this about?" she asked, looking out at the view, facing away from him.

"We need to talk." He walked to her side and stared out, his hands in the front loops of his jeans. "I have an apology to make." Suddenly, he felt hot and uncomfortable in his jeans and t-shirt. He stared at her profile, at her tightly closed mouth, noticing the way she avoided looking at him.

"You were right, about me, about what I did, manipulating things the way I did, to make sure you never left to go to that other job. It was wrong of me to do that, especially behind your back."

She turned to face him, slipping her hands into the back pockets of her jeans as she shifted from one foot to the next. They were like strangers around one another, awkward and uneasy. Gone was the easy familiarity, the closeness, the holding of hands, and touching. Perhaps it was right, under the circumstances but he still missed it. "I've been thinking about it and I understand now that you see it one way and I see it another way."

"Which way is that?"

"The way I try to make things fit. The way I like things to be a certain way—how I behaved when you told me you were going to leave. I knew you would still struggle the same, if not more, if you accepted that other position. I knew it wouldn't relieve you of your financial worries and I was in a position to change that for you—hear me out, Savannah," he said, when she opened her mouth. "Please," he begged. "Just let me finish. It was simple enough for me to see, but I had no right to interfere in your life like that, to take over as if you didn't have an opinion. I also know that I made that happen because of the way I behaved when you first asked me for an advance, the things I said to you racked me with guilt. I needed to make it up to you. You're right, the least I could have done was to give you that choice instead of making it for you and behind your back. I never intended to be backhanded about it and I've been meaning to tell you many times but we always ended up...not having dinner, or talking, but just getting down to...business..."

She folded her arms, a look of puzzlement coloring her features. She didn't interrupt, as he'd been expecting. Feeling brave, he continued. "I didn't want to lose you. That's the God's honest truth. I couldn't bear to lose you even though in those early days nothing serious had happened between us. Still, I had a gut feeling about you. It was what made me want to pursue you in the first place. I was being patient, waiting for things to take their own course, partly because, with you and Jacob, I wasn't so sure what it was I was looking for."

She looked more confused than ever. Maybe it would be better to show her. "Come," he said, holding out his hand. She placed her hands on her hips, and her hair fell around her shoulders as she shook her head more in confusion than by way of refusing him.

"I want to show you something, Savannah. It's important."

She put out her hand and he took it, guiding her up the glass staircase to the upper level. He walked silently to the far end where the master bedroom was and headed towards the door next to it—the one he didn't open often. He pushed it wide open and sunlight streaked in, bathing the blue and white walls of the room in a pale golden hue. The room was bereft of furniture and there was nothing in it except for the vinyl wall stickers that he and Ivy had put on one of the walls as soon as they'd found out.

Savannah walked in, her mouth dropping open as she looked around. It was obvious, even with its lack of furniture, what room this was. "This is a nursery?"

CHAPTER SEVENTEEN

He walked to the far wall with its stickers of cars, planes and trains, and ran his fingers over the outline of a red sports car.

Savannah's heart thumped as she walked slowly towards him; his back turned to her so that she couldn't see his face.

"Tobias?" She placed her hand on his arm, so lightly that she was sure he didn't even feel the pressure. Standing sideways, she observed the way the lines crisscrossed around the corners of his eyes, like tiny barbed wires. Her stomach churned slowly, making her queasy, but she waited patiently, not saying a word. The muscles around his jaw were tight and a vein around his temple corded, blue and ugly, raised above the skin. She could see that he struggled to hold it together.

"She wanted to name him Zach," his voice sounded distant. "But I wanted to call him Zachary."

"Zachary?" *Who was Zachary?*

"My son."

"You had a son?" Her voice barely audible, she stumbled backwards, her fingers numb, her chest tightening so that she had to work to breathe.

"We were going to have a son. Ivy was four months pregnant when the accident happened. That part, about the baby, we kept hidden from the media. Nobody knew aside from my family, and hers, and Matthias. We managed to keep that hidden because there are some things that are sacred."

He'd lost not only his wife, but his unborn child too. Savannah's heart ripped into a thousand pieces. But she had to be strong for this man whom she knew had been fighting to keep it together. She couldn't fall apart now when he needed her.

"I'm sorry," she whispered, hearing her own words and thinking how weak and pathetic they sounded given the weight of his loss. There were no words to convey what she felt.

His eyebrows inched together like angry caterpillars as his fingers continued to trace over the red car, over and over as if focusing on that helped to soothe him. The whole time, he never looked at her once.

"We were coming back late that night. It must have been 11:00 or something, and I remember driving along the empty road and thinking how quiet it was. We were five minutes away from home and it should have been an easy trip. We were laughing, talking about Christmas—he was due in October, you see, and it would have been our first Christmas that year. We were making plans for it, for our new family, and looking forward to it with our little boy. Ivy was laughing, I can't even remember what I said to make her laugh, but I remember looking at her and seeing her eyes sparkle in the dimmed light of the car. When I turned to face the road again, a man had stumbled out onto the road. He'd come out of nowhere. One minute the road was empty and the next second this stranger was just a few yards away from me. I remember thinking he was some homeless bum, or a drunk and what the hell was he doing walking onto the road. I swerved instinctively to avoid hitting him. But I hit the curb instead. We were headed towards a wall. I remember trying to turn the steering wheel even as that wall came at us. It all happened in slow motion, and I remember each second so vividly. My body locking up, the wall in our face and I knew it was going to hit her side. I spun the wheel but it was too late. There was a crash, the loudest noise that went on for the longest time."

He stared at the wall, his fingers stopped moving and he fell silent. Savannah's stomach felt hollow, as if everything had fallen out. The hairs on her arms stood up, and she felt suddenly cold. "Oh, Tobias," she whispered, moving her hand over his arm.

"I couldn't save her but I saved that bastard. And in saving him, I killed the two people I loved the most in the world."

His shoulders slumped. For a man who exuded intensity as though it were a new aftershave, Tobias looked as if the life force had zapped clean out of his body. His blue-gray eyes, sometimes so intense she had to look away, sometimes so serious, sometimes like the ocean, were now dull, lackluster and lifeless.

He looked like a dead man walking.

She shook her head. "It wasn't your fault. You didn't do this." He blamed himself, it wasn't only the weight of his loss that he'd been carrying around with him, but the guilt too, and that must have been as heavy to bear.

"But I did. It was me behind the wheel. I had the power to control it and I wasn't able to."

"No, Tobias," she lifted her hand to his chin, tilted his face gently towards her and forcing him to look at her. "This is not your fault. You cannot go on blaming yourself for something you didn't do on purpose. You did your best and you didn't know how it would end."

Tortured eyes stared at her blankly. "But don't you see? It should have been me. I killed them."

The hurt in his voice stabbed her heart and a chill slid over her. "It's not true," she insisted, determined to make him see. She had read about the accident but hadn't delved deeper. It had been bad enough discovering that his wife had died so young. Whenever she had checked up on his details online, Tobias's dark past was buried beneath the trivial speculation about his next girlfriend.

"You did no such thing. You didn't have a choice who would live even though you did everything—I know you would have tried to save her, Tobias. But you couldn't. Let it go. Don't you see? The fault isn't yours. The guilt doesn't belong to you. The blame isn't yours to bear. You have to stop hating yourself for the past." But she'd lost him. He stared vacantly at the wall, once again tracing his fingers around the red sports car, paying no heed to her words.

"Tobias," she said, shaking his arm gently. "You have to move on."

"I can't," he said softly, as if he was talking to himself. "I wasn't drunk, and of course the media went crazy. A rich kid and a bum and a fatal crash. They wanted to chew me up and spit me out. I wasn't as wealthy then, I was up-and-coming and I was ripe for a public takedown. But I was clean and it wasn't reckless driving, and despite the media circus, it soon blew over. I was innocent, but I've never *felt* innocent." His voice dropped lower as he hung his head. "That kind of guilt never leaves you; it eats you up, inch by inch, cell by cell, and you never get over it."

"Tobias," she murmured, his name a tortured whisper. She wanted to throw her arms around him, to heal his hurt, but he was solid and cold, his whole body a wall of metal. He wasn't letting her in even though he'd given her an insight into his demons. She took both of his hands and held them between hers, placing herself between the wall and him so that he had no choice but to look at her. "If you continue to carry the blame and guilt, it will consume you."

"It's easy for you to say."

"I know." A heaviness settled over her as if her body had been draped in a blanket of metal, weighing her spirit down and dragging it lower. As tragic as it was, she couldn't be weak. It would be up to her to make him see reason.

"Ivy wouldn't have wanted this for you," she said softly. She stared at the vein that pulsated along his neck and pressed her hand to his face. He'd aged instantly in front of her eyes in the reliving of that nightmare.

In one split second, something out of the blue had smacked into him and the course of his life had been changed forever. Whatever happened now, she would be here for him, it didn't matter what she thought of the past, of what he'd done—she now understood better the enigma that was this man. His actions, however controlled and calculated they seemed, she now knew where they came from; a place so deep down and buried in complete darkness that he would never heal unless he broke free from it.

Until now she had believed that she was the only one who was trying to escape from her past.

She wasn't.

Tobias Stone was trying to break free, too. He wasn't the man who had everything, nor was he the man who could have whatever he wanted. Tobias Stone was the man who had lost everything and was now trying to find his place in the world.

"You have to listen to me," she pressed her hands into his forearms, trying to elicit a reaction from him. "Your sadness doesn't have to destroy you, Tobias. It can be the source from which you can rebuild your life." Her voice wavered as she realized this didn't apply only to him. It was as profound a lesson for her.

He turned his face towards her again. "Then you and Jacob came along and... Don't you see, Savannah? I lost them, and I didn't want to lose you." She nodded, understanding at last. She pressed his hand and blinked back the tears she didn't want him to see fall.

"I had to do what it took to keep you here, at Stone Enterprises, not only because I believed it would be the better option for you, but because *I* needed you. After Ivy, after all those years, something about you drew me in. Zachary would have been four now. I used to ask myself whether I was replacing what I had lost with you and Jacob. The two of you fit right into my life. It was almost frightening how perfectly you both fit." He looked away from her. "I know that's what my Mom thinks."

His words landed like bullets on her shoulders. *He had told his mother about her?* "And were you?" She needed to know, even though now was not the time to ask such things.

"I'm still not sure. More than anything, it was myself that I saw in Jacob that day he peeked in through the window of the toy store. He wanted to come in, but he looked scared. I recognized that. I didn't have much when I was growing up, and I know what it's like to want things, living a life on the sidelines, watching others. When I saw Jacob, I was reminded of myself. But, yes, I do wonder what it would have been like if Zachary and Ivy had lived. And then I see you, and I see Jacob, and I know you're not Ivy and Zachary. You're both *you*. I know the distinction, Savannah. That's not what I'm setting out to prove. I wanted you to know why—in my own twisted way—why I couldn't let you walk out of my life. I wasn't ready to lose you, even though I wasn't sure if what we had was worth saving."

"It *is* worth saving. This, what we have. It's worth saving, Tobias. I promise you. I'll be here for you as long as you want me to. I'm not going anywhere." She meant it with all her heart.

As she pressed his hands between hers, seeking comfort, she realized that he no longer wore his wedding band.

She had already decided to let him know before she had any idea of the news he'd been wanting to tell her. During his absence, she had realized that she could not let this man slip away from her; this good, kind man—temperamental, but loving and caring—a man who put her first, always. She saw it even more clearly now that he had shared his past with her, now that he had let her see his vulnerability, now that he had confessed his feelings of guilt and the blame that consumed him.

The man before her had been stripped raw, to the bone and her heart filled with nothing but love for him.

"You see," he said, gazing into her eyes, "You pulled me out of that darkness and you made me feel again. How could I let you walk away?" His voice was soft, a hint of a whisper and she bit back her lip, stifling the lump that lodged in her throat. It was hard not to want to cry for his pain, for his was far worse than she had ever imagined. But she could not fall to pieces, not now when he needed her.

She put her arms around his waist and stared up at him, running her fingers around the prickly hairs around his chin. "I'm not leaving," she whispered. "I'm yours. Completely."

CHAPTER EIGHTEEN

The March sunshine, with its promise of spring, took away the grayness of winter as shards of warm sunlight danced into his apartment.

The heaviness that had weighed him down for so long was still there, but it had started to lift a little in the telling of his past. Over the years, he had allowed guilt and blame to land among the debris of his fractured life. He had become used to waking up each morning with a ball of regret in his chest, and a longing that could never be satisfied. But now he felt a little lighter knowing that he could move forward with his life once more.

They had made slow love for hours, safe in the knowledge of no interruptions, safe to heal and be healed, to love and be loved. Later, they had cooked lunch together and sat around, talking and doing the things that had been denied them for so long: spending time together in their own space, being truly alone, not just in bed, but connected, doing normal things like a normal couple.

Tobias lay on the couch downstairs in the living room with his arms around Savannah, who was on her side with her face on his chest, her fingers stroking his chest over his t-shirt. He ran his fingers through her thick hair, inhaling the fruity scent of her shampoo.

"Candace suspects—about us," she said.

"What makes you say that?" Not that it surprised him.

"She's been watching me like a hawk lately."

"Matthias was sniffing too." He had a feeling Candace had said something to him, which was why the man had been asking him more questions than Homeland Security. Savannah's eyes widened as she lifted her head up at him, forcing him to examine the amber specks in her eyes. *Like cat's eyes,* he thought. Wide and brilliant.

"They know, don't they?" she asked and he detected the hint of fear in her voice, as if it was something she wanted to keep hidden.

"Would it be so bad if everyone knew?" He was sick of hiding it. He wanted to be seen with her, to not give a damn what anyone else thought. But what she thought mattered to him, and for her sake, he was willing to do whatever she wanted.

"I need some more time, Tobias." He shifted up along the couch and kissed the top of her head.

"What are you afraid of?" Was it that goddamn asshole of an ex she was worried about? Because she didn't need to be; he would always keep her safe.

"I want to tread carefully, for Jacob's sake."

"Wouldn't it be great news if he knew we were together?"

"It's too soon. I want to be sure."

That hurt. "You're not sure of us?" But even as he asked, he was afraid that she was having doubts. Maybe she thought she'd become a substitute, a convenient replacement for the loved ones he had lost? Or that his interest in her was temporary. "Do you really think you're a replacement for Naomi?"

She shook her head. "Not anymore." Her thumb settled

over his lower lip. "It's not us that I'm doubting," she whispered, as if she'd read his thoughts. "I'm sure of us. Believe me, but I need a little more time. Everything in my life recently has happened so quickly. At times it feels too good to be true and I'm scared that something will come and take this away."

He put his arm around her and pulled her snug against his chest, holding her tightly, as if he couldn't bear to let her go. He knew only too well what that felt like, how quickly a life could change forever. "Take all the time you need but don't take forever, Savannah. Life is too unpredictable and too short to be scared."

"I'm not asking for a lot of time."

And that was enough for him, for now. He remembered what he'd wanted to give her and now seemed like the perfect time. "I have something for you," he said, getting up slowly so that she lifted her head and moved away.

"What?"

"Wait and you'll find out." He rushed to his study, grabbed the box and raced back to her to find her sitting up on the couch, looking perplexed. He handed her the box.

"What's this?" she asked, and stared at the deep red box, the size of her hand. "Tobias?" She looked at him, puzzled.

"Something for your birthday."

"Cartier?" Her mouth fell open.

"Open it," he urged, noticing that her cheeks were flushed. She opened the clasp and lifted the lid so that it stood up. Her eyes widened as she gazed inside the box. She gasped.

"It's beautiful." She looked at him, unsure again, making him wonder what that bastard man had done to her. Jacob's words were hard to forget.

To protect my mom.

"Take it out," he urged. "I bought it for you, Savannah." She lifted the delicate necklace out carefully as if it were made of ice and might melt. She shook her head.

"It's lovely, but it's too much...it looks so expens—"

"It would mean a lot to me if you'd accept it."

"I'm scared to try it on."

"Don't be scared. It won't break." Cartier necklaces didn't fall apart easily.

She lifted it up and examined it, a flush creeping along her face, her eyes flickering with awe. "It's beautiful." She stared at the necklace, made from white gold, with two entwined rings hanging in the middle. It was set with eighteen brilliant-cut diamonds. He'd stared at it for the longest time in the store, had debated with himself whether she might think it was too much, too soon, and whether it would scare her away. But he knew life was short, and had to be lived in the moment and at *that* moment, Tobias knew how he felt about this woman.

"I don't want you to think I've gone over the top. It's something small," he told her, as she lifted her eyes to his in silent gratitude. Right then and there he made a silent vow to take away the unhappiness from her life, just as her being a part of his life had started to take away his. "I don't want you to think that I'm buying you or anything but I wanted to give you something fitting. I hope you like it." He shook his head, finding it hard to explain. The store assistant had told him that it was called a 'Love' necklace, and the way the two rings were entwined, he thought it was the perfect gift for her.

He thought he heard a sigh escape her lips. Swallowing, she managed to utter a "Thank you." Then she reached forward and kissed him more slowly and more deeply than she ever had. It was a kiss that scorched his heart and when she pulled away, he knew they would end up in bed again.

She turned her back to him. "Would you fasten it for me?" Moving her hair out of the way, he fastened the clasp then placed his lips gently over her neck, closing his eyes to savor her scent, and the feeling of belonging she had given him.

"How does it look?" she asked, turning around quickly to face him and shattering the moment. She ran her fingers over the rings, as if she was getting used to the feel of the necklace as it hung around her neck.

"You look beautiful."

"It!" She laughed. "How does *it* look?"

"Stunning," he told her, pulling her towards him again. He dropped his mouth to hers as they fell into another kiss, deep and soft and full of promise.

"She called in sick," Candace announced, speaking into the phone while admiring her nails.

"Who?"

"Savannah Page."

"And I should care because?" Matthias sounded grouchy, she thought, and he appeared not to care. Yet this latest act only confirmed her suspicions.

"Because I told you they were up to something." Those two had been shady for a while now and that Page bitch strutted around the twenty-first floor as if she owned it.

"Good for them," Matthias returned smoothly, causing her growing irritation to snap.

"Tobias isn't at work either. According to Briony, he's chosen to work from home today." She thought she heard a woman giggling in the background. *Or was that two women?*

"What the hell are you doing?"

"Do you want me to answer that?" She withdrew her nails in disgust. "Did he say anything to you?" she asked. "Did you ask Tobias?"

Matthias sighed loudly, but she wasn't sure if it was in response to her question, or because of other distractions at his end. "Look, sweetheart, if you can't have Tobias, there's always the other Stone. If I were you, I'd let go of the idea that Tobias is going to wake up one day and see what a wonderful human being you are, 'cos it's not ever going to happen. He's out of your league, for one thing—I'm being honest here, sweetheart—Ivy is a class act to follow."

"That's exactly why I don't understand what he sees in *her*," she snarled. Was that a kissing noise she heard at the other end? She wrinkled her nose in disgust.

"That man's been through enough pain in his life," Matthias told her. "If he's finally found a little happiness, you should leave it be. I know how much that man has suffered."

"Is that all you have to say?"

"It sounds to me as if you're getting lonesome. I've told you before, I'm happy to oblige," Matthias replied in that smug, slimy way he had. "I might not be a Stone, but the offer still stands if ever you're lonely."

She ground her teeth. "I'm never *that* lonely," she snapped.

"In that case, sweetheart, do yourself a favor. You don't have a chance with Tobias. Now, if you don't mind. I'm busy." He hung up, leaving her insides tight with tension. She twisted her fingers, her upper lip twitching as if tugged by a thread.

Who did Savannah Page think she was?

Candace knew what she had to do. There was no way in hell that she was going to sit back and let that hussy walk away with the main prize.

THE OFFER, BOOK 3

The Billionaire's Love Story (#6)

CHAPTER ONE

Colt Brookes sauntered out of the rowdy bar and walked into the cool night air. He saw the parked car as he crossed the deathly quiet street and wondered why it was there. The street was a dead end.

As he neared the alleyway, he heard the voice. Thick and accented, and familiar. He almost shit in his pants as he turned around.

Santino?

What the hell did he want? In the dimly lit street, he could make out three figures. Santino stood with his hands in his pockets, looking as if he were admiring the view, while two men, as large as oak trees, stood on either side of him.

Colt's legs shook but somehow he managed to walk towards them—because he had no choice but to.

"Santino." The money wasn't due for at least another week and he was still trying to get it together.

"Brookes."

"Is something wrong?" He tried to keep his voice steady as the barnyard smell of Cuban cigar wafted over to him and stuck in his throat.

"You tell me," Santino replied.

"Nothing's wrong." He felt his bladder weaken. Something was off. Santino was early. Colt didn't like being here, in a dead-end street, in the dark. And there were three of them. "I'll make the payment." He needed them to know that, and he still had a few more days.

Santino made a noise that was between a snort and a laugh. "You'll have $500 by next week?"

"Five hundred?" He almost shouted, more in surprise than anger, but he knew better than to get angry or to show disrespect to these people. He still cursed the day his friend had introduced them to him. *Some friend.*

"Five hundred," Santino replied smoothly. "Why, you got a problem with that?"

"But I gave you three hundred last month." He should have known better, but at that time he hadn't been thinking straight. Now he was up to his eyeballs in debt and a whole heap of other crazy shit.

"You did, yes." Santino looked away, sniffed then looked back at him. "But that was three hundred, and that was *last* month's payment." He took a step towards him, forcing Colt to inhale the pungent cigar smell. His stomach muscles quivered, and he thought he was going to retch. From the fear, and the smell, and what was to come. He had heard about the things these people did.

"I'm talking about *this* month's payment." They owned him, with their insanely high interest rates, plucked out of thin air. Colt bit his tongue to stop himself from saying something rash.

"There is another way to help you with the debt," the man suggested, his eyes glittering dangerously under the splintered light from the windows of the bar.

Colt's insides turned to mush. He didn't want the *other way.*

"It must worry you," Santino said, "to carry the weight of

such a debt on your head?" But Colt already been forced to take 'the alternative' a few times before when he hadn't been able to make payment. Even so, the debt wasn't reducing. It was increasing. He had racked up $11,000 in online gambling debt and had sold everything except his TV as he'd struggled to make the rent, but the debt had more than doubled ever since he'd 'borrowed' money from these vipers. Now it stood at something like $25,000. It wouldn't have happened if she hadn't left him. If he hadn't lost his job. If he'd kept it together. But things were what they were, and he was trying to stay alive. That's all he was trying to do.

He took a step backwards. "I'll get you the money." All he wanted to do was to run into the alleyway and make it home in one piece.

"You know what Pedroza expects of me?" Santino asked, pinning Colt in place with his words. Colt shook his head.

"To look at the risk. You, Brookes, are a big risk. Because I don't think you can bring me the money by next week." He was about to reply when one of Santino's henchmen reached forward and a heavy, rough hand grabbed his wallet from his jacket. He was powerless to stop it, much less complain. They all laughed coarsely as he tipped the beat-up wallet upside down and a few dollars fell out.

"You'll have five hundred by next week?" Santino asked, as he stepped right up close to his face. "I don't think so."

"I will," Colt rasped. He had a few hundred at home, working odd jobs, stealing a few here and there. He'd been trying to scrape enough together each month, but increasingly it became more difficult, especially as they raised the payments higher every month.

"Think about it, Brookes. Make another trip and we can wipe one thousand off your debt."

A thousand dollars? He was tempted, but they would have

him by the balls. The way things were going, they already did. He would never be able to pay it off because they would always increase it and keep him dangling. He didn't know which was worse, prison or them.

One thousand dollars to run drugs to another state. Could he risk having the feds come after him? Crossing state lines meant it wouldn't be a simple police matter then.

He shook his head, determined not to sink even deeper into the mess. "I'll get you the money."

Santino laughed. "You're going to pull this money out of your ass?" The two men flanking him laughed. Santino sniffed. "You could make your life so easy, Brookes, if you did the run."

Colt shook his head. "I don't want to. I'm trying to straighten up."

"Straighten up? You?" He didn't like the sound of Santino's laugh. One of the men quickly pinned his arms behind his back.

"What are you—" but before he could finish, he heard the sound.

Whack!

A fist landed hard, like a brick across his cheek. The pain shot through his head and reached up into his eyeball, as if a fishing line was caught in it.

"Straighten up?" Santino asked him, as he adjusted his cuffs and flexed his fingers. He couldn't defend himself, not with his arms still pinned behind him. And even if he could, Colt knew he could not fight back. To do so would be fatal. For him. He couldn't bring himself to answer, and really, he had no choice. He watched as Santino flexed his fingers again and smiled. This time when his fist smashed into his face again, Colt tasted blood. Reeling back, seeing stars, he saw Santino wipe his hands with a handkerchief that one of his men had given him.

"You are a stupid man," said Santino. "One drug run a month and you wipe a thousand off your debt. But you are too stupid to see that." He sniffed again. "I tell you what. This time I will let you bring me the money but if you don't have it, I will slice off your finger."

Colt swallowed. He should have known better. Santino hadn't come to ask him for the money. Santino had come to tell him to do a drug run. He didn't have a choice but to do as they asked.

"I'll do it. I'll do the run."

"Good." Santino replied. "I knew you would make the right decision in the end."

CHAPTER TWO

Savannah lay back against him, sitting between his legs in the huge bathtub. Shiny bubbles bobbed gently on the surface of warm water as Tobias's arms encased her.

She felt loose all over, her body completely relaxed and her mind without a worry in the world. Being with Tobias had done this. He made her feel protected, wanted and loved—more than she had ever felt in her life. He wiped the soaked sponge over her body, letting it slide down her chest and stomach and into the water, before pulling it out and repeating the motion. This time he gently rubbed it over her breasts, and she squirmed, pressing her back further into his chest, as his hand lingered over her breasts.

"I could stay like this forever."

He teased his fingers around her breast. "I could stay like this for a *while*," he murmured, "and then I'd need to take you to bed..."

"Ummmmm," she mewled, arching her back.

"...and make you lose control again."

"Yes, please." The feel of him bare inside her had been

another first for them. She now had birth control, which meant no more condoms.

"Patience," he replied, and lowered the sponge back into the water. She gazed around the ivory-colored bathroom again.

"Your bathroom is bigger than my bedroom. It's even bigger than my living room. In fact..." she murmured gently, sighing as his hands cupped her breasts, "I think your bathtub is bigger than my bed." She dipped her head back and kissed the underside of his chin.

He squeezed her breast gently. "But your bed would be more comfortable."

She giggled. "That depends on which position you want me in." His lips curved into a sexy smile and she felt his hardness against her as she wriggled in the water closing her eyes and sighing, long and loud. Hours of slow and sensual sex would follow.

Heaven.

This, being in Tobias's apartment with Jacob over at Rosalee's and them not having to sneak around anymore, was pure heaven. Rosalee knowing about their relationship made it easier for them to spend one evening a week together. She would never sleep over, would never stay later than nine but at least they were able to spend some private time together.

This new arrangement of theirs had come about ever since he'd told her about Zachary. That day, something had deepened between them and Tobias had asked when he could see her again. Clandestine visits to the penthouse and weekends spent with Jacob weren't going to help their relationship, but this, a few precious hours after work once a week, helped cement their deepening bond. Earlier, they'd made love on the floor the moment they'd gotten back from work. Time was precious, scarce, and their desire, suppressed and hidden during the working day, exploded, needing quick release in the privacy of his apartment. Spent, sweaty but sated, they had decided to shower and she'd seen the candles as she had rifled through the closets in the large bathroom. Tobias had insisted on lighting them all. Candlelight danced around the room, infusing the air with the scent of fig and patchouli.

"I wish you could stay the night."

"*I* wish I could stay the night." The reality of that seemed so out of reach. She would never leave Jacob with Rosalee overnight, not only because it wouldn't be fair to her babysitter, but because she had never spent a night away from her son. Even so, the dream of spending a whole night with Tobias seemed more appealing each time she saw him, and more out of reach. As it was, she hadn't spelled it out to Jacob that she and Tobias were together and they were always careful around him.

They sat with their arms and legs entwined, in the warmth of the bathroom, unwinding and content in one another's company. At last Tobias spoke. "When was the last time you saw him?"

"Who?"

"Your ex-husband."

She tried to think. "Maybe a couple of years ago."

"Is he still there? In North Carolina?" She didn't remember telling him that, or had she?

"He's still there."

"Does Jacob miss him?"

She shifted in the bathtub, disturbing the calm water and making waves as dying bubbles parted. "No."

"Has he called again?"

"No."

An awkward silence opened up, eating into the tranquil mood they had created. Candles flickered and the bathroom lights had been dimmed, as if yellow silk had been draped over them. She didn't want to talk about Colt, or her past. Such talk contaminated the sensual ambiance around them.

"How was Candace today?" she asked, examining his fingers as his hand entwined with hers.

"No stranger than usual. Why?" Tobias sat up, forcing her to move forward as he reached over to turn on the hot water faucet.

"Do you want to stay in here longer?" she asked, always mindful of the time, not that she was in any way looking forward to getting out and leaving.

"Stay a little longer?" Tobias asked, turning the faucet off. The raised temperature of the water only served to make her more relaxed, as if she could almost fall asleep in his arms, if he'd let her.

"We could," she answered, turning around and kneeling to face him.

"Good," he replied, and settled back once more against the bathtub, his arms outstretched over the rim. "We still have time. We haven't even had dinner yet." His gaze fell to her breasts; she loved the power she had over him sometimes, usually only in the bedroom—or like now, in the bathtub. She loved that it took no more than a sneak of her naked to give him that hungry look again.

She stared back at him, at the alluring curve of his lips, the arch of his brows and the softness in his eyes. Ever since he'd opened up to her, it had been as if the weight that had been dragging him down had been lifted. She'd been given access to the inner chambers of his heart, and the workings of his mind, and along with it came the realization that he had revealed far more of himself to her than to anyone else. He slid his hands around her waist and pulled her on top of him. The soapy bubbles sloshed gently as she moved to straddle him, her knees hugging his hips.

"Why do you let Candace bother you so much?"

"She watches everything I do, and I don't like it."

"You're being paranoid," he said, kissing the sides of her breast and making her shudder. She bit her lip as he sucked the flesh gently, taking first one breast then the other.

"Again?" she murmured, smiling. She held on to his wet arms as she welcomed the throbbing sensation in the base of her stomach.

He pulled away for a moment, his wet face staring up at her. "I only have slices of time with you." And he knew how to make the most of it. The subdued lighting, the warm water and the scented candles made this their private oasis. It was always such a wrench to leave him at the end.

He sucked her breast harder, making her moan as their bodies, so close they were almost one, rubbed together slowly, taking foreplay to another level. Excitement crept along her back and stomach and tingled between her legs.

"I hate keeping us a secret, Savannah," he whispered.

"I know."

"How much longer?"

She didn't know how much longer. "You said you'd give me time."

"I will," he replied, sliding his hands around her waist. "Sometimes I get the feeling that you're scared."

"Of what?"

"I don't know. Why don't you tell me?"

"Tell you what?"

"About your past, Savannah. Let me in," he pleaded. "You can let it all out."

"Let what out?" She gave a nervous laugh as he looked at her for the longest time.

"The pain that can drag you down."

"Is that what it felt like?" she asked. "The guilt you carried, and the pain, about Ivy and Zachary?"

"Yes."

"And it helped to tell me?"

"Yes."

She knew what he was trying to get her to do. She was guilty of hiding her past, of trying to keep those memories buried and she had discovered that suppressing them didn't make them disappear. Perhaps she had to let them out, as he had done, but she wasn't yet ready for that. Not yet.

"In time, Tobias." She smiled as she felt his hidden hardness under the water.

"In time," he whispered as she leaned forward and kissed him, melting into his mouth again. He was so familiar, the taste of him, the scent of him and she knew every curve and ridge of his body, of his mouth, his lips, his hands and his most private places. She felt as if she'd been with him for years, not a few months. Their kiss started deep and slow and went deeper, turned more sensual, and she raised her body so that her breasts were level with his face, barely giving him the chance to lap at them before she slid onto him slowly, letting him fill her completely.

Her breasts tingled as he slid inside her, the feel of him making her shiver. "You feel so good." His words were slow, his voice strained, as she swallowed him to the hilt.

"Uh-huh," she murmured, closing her eyes and moaning in ecstasy.

He fit with her just right. He teased and tasted and touched and loved her more than anyone ever had.

His eyelids flew wide open. "I've been meaning to ask you..." he pulled his mouth away from her breast long enough to cause her distress. She stared at him in disbelief, unable to stop herself from moving up and down.

"What?" she gasped, as his fingers stroked her under the

water.

"The Gala dinner."

Oh, god, what? She couldn't think about anything right now, she could only *feel*. And the feel of him rubbing against her had already set her nerves on fire. "Don't talk," she begged.

And so he didn't. His hands held her steady around her waist, and she, lost and giddy from the feel of him inside her, clawed her fingers into his chest.

"How come you're always working late, Mommy?" Jacob asked as she put the book way.

"I'm not always working late," she protested with a playful laugh. *It was only one night a week.* "I had some extra things to do."

"Like what?"

"Like...stuff. The stuff I normally do. I had to get it done before Grandpa and Grandma come. I've taken a few days off work, and you and I are going to take them around the city."

"Awesome!"

"Go brush your teeth, honey," she said, putting away the book they had been reading together. She was taking four days of leave and spending three of those with her parents and Jacob and one day with Tobias. But to her parents, she was going to pretend that she was returning to work on Thursday. They didn't yet know about Tobias.

When he'd driven her back home earlier, when he had her full attention, he had asked her once more to consider the Gala dinner. "It's barely a month away, Savannah." Maybe he thought it would be enough time to get used to this. She wasn't so sure she was ready to step out into the world as the woman Tobias Stone was dating.

Jacob came running back into the room, smelling minty. "Can Grandma and Grandpa come to my awards ceremony?"

"Honey," said Savannah, soothingly. "They won't be here then but I know they would if they could. I think Grandma and Grandpa are working right up until Easter so that they can spend more time with you while you're at home."

"Are you coming?"

"*Am I coming?* Jacob Samuel Page, how could I even think of missing something like that?" She was so proud of him. He seemed to be settling in fine at this school despite the likes of Henry Carson. "I've told Briony that I'll be coming into work later that day."

"Did you see Mr. Stone today?"

She lowered her head and pretended to smooth out a wrinkle in the bedspread before answering and feeling brave enough to look at him. "He was in the office. Why are you asking?"

"I think he likes you, Mommy."

She tried to stifle the smile that itched at the edge of her lips. "What makes you think that?"

"We see him a lot and I think he likes talking to you 'cos he doesn't really know me."

"He *does* know you." She gave his nose a gentle tap. "He's bought you all the right toys, hasn't he?"

"I guess," admitted Jacob. "It's good that he spends time with us 'cos I really like being with him."

"It's fun, isn't it?"

"We never did stuff like that before."

"What stuff?"

"Like go out, with Daddy."

"No. We didn't do much of that," she recalled, her fingers touching the two intertwined rings on the necklace Tobias had given her. "Do you miss Daddy?"

"No." His mouth set in a firm line. "I like it with the three of *us*. You, me and Mr. Stone."

She felt relieved.

"When are we going to see him again?" Jacob asked.

As well as making time for one another once a week, she and Tobias had decided to spend at least one day on the weekend together, with Jacob. "This weekend."

"Really?"

She nodded. "Tobias has booked us on an Easter egg hunt." Jacob nodded his head excitedly. It had been Tobias's suggestion and it pleased her that he was so thoughtful when it came to her son. She hoped that the more time the three of them spent together, the more Jacob would get used to seeing her and Tobias with each other, before she told him about their relationship.

"But it's not Easter yet."

"Grandma and Grandpa will be over during the Easter weekend and Tobias won't be able to see us then."

"Why? Don't they like him?"

"It's not that they don't like him." *They don't know about him.* "It's more that Tobias wants us to spend time with your grandparents."

She'd have to tell Jacob soon, when she was ready. Her parents' impending visit was going to complicate things further and she would have to sneak around again. It was one thing Rosalee knowing she had a lover, it was a whole different thing if her parents found out.

That was why she couldn't think about the Gala dinner that Tobias seemed so eager on her attending. She wasn't ready to put herself on the arm of New York's most eligible bachelor. In fact, she wasn't sure she would ever be ready for that.

Not while the ghost of Colt Brookes still haunted her.

CHAPTER THREE

"I'll get these written up for you." Candace finished scribbling into her notebook. "It's going to be a busy few weeks," she commented, closing her folder.

"Every week is busy," replied Tobias. There never was a let-up or a slow week for him. Though lately, his mind had been more fixated by his recently revived love life than by the business which normally consumed him. He liked these new changes in his life and it put a smile on his face thinking about it.

"What's funny?" Candace asked, looking curious.

"Nothing," Tobias dismissed her comment. She still hadn't managed to drop that annoying habit of speaking to him as if she had a right to know about everything he was up to. He sensed that some news must have spread around the office because it wasn't only Candace who'd been asking subtly veiled questions.

Matthias had too.

He'd made a few comments which Tobias had thought were odd. He knew Savannah was justified in her mistrust of his PA, and rightly so. He sensed that office politics played a large part in her hesitation of making their relationship public.

Candace stood up. "Don't forget you're one of the keynote speakers at the Charity Gala next month."

"I know." Getting Savannah to come along was something he had to fix. "What's the exact date?" He opened his cell phone to check his calendar.

"April 9."

The dinner was a few weeks before his trip to Dextronics and he wondered if he could convince Matthias to stay behind so that he could take Savannah along with him instead. It would cause problems between him and Matthias, but he didn't care. He hadn't been able to manage it for the trip to Hong Kong, but if her parents were visiting, it seemed to be the ideal opportunity for them to go away.

One step at a time. He had to convince her to attend the Gala dinner first.

"You're sitting with Brigitte Obenchain."

"Why?"

"Because she's going alone, too, I imagine. She's also giving a keynote speech." Candace rifled through her folder. "Here's the table plan I've been sent."

He looked away, refused to take it. "I'm bringing a date." One way or another.

"Naomi?" Her voice rose in pitch.

"No," he replied, his voice tight. He didn't like it when Candace pried but he had to give some validity to the rumors he sensed had been going around. "We're no longer together."

She cleared her throat. "I see. Who shall I put you down with?"

"Plus one for now. That's all. You may go." He turned to his computer and started to reply to his emails long before he heard the door close. The corners of his lips curved upwards. Tobias could imagine the cogs of his PA's brain grinding together at full speed.

Maybe he'd get to ask Savanah tomorrow at the Easter egg hunt. Convincing Savannah Page to take a chance on him might not be as difficult as he first imagined.

CHAPTER FOUR

Chocolate spots dotted his mouth and chin as Jacob happily chomped his way through the one Easter egg that Savannah had allowed him.

"You look as if you're enjoying that, buddy," Tobias said, giving Savannah's waist a quick squeeze while her son was deeply engrossed in the egg. Jacob looked up, nodded in agreement and carried on.

If she'd let him have his way, he would have happily taken the entire basket of eggs he'd found in the Easter egg hunt. Tobias had booked the tickets and the event included a full buffet lunch as well as the privilege of having a photo with the Easter Bunny. This didn't appeal much to Jacob but she managed to convince him, not wishing to hurt Tobias's feelings. What she couldn't get Jacob to do was to take part in cupcake decorating. He made a face as if it were an unbearable activity though he happily sat down at one of the many craft tables that were set out.

They had enjoyed another relaxed Saturday and it seemed as if it was a normal family day out for them. She loved it, Jacob thrived on it, and Tobias looked more carefree and relaxed than ever. She watched him looking over her son's shoulder with interest, genuine interest, and more interest than his father had ever shown him. Spending the weekend with the two men in her life only reminded her what a long way she had come from when she had first arrived in New York.

After the craft session was over, they wandered over to the grassy area where Jacob was sitting on the ground looking over the bag of goodies each child had received. She and Tobias stood a few feet away, leaning against a low wall. She lowered her head onto Tobias's shoulder, enjoying the peace of the perfect moment.

"Hey," he said softly. "Tired?"

She lifted her head up and found Jacob looking at her. "I keep forgetting," she said, smiling at her son as she moved away from Tobias slightly.

"It's easy to do," he replied.

It was becoming increasingly difficult not only to hide their romance at work, but to remain detached and aloof around Jacob as well. They were tactile around one another and there were far too many moments where they had almost held hands or slipped their fingers around one another's waist or hips. In the office and around other people, Tobias maintained his control as well as his distance but whenever they were alone at work, their frequent glances at one another masked their desire to be closer. Candace suspected. Savannah knew she did. Briony hadn't said a word, but it was only a matter of time, Savannah felt sure.

At least things were less complicated where Rosalee was concerned. Savannah could tell her without lying why she was going to be late on the days she spent with Tobias. One less lie in an ocean swimming with them made a big difference.

The bigger worry was how she was going to tiptoe around her parents when they arrived. Savannah wasn't sure whether to be pleased or worried. Although she was excited by the thought of her parents coming to visit, she wasn't sure how long they were going to stay and therefore had no idea how this would impact her seeing Tobias.

"This isn't his kind of thing, is it?" Tobias asked. "I get the feeling he's bored."

"No, he's having a good time," she rushed to reassure him. She'd mentioned a few weeks ago in passing about doing an Easter egg hunt for him. Her idea had been to have it in their apartment since they had no yard. Unbeknownst to her, Tobias had taken it upon himself to book a proper event. She'd been touched, even though she had almost choked when she'd seen the price of the tickets. "Jacob's had a lot of fun today," she told him, nudging him playfully in the ribs and not wanting him to think the hunt had been a disappointment. "Look at his face all covered in chocolate. That's proof, if you want it." She was about to touch his face but she remembered just in time as she saw Jacob walk over to them.

"Can we go now?" he asked.

"We could go watch the Easter Parade," Tobias suggested but Jacob didn't look convinced. "Not your kind of thing, huh? What would you like to do?"

"Can we go to Bryant Park?" he asked. Tobias looked to her for an answer.

"We could," she replied, especially since she hadn't planned anything for today.

Jacob shrieked in excitement, causing Tobias to mess up the boy's hair playfully. Seeing the close bond that was developing between the two warmed Savannah's heart. But before she could ponder anything further, she saw him raise his hand at someone. She turned to look but couldn't make out who it was in the sea of faces milling around the park.

"Who're you waving at, honey?"

"Henry Carson." The moment he said it, Savannah saw the troublesome little boy. His unsmiling and sullen face was recognizable even from this distance. He stood next to a familiar-looking tall, thin man and woman—his parents, and she presumed that the adorable doll-like toddler holding her father's hand was Henry's sister.

Jacob had grabbed Tobias's hand and showed no inclination of going nearer. As for herself, Savannah smiled, and nodded her head.

"Don't you want to go over and say, 'Hi?'" Tobias asked, and was met with an emphatic 'No!' from Savannah and Jacob.

"Come on," she said, laying her hand on Jacob's shoulder. "Let's go to Bryant Park."

A short while later as they watched Jacob on the swings in the children's play area, Tobias asked her. "What's the deal with the boy from Jacob's class?"

"He's a little terror," she said, and explained the series of episodes beginning with the Christmas concert when Henry had said that Jacob's Dad didn't love him, to him laughing at her son for using his inhaler.

Tobias scrubbed his face, disbelieving. "I wish I'd have known. I'd have made sure we went over to say 'hello.' That's fucking insane." The last of his words floated to Jacob who was walking up behind him. Her son stopped, in shock. Tobias turned to see what Savannah was looking at. "What's the matter?" he asked Jacob. All she could see was her son's eyes because he had clapped his hands across his mouth.

"You used the F-word," Savannah explained, sighing.

Confused, he asked her. "The F-word?" Then understanding, his eyes widened. "*The F-word.* So I did." He turned to Jacob. "I'm sorry, buddy. I shouldn't have said that. I won't do it again."

Suitably appeased, Jacob lowered his hands. "Do you want to come to my awards ceremony, Mr. Stone?"

"Your awards ceremony?"

Damn. Not this. Savannah's throat dried up. "Mr. Stone is busy at work, Jacob. He can't just drop everything to attend things like this." *What would everyone think?* What would Lenny's parents think? Savannah laughed nervously. "It starts as soon as the school day starts," she told Tobias, trying to sound dismissive. "It's just a small event in the morning." She shook her head, implying that it was no big deal.

"It's not a small thing!" Jacob retorted. "I got the award for being a helpful member of my class." Savannah instantly regretted her words. She had wrongly trivialized her son's ceremony and all because she didn't want Tobias to attend.

"I'm sorry, honey." She rephrased her words. "It *is* a big thing. It's a great achievement, and I'm very proud of Jacob," she told Tobias. "But I know how busy you are." She hoped this last admission might explain why she hadn't mentioned a thing to him about it.

"Please, Mr. Stone. Please come."

"I would love to but are you sure it's okay for me to...?" He turned to her for clarification, for support, for her permission.

She twisted her hands together. "If you want to..." She couldn't say 'no.'

"I absolutely want to." Then in a lower voice and directing his words to her, "Only if you're okay with this." It was easy to see from the expression on his face that Tobias was eager to attend. Who was she to deny him? Who was she to ruin Jacob's moment? She knew exactly why her son had asked Tobias and for that reason alone, she had to accept it. It would be a morning ceremony and not as many parents showed up at those, preferring the evening concerts. Would it be too risky if Tobias was there?

"Come along," she replied. "It would make Jacob's day."

Jacob looked down at the grass. "But if you *really* don't want to, Mr. Stone, you don't have to."

"What makes you think that?" Tobias knelt down on one knee, his hand on the other.

"'Cos you didn't even ask me what day it was."

"That's because I'll be there, whenever it is, if I'm in the country."

"Really?"

"Really." Tobias assured him.

"It's next week."

"I'll be there."

CHAPTER FIVE

I t was around eleven o'clock that evening and Tobias was sprawled out on Savannah's couch, not wanting to go home, but aware that he needed to, at some point.

The problem was that Savannah had opened a bottle of champagne. "I'm hardly going to drink this alone," she told him. Apparently it was from the gift basket that he'd given her for Christmas.

"You won't be able to drive home," she'd whispered as she'd handed him his glass. But staying over wasn't an option, and he would get a cab home later.

They held hands, and talked, and drank champagne. The TV was switched off and Jacob had gone to bed hours ago. Savannah had switched on the lamp and the light in the room was soft. He felt relaxed and at home with her, so much so that he was loath to leave. At the end of every day he spent with her and Jacob, he felt more a part of their life. These two people, complete strangers until a few months ago, were becoming more precious each day.

His empty apartment had no appeal, it never had—which was why he'd spent so much time working and being away on business trips. Being with Savannah and Jacob had given him a taste of the kind of life he *could* have. Something fuller, meaningful and complete.

"What do you usually do on a Saturday night?" she asked.

"I usually spend it with you now," he replied.

"But what did you do before?"

"Good question," he replied, and tried to remember what life had been like pre-Savannah. "I often wonder that myself."

"I imagine you went out a lot, ate at a lot of fancy restaurants, met fashionable friends at fancy bars and nightclubs. Traveled a lot…"

"Is that what you think I did?" It was so far from the truth.

"Yes," she exclaimed, settling her head against his chest. "Why wouldn't you?"

"You have no idea how much I hated weekends before."

She held his hand firmly. "Not anymore, I hope."

Not anymore.

It had been difficult to overcome the emptiness of his days in the beginning. His business consumed his life but on weekends it seemed pointless going to an empty office building. He had been able to work from home which was what he'd done most of the time, and there was always lots of reading to do in his spare time, lots of financial papers to keep up with. But it still left countless hours where his mind would drift and he would remember. When the void Ivy had left behind had become too raw to bear, he had taken to drinking. Later, he had sought out Naomi. He still had friends, some his, some through Xavier, but back then, during the dark days, drinking and Naomi had been his salvation.

She lifted her head and kissed him. "Your loss is heavy," she said, running her finger across his cheek. "But with time comes acceptance." She kissed him again as if to remind him.

New life, new love, new beginnings had come along and

were helping him to heal. He loved this, what he had with her and Jacob. His heart already had a permanent place for them both, working on Savannah though, would take more time. She was hurting too, and she had to let that go. If only she would open up to him.

"What *did* you do?" she asked, just as he'd been about to ask her something.

"I worked out, I ran, I boxed, I read and sometimes I went out to eat—"

"Alone?"

"Not always."

"With Naomi?"

"When we were together, yes. Or I'd meet some business associates, or my brother or, occasionally, my parents."

"What about Matthias?"

"Not so much."

"I thought you were good friends?"

"We were, we *are* but we tend not to meet socially, unless we have to."

"Unless you have to?" She seemed surprised.

"He's a good friend, don't get me wrong. He's been there for me when I needed him but after a while, when you see each other all day at work, you don't need to socialize together. He has his own life."

"Does he have a girlfriend?"

Tobias laughed. "He has many girlfriends. Matthias doesn't want to settle down now, or ever, as far as I can see."

Something flashed behind her eyes; an unasked question, the one that seemed like a natural follow-up to what he'd said. *And do you?* He waited, but she said nothing.

"I always wondered if he and Candace ever..."

"They're friends who might flirt now and then," Tobias said.

"But I can't see them together. What about you? What did you do on weekends?"

"Clean the house, do some grocery shopping, go to the park sometimes. Watch movie, play board games. Do nothing. Come the weekend, I'd be so tired that it was great to do nothing." Seeing firsthand how full-on it was looking after a child, even one as well behaved as Jacob, had shown him how much time he had on his hands, as well as the luxury and bleakness of looking after nobody but himself.

"Do you see Briony much?" He wanted to know. She shook her head.

"We go out to lunch every so often, and she's always up for going out in the evenings but I can't fit her in all the time. She has Max but they have no kids, or pets that I'm aware of, whereas I have Jacob and ...and now I have you."

"Is it *that* much of a drag?" He made a sorry face.

"I never said it was a drag," she replied, grinning. "I never realized it before but you're what I've needed all along."

He liked the idea that he was needed by her. "Needed?"

She nodded. "I need someone to be good to me, for a change."

"I'll always be good to you, Savannah."

She said nothing, so he squeezed her hand. "Hey," he said, lowering his voice. "I mean that. I'll try to, and if I say or do something and don't realize it, I expect you to tell me." She was quiet and after a few moments he asked her. "What was Colt like?" her hands tensed up in his. "Savannah?"

"He wasn't the nicest of people," she replied. After a few seconds, she said, "As for Briony, we barely got together before you came onto the scene and now there aren't enough hours in the day."

She obviously wasn't ready to tell him and he reconciled

himself to playing the waiting game. She reached over and picked up their champagne glasses. She gave him his before taking a sip from her glass.

"You like that, don't you?" Tobias asked, moving off the couch to refill their glasses.

"It's good," she nodded and took another sip. He settled back against her again.

"I have a trip to San Diego later next month. We're planning to visit a company you did research on. Dextronics. Do you remember the name?"

"It rings a bell."

"We're meeting with the cofounders and probably a few other startups, if I can line up meetings."

"Oh?" She took another sip of champagne.

"And so," he placed his glass on the table. "I was thinking of going away for a few days after that and taking a bit of a vacation."

"That's nice..." she murmured. "You should." She set her glass back down on the table.

"I was hoping you'd be able to come along."

"Come along where?"

"Have you even listened to a word I've been saying?" he asked, messing up her hair playfully. She fended him off by grabbing his wrists then twisting her body to face him.

"You're going to see Dextronics next month and you want to take a vacation after that." She parroted him almost word for word.

"You were listening," he remarked, smiling. "It would be great if you could come along."

"What about Matthias?"

"He could sit this one out."

"Won't that annoy him?" she asked.

"I'll send him somewhere else." And before she accused him

of planning things to suit his needs again, he added, "We've got a lot of business to build up this year."

"Won't people talk even more if we go away together?"

"It's next month." How much longer did she need to keep their romance under wraps for? "Won't you be ready by next month, Savannah? Think about it, going away somewhere where nobody can interrupt us." She stared back at him and her eyes widened as the seed he had planted—days and nights together, just him and her alone—took hold. He embellished it further. "We could wake up together."

"And be together for the whole night," she murmured.

"We could walk around completely naked."

"We could do a lot of fun things completely naked." She giggled and her cheeks flushed.

"Think about it," he said, and moved so that he was lying down on the couch, fully outstretched. He pulled her on top of him and rested his hands on the curve of her lower back.

"Hmmmmm." She pondered the thought out loud. "A few nights?" she asked.

"Or as many as you want."

"My parents are staying for a few weeks. I'm not sure how long, but we could snatch a few days then. I'd feel comfortable knowing they were watching Jacob."

"Think about it," he told her, and clutched a fistful of her hair in his hands.

"What would I do when you're in your meetings?"

"You can do whatever you want. Go shopping, take a spa day, whatever."

She laughed. "I don't do things like that. I'd get bored."

"How do you know when you haven't tried?"

"I'm not like Naomi. I'm too used to being busy and juggling life and Jacob and work."

"Then why don't you give serious thought to the single moms' initiative you told me about?"

"What single moms' initiative?"

"If money were no object and you could do whatever you wanted to make things better, you said it would be good to set something up to help working single moms with childcare difficulties."

"We were only talking about it. You're not serious, are you?"

"What if you actually made it happen, Savannah?"

"But there are already places like that set up."

"So what? What's to stop you from setting up something similar?"

"How?"

"Don't worry about the 'how.' Concentrate on the 'why' and the 'how' will work itself out later." There was no reason why she couldn't. He'd help her. He'd fund it and get her the contacts, if she'd accept his help. He knew how stubborn and independent minded she could be.

"I don't know," she replied, shaking her head slowly. He wondered what it was, whether the scale of the idea overwhelmed her or the funding. "I hardly have enough time as it is and I already have a job."

Would she always want to work at Stone Enterprises? If things went the way he hoped they would…one day, if he was lucky enough, she might not want to be there.

If…

But the idea hadn't taken on form yet. He'd only known her for a few months, even though it felt like much longer. As much as Savannah hated his strategizing and planning, it was the way Tobias was built. He didn't leave life to chance, he planned for it. It was how he'd ended up running the successful business he had today.

He didn't see her working an admin job at his company forever. He saw another possibility; her by his side, with Jacob and more children. But if he told her this, she would back away.

"Think about it," he said. "Let the idea simmer."

CHAPTER SIX

"You've moved tomorrow's morning meeting to after lunch?" Matthias asked.

Probing again. "Candace said your calendar was clear," Tobias stated. "Why? Is there a problem?"

"No." Matthias coughed lightly.

Tobias observed his face carefully, but if he was waiting for an explanation, he wasn't going to get one. He had cleared tomorrow morning's schedule for Jacob's awards ceremony and it was none of Matthias's business.

"Candace says you have a plus one down for the Gala," his colleague continued.

"She told you?" Tobias asked, imagining the conversation between these two, rife with rumors and innuendo.

"She might have mentioned it."

Tobias nodded knowingly. Many people thought he was too focused on his work to be aware of what went on around him. It was a good cover, and he was secretly pleased that many people fell for it. He knew that Candace and Matthias were good workers and even better friends, and he was all too aware of his

PA's affinity and loyalty to Matthias. He guessed that his colleague, with his roving eye and appreciation for a pretty woman, was certainly taken by Candace's efficiency and business-like manner. It wouldn't surprise Tobias to know that his friend probably harbored fantasies when it came to her. But he sensed that his PA had other goals in mind.

Him.

She was in for a big disappointment.

"She'd make a good reporter for the *National Enquirer*," he commented drily.

"She's looking out for you." Matthias lifted his hands up to the ceiling and stretched out as he sat in his executive chair.

"You got back over the weekend and you're still not over the jet lag?"

"Who says it's jet lag I'm recovering from?" Matthias replied, his eyes glinting mischievously.

"Did you ever leave the hotel?" Tobias asked, wondering what else his colleague had been up to during his time in Hong Kong alone, aside from the obvious.

"I had to give housekeeping a chance to clean the apartment," replied Matthias, the big grin on his face growing. Ever since his return from Hong Kong a few days ago, Matthias had been busy catching up on matters and the two men hadn't had a chance to talk. But clearly Candace had passed on some of her suspicions to Matthias and he was up to date with recent events.

"You're still not going to tell me who your plus one is?"

"We're still discussing *you*," replied Tobias, anxious to move the conversation away from the topic of who he was bringing to the dinner. "You haven't finished updating me on what you did once I left Hong Kong. You must have spent some time out of bed, surely?"

"Obviously..." His friend rested his clasped hands on the desk in front and twiddled his fingers. "I'm not totally debauched, even if that's the image I like to create."

"You're not?"

"It's a carefully cultivated image," Matthias replied, shrugging. "It's not only that I have an appreciative eye for the ladies. I'm a shrewd businessman as well. Remember, I was number one in Schwartz's eyes until a certain child prodigy came along." Mathias's gentle poke about their past surprised Tobias.

"Of course, and you still are. Stone Enterprises wouldn't be where it is today without your input, Matthias. You know that."

His friend looked somewhat appeased. "But then again, I'm not a saint either." Tobias stood up and smiled, anxious to get away. Now that they had caught up on matters, he wanted to leave the office on time. Lately, he stopped working until eight or nine in the evenings, and had started to go home a few hours earlier, on evenings like today when he had another meeting to prepare for.

"Are you leaving already?" Matthias asked, sounding somewhat dismayed. Tobias tapped his foot on the floor. Savannah was coming over to his apartment tonight and he didn't want to waste any time at the office.

"I'm trying to get more of a work-life balance," he replied.

"I noticed."

"You *noticed?*" Tobias asked. "You've barely been here."

"I've noticed in the last few days. No more late nights for you, huh?"

"How was Yanling?" Tobias asked, diverting the topic smoothly again. "Did the great man offer to take you around or show you his hometown?"

"He offered both of those."

Tobias lifted his head. "I trust you had a good time."

"Strangely enough, he invited me to his house and showed me his Japanese Garden. I swear to god it was the most peaceful place on Earth."

"Interesting," commented Tobias. He'd never even seen the inside of Yanling's house.

CHAPTER SEVEN

Savannah waited anxiously, hovering outside the school gates a good fifteen minutes before the awards ceremony started.

She pressed a hand to her throat and her fingers settled on the necklace that Tobias had given her. Her insides knotted and she didn't know what she was more nervous about: Jacob going up to collect his award, or of Tobias showing up and walking into the school beside her.

What had she been thinking? He was doing it for Jacob, and Jacob knew no better, but *she* did. Lenny's mother would have a million more questions for her than Rosalee ever had. Her heart lurched as she saw the Carsons walking towards her.

Damn.

She tried hard to turn her wince into a smile as they walked past her, and once they were out of sight, she looked around again for Tobias. She'd told him to park on the road and walk up through the school gates. He had assured her that he wasn't a well-known figure, not a pop star or movie star, and that she need not worry about this making it into the papers. That's when she'd become nervous. She'd been so anxious worrying about the other moms and teachers that she hadn't given any thought to this incident leaking out into the press.

But last night hadn't been the time to tell him not to come. She turned around, glanced at her watch, looked at the doors of the main entrance to the school and placed her hand over her stomach, as if trying to calm her insides down.

"Hey," Tobias tapped her on the shoulder from behind.

She spun around. "I wasn't sure if you were going to show up."

"Relax, Savannah." His smile, soft, and wide and full-lipped, made her worries vanish as he took her hand. She grasped it firmly, squeezing it for sheer comfort before releasing it.

"I'm trying," she replied. He was here because they were together. It couldn't get any simpler than that. "Did you drive here?"

"Morris is parked along that road." He pointed behind him. Horrified, she glanced over his shoulder.

"You came in the *limo?*"

"No, did you want me to? I would have if you'd asked." He smiled at her sweetly.

"You're not helping to calm me." She smiled as a few moms walked past, their gazes lingering on Tobias.

When they had passed, he moved his head towards her. "I told him to bring the Merc," he murmured, his lips hovering around her ear before he pulled away. "Come on, Savannah. I don't want to be late." His fingers reached out for her hand. "May I?" And she let him hold it.

They walked into the auditorium and looked for empty seats. She whispered to Tobias, "this way." Heads turned and people stared at them both as they made their way. She smiled and nodded at the faces she recognized, some teachers, including Jacob's class teacher, whose smile looked as if it would light up the auditorium.

She let go of Tobias's hand as they sat down and even then people on either side of her, and across the auditorium, continued to stare at them both.

He leaned in towards her, "Relax, Savannah."

Easy for you to say, she thought. The way these women were ogling Tobias, she didn't think she could ever relax again.

"There he is," said Tobias, oblivious to the fact that all eyes were on him as he happily waved to Jacob. She turned and saw Jacob's teacher leading the children in from the hall. Jacob had seen them and if the smile on his face grew any wider, he would need stitches to sew up the sides of his lips. He waved at them, a tiny wave, but he looked so happy that Savannah was happy Tobias was here. She looked at him beside her. He looked proud, smiling as widely as Jacob, and she realized in that moment that she was secondary to this. Tobias had come for Jacob—she'd known it on a deeper level but only now did she understand it at a heart level. She watched Jacob nudge Lenny who followed him like a lapdog.

In that moment, she relaxed, because it no longer mattered to keep their liaison a secret. Things were unfolding as they should, if she allowed them to, if she stopped worrying and got out of her own way. She settled down and watched the ceremony unfold.

"Better now?" Tobias asked.

"I'm fine," she replied, looking at his blue eyes, soft and shiny, and the expression on his face gentle. It was going to be fine because Tobias was by her side.

They watched as the children from Jacob's class filed to the front and were honored with awards for exemplary behavior, working well, putting forth good effort and attaining achievement. Soon it was Jacob's turn and Savannah watched, pride spilling out of her, as he walked up to the principal. He beamed back at her as he received his certificate. She took pictures, as many as she could in that three-second slice of time.

"I got a few nice shots," Tobias whispered, putting his cell phone away. She hadn't expected him to be as excited as he was. And then she realized: he'd never had a chance to do this before.

He almost *could* have, had life not conspired against him. Savannah's chest tightened. Today must have been tough for Tobias, but she'd been too embroiled in her own worries to pay him any notice. Maybe he had been thinking of Zachary and the other life he might have had? Had Ivy lived, this could very well have been his life, only with a different woman and a different boy. Savannah swallowed, pushing the thought away, trying to bury it before it wormed its way back to the forefront of her mind.

She wanted to enjoy this moment, Jacob's moment, and not dwell on painful thoughts; like the guilt she sometimes felt for being lucky enough to have Tobias, knowing that he had once belonged to someone else. Watching him as he smiled through it all, she was none the wiser as to what he really felt inside. Slowly, she reached out for his hand, covering it with her own.

"*You're* Jacob's mom?" a woman to her left asked her. Savannah didn't recognize her and the woman elaborated. "I wasn't sure until I saw you take his photo. I'm Dean's mom, Cindy."

Savannah vaguely recollected Jacob mentioning the name. "It's nice to meet you," the woman whispered. She looked at Tobias. "Is that your husband?"

"No," Savannah replied and turned her attention back towards the front of the auditorium. Henry Carson got up to receive his award and his father cheered loudly—the only parent to have done so—before getting a stern look from the teachers' row.

Jacob's class members walked away and sat back down again. It had lasted no more than an hour and at the end, the principal closed the ceremony and wished them all a good Easter break. As soon as it ended, parents stood up and started to follow the children as they filed out of the auditorium. She and Tobias also started to leave and she saw Jacob looking at them. She pulled her hand away from Tobias's and waved back. There was a time and place for her son to find out about her and Tobias and this wasn't it. He waved as if he'd won a ticket to Disneyland before soon disappearing from view.

"Shall we go?" Tobias asked, placing his hand on the small of her back. She nodded.

"Savannah?" She turned and saw Lenny's mom behind her.

"Julia." The two women hugged briefly.

"The boys did well, didn't they?" Savannah remarked as they stepped to the side, out of the way of the outgoing parents who suddenly seemed in a rush to leave. Lenny had also received an award for being a good citizen.

"They certainly did." Lenny's mother replied. "I'm so proud of them. Jacob did well settling into a new school and being a model student." She held her hand against her chest, her gaze darting to Tobias, who stood and smiled politely by her side. "And this is—?"

"This..." Savannah turned to Tobias. "This is Tobias Stone."

"We certainly know who you are, Mr. Stone." Lenny's mother flashed him her brightest smile as she moved her bangs out of her eyes. "It's great to meet you." She gave Savannah a why-didn't-you-tell-me stare. "What a treat for Jacob!"

"Jacob asked me," Tobias replied. "And it was an honor to watch him collect his award." Savannah's attention diverted as she caught sight of Henry Carson's parents eyeing them like hungry hyenas. The couple sauntered past them, looking straight ahead.

"Would you ladies excuse me?" Tobias gave her an apologetic glance as he fished his cell phone out of his pocket. He gave Lenny's mom a smile that would have made her toes curl. Savannah couldn't believe it when the woman's face turned pink.

"Savannah?" Julia asked, her eyebrows lifting. "I had no idea you were with *him*! Why in God's name didn't you say something before? How come nobody knows? News like this doesn't stay quiet for long."

Savannah put her finger to her lips. She had no excuse, at least no excuse that Julia would understand. After all, who else would keep a relationship with someone like Tobias a secret? "It's a relatively new development," she mumbled, tucking her hair behind her ears.

"We need to meet for coffee."

"I'm working," Savannah replied.

"Let's get the boys together one weekend, then."

"That's a great idea," Savannah replied, and started to move out towards the main doors.

"I'll call you!" Lenny's mother shouted.

Tobias was still on his cell when she walked out. He grabbed her hand as soon as she got near and she didn't try to wrestle it away.

CHAPTER EIGHT

"That wasn't so bad, was it?" he asked.

"No. It wasn't."

"Easier letting people know, don't you think?" Tobias placed his hand on her thigh as Morris drove away.

"People were staring."

"You're beautiful. Why wouldn't they stare?"

"You charmer," she replied, shaking her head. "They were staring at *you*."

"Were they?" He hadn't been paying much attention to anyone else. He'd been busy looking out for Jacob, had wanted to see the boy's face and reaction when he saw that Tobias had come.

"You must be used to it."

"I must be," Tobias replied. "What made you take my hand back there, towards the end? I thought you didn't want to draw attention to us as a couple?"

"It's getting harder to do that." She rested her head against his shoulder. "The moment you showed up at the school, there was no other conclusion for them to draw. Maybe subconsciously I want everyone to know, so we can go about living our lives."

He liked her reasoning. "Maybe."

"I'd like to tell Jacob soon, but I'm not sure when it would be the right time." She lifted her head sharply. "Jacob can't keep a secret and he'll let it slip to my parents."

Tobias grabbed his moment to press the idea home. "Would it be so bad for them to find out? Think about it, Savannah. You could see me in the evenings without having to lie to them. We could even go away."

"Let me think about it some more."

"Okay." He kissed her on the lips, knowing that their pretense would begin again as soon as they walked into the office. "Thanks for letting me come today."

"Thanks for coming. It meant a lot to Jacob that you did. Was it difficult for you—being there?"

His eyebrows pushed together. "Why would it be?" He was happy to have been asked. "I was so proud of him."

"It's just that I wondered if it might remind you of Zachary," she said in a quiet voice. The thought had occurred to him when they'd been sitting in the school auditorium and he'd seen the rows of children sitting obediently. For a moment, he wondered what it might have been like if he'd come to Zachary's school. But then he'd seen Jacob, and the thought had floated away as easily as it had come to him. "I was more sad when Jacob first asked me to come, that time in the park. I went home that evening and thought how different my life might have been if Ivy and Zachary were still alive."

Savannah looked at him with sad eyes. "But thinking about it isn't going to change a thing," he told her. "I've accepted it and I'm moving on." Now that he had met this woman, perhaps he had another chance at finding happiness.

She said nothing.

"Don't be sad," he cautioned. "It doesn't make much sense to expect to be happy if I think about the past. We have to be grateful for all our blessings, for what we have, and right now, I've got you and Jacob. I do, don't I—have you and Jacob?"

She smiled. "You do."

When the car stopped outside the Stone Building, Morris turned the engine off and waited quietly, almost invisibly, as if he was a part of the seat. "I'm not sure this is a good idea," she said, looking out of the tinted windows. "What if someone sees you and me get out together?"

"Would it make you feel better if I got out and Morris drove you around the block and dropped you somewhere close by?" She gave him a grateful look. "Morris, would you please drop Ms. Page around the block?"

She stared at the conglomeration of people lurking near the elevator bank as she got out. Trust her luck to walk straight into a group of managers.

"Hey," Briony gave her a welcoming nod. "How was it?"

"Good," she replied, nodding at Matthias who stood by her side.

"Have you seen Tobias?" he asked. Savannah didn't know whether to shake her head and lie or hide her face.

"I only just got here," she blubbered, thankful that Morris had dropped her around the block thus preventing her and Tobias from walking in together.

"Why are you all gathered around here?" Tobias asked, appearing from around the corner. He cast a dubious eye over the congregation of managers. Savannah was relieved to see that he avoided looking at her.

"We thought you might have disappeared into your

penthouse," she heard Matthias say as she slipped away to her office.

About an hour later, Briony entered her office. "So?" she asked, pulling up a chair, as she usually did when she wanted to chat. She settled herself down and placed her folder on Savannah's desk. "What's the latest?" Priceless first words.

"Jacob got an award for being helpful." Pride echoed in her words.

"I have yet to meet this boy wonder," replied Briony.

"We should set something up in a few weeks' time. My parents are coming down on Sunday for a few weeks so we're going to be busy for a couple of weekends, but definitely, it's about time you and Jacob met."

"I should think so! I already feel as if I know him, from all the things I've heard about him," Briony replied. She cleared her throat as if she was going to say something important.

When she didn't, Savannah asked, "How was your meeting?"

"Boring. Maybe I shouldn't say that," she corrected herself. "I mean, it was perfectly fine, as far as these things go. Matthias had a couple of new ideas he want to discuss." She rolled her eyes. "These men come back from their trips with a million things for us to do. It doesn't seem fair."

"I thought he was on vacation that second week?" She knew that Tobias had returned early from Hong Kong.

"I expect he was," Briony replied, yawning. She was clearly not interested in discussing the matter further. "What's going on with you?" There it was again, the humongous elephant in the room. It was obvious to Savannah that the rumors had reached a certain level and now needed confirmation. She wondered whether Tobias had inadvertently mentioned something.

"Nothing much," Savannah replied, shaking her head for

double impact. "I'm taking a few days off next week to show my parents around the city."

"Just you?"

"Just me?" Savannah asked, wondering what her friend was getting at. "And Jacob."

"And Jacob..." Briony said, squaring her shoulders, as if she was expecting more and when Savannah chose to remain quiet, "Nice necklace," she commented, staring at the chain which lay over her blouse. Savannah usually hid it inside her clothes, especially when she was at work.

"Thanks," she replied.

"If you want to do lunch or anything, you know, to *talk* about things," Briony said, "you let me know." She got up to leave and her brief visit surprised Savannah.

"I will."

She stopped at the door and shook her head, as if she couldn't keep it in any longer. "You need to know that Candace has been talking." Nothing new there.

"And?"

"You know I don't like gossip."

But still. "What did she say?"

Briony breathed out loudly. "I'm just saying that if anything is going on, anywhere, with anyone, it needs to be denied or confirmed. That's all. I just thought you should know."

"Kind of vague, don't you think?" Savannah asked, amused.

"We both know what a conniving little witch that woman can be."

"Noted." She really was running out of time.

"We need to make a shopping list," she told Jacob later that evening when she had finished clearing the dinner dishes. They needed to do a lot of grocery shopping now that her parents would soon be here. She had made plans for a lovely lunch for Easter Sunday.

"Shall I do it, Mommy?"

"Sure," she said, giving him the notepad. She looked forward to deciphering his scribbles later. They would need ham, and some mashed potatoes, broccoli, cauliflower, biscuits and asparagus. Maybe she would get some deviled eggs. She listed the items one by one and watched him concentrate.

"Are you looking forward to Grandma and Grandpa coming over?"

His eyes gleamed. "I can't wait. How do you spell potatoes?" She told him, then waited.

"We won't be able to see Mr. Stone as much when they're here."

Jacob looked up. "Are his parents coming to see him?"

"They might be," she replied. "I don't know."

"Grandma and Grandpa don't really know Mr. Stone, Jacob, so let's not talk about him when they're here."

He looked disappointed. "Can't I show Grandpa my Marvel Quinjet?" It was the toy that Tobias had given him for Christmas. Her insides churned. Expecting Jacob not to talk about Tobias was futile. Her son was bound to mention Tobias at some point.

She tried again. "Sure, you can. It's just that they might worry because they don't know him, and we wouldn't want them to worry about us, would we?"

"Why would they worry? Mr. Stone is so nice."

She didn't have an answer for him.

"What's next?"

"Huh? Oh, broccoli."

"B—r—ok...how do you spell it?"

She spelled it out for him and let the matter rest. All she could do was hope for the best and hope that out of sight meant out of mind as far as Jacob was concerned. It made her anxious about leaving her parents alone with Jacob while she was at work but she needed their help, and they seemed eager to give it.

There was nothing she could do except tell everyone the truth. Why was she so afraid of people finding out? Colt was in her past and he couldn't get to her now. They were divorced and he'd shown no interest in getting to know Jacob. It was fear itself that kept her from moving on. Fear not just of Colt, but fear of getting in deeper with Tobias, of being vulnerable and opening up to him. Fear of getting hurt. Perhaps that's all it really was and she was using Colt as an excuse to stop herself from moving forward.

She got up and realized she'd forgotten to put the detergent tablet in the dishwasher.

"What's a gold digger, Mommy?" She turned around in shock to find Jacob embellishing the shopping list with doodles.

"Why?" Her insides hardened like ice.

"Henry Carson said you were a gold digger." Her heart plunged to the ground. She crouched beside his chair.

"Why didn't you say anything earlier? Why didn't you tell me as soon as I got home?"

"Miss Yates already told him off for it." He seemed not in the slightest bit upset by it.

"Good," she said, her lips twisting as she tried to hold back the list of words that seemed fitting to describe that troublesome little brat.

"But I kicked him when he said it," he said proudly.

"Jacob!"

"He told Miss Yates I kicked him and she asked me why I done that and I told her. I didn't think it was a nice word even though I don't know what it means."

"What did Miss Yates say?"

"She told Henry off and then she told me not to worry and that she was sure Mr. Stone was a nice man." *I bet she did*, thought Savannah, remembering the way his teacher's eyes hadn't left Tobias's face.

Had that come from Henry's mother? Savannah had underestimated how well known Tobias was and how much attention he seemed to garner. To her, he was just Tobias, a man she was involved with, but to everyone else, he was obviously a prize catch, especially in a city where status and wealth were so highly coveted. Or perhaps it was the domino effect? One person had recognized him and the news had spread through the school like wildfire.

"What does it mean, Mommy?"

She got up and sat on another chair. "Come here," she said, patting her lap for Jacob to come and sit. She put her arms around him and held him, knowing already that in a few years' time he would be too long and lanky and too big and heavy to hold. She hugged him tighter. "It's a bad word, not as bad as swear words, but it's not a nice word, that's for sure."

"But what does it mean?"

"It means...it means..." She didn't know how to explain it. "It's for when a woman is—" she almost said '*dating*,' then stopped herself. "It's when a woman is friends with a man who has a lot of money, and other people think that the woman only wants to be friends with that man because he is rich."

Jacob frowned. "So you *are* a gold digger?"

"Honey, no. Just because I'm friends with Mr. Stone, it doesn't make me a gold digger."

He looked confused. "But you said—"

"People say it when they are jealous of other people and when they think someone, usually a woman, is friends with a man only because she wants the man's money or she wants him to buy her things."

"But Mr. Stone gives you those things."

"Uh, not exactly. I don't *ask* him for money." The advance for the hospital bill didn't count. She squeezed her eyes. "And those gifts he gave us, well, that's because he wanted to and not because I ever asked him to." She cringed inside, feeling herself sinking into a deeper hole with each passing moment. She tried another way. It was wrong to explain it like this but it was probably closer to the truth. "Maybe Henry's parents saw us at the Easter egg hunt and at the awards ceremony and they got jealous. Maybe they thought the only reason a man like Mr. Stone would want to be friends with someone like me was because..." *Of sex?* No. She couldn't explain it that way either. She tried again. "Some people can't understand that there are perfectly good reasons why Mr. Stone is our friend and so they think I was being extra nice to him because I wanted things from him. All I want from him, honey, is his friendship. He's good to us, isn't he? And he likes being with us? So he gets something from being our friend too."

Jacob nodded, but she wasn't sure she had explained it well. "Take my word for it, Jacob," she said, frustrated by the turn of events, "some people in this world are just born mean."

"I'm glad I kicked him."

"It's still wrong." But she was glad nonetheless.

CHAPTER NINE

She was forced to push Tobias to the back of her mind when her parents arrived.

It was wonderful to have them over and it made Savannah realize how much she and Jacob had missed them not being a part of their lives.

She had prepared a lovely Easter Sunday lunch and sitting around her small dining table with her parents and Jacob, Savannah felt truly blessed. Tobias had filled another need but her parents had always stood by her and supported her in her darkest hours. To have them back in her life again was a wonderful blessing.

In the days that followed, she gave her parents a whirlwind tour of the city and of the typical visitor attractions. They eventually went to see the top of the Empire State Building after a two-hour wait and navigating the labyrinth of ropes in the waiting area. They were overcome by sadness and touched and silenced as they visited the 9/11 Memorial and Museum. She watched her father struggle to explain to Jacob what had happened on that day.

Another time, they took a city tour which showed them around Times Square and Central Park and took them on a ferry ride to see the Statue of Liberty.

On the third day, she took them to the Brooklyn Botanic Garden which Tobias had mentioned. It was the first time she had visited this place and the sight of the cherry blossoms and the lake was one to be admired. The wind carried the cotton candy pink petals like fluttering confetti; it was breathtaking and she decided she would revisit this place with Tobias later on.

The days she had spent with her family lifted her already happy mood. Life was beautiful, and she was more than fulfilled. Her cheeriness caused her mother to comment as they wandered around the garden among the pink and white magnolias.

"You're looking vibrant, Savannah," her mother remarked. "Healthier and happier than we've seen you look in a long time."

"Starting over in a new place has worked out well."

"I can see that." Her mother paused. "Is there more to it?" Her mom's choice of words made her turn her head sharply as the two of them strolled along. Jacob had rushed on ahead with his scooter and her father kept a watchful eye on him.

"More?" She tried to affect surprise. "Mom, I have a wonderful job, Jacob loves his school. I don't have Colt to contend with, and look at this. Isn't it beautiful? We've been spending a lot of our weekends at the park."

"So Jacob's been telling me."

She tried to read her mother's expression. "Oh?"

"He seems obsessed by a certain Mr. Stone."

"Oh." How could Jacob not talk about Tobias, when they had spent so much time together lately? She said nothing as they continued to walk among the flowerbeds. Further along, she saw signs for the Japanese Garden. "Dad might want to see the Japanese Garden. Shall we go there next, before we see the rosebushes?"

"Even when you were a teenager, Savannah, I could always tell when you were hiding something."

She turned to her mother and didn't miss the wry smile on her mother's face. "I'm not hiding anything."

"It's the way you suddenly change the subject to something completely unrelated."

"Mom, Mr. Stone is someone from work."

"We gathered that." She wondered what Jacob had told them.

"He's nice and he's kind and he understands that my son is my first priority." Her mother made an approving noise in her throat.

"Your father, you know what he's like, he worries about you. You're out here all alone in a big city with a small boy, and trying to work as well as look after him. You don't even have any family close by."

"I have Rosalee."

"At least that's something."

"It's better than being alone. She's a great help."

"I gather she is. Jacob seems very fond of her. But it's not her we're worried about."

"Why are you worried?" Savannah asked.

"We don't want you to make another mistake again."

"I'm taking it slow this time." It wasn't love at first sight as it had been with Colt.

"You *are* seeing him then?"

"Sort of. We're in the early stages, Mom." Her father waved at them from up ahead, and as she had predicted, when he'd come to a fork along the pathway, he signaled in the direction of the Japanese Garden. She waved back and gave him the thumbs-up.

"Dad wants to see the Japanese Garden," she said to her mom, hoping and knowing at the same time that it would be impossible to throw her mom off the trail now that she had smelled something.

"Your father and I were planning on staying for three weeks."

Three weeks? She'd assumed it would be two.

"But we weren't sure if it might be too much for you both," her mother continued. "We've managed to get the time off but your father told me to run it by you first, to see if you had made other plans."

"Other plans?" she laughed. "I don't have other plans." Apart from a few nights here and there with Tobias but the more she considered it, the more she liked the idea. "Why didn't you tell me sooner?" she asked. Not that it mattered.

"Your father wasn't sure if he could stay that long, you know how much he likes being in his own home, and his chest can be prone to acting up if there's too much pollution. He was worried about the city."

"But he's been okay."

"He's been fine. He's loved, *we've* loved seeing you both. We miss you so much, dear, and that's why we wanted to stay longer, if that's all right with you."

Savannah smiled, happy to know her parents were so eager to stay. "I'd love for you to stay. Jacob would, too."

"What about your friend?"

"Tobias?" Would it open a can of worms if she told her mom that she was actually spending tomorrow with him and not going to work? She couldn't; not when she hadn't broken the news to Jacob and she felt that she owed it to tell her son first. "What about him?" she asked. "The length of your stay has nothing to do with him." Even though it opened up the possibility that she could go away with him.

"If you're sure."

"I'm sure."

"We don't want to get in the way."

She looked surprised. "You won't get in the way. This is new for me and I don't know where it will go." Even though in her quiet moments late at night, she dreamed of a future with him. "Jacob doesn't even know yet, so please don't say anything to him."

"But Jacob says you've been spending a lot of time together."

"Tobias hasn't stayed over." She let that sink in, hoping to win Brownie points for her good behavior. Her mother looked mildly relieved.

"You're being very careful, dear. I suppose you have to think about Jacob. I'm sure this will put your father's mind at rest."

"Jacob feels comfortable around Tobias, and that was the most important thing for me."

"From what we've heard, he dotes on the man."

"Tobias is good with him."

Her mother looked suitably appeased. "Then I'm thrilled for you, dear," she replied, hooking her arm into Savannah's.

It had been a packed three days and when they returned home later that evening, she sensed that her parents were relieved she was going to work tomorrow. Even if, in reality, she was going to Tobias's apartment.

"There's still the Rockefeller Center and Central Park Zoo," she said, handing them the leaflets she'd picked up. A twinge of guilt pricked her conscience for lying to them.

"We're not as young as you, Ruby Red," her father cried out, sitting down on the couch and grabbing the TV remote. He looked especially weary as Jacob snuggled beside him. It was clear to her that in her eagerness to show them a good time, she had possibly overdone it.

Maybe tomorrow they would both get a break. Her parents would get to spend the day as they pleased with Jacob for company, and she would get to spend the whole day with Tobias.

She'd missed him.

CHAPTER TEN

"You, a gold digger?" Tobias shifted his head sharply, as he picked up their empty wine glasses. "Who the fuck said that?"

"The same child from Jacob's class; the one Jacob waved at when we were at the Easter egg hunt." He tried to recollect. *That* child. The one who'd laughed at Jacob because he had an inhaler?

"He's not a pleasant child at all," Savannah added, walking into the kitchen. Tobias placed the glasses on the countertop, his face stern and his hands now resting on his hips.

"That spoiled little shit." Tobias's insides burned.

Savannah stared up at him as she opened the dishwasher door to load it. "Why're you so mad?"

"I didn't know kids could be so nasty. How did Jacob take it?"

"Much better than you."

"Can you stop that, please, for one moment?" This kind of cruelty reminded him of his own school days. "You don't have to clean up after us, Savannah. My housekeeper comes every morning."

"I'm not used to leaving the kitchen a mess."

"I pay her to clean it up."

"Can I just tidy it up a little?"

"You want to tidy up for the housekeeper?" He rubbed his eyes. "Please? It's something you're going to have to get used to. I'd rather spend time talking with you than wasting it doing *these* things." He closed the door to the dishwasher. "It's unacceptable," he said, folding his arms. "I want the school to take care of it."

"Take care of what?" she asked. "Some kids are like that and this one seems to have had it in for Jacob from the start." Tobias narrowed his eyes, wishing he could get his hands on the boy now. It wasn't right.

"Do you understand now why Jacob wanted you to come to his awards ceremony? He wanted to show that he had someone like you in his life."

"Someone like me?"

"Like a father figure...I mean. That's why." Tobias smiled.

"I see why," he said softly. "I'm glad that boy saw us all together." It made sense now that he recalled that day at the Easter egg hunt, when Jacob had grabbed his hand. Tobias rubbed his chin, his brows furrowing.

"Don't," Savannah warned.

"Don't what?"

"Don't do whatever it is you're thinking of doing."

"I could pick up Jacob from school in Xavier's Ferrari one day. When does school start again?"

"Next week." Savannah shook her head. "I think he'd settle for your Porsche but remember, his gold-digging mother is embarrassed by such obvious displays of wealth."

"You're not like that at all." He pulled her to his chest and held her, and when she stared up at him, he couldn't help but kiss her. She tasted like red wine. Her hands trailed slowly down his stomach and he couldn't help but slip his hands over her bottom and kiss her again. "How long did your parents say you could stay out for?" Now that dinner was over...

"They think I'm at work." She chewed her lip. "I didn't mention anything about staying late."

He raised an eyebrow. "Aren't you too old to be sneaking around?" People in the office would have more to talk about now, especially since this was another occasion when both he and Savannah were away from the office. It was news enough that he was working from home, when for the past few years he had been coming into the office and working late every single day unless he was away on business.

The priorities in his life, and how he spent his time, were slowly shifting. He didn't care for anyone's opinions on the matter but understood that things would be different for Savannah. Yet he still wondered how much longer she wanted to keep this charade going on for.

"My parents know about you, courtesy of your number one fan."

Tobias's eyes shone. "You told them?"

"Jacob did."

"Ah." Tobias's heart warmed.

"My mom thinks we haven't even had sex."

"Why would that even come into the conversation?"

"Just that, well...I told her you hadn't stayed over. She was wondering how serious it was."

"What did you say?"

"That we're in the early stages. I wasn't ready for the conversation and it kind of caught me by surprise. She asked me because Jacob can't help but talk about you. They're worried. It's only natural, after Colt."

"After Colt?"

She lowered her head. "They weren't so keen on him towards the end."

"Why was that?"

"For a whole heap of reasons," she said, trying to wriggle out of his embrace.

Walk away again, thought Tobias, letting her go. She walked away and stood leaning against the kitchen island with her arms folded. "So your parents have no idea that you're sleeping with your boss." He cocked his head, curling his lips at her and braving a smile, knowing this might set her off.

But she gave him a cheeky smile instead. "No," she replied. "Though I've been tempted to tell them how you paid me for my favors. Of the presents you enticed me with when I was nothing but a bright-eyed new temp at your firm."

"I will be forever grateful that you showed up."

"I will be forever grateful for getting the job."

"And as a sign of your gratitude, have you decided yet?"

"Decided what?"

"Whether you're going to attend the Gala dinner?" They had started to discuss it this morning but having a whole day together out of the office was such a luxury that it had pushed certain other priorities further up the list. "You told me that your parents are staying for a few weeks so you won't have to worry about Jacob."

"Is it a fancy occasion?"

He nodded.

She looked anxious. "I don't have anything to wear—"

"Don't worry about the clothes. I'll have someone at Saks Fifth Avenue take care of you...*if* you want advice or anything, and don't worry about the cost." He didn't want trivial matters such as that to be the reason she wouldn't come. "If you're worried about people seeing us, it's inevitable, Savannah. People have already seen me at Jacob's school. People at work know that both you and I are away from the office today."

She said nothing.

"Or is it your ex-husband you're afraid of?" He stared into her eyes looking for the answer. "Because you don't need to be."

"You don't know him."

"Then tell me about him."

She shook her head. "There's nothing much to tell." Then after a few moments, "When is it?"

"The dinner?" he asked. "The weekend after next, on Saturday."

"That's short notice."

"I've only been asking you for a month."

"I know."

"All you have to do is show up."

"And find something to wear," she said, making him hopeful. This was the most he'd ever gotten from her. She seemed to be thinking about it.

He'd been giving the matter more thought. Instead of trying to persuade her to go on a business trip, why not just go away and take a real break instead, something not business related? He loved his waterfront home in Miami. It was an oasis of calm. It was exactly what they would need after the Gala dinner. "We could even go to Miami for a few days afterwards," he suggested. It would make sense to stay away while the media speculation mushroomed. He wasn't sure to what extent it would blow up, but if he warned Savannah, she might get scared and back off. He couldn't afford for that to happen.

"Miami?"

"For a few days, after the dinner."

"Just you and me?"

"Jacob could come along."

"He has school and I don't want him to miss any days."

"It seems the universe is conspiring to provide us with the perfect opportunity."

"It would be wonderful to get away," she whispered, as if she were talking to herself. Her eyes glittered and he could see she was sold. Lowering his head, he kissed her lightly on the lips. "Would five days be all right for you? We could leave the day after the Gala and be back on Friday evening. Or we can make it as short a trip as you want. It's entirely up to you."

Her brows knotted. "Surely it's up to you? Don't you have a company to run?" he did but she was becoming more important to him. The company would continue to run without him. But what they had was growing stronger and he was falling deeper. No longer was he content with snatched pieces of time with her. He needed days and nights alone with her and he would savor as many as she would let him have.

"I've never been to Miami."

"Then this would be a good time to see it, although we can also go someplace else, if you'd like."

She shook her head. "I'm happy with what you've decided."

It was settled.

"My parents are going on a cruise in the summer," she told him. "They're going from Miami to the Bahamas. My dad booked it as a surprise for my mom's sixtieth birthday."

"They're more than welcome to spend some time at the house in Miami," he told her. He'd make sure his housemaids were available.

She laughed, dismissing the suggestion. "We'll see where we are by then."

"Stronger," he replied. "And still together." He told her, speaking with a conviction she didn't yet share. She traced the outlines of his lips with her fingers.

"Let's take it a day at a time," she replied, touching his lips.

"Five days in Miami." His insides stirred with excitement.

The lure of being with her completely warmed him inside. It told him something—that he had come a long way, that he had healed and was now ready to move on.

"Five days," she murmured, and lifted her face towards him.

"Is that a yes?"

"For going away?" she asked.

"To both?"

"Yes," she replied, suddenly smiling, as if making the decision had lifted a weight off her. "To both."

His gaze fell to the necklace he'd given her. She wore that all the time now, he noticed. He kissed her deeply then. Flames of fire crept along the backs of his legs and spread throughout his body. He was powerless to pull away as he sank deeper into her kiss, tasting her mouth slowly as his hands slipped underneath her blouse and his fingers moved along her skin and the satin of her bra. With an urgency that shot along his body, he hoisted her up onto the countertop and stood between her legs, his hands pulling her skirt up until he could see her panties. She had her hands on his shoulders as he began to kiss her again, slowly undoing her blouse. He nibbled on the skin above her bra, his hands doing double duty as one hand caressed her thighs, raising goosebumps along her skin.

"Cold?"

"Excited." He felt her thigh muscles flex as his fingers traced over her inner thighs.

"Let's see how much." He peeled the fabric of her panties to one side, exposing her nakedness, then rubbed his thumb around gently, making her sigh in the way he had come to know so intimately. She mewled softly.

"Don't stop," she pleaded, as his thumb circled around her most intimate part.

"I don't plan to," he croaked, his own excitement building. She slowly undid the belt of his jeans and unzipped him.

"What's there to do in Miami?" she asked as his fingers slipped inside her, making her shudder. Her hooded eyes glistened and he pulled back to look at the expression on her face.

Stilling his thumb, wanting to prolong her build-up, he leaned forward and whispered. "We could do this, all day long."

Her breath was hot against his face as she sighed, opening up to him and pleading for more.

CHAPTER ELEVEN

"How're your parents finding New York?" Briony asked, when she returned to work the next day. It seemed strange to show up for work on the last day of the week but as much as she would have liked to have seen Tobias again, she needed to preserve her holidays.

Especially now that she had made up her mind to go away with him. She didn't even care where it was, she'd have happily spent the entire time at his apartment, but she'd never been to Miami, and it added an additional layer of excitement to the trip.

"They're loving it. I might have overdone it with the places I squeezed in during the three days. They stayed at home yesterday and they're taking Jacob to the park today."

"You were off for four days, not three," Briony said.

"Yes," she replied, "I was." She wondered if now was the time to come clean. "I was at Tobias's yesterday." To her surprise, Briony didn't move a muscle.

"Was it a 'Tobias day,' you mean?" Her voice was smooth. Too smooth.

Savannah's face colored as she stared at her shoes. "Not exactly. I took a day's leave."

"Huh," Briony made an unconvincing sound. "You did?"

"Yeah," Savannah looked up slowly.

Briony smiled as if she'd uncovered a great secret. "I was wondering when you were going to tell me. I could *feel* the vibes between you two." She shook her head, grinning.

"Oh, puh-lease." Savanna waved her hand at her friend and hoped the color from her cheeks had faded.

"All these days away—"

"Only a few!" Savannah protested.

"The body language, the looks," Briony rolled her eyes for dramatic effect.

"Stop it," Savannah warned, feeling her cheeks heat up again.

"The sizzle!" She shimmied her body like a dancer from the '50s.

"Now you're making it up."

"I'm not," Briony insisted. "There was definite electricity between you both."

"How could you tell?" Savannah asked. "I thought you were only tuned into—"

"My instinct is almost always spot on," Briony declared. "I thought I'd get electrocuted if I got caught up in the sexual tension between you two lovebirds."

"Okay, enough!" Savannah insisted.

"But seriously, you've both been looking relaxed lately, and it suits you. It was about time Tobias lightened up."

"Does everyone know?" Savannah asked. "Chloe and the others?" This had been her main worry, the other women in her office. And, of course, Piranha Queen herself, Candace.

"The rumors have been spreading faster than herpes in a brothel," replied Briony. "You know what this place is like."

"I can imagine."

"I've wanted to tell you for a while," said Savannah, "but I wasn't sure of what you might say and I didn't want it getting out while I was still getting used to the idea. But now people are noticing and it's getting harder to keep it a secret."

"I understand," replied Briony. "I had the same thing myself when I first came out. Trust me, the people who mind don't matter, and the people who matter don't mind."

"That is so true. I'll have to remember that. Of course now I need to tell my son. He's going to find out next weekend anyway."

"Next weekend?" And before Savannah could answer, Briony replied. "He's taking you to the Gala event, isn't he? The rumors have been circulating for days."

"I need your help."

"For what?"

"I have no idea what to wear."

"Max will. Leave it to her."

———

Another Friday afternoon managers' meeting had finished and Tobias gathered together his papers. Matthias was busy on his cell phone.

"Something up?" he asked, putting his hands into his pockets as his colleague ended his call. Matthias looked up as he put away his cell phone.

"No. I was simply waiting for you." He got up and the two men hovered around the large conference table. "Have you ever considered looking into the telecom sector?"

"I keep my eye on it," Tobias replied. "Why? Has something caught your eye?"

"There are a lot of new startups in San Diego we could

check out, since we're going there to meet with Dextronics in a few weeks' time."

"Put something together and I'll take a look."

They started to move towards the door when Matthias stopped and asked him, "Are you going to reveal the identity of your Gala dinner date?"

"To reveal would imply that you don't already know, Matthias." *This* was why his colleague had been waiting? Matthias leaned forward and stared at Tobias.

"She's a very lucky lady, that Savannah Page."

Tobias nodded and returned the smile. "So you're still guessing?"

"Isn't it Savannah? You've set tongues wagging with your days off. The two of you have been AWOL from the office on more than one occasion."

"Who's counting?"

"Does it matter? Think of it more as a collective observation." Matthias replied, and laid his arm on Tobias's back, almost congratulatory in its placement. "It's good to see you looking happy. It's been long overdue."

Tobias lowered his head and took a deep breath. "I don't want it to be awkward for Savannah. She feels odd about people finding out and acting differently towards her. Her son's already had some comments from the kids at school."

"It's serious then," Matthias commented, with a grin, "if schoolchildren are involved. What sort of comments?"

"The kind of comments that label Savannah a gold digger," Tobias replied. "I went to Jacob's awards ceremony at school a few days ago. I thought it would be low-profile, turns out, some people recognized me."

Matthias laughed. "What makes you think anything you do is going to be low-profile? With your looks and wealth—you're a babe magnet for every pussy in New York City."

Tobias squeezed his eyes shut. "Must you determine a woman's worth by the—"

"I'm only stating the facts, my man. Just the facts."

"That's not why I'm with Savannah."

"I'm sure it isn't but the fact of the matter remains. More pussies gravitate towards you than is statistically fair. And that, on top of your billions and your movie star looks, is a fucking pain in the ass for mere mortals like me." Matthias patted him on the back. "But I'm happy for you, buddy. I really am. God knows it was about time you met someone who made you happy and if Savannah Page failed to appreciate my wit and charm, I'm glad to lose her to you. It's her loss anyway."

"I'm taking her to the Gala dinner next week," Tobias said. "It seemed to be the place to announce it, not that I care to make announcements regarding my personal life, but working here complicates matters and it's better to come out with these things."

"Stepping out in style," said Matthias. "Does she know she's going to lose her anonymity from that moment on?"

"People will lose interest in a few days' time. I don't party or go out. We'll still maintain a low profile. Actually, we're going to Miami the following week."

"The week before we go to San Diego?"

"It's only five days. I'll be back in time for San Diego."

"The break will do you both some good," Matthias agreed. "It could get crazy once news gets out."

"I doubt it."

"You underestimate your fame."

Tobias shook his head. Leaving the day after the Gala would be a good way for them to be out of the public's eye. He didn't doubt that there would be a lot of press interest in the beginning. It would no doubt be the same in the office. He could already see the rumors spreading around each office in the building and beyond.

They walked out and headed back to their respective offices. Tobias stuck his head inside Candace's office seeing that her door was wide open. "I'm sure you're already aware of this," he said, "but just to confirm, Savannah Page will be accompanying me to the Gala dinner next week." Candace looked up, caught completely unawares.

Her mouth was still wide open as he turned and left.

CHAPTER TWELVE

"Rushing out again, Ruby Red?" Her father looked up from his newspaper as she rushed into the kitchen to pour herself a glass of orange juice. "Sit yourself down," he said, putting away his paper and getting up from the table.

"But Dad, I need to get Jacob up and—"

"Mom and I are here and we'll take care of Jacob."

"But I was going to get him ready—" She glanced at the hallway and saw her mother disappear into Jacob's bedroom, which she was sharing with her son while her parents were visiting.

"Your mom will see to him." She didn't want to completely relinquish her responsibility to her son, nor did she want her parents to do everything. This was supposed to be a break for them as well but they seemed to be adamant.

Yesterday, on his first day back to school after spring break, she'd gone into work a little later in order to show her parents the route to school and where to drop Jacob off. He wouldn't need to go to the Breakfast Club and they would also pick him up at the end of the school day. Rosalee would have a few weeks free from childcare.

"You don't need to worry about him. Your mom's got it under control. Now, what'll you have? Fried eggs on toast?"

Fried eggs on toast this early?

"No thanks, Dad." He gave her a look that told her he wasn't going to let her go until she'd eaten something.

"I'll have cereal."

"Coffee, dear?" Her mom scurried into the kitchen, fully dressed.

"I'll get it, Mom." Savannah got up but her mom had already poured her a cup, and when she sat down at the kitchen table with her, Savannah felt as if they were sitting her down to discuss something.

Her father cleared his throat. "How's your—" Hrrph. He coughed again. "Your friend? Mr. Stone, is it?"

Since that day at the Brooklyn Botanic Garden, her parents hadn't said a word about Tobias.

"He's fine. Why?" She hadn't been wrong in her assumption.

"We'd like to meet him," her father said.

"Why?"

"We thought he was someone who worked alongside you, dear." Her mother looked worried.

"He is," Savannah replied, looking at them both and trying to figure out what they were getting at.

"Jacob says he owns the company," said her father, sitting down with his fried eggs and toast.

"And what if he does, Dad?" Her father stopped cutting into his toast and stared at her, speechless.

"How old *is* he?" She could tell from her mother's voice that she assumed Tobias was some kind of aging Hugh Hefner. The idea made her laugh. It fell into place, this early morning interrogation. She looked at them both, pleased to be able to put their minds at rest. "He's a year older than me. He's twenty-nine."

"He inherited the company, did he?"

Flustered, she raised her hands. "Why does it matter? And no. He made his fortune himself. He's a smart businessman."

"Jacob says he drives a very flashy car."

"It's not *that* flashy." She stood up, having drunk her coffee quickly. "Are you two worried about me?" She spread her hands on out the table, palms down as she leaned across, examining her father's face carefully. "Daddy?"

"Ruby Red, it's not that we don't trust you, but this relationship of yours makes us nervous."

"Did he try it on with you?"

"Mom!" Savannah was mortified. "He didn't take advantage of me, if that's what you mean."

"Jacob says he bought you gifts, flowers and gift baskets and he bought Jacob toys. That's how it all starts."

"How *what* starts?"

"Grooming."

"Grooming?"

"He's after *something*."

"Mom!" She couldn't believe her ears.

"You said you hadn't had sex yet." Her father almost choked on his toast. "He's not buying you gifts for nothing. Some men have ulterior motives."

"It's nothing like that."

"Why is he so interested in your son? Jacob says he went to the awards ceremony at his school. It doesn't sound right to me or your father." Savannah hung her head in shock. Of all the assumptions her parents could have reached, this hadn't been one of them.

"He is the kindest and most sincere man I have ever met. He

cares deeply about me, and I'm lucky that he cares so much about Jacob."

"His interest in you both sounds unhealthy."

"As opposed to..." She took a few steps back from the table. "As opposed to someone like Colt Brookes? Am I only suitable for the likes of people like him?"

"That's not what we're saying, Ruby Red." Savannah shook her head. Her parents didn't know anything about his background and she didn't feel at liberty to tell them what he had revealed to her in confidence. Even if she explained it to them—about his wife and unborn child—she didn't think her parents were in the listening mood. She could partly understand their concern, given her past experience with Colt, but Tobias Stone was nothing like that man.

"I know you both love me, and you're saying all of this because you're worried and you don't want me to get hurt, but Tobias is a good man. I didn't go looking for him. We just..." she stared down at the wooden table. "We just found one another, it's like we were meant to be together. I know you might not understand that."

"You're old enough to know what you're doing, Ruby Red. You have a son to think about."

"Do you think I don't know that?" She turned to her father. "I am being careful and I think I'm going to have to tell Jacob tonight, because," she took a gulp and stared at them both.

"Because?" Her mother asked, glancing at her stomach. Savannah's insides pinched with irritation. Trust her mother to think she was pregnant.

"Because Tobias has asked me to accompany him to a Gala dinner this weekend, and I said yes."

"A Gala dinner?"

"It's a black-tie event in some fancy hotel. It's a big deal for me because we've avoided being seen together in public. Tobias didn't want to hide our relationship from anyone but I did. I guess I was scared of Colt finding out."

"What's this got to do with Colt?" her father asked. "You don't have to worry about that man, Savannah."

"It's hard to shake him off, Dad. Tobias is well known. If we're seen in public, the chances are high of news leaking out." She was at a loss of how to explain to her parents the far-reaching effects and power of social media. "Colt would know where to find me."

Her father reached over and placed his big, rough hand over hers. "Why would he come looking for you? He's gone from your life and a loser like that isn't coming back. Don't you stop living because of him."

Her father was right but Colt's calls a few weeks ago had made her unsettled. She knew him better than anyone and she didn't trust him.

"I will say this," her father continued, "as much as I still worry about you, I can't say I've ever seen you look this happy before." Her father gave her mother a testy glance. "You go to the dinner, Ruby Red. Don't worry, we're here to look after Jacob."

She was never going to get a better opportunity to ask now that they were on the topic. "We were also thinking of going away together. Just the two of us. Tobias wants to take me to Miami."

"Miami?"

"For a few days. Would it be okay for you to look after Jacob while we were away? I won't leave him with anyone else." Her parents looked at one another. "I can get Rosalee to come over and help," she offered, "and you'd still be able to go sightseeing during the day while he's at school. I know it's a lot to ask."

"You're not asking a lot. We'd like to spend more time with Jacob, and this sounds like the perfect chance for us to do that."

"Thanks. And I'm going to be coming home a little late every day this week." Max had told her it would be a tall order to find a dress for the Gala within a week.

"Darling, you can't wear this! You'll look like someone from a reality show!" Max shrieked.

Savannah agreed, if she'd been left to find her outfit for the Gala dinner herself, she probably would have.

Asking for their help with only a week before the event had been foolish. This, coupled with her insistence on paying for everything herself, did not bode well for a stylish red carpet debut. When she'd first emailed Max and Briony the types of dresses within her budget, they'd almost had seizures. Their forceful objections had her reconsider her honorable stance. Tobias had been insistent that she let him pay for her dress and shoes and accessories, and she'd been totally against the idea. But over the next few days as the three of them trekked around the luxury department store, all the best dresses had thousand-dollar tags. She couldn't bring herself to pay that much.

"Tobias would want you to look amazing," they'd told her.

But still she didn't feel right about it. "You're going to be photographed, you'll be seen arriving and leaving his limo. You'll be in the public limelight. Do you seriously want people to think you put your outfit together from Wal-Mart?"

"What's wrong with Wal-Mart?"

Max rolled her eyes. "Now you're trying to be funny." Max took fashion so seriously it was scary. "People expect Tobias to be with some chic and classy beauty from New York society."

"Well, tough," she'd replied, knowing Tobias well. "He's with Savannah from North Carolina."

But the outfits she had tried on, the ones she could afford, didn't look that great. The only thing they had going for them was that they were in her budget.

In the end, panicking, and with so much going on at work and at home, Savannah was running out of time. It made sense to listen to Max and Briony.

Now as she looked in the mirror, with the dinner a few days away, she was glad she had.

"Next time, a few more weeks' notice would be appreciated. We're not miracle workers, darling." Max tut-tutted loudly.

"I know. I'm sorry." Savannah mumbled, walking around in the Christian Louboutins which were surprisingly comfortable given that the heels were the width of a pencil. *So this was what wearing thousand-dollar shoes felt like?*

"But we did it. Cinderella *will* go to the ball. What do you think, darling?" Max turned to her partner. Briony's eyes sparkled as she stared at Savannah.

"You and Prince Charming are going to blow them away. Candace Oakley, I hope you choke watching her on TV!"

"TV?" Savannah asked, distracted. She was still unsure about the shoes. The shoes were the final piece of the ensemble.

"Doesn't she look amazing?" asked Briony.

"She does." Max nodded her head, appreciatively. "She was already halfway there. It wasn't such an impossible task, not with that kind of skin and cheekbones, and that hair. No wonder Stone wants you and no wonder he wants to take you to Miami," Max purred.

"I can't imagine the torment Candace must be going through," remarked Briony, smiling like an imp.

Savannah shook her head. She couldn't think about Miami just yet. She needed to get this dinner over with first. "Thank you both," she said. "When I get back, we'll go out for dinner somewhere. On me. I would never have looked like this if it had been left to me."

Max laughed. "Believe me, darling. We know. We'd never have risked leaving it to you." They all burst out laughing. If it had been left to her, she would have shown up in a garish cheap satin number, most definitely black, most definitely knee-length and most definitely with a wide scoop neck.

She didn't think anyone could ever convince her to wear red yet Max had. She felt like a fire truck with the attention the dress had drawn when she'd tried it on but it looked stunning. She looked stunning; like one of those women who stepped out of sleek, black cars at the big awards nights she'd seen on TV. Red carpet, black tuxes, long dresses and plenty of bling. She could finally compete.

But gold shoes? That was overkill. "I'm not sure about the shoes," said Savannah.

"You can have red shoes to match," Max shot back. "That's your only other choice."

Gold shoes it was.

"How come you've been working so late all week, Mommy? I don't even get to see you anymore." She sat by Jacob's bed, still in her work clothes.

"I'm sorry, honey," she replied. "I didn't mean to leave you with Grandma and Grandpa all the time." Getting her outfit had taken up most of the week, and now she wondered if it would be fair to her son if she went away with Tobias for almost a week. She was neglecting her son. As the week wore on, she realized how big a deal the dinner was and she was beginning to freak out a little. Only her parents kept her calm. Kay had called for her but she'd been out shopping with Max and Briony and hadn't been able to call her back.

She hadn't even seen Tobias, but she didn't feel too bad about that. But this, she stared back at her sleepy son, this was what she felt most guilty about.

"Are you having fun with your grandparents?"

"Yes." He yawned loudly. "But I wish you would come home early." She dropped a kiss onto his lips.

"I had to go shopping with some friends. I was looking for something nice to wear."

"Okay." He yawned again. "Goodnight, Mommy."

"I want to tell you something, Jacob." His eyelids flickered open. "The dress is for a special occasion, a big party and Tobias is taking me."

"Will you get party bags?"

"No. It's a grown-up party." He stared at her blankly. "And the reason Tobias is taking me is because...because we are seeing each other, as in...we're dating." Still he continued to stare at her, and for a moment she wasn't sure if he'd heard her properly. "He likes me and I like him."

"Do you have to kiss him?"

"Uh...not if I don't want to."

He seemed to consider this.

"Do you understand what I'm telling you?"

"Yeah."

The conversation wasn't going the way she had expected it to and even though she had already told him that she was going away with Tobias next week, he hadn't asked any questions about it.

"How do you feel about me going to this party with him?"

"Can I come too?" he asked.

"It's a grown-up party, honey."

"Okay."

"And afterwards, you and I can spend all of Sunday together. Then Mr. Stone and I are leaving for our trip, remember I told you about it?"

"I remember." But his voice had a somber tone to it, not the type of tone that made her feel good. Her doubts were beginning to creep in, especially since he seemed to be unsure about it. She didn't understand it. A few days ago he'd been fine about it all. Inside, it felt as if pins were digging into her chest.

"Would that be okay with you?"

"What?"

"If we still went away?"

"Can I come with you?" Her heart nosedived to her stomach.

"You'll still have school."

"Who's going to look after me?"

"Grandma and Grandpa, unless you don't want them to." Or she could cancel the trip. "I don't have to take this trip. I can stay behind if you want me to."

He pursed his lips into a tight line, as if he wasn't sure. "Do you like him more than you like me?"

It was as if she'd been hit with a baseball bat. The shock of his words knocked the air out of her stomach. "Honey, no!" She threw her arms around him, lifting him up so that he was in her arms, slumped across her chest. "Oh, Jacob." She kissed his hair, then moved her face away. "Is that what you think? You're the most important person in my life. I love you more than anything." The palpitations ricocheted inside her ribcage and she closed her eyes, wondering how she hadn't seen this coming. It had been one thing after another: she'd been spending more time with Tobias, then she'd been so engrossed in getting her dress and worrying about the dinner, not to mention what to pack for their vacation. She'd been so swept up in it all that she had lost sight of how Jacob might have felt. No wonder her son thought he no longer mattered. "*You* are the most important thing in the world. Do you understand that?" Her stomach twisted into knots. "I don't love anyone more than I love you."

"Not even Mr. Stone?"

"Not even Mr. Stone, and what makes you think I love him? We're just..." *Dating.* But what would Jacob understand?

"Your face is always happy now, Mommy, and you're always laughing. I know Mr. Stone does that to you."

She gulped, her heart doing one hundred. Sooner or later it would come out...that she was in love with the man, because keeping it hidden and tucked away in her heart was becoming harder to keep down. She didn't know what to say to Jacob, so she ignored the comment completely. "I don't have to go away next week, if you don't want me to. I can stay here and we can do lots of fun things together instead." She would still take those days off.

Jacob shook his head. "I don't want to make Mr. Stone sad. You make him smile, Mommy. He doesn't look sad anymore."

"He doesn't, does he?" she replied softly.

"Does this mean you're going to get married?"

"Not next week," she replied, saying the first thing that came to mind. She squeezed her eyes shut and considered the absurdity of her words. When she opened them again, she found Jacob looking at her, concerned. "He hasn't asked me," she replied, hoping to allay his obvious concern.

"But *if* he asked you?"

Her face flushed at the idea of it. "Then I would say...yes."

Jacob smiled. "You would?"

"Uh....Yes."

He smiled back and she kissed him again. "Then I 'spose it's okay if you want to go away with him."

"Thank you, honey."

CHAPTER FOURTEEN

Briony and Max had been *so* right. When she finally stepped out of the master bathroom and into his bedroom, knowing that he'd been waiting, Tobias's mouth fell open in surprise. For a few seconds, he said nothing. He didn't need to. She only had to look at those shimmering blue eyes to know that she had hit the mark.

"Sweet Jesus, Savannah," he breathed. "You take my breath away." Goosebumps erupted along the back of her neck and arms. It was what he didn't say, the way his eyes held her, that said it all.

He didn't look so bad either in his black tux. In fact, he looked insanely handsome. They stared at one another, all dressed up, like A-list celebrities, ready to reveal their secret.

She'd been shocked when she'd finally stepped in front of the mirror with the whole outfit, the dress, shoes, small clutch, and with her hair and makeup fully done by the stylist. She didn't recognize the svelte and polished woman who stared back at her. The other Savannah was still there, but her features seemed more defined; her skin flawless, her lips fuller, her eyes bigger, and a deeper green, like velvet moss.

And the dress. A sleek, full-length evening dress in scarlet, cut high to the thigh on one side and off the opposite shoulder. It showed off her figure, made her breasts look bigger—a little more than she was happy with—but her height, especially in the shoes, gave her frame a good length. Max had insisted that she have her hair put up in a sleek chignon and she'd tried to resist the idea, preferring to wear it loose and tousled as she normally did. But she'd ended up listening to Max again and now she was thankful she had. She looked drop-dead gorgeous.

"Nervous?" he asked, as the car pulled up outside the Waldorf Astoria. She peered out of the tinted windows and held onto his hand. A crowd of people had gathered outside but were held back by security men and metal cordons. "My men will always be behind us," Tobias assured her. "And one of them will open your door." He dropped a gentle kiss on her lips before taking leave of her hand. "Don't worry, Savannah, I've got you covered."

Sure enough, a tall, bulky, beefcake of a man opened the door on her side and she climbed out, then turned, to see the cameras and flashes light up like lightning. It was still daylight outside. Tobias blinked as he got out.

"Mr. Stone!" She heard the cries, saw the people turn their heads at him, saw the photographers rush to his side and watched as reporters shoved their huge lollipop microphones towards him.

She heard him answer a few questions before he turned and swiftly made his way to her side. Taking her hand, he led her towards the hotel. They followed the two guards, one in front and one behind.

The flashes came fast and furious after that and she almost tripped as the light, so bright and right in her face, blinded her. She blinked as she moved forward and beside her she heard Tobias mutter something. "Gone insane," she thought he said, as he gripped her hand tighter. How she managed to walk on those pencil-thin-heeled shoes, she didn't know. It was a miracle that she hadn't tripped or the heel hadn't snapped as she tottered beside him towards the doors. Soon they were inside and safe.

He pulled her to one side and put a hand to her cheek. "Are you all right? That was a bit crazy."

"A bit?"

"I don't know what happened."

"Is it always like this?"

"Never like this," he told her, adjusting his cuffs. "They'd have let me walk in unencumbered," he told her. "That was all *you*. I don't blame them for getting excited." She felt her heart thrashing and felt the hair on her skin creep to standing. It was exciting and scary and she was relieved that Tobias didn't let go of her hand for one moment.

"Come on," he tugged at her hand. "Let's get this over with."

She walked around in a daze, staring at the beautifully adorned tables, the delicately lit lamps, admiring the calla lily table arrangements. She watched people, stunningly made up and wearing their finest clothes and jewels, as they greeted Tobias as if he was their best friend. When he introduced her to them, they treated her as if she was their long lost friend.

She never let go of Tobias's hand as he walked around, a lesson in charm and graciousness as he introduced her to almost everyone. He seemed to know them all.

Every so often, he would tell her that so-and-so was the head of this charity or that, and she could barely remember their names, let alone what they did. Sometimes her attention fixed on the way the women stared back at him, as if they were grateful for even a morsel of his attention. Then she would tighten her hold on him even more, as a feeling of jealousy coursed through her veins, something she had never known before.

Suddenly, she no longer felt like a stranger or someone who watched these types of snippets on the evening news. She was a part of it, and proud to be by Tobias's side, feeling like the luckiest woman in the world when he looked at her the way he did, as if she belonged to him.

Soon they were seated and over the course of their meal, she made polite conversation with everyone. After a while, Tobias got up and walked to the stage to deliver his speech. The muscles around her heart clenched as she watched him on the podium speaking easily and addressing the crowd, with an impassioned speech. He spoke of what a privilege it was to honor those who strived to make things better for others less fortunate. He didn't mention his own work with the adoption centers, but instead he concentrated on the tireless workers whose selfless determination, and in many cases volunteer work behind the scenes, made life bearable for others. She found herself caught up in him, in the way he spoke, in the way his eyes held everyone captive. She looked around at the audience to see everyone watching him with rapt attention. When he finished his speech, it was to thunderous applause.

"You were brilliant," she whispered, when the audience had stopped clapping. Then one of the women from their table got up and delivered her speech so eloquently that Savannah felt almost envious of her confidence.

They sat through a round of more speeches and presentations and the evening felt surreal. She still found it hard to believe that she was sitting here, at a Gala dinner with this man. She kept expecting the dream to end.

He leaned in closer, nipped her ear, making her smile as she tilted her head towards his face. "Your parents aren't expecting you back tonight, are they?"

She hadn't said anything to them about what time she would be back but she knew that Jacob would be waiting up for her. "I can't come over," she said, making an apologetic face. "Jacob's waiting up for me."

He grimaced. "Then you must get back. We've got all week to make up for lost time, starting tomorrow night."

Tomorrow night.

She had barely caught her breath from this evening, but the reminder that she had a week with Tobias away from this craziness cheered her up even more.

When they left the hotel, the crowd outside seemed to have doubled in size. "Word got around fast," she heard Tobias mutter as he pulled her to his side and slipped a protective hand around her waist. This time the cameras didn't stop flashing for one second. The blinding lights suddenly made her feel nauseous.

"This way, ma'am." The security guard led them quickly to the waiting limo and opened the door for her.

This time Tobias got in alongside her. The doors closed and Morris drove off. Even through the tinted windows, she could see the camera flashes lighting up the darkness like fireworks gone awry.

CHAPTER FIFTEEN

"You were on TV, Mommy!" Jacob leapt at her as soon as she walked through the door. Then he did a double-take, his eyes widening as he looked her up and down. "You look awesome!"

"Thanks, honey," she said, hugging him. "How come you're all still up?" She wasn't sure what she expected, but not for all of them to be wide awake at nearly midnight.

Her mother and father stood up and looked at her in awe. "You look so different," her mother exclaimed, holding her hands together in front of her chest. "Savannah, dear. You look so..." She shook her head.

"You look beautiful, Ruby Red," her father said. "Didn't Mr. Stone want to come in?"

"I didn't think to ask him, Dad. It was so late." She took her shoes off with Jacob still stuck to her side, his arms around her waist. "Let me put my things down, Jacob." Morris had stopped by Tobias's condo so that she could rush inside and grab her things. She could have changed back into her jeans but she wasn't ready to take off her glamorous dress yet.

"Mr. Stone looked so cool! And you looked so beautiful!" Her son was still ecstatic.

"I hope Grandpa hasn't been giving you sweets?" She looked at her parents and wondered if they'd spoiled him with a bowl of M&Ms again.

"You look so beautiful!" Her mother's eyes gleamed.

Jacob giggled. "Grandma found you on the TV channel."

"The celebrity channel," her mother explained. "You looked like movie stars. He really is a dashing young man, isn't he?"

"And Grandpa Googled you," Jacob told her. She stared at her father in disbelief, unaware that he even knew the Wi-Fi password. "I told him how to," Jacob explained.

"You're on the internet, Ruby Red. I found some sites with a couple of pictures of you both getting out of the car." Her father had that worried look about his face. She wanted to tell him not to be, that Tobias would keep her safe, that he had security, that Colt could never touch her now, but she didn't want to say this in front of her son.

"Hush now, Dale. They looked so good together."

"You went in a limousine, Mommy?"

She nodded.

"I sure hope Henry Carson saw that."

"Jacob Samuel Page," replied Savannah, walking towards the couch. Under her parents' gazes, the thigh-high cut on her dress and one bare shoulder revealed too much. She suddenly felt self-conscious. She placed her hands on her son's shoulder and sat down so that their faces were level. "I know you're excited that Mommy and Tobias are..." How to put it? "Are good friends."

"He's your boyfriend, Mommy." Jacob said. "Lenny's sister has a boyfriend and she says it's a big deal." Savannah narrowed her eyes. Lenny's sister was eight. "Honey, I don't want you showing off, or bragging about me and Mr. Stone. Do you hear me?" He made a face as if his hopes had been crushed. "Did you hear me, Jacob Samuel Page?" He stared at her with puppy dog eyes. "Because if I so much as catch a whiff of it, I will not be a happy Mommy."

"Okay," he replied, his mood deflated.

"Weren't you cold in that dress?" her father asked. "It looks like it's been ripped to shreds."

"Nonsense, Dale. She looks lovely. That's what they call high fashion, isn't it, dear? Tell us all about it," her mother made herself comfortable on the couch.

"Jean, I think it's getting late. You can find out all about it tomorrow. And you, young man," her father looked at Jacob. "I think it's time you went to bed."

"Grandpa's right," said Savannah. She wanted some time to herself, to climb down from the high of the evening. "You go to bed, and I'll be over in a while."

But the landline rang. For a moment she was paralyzed, wondering who would call this late. For a short, terrified moment, the image of Colt flashed up. But he didn't have her home number. She answered it without thinking.

"Are you freakin' serious?" Kay shrieked. "Tobias Freakin' Stone and YOU?"

Oh, shit. Kay, and she hadn't said a word to her cousin at all.

"Is it true? How can you? How can you date THAT MAN AND NOT TELL ME?" Kay sounded almost hysterical. Then, calm again. "Is it true? Or is that your doppelganger? They haven't said who she is but I swear it's the spitting image of you. I mean you look identical. You look *freakin' amazing.*"

Savannah held the phone a few inches away from her ear. "It's Kay," she mouthed to her parents and Jacob, who were staring at her. As they slowly shuffled off to bed, she put the phone to her ear again.

"I was going to tell you," Savannah began, but her words

were weak and her voice bore no conviction. In all the rush of the past week and the nervousness and excitement around the event, she'd completely forgotten that she had intended to forewarn Kay, to tell her gently. "I got really busy trying to find my—"

"I ask myself: how the hell can my own cousin *forget to mention* that she's dating THE HOTTEST MAN IN NEW YORK? My cousin wouldn't do that to me, WOULD SHE?" Savannah slumped further into the couch and listened. Kay continued, "And if she was DATING THE HOTTEST MAN IN NEW YORK, maybe she'd have the decency to tell me first instead of it showing up in my newsfeed!"

"I'm sorry I didn't tell you. I meant to tell you a few days ago —Mom said you'd called, but things got hectic. I only had a week to find something decent to wear."

"How long has this been going on?"

"A few weeks...or months."

"MONTHS?"

"Two months, maybe three." It depended when she started counting it—from that first kiss, or from the first time they'd made love? Or had it all started long before that first kiss?

"Three freakin' months and you couldn't find a minute to pick up the phone and TELL ME THAT YOU WERE SLEEPING WITH TOBIAS STONE?" Kay was beyond hysterical.

"I wasn't sure myself!" Savannah shot back. "I wasn't sure and then we kind of didn't get along, and then we kind of did."

"Unbelievable," her cousin muttered.

"Why are you so upset?"

"I'm not, I'm happy for you but I'm pissed that I found out through the 'net. I don't understand it, Sav. I've been going on about this hot guy ever since you told me you worked in his company, I've been joking about meeting you at work—"

"Joking?"

"I was getting all excited that I might get to see this guy when I met you at work or something. But to find out you've been secretly dating him. You could have said *something*."

"It's been complicated."

"I don't believe you."

"It hasn't been easy," Savannah insisted.

"Is he good in bed?"

"Kay!"

"What? It's a valid question. Have you been in his private jet yet?"

Savannah wasn't sure that now would be the right time to tell her cousin that they would be flying to Miami in the private jet tomorrow. "No," she replied truthfully. "We've been keeping it quiet."

Kay puffed out loudly. "Not any more. Someone posted pictures online. You look freakin' amazing."

"Thanks."

"Does this mean I can hang out with you guys when I come back?"

CHAPTER SIXTEEN

"Jacob would love this," she exclaimed, wandering around his private jet, trying to tone down her obvious awe.

"Then next time we must bring him," Tobias said.

She'd never known a plane to have large tables, or a bathroom, or a toilet that looked like this, let alone a bedroom with cupboards and side cabinets. She had never in her wildest dreams imagined that the inside of a plane could look like a luxury condo.

When he'd shown her the bedroom, she had almost laughed at the strangeness of it.

A bed, in a room, with carpet. A normal bedroom, but in a *plane.* Jacob would have loved it. She'd taken him ice skating in Bryant Park this morning, while her parents had stayed at home. She'd wanted to spend as much of the day with him, precious one-on-one time for them after a week in which she'd felt she had neglected him. Jacob seemed happy that she was going with Tobias—in his little mind he already had a plan for how things would turn out, and she worried about that. She especially worried about how high his expectations were for them.

By the time they came home late in the afternoon, he was

exhausted but happy. It had made her departure easier. What made it even easier was her parents' approval of Tobias, despite not having met him. Her father's online investigations into him seemed to have left his mind at ease. She had wanted them to meet Tobias but the last two weeks had stormed past like a hurricane and she didn't want their first meeting to be rushed.

They had taken off from New York an hour ago, and now sat facing one another in the big, cream comfortable leather seats. It was a world away from economy class.

"What is it?" she asked, seeing Tobias shaking his head as he looked at his cell phone.

"Matthias commenting on the Gala dinner. He says his latest girlfriend was talking about us."

"Latest girlfriend?"

Tobias waved his hand. "I can't keep up. He doesn't mention names, they change so frequently, and I don't ask."

"What did she say?"

"She liked your dress."

Savannah smiled. "Kay called me when I got back last night."

"Kay?"

"My cousin."

"The one in Hong Kong?"

Savannah nodded. "She was upset that I hadn't told her about us."

"Upset? Why?"

"Just..." She couldn't divulge why without telling him about his Stone groupie. "We're very close and I guess I would have, but this last week I didn't get a moment to catch my breath."

"Imagine if you'd come with me to Hong Kong and run into her."

"Thank goodness I didn't." She didn't want to think about

the consequences of meeting Tobias and her cousin face to face. Dealing with her on the phone had been hard enough.

"You should have heard her last night. Talk about whining. Anyway, she's returning to the city in the summer and maybe I can introduce you both then?" She would need to make that happen because it was the only way she could see that Kay might forgive her.

"Maybe you can come with me if I return to Hong Kong?" he asked.

"Will you be returning?" Savannah asked. "I thought you and Matthias had a difference of opinion regarding the Far East."

Tobias shrugged. "It's more than a difference of opinion."

"What, specifically?"

"Things are unsettled globally at the moment. The markets are shifting everywhere and there's a lot of uncertainty and gloom. The EU in Europe is in danger of collapsing and the Far East has its share of problems. I don't want to expose myself to those types of risks—not for my customers. From the work you're doing for me, you know we've been focused heavily in a lot of tech startups. Matthias and I have been visiting them over the past eighteen months, trying to diversify our investments. I want to move away from relying on an economy that seems shaky but Matthias seems otherwise convinced."

"If you've always trusted your gut, then why don't you now?"

"Because Matthias always has a good reason. There are times when I can't see the wood for the trees, but Matthias, he always sees the bigger picture."

"But if your own instinct has gotten you to where you are now," she persisted, "doesn't that tell you something? I mean," she was out of her depth, she didn't completely understand about stocks and portfolios but what Tobias was telling her was simple; that he was ignoring his own feelings. "You have your doubts about China and this Yanling guy as well as your investments overseas yet you're willing to push them to one side. Does Matthias really carry so much weight?"

"He's my equal and I trust him implicitly." She nodded, keenly aware of that fact.

"He was the hotshot until I joined a small investment management firm owned by Becker Schwartz, the man who was to become my mentor. He did something that nobody had done before."

"What was that?"

"He believed in me. I'd come from a school system in which teachers didn't have much time for me. I had a few special classes here and there but I still struggled with my lessons. I'm mildly dyslexic," he explained, "and so reading and spelling and writing were a chore. Numbers were easier, but only just. But when I worked for Becker, the graphs and charts all started to make sense. I could analyze them and see patterns. It was almost as if I could 'read' the data. The systems he taught me and the pointers he gave me started to make sense. It no longer felt like a struggle to make sense of things around me. He didn't treat me like an idiot or someone who was slow. His belief in me made all the difference." She couldn't imagine Tobias Stone ever not having unshakeable faith in himself and his admission surprised her. "I could finally do things, make judgments, predictions, and they were usually right. That's when Becker started to spend more time with me than with Matthias. He seemed to value my opinion more and he concentrated more of his time and attention on me."

"That's why you feel guilty."

"I never said I feel guilty."

"You didn't have to."

Tobias gave her a look that was expressionless, as if he

refuted what she'd said. She tried to frame it differently. "Maybe not guilty but maybe you feel you might have overshadowed him and that's why you overcompensate."

"Overcompensate?" Tobias's jaw tightened as if he didn't share her view. "Matthias is more like a brother to me. I won't ever *not* consider his opinion."

"I'm sorry," she said, crossing her legs and placing her arms over the soft, plush armrests. She hadn't meant to make the atmosphere awkward, not now at the start of their vacation, but she didn't know Matthias and she wasn't sure she trusted him as much as Tobias did. Still, they went back a long way. They had history.

"I know you might not warm to him, Savannah, and I'm aware that he has a certain sexist side to him that grates on most women. I don't blame you for feeling wary around him. Plenty of times, he's made me want to throw up, but the man isn't *all* bad. Most of it is a front."

They sat quietly for a few moments, letting the awkwardness dissipate.

"Where will you live when she gets back?"

"Who?"

"Your cousin."

"I'll figure something out," she replied, even though it was starting to worry her.

"You will." Tobias seemed sure of it but she had her doubts. The onset of spring with its blooming flowers and falling cherry blossoms was a sharp reminder that time was passing quickly. She wanted it to slow down so that she could make the most of each moment with this man but summer would be upon them soon enough.

She had no idea how things would develop between her and Tobias. Her idea of moving out of the city to the suburbs where she could afford the rent seemed less and less appealing, especially since it meant she might have to change jobs. Anything that was an hour's commute from work and with no Rosalee around to help her, in addition to the prospect of Jacob having to change schools again, gave her nightmares. She didn't want to think about it.

"I've had a lot of crazy messages from Briony and Max about the Gala," she said. "I told them they ought to consider a career in becoming personal stylists. I don't know what I would have done without their help."

"You still would have looked amazing."

She shook her head. He had no idea. "I doubt it."

"Glad I convinced you to come?"

"Naturally." She was. The secrecy was gone and it was out in the open, that she and Tobias were an item. She didn't relish the thought of returning to work and was pleased that they had taken this week and gone away. It saved her from dealing with people's immediate reactions. Hopefully, by the time they both returned to work, the shock and surprise of her and Tobias being an item would have died down.

"Don't you get scared to speak in front of people?" She had been filled with pride when he had made his speech. Public speaking frightened her more than the thought of dying.

Tobias shrugged. "I'm used to it now but it didn't come easy at first. At first I was so concerned about trying to look confident, trying to be slick and professional. I didn't want to trip up while reading, so I always practiced for hours, days sometimes, until I knew the speech by heart. Back to front, upside down, you name it." Savannah tried to imagine him lacking confidence, and being unsure. Tried and failed. Tobias was the epitome of cool self-possession. Resolute, poised and fearless—she couldn't see him as anything but that. And yet he was telling her he hadn't always been like this. "After a while, it's like most things, you become used to it. When the message you want to deliver is more important than the way your gut is churning, you forget the physicality of the moment and deliver the words. These days, when making speeches for events such as the Gala dinner, I still have to do my homework and prepare well. I make sure I have my facts correct, but when I'm giving presentations about our business and speaking about the markets and financial analysis, I don't have to have it written down. I know what I'm talking about, and when you know that, it gives you a confidence that's on another level altogether."

"You captivated the audience."

"That's odd," he remarked casually. "Because I was looking to mainly captivate you."

"You did that already, the moment I stepped out of your bathroom."

His eyes sparkled and his lips almost turned into a smile. Almost. He put away the newspaper that he'd been reading. "I don't want to talk about work or our colleagues. This vacation was supposed to be downtime for you and me."

He got up and held out his hand. She felt a rush of warmth pass over her stomach as he headed towards the bedroom, her heart starting to race, making her skin tingle. She had missed him in her bed last night, and felt as if their Gala evening had been cut short the moment Morris had dropped her off at home. But now they had five glorious nights together. As soon as he pulled her inside and closed the door, his lips were instantly on hers. She tasted mint and sweetness as he pushed her against the door and pressed his body against hers. She wondered if he could feel her heart thumping as his chest pressed firmly against her breasts.

"What about your pilot?" she asked nervously, eyeing the bed.

"He's in the cockpit," Tobias replied, his feverish tongue and lips teasing the dip at the base of her neck. He stopped for a moment. "He can't see a thing." Slipping his hands around the hem of her A-line summer dress, he lifted it high above her head and pulled it off. She started to undo his belt, her hands trembling as he unclasped her bra.

"Slow down," she whispered, trying to pry open the stubborn button on his jeans.

"I can't," he croaked, and rolled her panties down to her ankles. "I need to be inside you." He'd already beaten her to it. Within minutes of getting her into the room, he'd stripped her naked while he himself was still fully clothed.

He lifted her up and strode over to the bed with her legs clamped firmly around his waist. Throwing her onto the bed, he pinned her in place with his scorching gaze as he peeled off his shirt. His hungry, roving eyes slowly took in every inch of her naked body as if he was going to devour her completely.

She could barely wait.

CHAPTER SEVENTEEN

"What news channel?" Colt asked, zipping up his slacks as the hooker wiped her mouth. She grabbed the bills he threw at her as if they were her next meth fix.

They probably were. The door slammed behind her.

"Sheryl says you might wanna see this. Happened over the weekend, looks like." His friend hung up.

Colt switched over and blinked at the celebrity couple walking past a sleek black car. What the hell was this? Merle's wife was a celebrity-whore, always buying the latest magazines and following celebrities online like a faithful Chihuahua. He peered closely at the screen, expecting enlightenment. Then he peered even closer. The sexily dressed woman looked familiar.

She looked like Savannah.

Heat numbed as it spread across his face. He tried to swallow but his throat stopped working. It *was* Savannah. He turned the sound up. Those eyes, those legs. That was his goddamn ex-wife. And who the fuck was *he*? Colt stepped closer to the screen, his eyes narrowing on the man beside her.

Who the hell and how?

"Hearts are breaking everywhere now that it's official, news that the billionaire New York hedge fund owner, Tobias Stone, has a new woman in his life. Rumors continue to spread, but sources close to the billionaire remain tight-lipped. Tobias Stone has rarely been linked publicly to anyone since the death of his wife in an automobile accident four years ago. He shies away from the public eye and continues to remain an enigma, as well as a heartthrob to many. However, it is claimed that this new sighting might mean true love at last for the reclusive billionaire. His new girlfriend, rumored to be an employee at Stone Enterprises, is a single mother with a young son. The couple attended a charity dinner at the Waldorf Astoria over the weekend before leaving yesterday for Miami where Mr. Stone owns a multi-million dollar home. Let's wish these lovebirds well. Moving onto other news..."

"I'll be damned," Colt rasped, blinking at the images before him. She'd been lying to him the whole time.

She was screwing a billionaire?

Since when?

He guessed she was putting out dirty favors. Women could do that—reel men in with their pussies, while here he was, drowning in debt and risking his life by transporting drugs out of state. Santino more or less owned him.

Screw that.

Colt Brookes scratched his face and pondered how he could turn this new discovery to his advantage. Somewhere in all this lay the solution to his problems. He knew she would never leave Jacob alone for more than a few days. He needed to get to New York; hitch a ride with one of his trucker friends for part of the trip then hitch rides the rest of the way. It would take about a day, he guessed.

His next payment to Santino was due next week. He needed a day to get to New York, a couple of days to figure out how to convince his ex, and a day to get back.

He could do it in a week.

A week to get his life back.

It could work.

It had to.

He imagined the new life he could buy for himself if he convinced her into a little loan. Or even a big one. Not a loan so much, as an offer—if he promised never to see her or the boy again.

How much would a deal like that be worth to her?

Colt grunted like a pig, barely able to keep still as the plan started to come together. The rich dude would soon get bored of her, and so he had to act fast. Better to take advantage of the situation while he still had the chance.

He smiled to himself, loving his new plan more with every second. It was obvious his ex wanted nothing more to do with him. Why had she buggered off and never told him where she was? Why else did she always sound so pissed off whenever he called her?

He could disappear from her life forever. Something like that had a price and he figured Savannah Page would be willing to pay it, especially when she had access to the kind of money she did. Even if the money wasn't technically hers.

He just needed to find a way to get to her.

CHAPTER EIGHTEEN

Only two days into their vacation and she was already imagining a life in which every day was like this. Waking up with Tobias was beautiful. Going to bed with him for the whole night was even better. She had never known such complete happiness away from her son.

Tobias had made it possible for her; he'd given her a life, an inner peace she had not known for so many years and it felt strange to her even now, as if at any moment now it would all be taken away from her.

Many times during this trip, she'd looked around, turned to see if the security men were there, even prompting Tobias to ask her what she was worried about. How could she tell him she was scared this would vanish into thin air? This happiness, this deeper love she felt for him, it made her feel whole again. She thought she only had enough love for her son, but she had more.

Sometimes she would watch Tobias sleeping, and her heart would sing. He told her often that she brought him peace, that she did things to him, but he had no idea of the things he did to her, of the happiness that being with him gave her.

"Is that new?" he asked, casting an especially hungry glance over the new hot pink silky satin slip she wore. She twirled around, letting him see the low-cut back with the crisscross straps.

"Do you like it?" she asked, unafraid, and no longer self-conscious. She liked the way his gaze raked all over her, as intimately as his tongue. She knew that look in his eyes; knew that they would make love all night until their melting bodies succumbed to sleep in sweat-streaked sheets. Then he would wake her up again, as he had done this morning in the most sensual manner, making her smile before she'd even opened her eyes. There was no other man for her. Ever.

"Do I like it?" he answered slowly.

Her hand tugged on the towel that hugged his hips. "Something tells me you like it," she murmured, running her fingers over the solid muscles of his torso. He drew out a breath and slid his hands over her back, then frowned as his fingers went back over the contours of her bottom.

"No panties?" he asked, reaching down to confirm his suspicions.

"No point," she whispered. He'd have them off in no time.

"You're a fast learner."

"You're a good teacher."

"You're a big tease." He told her.

"That's exactly why I do it," she murmured, her voice low but not quite a whisper. Emboldened, she slid her hands into his damp hair, inhaling the clean and freshly showered scent of him. She dipped her tongue into his sweet and warm mouth as their bodies pressed together with a familiar urgency. His fingers explored her body, teasing, and prying as blood rushed through her veins, pumping around her body and heightening her senses.

Making love with Tobias was unlike anything she had ever experienced with Colt. With him, it had been mostly one-sided, even back in the days when the sex had been consensual. There hadn't been much in it for her, and she had used the time to compile to-do lists in her head of things that needed her attention later. With Tobias, she experienced a whole new world of sensations and feelings the like of which she had never before known. With him, she wasn't afraid to lead or to instigate it.

Three more nights and it would be over. She didn't want it to end and so she lost herself in the moment, in the white-hot heat and desire that bound them together. She placed her hands along the towel that hugged his hips. Her fevered fingers slid along almost-damp skin above his waist before moving along his corded arms then down his iron-hard stomach. After carefully examining the hills and ridges of his stomach, her fingers slid lower then tugged off his towel, leaving him completely naked. She stroked and rubbed him until his breathing was heavy, then pushed him back and onto the bed, staring at his body, her mouth open, her heartrate sky-high.

"Come here," he murmured, propping himself up on his forearms. She could see that he was desperate to get his hands on her, to feel her, to do those beautiful things he always did. Except that tonight, she wanted to do those things to him.

"No," she replied, licking her lips as she climbed onto the bed. Placing herself sideways across his body so that both her knees were by his waist, she began to slowly kiss his chest and stomach.

"Kiss me," he urged, making her lose concentration. She allowed him that, and moved her face up to his, to let him have a taste of her lips. The moment their lips met, his hands were on her breast, one hand there and one sliding under her slip, settling against her, making her lose concentration again. She stared into his face; at the face she knew as well as her own.

Every wrinkle, every line. A face she had come to love, a man she had come to love. A man who had stolen her heart.

She moved his hand away. "I want to touch you," he begged.

"Me first," she replied, coolly ignoring his irritation as she moved down and bent over, her hair falling onto his thighs as she lowered her mouth.

The busy internet cafe near Times Square reeked of fried fat, bubblegum and body odor. He couldn't wait to leave this shithole. People talked about New York like it was some magical place.

Not from what he'd seen. If his ex wanted to live here, good luck to her. Colt Brookes hadn't wasted any time. He'd arrived here a few hours ago and had found a place to stay but he didn't want to stay here longer than he had to, not in this dirty cockroach-infested hostel.

He'd been surfing online, trying to find out things about Tobias Stone. It was so much easier to find things out when the guy was rich and famous. And Tobias Stone was stinking rich.

No fucking wonder his ex hadn't been returning his calls. She'd been busy doing other things. He stared as the pictures of her and that man filled the computer screen. *She'd been his once.* Pain shot through him, as if someone had aimed a dart at his chest. It only lasted a moment, a short-lived memory that was gone in an instant. It could have worked, if the economy hadn't folded. If he hadn't lost his job. If life hadn't been so tough. It wasn't his fault things had turned out the way they had.

But life wasn't fair. And he was trying to get by.

He'd looked up the phone number for Stone Enterprises and scribbled it down on the dirty napkin with which he'd wiped his greasy cheeseburger hands. If his ex was going to ignore his calls on her cell phone, he'd have to call her at work. Hopefully, she'd be back by then, or the day after. He couldn't see her leaving Jacob with a babysitter for too long. She might have been a lousy wife, but she'd been a good enough mother.

He slipped the note into his jacket pocket. It was after office hours now, but tomorrow he'd make sure he got in touch with her. Each extra night here cost him money he didn't have. Santino's money. If everything worked out as he envisioned, by this time next week, he'd have a new life and nobody would ever own him again.

He'd clean up, sort himself out and move someplace else if he had to. He'd lived in his hometown all his life and maybe it was time for new beginnings. If his ex could do it, in a city like this and with a child, so could he.

All Colt had to do was to tell her the truth: that he was up shit creek and he'd get killed if he didn't make good what he owed. Things might have broken down between them but Savannah had a heart and there was no way she was going to let the father of her child get killed.

He'd ask her for the money in exchange for never contacting her again. It seemed simple and he saw no reason why it wouldn't work. Being desperate and running out of time, he had no option except for it to work.

Still, he found himself staring at the pictures again. She looked so goddamn pretty, not like the woman he remembered. He examined the man's height and build and rubbed his greasy fingers across his brows.

She'd done well for herself.

It was a good thing, because it could work out well for him, too, if things went according to plan.

CHAPTER NINETEEN

Candace was in no mood for this. "I don't accept calls from salespeople. Can't you get rid of him?" People who didn't have her direct number were cold callers and no better than parasites.

"This caller sounds real angry and keeps calling back. Please take it," the receptionist begged. "He says it's an urgent inquiry regarding Savannah Page and he can't get hold of her."

Candace sat up and pressed the receiver close to her ear. She closed the screen images she'd been looking at during her lunch hour. Images of the two of them on vacation in Miami. "Put him through," she said, sucking her breath in irritation. "Candace Oakley. How may I help you?"

"About damn time too," the male caller sounded annoyed. "I want to speak to Savannah Page."

"I'm afraid Ms. Page is away until Monday," Candace replied testily. It should have been *her* in Miami, not that bitch.

"Monday?" The man's voice had a rough edge to it, and she wondered what he was after.

"Is there something I can help you with?" Candace asked, sensing this wasn't a normal cold caller.

"It's personal."

"A personal matter?" Her ears pricked up. "Do you have her cell phone number?"

"I've tried, but she ain't answering. Could be 'cos I'm her ex-husband." She heard a coarse laugh.

"You are?" Candace sat back in her chair and rubbed her fingers together. Her day had instantly brightened.

"Yes, ma'am."

Candace's voice melted, and she smiled. "Is there anything I can do to help?"

"I'm not sure." The man's voice suddenly dimmed, as if hope was lost. "I was in town and I was hoping to meet up with her and my son."

"Unfortunately, Ms. Page is away with Mr. Stone. I could let her know you called."

"I was looking for her address. You wouldn't happen to know it, would you?" he asked. Candace laughed at the suggestion.

"Her address?" Her fingers trembled as she clicked the mouse and retrieved Savannah's personal file, something that only a few people outside of HR had access to. "Why, of course," she stared at the details on the screen, her heart pitter-pattering away. "This information is strictly confidential, you understand, don't you?"

"I swear I won't tell anyone. You'd be doing me a huge favor, ma'am. I hitch-hiked for over ten hours just to come see them."

Hitch-hiked? She wrinkled her nose in disgust. "I hope you understand what a huge risk I'm taking."

"I'd be mighty obliged and thankful to you. My ex-wife won't even let me see my son. Do you know if Jacob's gone with them?"

Candace couldn't believe her luck. She cleared her throat.

"I believe it's a personal vacation they've taken. Again, I've already said more than I should have."

"Who the hell's she left my son with?"

Candace smiled at the anger in his voice. "I believe Ms. Page's parents are here. Again—I've said too much."

"Thank you, ma'am. I ain't heard nothing from you. If you could give me the address." Candace lowered her voice and read it out to him.

CHAPTER TWENTY

As they left the restaurant, a couple of photographers scurried out from behind the trees and took some pictures.

"Not so close," Tobias heard one of the security men warn them. These were things he had become used to but would Savannah put up with this? Would she want to subject Jacob to this?

"Don't mind them," he said, as they walked hand in hand again, along the streets as darkness fell. Their time together was flying by and now he wished they had longer. He had mentioned a few places to visit, but she'd shown no interest in any clubs or bars, and except for a private sailing trip around Biscayne Bay, most of their time had been spent at his house, outside on the sun loungers, relaxing by the pool.

They didn't need to be out doing things in order to enjoy the day. The luxury of spending time alone together was more than enough. The only intrusion in this idyll had been phone calls. Candace and Matthias knew better than to disturb him with trivial matters.

Work hadn't been the problem.

It had been his mother. Surprisingly, he hadn't heard from Xavier and he felt sure his brother would have known by now about him and Savannah. When his cell phone went off again, his insides locked and he dreaded seeing his mother's name on the caller display. She'd called a few times. Five, to be exact, and being with Savannah and not wanting the intrusion, he'd let it go to voicemail.

But now he couldn't *not* answer it.

Not when it was his dad calling; phone calls from his father weren't as easy to send to voicemail.

"Hi, Dad," He turned to Savannah and shrugged.

After the usual polite greetings, his father cut right in. "The papers have nothing but news of the new woman in your life, son. Is it true?"

"It's true."

Ellery Stone made a satisfactory grunt. "That's all I needed to know. It was more your mother who wanted to make sure." With those few words, his father absolved himself of the reason for his call.

"You can tell Mom not to worry."

"I'll do that. Your mother wanted to know if this is the lady with the son?" Tobias drew his mouth into a straight line and swallowed. He could almost see his mother in the background, whispering. "Don't put her on, Dad. I'm with Savannah." He felt the gentle tug of Savannah's hand. She made a face, obviously wondering why they were talking about her.

"She's not here. She's out playing bridge with the ladies from the club." Tobias breathed easier. His father was wise and sensible, and called when the coast was clear.

"Then please be sure to tell her that it is."

"Your mother doesn't mean to interfere," said his father. "She worries about you, Tobias. If you're happy, I'm happy.

Don't worry about your mother's meddling. She has too much free time on her hands and not enough things to keep her busy."

"Thanks, Dad," Tobias replied, amused.

"I'll let her know I spoke to you and that the world hasn't ended."

"Thanks."

"Will we get to meet your new friend sometime?"

"We'll see."

"What was that about?" Savannah asked, when he hung up.

"The news spread, and my parents wanted official confirmation that we were together."

"What was it that you didn't want to discuss in front of me?"

"Nothing. I thought my mother might be hovering in the background and I wasn't in the mood to talk to her right now. She can be a little trying sometimes."

"Trying?"

"She's an acquired taste," Tobias explained. "Harmless, but definitely an acquired taste."

Savannah looked at him, unsure. "Acquired taste?"

"You'll see when you meet her. I won't subject you to them yet, don't worry. I've learned from my brother's experience."

They continued walking and came across another sprawling estate which was set back from the street and gated, as they all were on this private road. But the front of the mansion glowed and was brightly lit up in brilliant purple. A party was in full swing and the music, loud and electric, blasted out into the night. Walking past, they turned and stared at the building that was only five minutes from his house. Tobias cocked his head to listen then smiled as he recognized the tune. The synthesizer chords and pulsing kick-drum of the song vibrated in the air—it was one of his favorites. Prince's 'Little Red Corvette' screamed out towards the heavens; the singer's vocal acrobatics electrified the night sky, touching it with its magic. The music faded as they walked away and the night was silent again.

Once inside, and as his security men patrolled outside checking the perimeter of the building, they walked through the house to the back. Tobias opened the doors to the yard and the pool. "Let's sit out here for a while," he suggested, turning on the outside lights which illuminated the pool and the area around it. In the balmy night the pool lights glittered like stars. He loved his exotic yard with its gurgling water features and delicately fringed plants. It centered him, giving him a sense of calm that was hard to find elsewhere. These past few days, he and Savannah had spent most of the time out here, by the pool. It was where they'd eaten most of their meals.

This was one of his favorite places away from New York, not only because of the weather, but because it was on the waterfront and there was water all around. After spending so much time cooped up inside, either in his office or his apartment, being able to sit outside and work, or do nothing—a rarity for him—was something he enjoyed.

They settled down on one of the super-sized sun loungers, the size of a double bed. Tobias lay back as Savannah curled into him. He loved it when she rested her head in the crook of his arm. It was how they slept most of the time.

They lay back, enjoying the peace and tranquility as light danced on the water surface of the pool.

"Are you thinking about Jacob?" he asked, breathing in the scent of her hair.

"I spoke to him earlier, when you'd gone for your run. He's having a great time. My parents are overindulging him and spoiling him rotten."

"I can't imagine Jacob ever being a spoiled child. You've done well the way you've brought him up."

"It hasn't always been easy but I'm glad we got away."

"Got away?"

"Left North Carolina."

"I'm glad you left North Carolina."

"It was worth it, making the new start."

"Was it hard? Getting away?"

"I should have done it sooner," she said. "I tried to, many times, but I was powerless. It wasn't easy with a young child and I had no money, no savings and I didn't want to tell my parents too much. They'd only worry." His gut tightened as he listened to her. "It was the biggest help having my parents close by, but I kept things from them. I never told them about what really went on."

"And what was that?"

At first she was silent, and he felt the vise tighten around his chest, as if it was stopping the air from getting into his lungs. "Uh, you know, the fighting."

The fighting?

"Not all the time. He wasn't always physically rough," she said quickly. "He was never like that before." She was making excuses for him. He didn't like that either. "It started when he lost his job and then he grew bitter and frustrated when he couldn't find anything else." She stopped talking, letting silence fill the air. "It only happened when he'd had too much to drink. But it was as if he hated the sight of me, as if it belittled him that I was out earning money and still had a job."

"Why couldn't he find work?"

"It wasn't easy," she replied, and he could hear the defense in her voice. A chill iced over his skin. *Hitting a woman was easier?* He managed to stop himself from responding and instead listened while she told him of how her ex had lost his job and had never recovered from it; how he'd scraped by on odd jobs as a handyman.

"He resented me for still having a job and being able to

support us. Then we would fight. It was mainly verbal in the beginning, and it was only later, with the alcohol, that he would lash out at me. While Jacob was a baby, it didn't matter."

Didn't matter? Tobias struggle to listen. It had suddenly become harder to breathe because the vise clamped inside him would not open. He held her tighter, his jaw solid as he gritted his teeth. "But surely Jacob must have been frightened of him?"

"He was too young to be frightened. In the beginning, he was a toddler, but when he turned three, the fighting would make him cry."

"And the fighting..." He forced himself to ask, needing to know, yet not wanting to at the same time. "How bad?"

"I don't remember. It wasn't all the time. It was mainly shouting and him pushing me around. But one time, I remember." She paused, for more than a few moments. "One time it was really bad. I stubbed out his cigarette because Jacob suffered. He had problems with asthma from a young age, and I couldn't get Colt to stop smoking. So I got really mad and I stubbed out his cigarette and he got angry. His hand was like a rock across my face. I couldn't go to work for days because I didn't want anyone to know and I didn't want my parents to see me. I used to leave Jacob with them."

He hugged her to him, hugged her tighter than ever, as if he couldn't bear to let her go. "Do you know what I remember most about it?" she asked him. "Not how much it hurt, but the look on Jacob's face. He must have been three, I think, or just under, but he was old enough to know something bad had happened. That's what I remember about that night. The look on Jacob's face."

"So you left him?"

"Not then, but I learned not to make a noise. I learned to take the punches quietly." Her words settled over him like metal chains, cold and heavy.

"But one day he ended up hitting Jacob by accident. I'd been putting him to sleep and we both dozed off on the bed. Colt was beside me when I awoke and we wrestled. His hand slipped and instead of hitting me, he smacked Jacob by accident instead. That was the day I decided enough was enough."

"Why was he trying to hit you when you were sleeping?"

She shifted in his arms, but this time he wasn't going to let her escape easily.

"Savannah?"

"Because...he..."

Tobias knew. His mouth ran dry.

"Because he wanted sex and I didn't." His thoughts, like metal splinters, shot outwards in all directions, imagining the situation, seeing her, and Jacob as a baby, powerless to do anything. He gritted his teeth together so tightly that his entire body tensed.

"I left him that day," she said quietly. "I went to my parents and still I didn't tell them everything. I didn't need to, but I stayed with them for a while and slowly turned my life around."

He heard how she'd moved to Pennsylvania then to New York to look after her cousin's apartment, in order to get away and start fresh with a new life for her and Jacob. The insides of his stomach turned hot, like molten metal. He heard her words but they faded away, as his mind lingered in the frightened, dark places of her past life. "I'm sorry this happened to you," he said.

"It's not your fault."

"I'm still sorry. You don't deserve this. No woman does."

"It's all over now," she said, staring back at him as he kept his arms firmly around her back. He knew there was more to it and he wasn't sure how he would be able to listen to it but he would, because he wanted to know everything.

"Things have turned around for me. I like to think that we turned a corner." She *had* turned a corner. She was here and she was his, and she would never again know that kind of life. He could never bear to see her hurt again, or the boy he had come to love as his own. He would make sure of it.

"You don't have to worry about that anymore, Savannah. You and Jacob, you're going to be fine. Nobody will ever lay a finger on either of you again, and your ex," he swallowed, "he's out of your life now. Forget about him."

In the dusky hue of the amber-colored pool lights, her eyes glittered as she stared back at him. He ran his hand down her arms, pressing her closer to him. "I'll keep you safe," he vowed.

"I believe you."

He had the money, the security, the wealth and the power, and he would make it so.

CHAPTER TWENTY-ONE

He'd waited outside since seven thirty this morning, not daring to risk missing them leaving for school. He was mildly surprised to see Jean again. She was taking the boy to school.

Her parents really were here. That explained why his ex had been away for more than a couple of days. He noticed that the boy had grown. Now he was an even lankier, string bean of a child who looked more and more like his mother, except for the color of his hair, which at least he'd inherited from his father. Colt sniffed, wiping his nose, and inhaling sharply.

This morning, he'd kept a good distance behind them, skulking in the shadows as he followed them to the school gates. Now he knew where the boy went to school. It was sort of coming together. His plan wasn't solid, how could it have been when he didn't know much, and didn't have much time? How was he to know she was going to spend the whole week away? He hadn't planned for any problems, nor could he afford to fail.

Not with Santino breathing down his neck.

But even so, because of the fuck-ups, a new and better plan

had formed. He'd spent the whole day wandering around the stores and sitting in cafes, waiting for the day to end; keeping himself busy surfing the internet, seeing what Savannah and lover boy were up to.

It was finally time. The end of the school day was here and this was his moment. With his heart thumping underneath his chest, Colt stepped out from the shadows of the trees and walked slowly towards the school gates, towards the sea of mothers with their young children. It was harder to pick out Jacob in the crowd but Jean was easy enough to spot. She was one of the few grandmothers in the throng of younger moms.

"Hello, son," he said, planting himself directly in front of them as they walked away from the school gates.

"Dad?" Colt noted that the boy gripped his Grandma's hand.

"Colt?" Jean narrowed her eyes, her voice shaky. "What are you doing here?" She backed away a few steps, pulling the boy behind her.

"I had a job out here," he told her. "I was in the area and thought I'd come by. I called Savannah a few weeks ago to let her know. I've called her a couple of times but she's not answering." He waited to see if his ex's mother would tell him.

"I expect she's busy," she replied, and looked at him as if she was waiting for him to leave.

"There's no need to be cold, Jean. I only want to see my boy so please don't make this any harder for me. I went through a bad time back then and I'm sorry for the things I'd done. I love him, 'cos he's my blood. Think what it's like for me, going all this time without seeing him." She stared at him as if he was a convicted felon, keeping Jacob's hand firmly in her own, but her mouth twitched, as if she was deciding.

"We need to get home, Colt. Please don't cause a scene. Dale's expecting us any moment now."

"Give me a chance, Jean."

Come on, he thought, smiling at them both. Because in that boy lay the answer to his problems. His ex being away had worked out even better for him. It had paved the way for an even better plan and one that would not fail.

This time Savannah wouldn't be able to refuse. She might not have been willing to help him, even if she'd been here and he had managed to convince her to meet him. Not so with Plan B. For Jacob, she would pay up.

She would get the boy and he would get to start over.

Thank you for reading THE OFFER, BOOKS 1-3! Tobias and Savannah's rollercoaster love story comes to a thrilling conclusion in **THE VOW, Books 1-3.**

She's falling deeper in love. He's getting over his tragic past. The future belongs to them. Or does it?

A secret from Tobias's past threatens his new-found happiness. Suddenly, the odds are stacked against him. He lost everything once before and he won't make the same mistake again.

Because sometimes you only get one chance to find your soulmate.

Get THE VOW, BOOKS 1-3 now!

SIGN UP FOR MY NEWSLETTER to find out when new books release!
http://www.lilyzante.com/newsletter

I appreciate your help in spreading the word, including telling a friend, and I would be grateful if you could leave a review on your favorite book site.

You can read an excerpt from **THE VOW, BOOKS 1-3** at the end of this book.

Thank you and happy reading!
Lily

AN EXCERPT FROM THE VOW, BOOK 1

"Just half an hour with my son, please, Jean. That's all I'm asking for." He'd won his ex-wife's mother over once before and he knew she had a soft side to her.

Colt smiled at Jacob. The boy had grown big. It had been two years, maybe longer, since he'd last seen his son. For one fleeting second, he remembered the chubby toddler in his crib, when they had all lived together, when he'd still been married to Savannah.

Looking back, life hadn't sucked as much as he'd thought.

"We need to go," his ex-mother-in-law said.

"Twenty minutes?" he pleaded. "It's been a while hasn't it, son?" He put out a hand to ruffle the boy's hair and hated the way Jacob moved away from his touch as if he were a leper.

"Don't be scared, Jacob. I'm your Daddy. I won't hurt you."

His ex-mother-in-law spoke, "He doesn't know you."

He gave her a hard stare. "See what happens when your daughter won't let me see my son? He can hardly bear for me to touch him."

"It's not as if you've been beating down the door to come see him."

"Look how far she moved."

"She needed a fresh start."

"I've been trying to come for a visit but your daughter won't let me."

"I can't say I blame her," Jean said, obviously not backing down. "You didn't make much of an effort even when you were married."

He exhaled slowly, trying to remain calm. "I was going through a tough time back then. I'm not here to argue with you, Jean."

"Then why *are* you here?"

"I already told you, I was in town."

"Savannah's not here."

"No?" He feigned surprise. "That's too bad. I wanted to let her know I was here for a couple of days." He hoped to get the money and leave, especially if he was to have a chance of leading a normal life again. Without any body parts missing.

"Why don't you come by on the weekend?"

"'Fraid I can't, Jean." He shrugged and gave her his best look of disappointment. "Can you let her know that I dropped by?"

"I'll do that."

"I was hoping to buy Jacob an ice cream and maybe a comic or a toy. I saw a few stores a couple of blocks away. Are you still crazy about them Ninja Turtles, boy?" Jacob shook his head, and he hadn't yet let go of his grandma's hand.

"All I'm asking is to buy my son a small gift. Can't you find it in your heart to let me? What do you say, Jacob?" But the boy looked at him silently with big green eyes that barely blinked. "Don't be scared. I promise I'll walk by your side, and you can stay close to your grandma."

"One milkshake," Jean insisted.

"Just the one." That's all he needed.

In the beginning, she'd wanted them to try to make a go of

their marriage, but that had changed later on, probably when Savannah went whining back to her parents. He was going through a bad time and she couldn't deal with it. But sometimes he wished he could turn back time. It didn't happen often, just lately, now that he was caught up in all this shit.

Because life the way it was now was complete shit. Seeing Merle and his wife and kids shook him sometimes and made him think about the life he'd let slip by. If he'd still had his job, if he was still earning regular money, if he hadn't turned to alcohol, things might have been different. He couldn't help but take it out on Savannah sometimes when the frustration mangled his self-esteem. She hadn't exactly been supportive and wasn't there for him the way a wife should have been. She was always too tired for him but had plenty of time for the kid. He'd been a douchebag sometimes, but not all the time.

Once she left him, though, it was crazy how quickly his life had spun out of control. Small mistakes had ballooned into bigger problems and now he was in shit so deep that he almost couldn't believe it.

Coming here was his one final chance to fix his life and it was all thanks to Savannah and her new lover.

They walked behind him and he turned around every now and then to pass the time by making small talk. "Where is she?" he asked, wanting to hear what the old woman had to say about it.

"On a business trip."

"A business trip?" He laughed politely. *With her lover in Miami?* Now that was some kind of business trip, living the good life and servicing her boss. He had a feeling it was going to work out better this way, with Savannah not being here. The more he thought about it, the more he realized that his initial plan might not have worked. She might never have agreed to meet him, might never have given him the chance to hear his sob story. The woman was too smart to fall for anything like that—even though his story, the parts of it he chose to reveal, was true.

"That's right." Her mom was being careful. "A business trip."

"She sure sounds busy," Colt commented. "Looks to me like she's doing good." She had landed on her feet. *Or on her back.* Either way, she was doing better than he'd ever hoped.

Screwing the billionaire.

If he played his cards right, her good fortune would soon be his now that life had given him a chance to put things right. His prayers had been answered and with the boy as collateral, he had the perfect solution to his problems.

He looked at the boy again and still couldn't see any resemblance of himself, except for the hair color. Jacob had eyes like his mother's. His were more of a brilliant green where hers were a murkier shade. Hazel, she called them, not brown like his own.

The boy caught him staring, so Colt smiled at him, and the boy almost smiled back. A tiny prick of guilt nudged at him, at what he was doing. He wouldn't hurt the boy but even so, this was as dirty as it got, holding his own son for ransom. It was as low as being a drug mule.

He hadn't had much to do with his upbringing, but blood was thicker than water, and there was a bond, even if it was weak. Now that he was with him again, he felt it more. Seeing his son reminded him of what he had missed out on and what he would never get back. Flashes of these moments stabbed at him as they walked down the street to the parade of stores nearby.

"Can we call Mommy?" Jacob asked his grandma.

"Let's call her," offered Colt and called the number to his own house. "She's not answering," he sniffed. "Mommy might be busy, or in a meeting or something," he replied, giving Jean a friendly smile.

"Maybe Mr. Stone took her somewhere nice. He always takes us to nice places," Jacob said.

Colt forced a smile. "That's mighty kind of him, ain't it? It's not fair that they're having all the fun. How about we get a milkshake or an ice cream?" he asked. "I feel like I'm missing out on you growing up, Jacob. Sometimes it makes me real sad." The boy attempted a smile.

"We can't stay out too long," Jean cautioned. "Dale will be wondering where I've gone. Maybe I should call him." She reached into her bag and pulled out her cell phone.

"We won't be long, Jean," said Colt quickly. "There's no need to call him. Dale hates me and you'll only make him worry if you tell him I'm here. He'll probably charge right over and take you both home."

She put her phone back into her bag. "Okay, but hurry up."

"How about a nice chocolate ice cream?" Colt asked the boy. "This store looks like it might sell some." He was familiar with the parade of stores because he'd been hanging out around here while killing time during the day.

"Come on," he beckoned to them both and walked in. "What can I get you, Jean?" But Jacob's grandma politely declined and in the end he bought the boy a double scoop of chocolate ice cream and picked the cheapest ice pop for himself.

"How's school?" he asked, as they walked out.

"Okay."

"Just okay? Made any friends?"

"Yeah."

"Yeah? Do they have names?"

"Lenny."

"Lenny?"

"He's my best friend."

"Lenny." He turned to Jean. "He seems kind of settled in."

"He is," Jean replied. "They're both settling in just fine."

She glanced at her watch again and looked as if she couldn't wait to get back home again. As if she couldn't wait to be rid of him.

He attempted to set her mind at ease. "There's a store along here that sells toys. I want to buy him a gift, and I promise I'll leave you both in peace." He pretended to look at his watch. "I didn't realize it was that time already. I'd better get back."

"All right," she replied. After a while she asked him, "What kind of work are you doing now?"

A bit of this and a bit of that. The truth wouldn't sit well with her, so he lied. "Trucking. I was helping a friend out part of the way, that's how I got here."

"Part of the way?"

"We drove up to Philly and then I got a ride here. It was the only chance I was going to get to come to New York. Seemed a waste to come so far and go back without seeing my boy and Savannah."

Jean wrinkled her brow. "Philly is still a couple of hours away."

"Like I said, I was close by. Closer than being ten hours away."

Jean's mouth twisted, as if she was watching what she was saying. "Helping a trucking friend doesn't sound like a consistent way to earn money."

"I keep my hands in a lot of pies, Jean," he told her stiffly. "It's tough. I never found a stable job that paid as much as my foreman job did but I'm doing the best I can."

Crazy old cow, he thought. She never lets up. Always interfering, always thinking her daughter was too good for him. He turned to Jacob. "What kinds of toys are you into now?"

"Marvel superheroes," the boy mumbled. Jean had paused at the entrance to a small grocery store.

"Do you need to get something?" Colt asked. She frowned,

as if she wasn't sure whether to go in or not.

"I need to pick up a few things for dinner."

"Go right on in," Colt urged her. "We'll wait."

"I won't be long. Those avocados look nice and ripe."

"You might as well get them now," Colt insisted and watched as she wandered into the store. "You still like model cars don't you, Jacob?" The kid had liked them when he was three. But the boy shook his head.

"No?" Colt asked. "What do you like?"

"Iron Man, but you don't need to get me anything. The ice cream was enough." Refusing to give in, Colt pulled out his cell phone and scrolled to some photos of his ex and the billionaire that he'd found online.

"Look," he said, "Mommy sent me some pictures."

Jacob looked, then wrinkled his nose. "That's not a picture," he said. "That's from a newspaper."

"So it is," mused Colt. "I had some she sent, wait a minute." As he started to scroll through his cell phone once more, a cab turned the corner and slid down the street, coming towards them. He had a split second to decide.

Why wait to lose Jean later?

This was it. His only chance. He hailed it down, his heart thumping like he was on drugs. The cab slowed, and he glanced quickly at the store entrance, saw Jean with her back turned and walking away to another aisle. "Mommy has a surprise for you, Jacob. She's coming home early and she wanted me to bring you to the airport."

Jacob looked and made a face, his eyes dubious. He looked at the grocery store. "What about Grandma?"

"She'll come later." He opened the cab door quickly. "Come on, son."

"But Grandma said—"

Screw Grandma. "It's a surprise." He grabbed the boy's arm and pulled him towards the taxi door and in his haste to get the boy inside, Jacob dropped his ice cream. "Don't worry, I'll get you another one." He shuffled the boy into the cab and slammed the door shut. Sweat licked at the hairs on the back of his neck.

"Drive," he barked, because he had no idea what the hell he was doing.

Jacob looked out of the window, his lower lip trembling, "But Grandma—" He looked at Colt and shrank towards the car door, moving away from him.

"Don't worry about Grandma, son. I promise you Mommy wanted to surprise you. Here, speak to her yourself, if you don't believe me." He got out his phone and it seemed to settle him a little.

Once again he called his own home number. Colt shook his head. "She's still not picking up." *Stay calm,* he told himself, even though his heart rocked violently against his chest. But he knew it wouldn't be long before Jacob figured out he was lying. And he only had a small window of time before Jean raised the alarm.

"Tobias has his own airplane," said Jacob, with a touch of defiance in his voice. This lie wasn't going to last much longer.

"His own airplane?" asked Colt, swallowing hard. The fucker had his own jet, did he? In that case, thought Colt, shrewdly, why not ask for more?

Forty thousand dollars.

It would buy him a pretty good life. It was enough money to pay off Santino and disappear to a new town to start over again.

"Why would Mommy tell you to come to the airport when she's got Mr. Stone now?"

"I told her I was in town," Colt replied, the muscles around his neck cording as he fought to remain calm. "I like the sound of this Mr. Stone," he said, smiling at his son. "He sounds like a good man."

BOOKLIST

The Seven Sins:(New Series) A series of seven standalone romances based on the seven sins. Steamy, emotional, and angsty romances which are loosely connected.

Underdog (FREE prequel)
The Wrath of Eli
The Problem with Lust
The Lies of Pride
The Price of Inertia

The Billionaire's Love Story: This is a Cinderella story with a touch of Jerry Maguire. What happens when the billionaire with too much money meets the single mom with too much heart?

The Promise (FREE)
The Gift, Book 1
The Gift, Book 2
The Gift, Book 3
The Gift, Boxed Set (Books 1, 2 & 3)

The Offer, Book 1
The Offer, Book 2
The Offer, Book 3
The Offer, Boxed Set (Books 1, 2 & 3)
The Vow, Book 1
The Vow, Book 2
The Vow, Book 3
The Vow, Boxed Set (Books 1, 2 & 3)

Indecent Intentions: This is a spin-off from The Billionaire's Love story. This two-book set consists of two standalone stories about the billionaire's playboy brother. The second story is about a wealthy nightclub owner who shuns relationships.

The Bet
The Hookup
Indecent Intentions 2-Book Set

Honeymoon Series: Take a roller-coaster journey of emotional highs and lows in this story of love and loss, family and relationships. When Ava is dumped six weeks before her Valentine's Day wedding, she has no idea of the life that awaits her in Italy.

Honeymoon for One
Honeymoon for Three
Honeymoon Blues
Honeymoon Bliss
Baby Steps
Honeymoon Series Boxed Set (Books 1-4)

Italian Summer Series: This is a spin-off from the Honeymoon Series. These books tell the stories of the secondary characters who first appeared in the Honeymoon Series. Nico and Ava also appear in these books.

It Takes Two
All That Glitters
Fool's Gold
Roman Encounter
November Sun
New Beginnings
Italian Summer Series Boxed Set (Books 1- 4)

A Perfect Match Series: This is a seven book series in which the first four books feature the same couple. High-flying corporate executive Nadine has no time for romance but her life takes a turn for the better when she meets Ethan, a sexy and struggling metal sculptor five years younger. He works as an escort in order to make the rent. Books 4-6 are standalone romances based on characters from the earlier books. The main couple, Ethan and Nadine, appear in all books:

Lost in Solo (prequel)
The Proposal
Heart Sync
A Leap of Faith
A Perfect Match Series Books 1-3
Misplaced Love
Reclaiming Love
Embracing Love
A Perfect Match Series (Books 4-6)

Standalone Books:

Love Inc
An Unexpected Gift
An Ordinary Hero

ACKNOWLEDGMENTS

My wonderful group of proofreaders check my manuscript for errors, typos and other weird things that sometimes find their way into my story. I would like to thank the following ladies for their time, help and support:

Sherrie Brown
Marcia Chamberlain
April Lowe
Dena Pugh
Charlotte Rebelein
Carole Tunstall

A big thank you to Tatiana Vila for creating my awesome covers: **www.viladesign.net**

ABOUT THE AUTHOR

Lily Zante lives with her husband and three children somewhere near London, UK.

Connect with Me

I love hearing from you – so please don't be shy! You can email me, message me on Facebook or connect with me on Twitter:

Website http://www.lilyzante.com

Email lily@lilyzante.com

facebook.com/LilyZanteRomanceAuthor

twitter.com/lilyzantebooks

instagram.com/authorlilyzante

goodreads.com/authorlilyzante

bookbub.com/authors/lily-zante

amazon.com/author/lilyzante

tiktok.com/@lilyzantebooks

Printed in Great Britain
by Amazon

59552931R00223